W9-BAL-964

SKY WOMAN FALLING

SKY
WOMAN
FALLING

KIRK MITCHELL

BERKLEY PRIME CRIME, NEW YORK

This is a work of fiction. Names, characters, places, and incidents either are the product of the author's imagination or are used fictitiously, and any resemblance to actual persons, living or dead, business establishments, events, or locales is entirely coincidental. The political and administrative settings of this novel are not meant to represent the actual policies of any tribe or law enforcement agency.

SKY WOMAN FALLING

A Berkley Prime Crime Book
Published by The Berkley Publishing Group,
a division of Penguin Group (USA) Inc.,
375 Hudson Street, New York, New York 10014.

First edition: November 2003

Library of Congress Cataloging-in-Publication Data

Mitchell, Kirk.
    Sky woman falling / Kirk Mitchell.—1st ed.
      p. cm.
    ISBN 0-425-19191-5 (alk. paper)
    1. Parker, Emmett (Fictitious character)—Fiction. 2. Turnipseed, Anna
(Fictitious character)—Fiction. 3. United States. Bureau of Indian Affairs—
Fiction. 4. Indians of North America—Fiction. 5. Government investigators—
Fiction. 6. New York (State)—Fiction. 7. Oneida Indians—Fiction. 8. Indian
women—Fiction. 9. Land tenure—Fiction. I. Title.

PS3563.I7675S57 2003
813'.54—dc21

                                                                  2003051935
PRINTED IN THE UNITED STATES OF AMERICA

10   9   8   7   6   5   4   3   2   1

SKY WOMAN FALLING

1

ANNA TURNIPSEED AND EMMETT Parker left their FBI loaner car beside New York State Route 8 and started side-by-side down a frozen dirt lane. Anna thought it felt as hard as concrete under her shoes. It was overarched with oak and alder branches, black against the overcast. The sky itself was a festering gray that pressed nearly all the way to the ground, as if, with the coming of night, the heavens were too dark and heavy to stay up.

A field began to show through the leafless woods. It was blotched with snow. Out in the middle of this fallow expanse, an amber light winked on and off, on and off. A cop car, waiting for them.

They broke from the trees, still silent.

The summer crop had been Indian maize, for littered among the stubble were ears of corn with calico-colored kernels, gay and festive-looking. Anna realized that the expectation of seeing something horrific makes the mind seize upon fragments of beauty, things that otherwise go unnoticed.

Emmett Parker's breath streamed whitely over his shoulders. Tall and robust, he looked impervious to the cold. Yet, after a little more than a year as an investigator, Anna now knew that nothing was as fragile as human life. The world was an anvil on which life was smashed and broken.

They came to a sunken place in the road where the snow-melt had pooled and refrozen. She shortened her stride, but still slipped. Emmett grabbed her, firmly held her until she got her balance again, then let go.

"Thanks," she said quietly.

Emmett kept his silence. He'd insisted on walking in from the highway instead of driving. A previously staked-out crime scene could be like a road sign pointing in the wrong direction.

Anna checked her wristwatch: 1:34 P.M.

Frowning, she reset the time to 4:34. Her day had begun at home in Las Vegas with no idea that she'd end it in upstate New York, robbed of three hours by the time change and wondering who she could call to empty out her refrigerator if this unforeseen assignment went longer than expected. Emmett had departed Sky Harbor International Airport in Phoenix within minutes of her leaving Las Vegas, and they'd rendezvoused in Denver for the connecting flight to Syracuse. Together, they'd left the turquoise skies of the Far West behind. Perhaps for weeks.

Sky Harbor—an oxymoron. Apparently, judging from the initial information about this case, there were no safe harbors in the sky.

The road split into two branches. The sheriff's cruiser was parked in the fork of these branches, engine running. The deputy reluctantly got out of the warm interior. Pulling down the earflaps to his fur shapka, he nodded an unsmiling hello as the partners presented their credentials to him. A fleshy nose with burst capillaries. He meticulously compared the photographs to the live Indian faces before him. Anna's agency, the FBI, gave him no pause, but Emmett's outfit made him smirk. "What the hell is the Bureau of Indian Affairs doing here?"

"You'll have to ask the Attorney General of the United States," Emmett said indifferently.

"You a *cop*?" the deputy asked.

This didn't feel like Indian Country to Anna, with its bucolic Washington Irving landscape. She associated native lands with those of her childhood, with wind-swept emptiness, seas of sage or rocky wastes stretching off to the horizons. But here it was as in much of the rural West—surprise that natives had been entrusted with responsible law enforcement positions.

"You a sworn peace officer?" the deputy pressed.

"What do I look like?" Emmett asked, scowling. "A goddamned nun?" The whites of his eyes were inflamed by sleeplessness. He'd told Anna he had been up all night investigating a drive-by shooting on the San Carlos Apache Reservation east of Phoenix when the A.G.'s office in Washington asked him to proceed to New York state without delay.

Obviously, the Oneida County deputy wasn't familiar with Emmett Parker's legendary fits of temper. She stepped in before things started badly here and asked, "Who made the discovery?"

The deputy pointed across the stubble at a cluster of farm buildings set against the smoke-like fringe of winter woods. "The farmer."

"He home right now?"

"Suppose."

Down the left branch of the road, a generator grumbled to life and floodlights broke the deepening gloom. Human figures flitted back and forth in the confluence of the beams—the cops first on the scene. The fact that the crime scene was no longer virginal might have had something to do with why Emmett paused to look up the right branch of the road. It ended at the farm buildings, and it was in this direction that he inclined his head for Anna to follow.

Away from the scene, for the time being.

The only sounds she heard were those of the generator and their shoes scuffling over the iron-hard road. She glanced at Emmett. They were launching yet another far-flung investigation when their caseloads at home were already crushing. When certain things occurred in Indian Country, which included parts of all fifty states, the U.S. Attorney General spun his Rolodex to their dog-eared card. It no longer felt like a compliment.

The old farmhouse appeared not to have been painted in a generation. The roof was encrusted with moss. A mudroom led into the kitchen, from which the only light spilled. Emmett started for the front of the place, but Anna guessed that the back was the winter entrance. She knocked on the storm door there.

The response was prompt and suspicious. An old man in coveralls appeared from the kitchen and stood behind the grimy pane of door glass. His ear canals and nostrils bristled with hair. His pale blue eyes shifted from partner to partner, then fixed on Anna's. She noticed that his ruddy hands were balled up. Emmett had taught her that human intentions are more clearly telegraphed by the hands than the eyes, and so now she watched hands when she first met anyone, on or off the job. Hands were the true windows of the soul, especially violent souls.

Raising her voice, Anna said, "Federal officers. We'd like to talk to you, if you don't mind."

That persuaded the old man to crack open the storm door, but only wide enough for conversation to be heard at normal volume. "I told everything to the deputies," he declared in a scratchy tenor.

"I'm sure you did," she said, "but we'd appreciate getting our own information from the source."

"Am I a source?"

"The only one we've got so far."

After a few seconds, the farmer unfisted his hands and opened the door for Anna and Emmett to enter.

A wood-fed cookstove was going in the kitchen, making the room comfortable, but the farmer led them down a hallway with creaking oak floors to a chilly parlor. He parted the curtains, letting in a light so wan he had to turn on a floor lamp. The furniture was dusty and the rooms beyond still, which suggested to Anna that the farmer was a widower.

The old man gestured for the partners to take the sofa as he sat opposite them in an armchair. "You're Indians," he observed with a myopic stare.

"How about that," Emmett said tonelessly.

"Never seen either of you before, have I?"

"Doubtful."

"Not Iroquois, are you?"

"No," Anna replied, sensing that this was a distinction she'd have to make repeatedly in the coming days. "Investigator Parker is a Comanche from Oklahoma and I'm a Modoc from northern California."

"You say *Mohawk*, lady?"

"No. Modoc."

"I've heard of Comanches. But not Modocs." He waved languidly at a bookshelf in the corner, inferring that Indian studies were included among the tomes stacked helter-skelter on the shelves. And that's where Indians belonged. Books.

She felt no urge to explain the many differences between the Comanche and Modoc—his people blunt and straight-forward, hers more introspective and circuitous; his tribal history one of speedy acculturation to white ways, especially commerce, hers one of resistance and isolation. All the interest here seemed to be in the Iroquois. And it didn't feel positive.

"You two out of Albany?" the farmer asked.

"No," Anna said. "I'm from the FBI Las Vegas field office and Investigator Parker's from the Phoenix area Bureau of Indian Affairs. We're here on special assignment."

"But you got pals among the Oneida," the old man said accusatively.

"None," Emmett said.

"Friends among any of the six Iroquois nations?" He meant the Cayuga, Oneida, Onondaga, Mohawk, Seneca and the Tuscarora.

"A few, but no Oneida," Emmett replied. "Didn't catch your name."

"Clifford Van Hastart." To prove that he'd been pestered repeatedly by law enforcement over the past twelve hours, Van Hastart then spelled his last name with as much precision as his ill-fitting dentures would allow. "Why's the federal government sending *Indian* cops up here?"

"Why not?" Emmett said, yawning.

"What call do Indians have to look into anything off the reservations?"

Anna believed that Emmett was about to explain the joint-jurisdiction both the FBI and the BIA had in cases that involved an Indian either as a suspect or victim. And by federal definition, Indian Country was more expansive than the reservations themselves. But instead of wading into this, Emmett sat back and folded his big hands over a knee, his tag-team signal for Anna to take over the questioning.

"You raise Indian corn, Mr. Van Hastart?" she asked pleasantly.

"For Thanksgiving decorations. Nobody can digest these varieties anymore. Even you folks don't have the gut for it. Some Cayugas tried, and it made 'em sicker than dogs. I warned 'em, but they wanted to go traditional. That's the rage, isn't it? Going traditional?"

"I suppose," she said. "Is this your farm, or do you work it for somebody else?"

"Mine. 'Til the goddamn Oneida—with the help of you feds—steal it. The Iroquois are like Jews. They love money. To them, land is nothing more than money, even though they say it's their sacred homeland that matters. Their Mother Earth. But it's money, money, money. That's the game here. It's always the game."

Anna sat back to tell Emmett that he might as well take the lead again.

"And they don't just want some land," the old man ranted on. "They want *all* the land. Why, everybody knows they were paid fair and square two hundred years ago by the state. Even they admit that. Not even an issue. Nobody shoved those deals down their throats. They shook on it because they love money. They drank it all up or gambled it away in no time, but they still love money. Now, all of a sudden, they're claiming the thousands and thousands of acres that were bought honestly by my ancestors and all the other pioneers here in Oneida and Madison Counties. The money's gone, so now they want the land back. I suppose it makes me sound prejudiced or something, but don't that make your Oneida brethren *Indian-givers . . . ?"*

Emmett interrupted, "How'd you become aware of what happened out in your field?"

Van Hastart paused, his eyes turning ruminative. "The sound."

"What kind of sound?"

But the old man seemed to have only half-heard Emmett. "About three in the morning. It angled right over the house."

"Angled?"

"Dropped out of the west. Then a thump, like a watermelon falling off the back of a wagon. Followed by nothing. Dead quiet."

"What'd you do?"

"Phoned the sheriff's office. They said a squad car was on the way. But it was going on four-thirty when I saw a spotlight shining through the woods from the highway. The sheriff's car never turned off the county road, and the deputy never got his fat ass out of the car. His spotlight went off after just a couple minutes, he drove off, and I phoned again. They said the deputy saw nothing to account for the sound. So, come dawn, I went outside to have a look on my own." He paused again.

"And, Mr. Van Hastart?" Anna prompted.

"Halfway to the creek, I saw steam rising out of a low spot in the stubble. I think you know the rest."

Anna didn't, not entirely, but Emmett prevented her from asking. "What kind of sound angled down over your house?"

A facial tic jerked at one corner of Van Hastart's mouth. "It was a *howling.* Like the wind screaming, except it was the most god-awful thing I ever heard in my life."

"Some kind of aircraft, maybe?"

"No, no—nothing like that. It made me jump up in bed. A plane wouldn't make me jump up in bed. It *howled* like the devil himself. I never want to hear anything like that again."

Shock was a cold wind that blew through you. It was best not to fight it. Just let it pass through you and be gone. Then you could start thinking. Emmett remembered this as he and Anna stepped up to the yellow police tape marking the scene. Beyond lay a circle of trampled earth filled with detectives and technicians, the latter the better part of an FBI Evidence Response Team. A man of medium height in a charcoal-colored overcoat broke away from the others and approached Emmett and Anna. He was in his late twenties but already had an old man's face, soulful and vaguely sad. "Turnipseed and Parker?" he asked, squinting against the floodlights as he reached over the tape to shake.

"That's us," Emmett answered for the two of them.

"Leo Manoukian." Their contact with the Syracuse satellite office of the FBI. Apparently, he'd tracked their walk in from the highway, for he asked with concern, "You find your loaner car okay at the airport?"

"You bet, thanks," Emmett replied. "Just felt like stretching our legs after our flights."

Special Agent Manoukian's chameleon face turned young again—with relief. He obviously liked to please, an urge he'd have to rein in if he planned to remain in the business. A cop pleased no one, including himself.

Manoukian hooked his thumb around the tape and lifted it so Emmett and Anna could pass under. "Come on in."

Anna stopped dead in her tracks, staring.

For a moment, Emmett focused on her, not what lay just beyond. Pretty, petite, bobbed brown hair and cinnamon complexion. Plus the physical attributes especially prized by her people—large eyes, a straight nose, graceful limbs. *Christ, I'm needlessly obsessing on her again.* This also made him realize that he wasn't completely ready for one more all-consuming case. His mind was putting it off.

But then, surrendering to the moment, he gazed back toward the farmhouse, imagining old man Van Hastart's described howling descending out of the western sky toward him. That sky was now a mute slab of gray. Yet, last night, if the farmer's impression of the events was accurate, it had been split by an unnerving sound that had *angled* down over the farmhouse and ended in a thump.

Here.

Finally, Emmett looked at the body.

Intermingled with the unavoidable revulsion was a mental note—*check on last night's weather conditions.* In its present frozen state, the field couldn't have been indented by anything lighter than a Volkswagen. Yet, the corpse had left a definite depression in the cornfield. Oblique, like that left by a glancing meteorite—substantiating Van Hastart's belief that the sound had angled over him.

Emmett couldn't recall having seen a body so broken and shattered by impact, even during his days of traffic accident investigation with Oklahoma City P.D. Compound fractures to all the limbs. Gross deformities that almost robbed her of her humanness. Her. Undeniably female. Chunky build. She wore a pantsuit and light sweater, totally inadequate for braving an upstate New York January night.

The most appalling thing about the corpse was the condition of the head, and Emmett heard Anna whisper as she studied it, "Jesus." Impact, in addition to caving in her right shoulder, had forced most of the bodily fluids in her upper body to the top of her head, distending it as much as four inches. This sac gave her an alien, otherworldly appearance.

"Medical examiner used to sky-dive," Manoukian quietly said. "He thinks she tumbled through the air as she fell. Still, she probably achieved maximum acceleration in a freefall before slamming into the earth."

"Chance a light plane or helicopter was involved?"

"Don't know yet," Manoukian admitted. "We've just started on this. Believe it or not, she boarded a commercial jetliner in Syracuse last night."

Emmett hid his disbelief.

He knelt for a closer look, the chill of the ground penetrating his trouser knees.

The victim had raven-black hair, not unlike his own in earlier years, although at age fifty-five, she was a decade and a half older than he. A dye job perhaps, recent enough for no gray roots to have re-emerged. The A.G.'s office had supplied Anna and him with a bare essential of vitals: Brenda Two Kettles, an Indian adult female. Sixty-two inches tall, 140 pounds. Born in

1948, she had resided on the federally-recognized reservation just south of the city of Oneida, New York. Approximately twenty-five air miles to the northwest of here.

This all has to be pondered in air miles.

Anna knelt beside Emmett. He silently congratulated her: The shock of confronting violent death no longer registered on her face. Her eyes seemed a bit pinched, but that was to be expected; the floodlights were blinding. Since he'd met her on a case in the California desert a year ago December, she'd made her peace with horror. Now the trick was to not let speculation run away with her. To sip information, not gulp it.

"No question about the victim's ID?" Emmett asked Manoukian.

"None. Midday, we rushed her prints to Identification Division. Positive match. Tribal police made the death notification to the family on the rez."

Anna asked, "Husband?"

"Deceased. Family consists of two grown daughters and some grand-kids, who last saw Ms. Two Kettles at around five yesterday evening . . ." It had been too soon for the Oneida Nation Police Department to have taken a missing person report. Then, before twenty-four hours had elapsed, Van Hastart had seen steam rising from a slight depression in his cornfield.

"Examiner says her wounds bled some," Manoukian noted.

Lovely, Emmett thought. Brenda Two Kettles's heart might have been pumping in the split-second her consciousness had been jarred out of her. Had she died against her will? *Yes.* Emmett realized that, viscerally at least, he'd made up his mind that this was a homicide.

He rose and brushed the icy slush off his knees. "Shoes," he said under his breath.

"What?" Anna asked.

"Where are her shoes?"

2

ICE CLOUDS WERE RUNNING transparently over a half moon as Johnny Skyholder inserted his key in the door lock at the service entrance to the Shako:wi Cultural Center. His abnormally long fingers made minute tasks such as this difficult, and he fumbled in the darkness of midnight. Behind him in the distance, headlights twinkled on the Thomas E. Dewey Thruway, but here in the Oneida Nation the streets were empty, and the only vehicle in the cultural center lot was his old van. The wheel-arches were salted out, and his foreman had described its color as being baby-shit yellow. But the vehicle got him from his duplex in the woods to work and the supermarket and back again, the limited orbit of his world.

The lock refused to budge.

Sighing, he looked up. The night sky. It was more than a vast shadow. It was the velveteen underbelly of heaven, and the stars were holes in that soft belly, revealing the never-ending golden light that shone in paradise.

Johnny slid out the key and breathed on it, then tried again.

Success.

He pushed open the heavy steel door. Swiftly, as swiftly as his massively-boned legs could carry him, he homed in on the blinking red light to the security panel. He switched off the exterior alarm and deactivated the motion sensors out in the galleries.

Get to work, you lazy little redskin. To work, to work, to work.

Inside his closet, he pulled the chain to the overhead light. A cracked mirror from the women's lavatory had been stored inside. Against his wishes. Catching a glimpse of himself was unavoidable, even if he focused away from the dusty, reflective surface. He didn't care for his cow-like face, his maudlin eyes with chocolate brown irises bleared by the lenses of his horn-rimmed glasses. The sight, even the fleeting sight of his own reflection shamed him. He wasn't worth looking at. Hurriedly, he wheeled his janitor's cart out of the closet and left himself behind.

To work, get to work.

Smells of antiquity filled his nostrils. They were wafting off the exhibits—cornhusk dolls, rattles made from mummified turtles, tobacco pipes and woven baskets. He especially liked the vanilla scent of the sweet-grass baskets.

Get to work, Injun baby!

He glanced into the semi-darkness of the galleries along the way. All but one. That was the chamber reserved for the masks, or *false faces* as the cards called them. These were the likenesses of the Forest People, half humans with wild hair and heads that could float free of their bodies like talking balloons. Their expressions were mocking, their teeth an angry black or red, their eye holes penetrating in their vacancy. He didn't care for this gallery and made it his habit to clean the smudges off the glass cases and vacuum the carpet as quickly as possible. Sometimes, if he lingered too long here, the masks hissed to life. A babble gushed out of the gaping mouths. Voices accused him of doing incomprehensible things. *I'm the Good One,* he would protest, but the voices went on babbling to his back.

Johnny came to the main gallery just off the foyer and gift shop. A happy place for him, for here a silhouette with waist-length hair awaited him.

"Hello, Grandmother."

She stood stock-still, but the glints of her eyes invited him to step up onto the elevated platform and kiss her unyielding latex cheek. "Sorry I missed last night's story time," he apologized. "But I'm ready now. I have all the time in the world for you now, Grandmother."

He thumbed a well-worn button on the hand-rail and sank onto the cushioned bench closest to her.

A floodlight poured down on Grandmother. Her crinkled eyelids blinked twice, and her brown cheeks broke into a pretty smile. *"Sheko:li!"* she said sweetly, shifting right and left as if talking to a room full of people. "That is our word for *Greetings!* We the Oneida are one of the Six Nations of the Iroquois, the *Haudenosaunee,* or *the People of the Longhouse.* The longhouse was our communal dwelling. And we Oneida call ourselves the *Onyotaa:ka,* which means the *People of the Standing Rock.* This is because the Father Spirit placed a large boulder wherever our people made their principal village . . ."

Principal village, Johnny silently mouthed her words, his homely face bright with pleasure.

"We *Onyotaa:ka* have been in this part of what you call New York for a very long time. Ours were the rich and forested lands between those of our brothers, the Onondaga and the Mohawk. These lands stretched all the way from Canada to Pennsylvania. But in the beginning, New York, North America, the earth itself looked very different from the way they appear now. In the beginning all was darkness and water. In the heavens above, the Father Spirit looked down on this world and was not pleased with it. It was not complete. So he uprooted a white pine, which is sacred to us, creating a hole in the heavens. You can see this hole, which is often mistaken for the morning star. Then he spoke to his daughter, whom he loved very much. He told her to go below into the world of darkness and water. Finally, he picked her up and dropped her through this hole in the sky. This woman, who would be called Sky Woman by all the water creatures below, began falling. As she fell, the animals gazed up in wonder and fear. Far above them they saw a radiant light that was Sky Woman . . ."

She totters blindly on the balls of her feet, leaning out over the lip of a precipice at the edge of a bottomless void. Then, undeniably, she is falling. She can see nothing, but she has the tingling sensation of falling. Her arms flail and her hands grab at the blackness, but she plummets with ever increasing speed. The night air is like fire on her face. Her body howls down through the void, and a scream is pulled from her lungs. Then she has no air left to scream. She begins to tumble end over end, making a whiffling noise as she somersaults faster and faster.

She spreads her arms like wings, trying to stop spinning.

But then there is a burst of light as she strikes the ground with a terrible, bone-splintering thud. She hears the crunch of her bones shattering.

After a moment, she lifts her head. She expects it to ache, but it doesn't. If anything, she feels a strange, sensual pleasure. An inexplicable pleasure.

Farmer Van Hastart's frost-blasted cornfield surrounds her. She looks down at her own body. It's torn and mangled beyond repair. She wants to turn her face from the sight, but can't. Steam rises off her as the life cools out of her. The heaviness of death fills her like wet cement, solidifying all possibility of movement, freezing her in place.

But the peculiar pleasure persists.

She hears someone crying. Who?

Finally, she realizes.

She herself is crying.

Anna awoke.

Her heart raced as her damp eyes searched the darkened hotel room for reality. It revealed itself in a pencil-thin stripe of gray daylight between the drape panels. And the digital clock. It read: 7:56 A.M.

She threw off her covers, swung her legs over the side of the bed and sat a moment with her head cradled in her hands. A dull, jet-lag headache thumped at her temples, and her face had been chafed raw by last night's hours of cold in the cornfield. She wanted to flop back down, but there was too much to do today.

She rapped lightly on the connecting wall.

Immediately, Emmett answered from the other side with a sharper knock. He was already up.

Day Two began.

Day One had yielded nothing more than the inarguable logic of a corpse.

Twenty minutes later, Emmett and she waited in line at the cappuccino cart in the lobby.

Turning Stone Casino Resort, a four-star hotel, was owned and operated by Oneida Nation Enterprises. Only about a thousand Oneida Iroquois remained in New York, but not a single member of the tribe was visible among the mostly white employees and guests. The place smelled new, as new as the scattered pockets of native prosperity that were cropping up across the country, thanks to gambling.

"Just coffee," Emmett told the server, dismissing the more complicated choices on the menu board.

Anna considered those choices, but then dittoed Emmett's order. She took a brochure off the cart and leafed through it. Olmec Gold, a trademarked blend, was grown by Indians of southern Mexico and marketed by Oneida Nation Enterprises, ". . . *reviving that grand tradition by which Native people traded goods from Canada to Mexico and mutually prospered.*"

Served at last, Emmett turned on his heel and strode for the entrance of the resort. Stealing sips from her own cup, Anna followed. Olmec Gold was very good. Rich and misty, like a rain-forest. She wondered if this cup constituted her breakfast. It was no idle speculation. Her dream made it important. The Modoc believed that a person's death was foretold if he or she remembered crying in a dream. That death could be avoided only if the person scrupulously avoided mentioning the dream before breakfast.

As they waited for their FBI loaner car to be brought around by the parking valet, she looked at Emmett. Forty-one years old, and he looked it this morning. Flecks of white in his black hair. Crow's-feet astride his weary eyes. "You want to grab a bite somewhere?" she asked.

"No, not unless you want to."

"I'm fine." That settled it: Her dream would go unmentioned. This was breakfast. All was well, for the time being, and her dream metamorphosed from omen to simple warning. *Be careful.*

She shifted her gaze up to the bold, curving lines of the modernistic hotel. A sign in the lobby claimed that the structure had been inspired by the Iroquois longhouse. She couldn't see the resemblance. But the four golf courses snaking around the resort complex did masquerade as snowy meadows, suggesting the aboriginal feel of this rolling and wooded country. It was another day with low overcast, making her miss the inter-mountain West, where even persistent storms failed to bog down into this kind of stifling grayness.

Their car pulled up with a squeal of brakes.

The valet was holding open the passenger door for her when she realized that Emmett had not stepped around to the driver's side. He'd been delayed by a man in a black overcoat and matching fedora. He was mildly overweight, but his face was hard and angular.

"Investigator Parker?"

"Yeah. Who're you?"

"William Jordan, U.S. Marshal's Service." Jordan offered a manila envelope in his right glove and his credentials in his left. "I've got your deputization orders."

"My *what*?"

"I'm sure you've been deputized by us before."

Emmett paused. "Yeah, a couple times. Why now?"

"Somebody thought it might be prudent." Just when Anna didn't think Jordan knew who she was, he touched a glove to the brim of his hat and said, "Ms. Turnipseed."

Emmett asked, "You out of the local district?"

"No, Louisiana." Jordan took a business card from his credentials holder and presented it to Emmett. Reading over Parker's shoulder, Anna saw that Jordan was a *chief* deputy marshal. Gesturing at a yellow cab idling behind him, the man added, "I apologize for this hasty introduction, but I've got to be back at my desk by early afternoon. Take care." Without a word more, he went to the cab, ducked inside and was driven off.

Emmett slid the authorization out of the envelope, examined it briefly, then stepped around the grille to take the steering wheel. She didn't argue. The roads were icy, and her mind was too full to concentrate on holding down her speed. Too full of Brenda Two Kettles. Too full of her own dream of falling to her death and the inexplicable pleasure that had given her.

"You see Jordan at the crime scene yesterday?" Emmett asked.

"Nope."

"Me neither."

"What's a marshal from Louisiana doing in New York?" she asked.

"I'll bet he's out of their Special Operations Group at Camp Beauregard, though his card doesn't specify."

She agreed. SOG handled major fugitive apprehension, dignitary protection, court order enforcement—most of their high-profile details throughout the country.

"So why's he here?"

Emmett shrugged.

Anna could already guess one possible reason for the U.S. Marshal to deputize Emmett through an agreement with the Department of the Interior. BIA investigators didn't have the broad jurisdiction of FBI agents and federal marshals. Theirs was limited to Indian Country, unless the commission of an allied agency was extended to them. Did this mean the A.G. didn't want Parker to be hog-tied in the course of this investigation? Or was the Marshal's Service keeping an eye on him for somebody highly placed?

Emmett Parker had a reputation.

"Well, whatever," he mused out loud, "Jordan planned a quickie ambush so he didn't have to talk with us any longer than necessary. If he keeps that up, I may wind up liking the son of a bitch. First goddamned marshal I ever met who apparently doesn't love the sound of his own air escaping. I'm impressed."

Just outside the highway entrance to the resort, two white protesters trudged back and forth, holding placards. The elderly men were bundled up and wore mittens against the cold, yet they still looked miserable. Their hand-lettered signs read: DON'T SUPPORT THE LAND CLAIM WITH YOUR GAMBLING DOLLARS! and BACK C.U.E.! The two hunched, shuffling figures gave off the impression that they had been picketing for months and would go picketing for years. "What's C.U.E.?" she asked.

"Committee for Upstate Equality." Emmett sped onto the westbound ramp of Interstate 90. "Local white backlash. Old man Van Hastart had a C.U.E. pamphlet on his kitchen table."

Struggling to fall asleep last night, Anna had read the Oneida position on the land claim controversy. It was laid out in the guest services book. Early allies of the rebellious American colonists, the Oneida broke with the other pro-British tribes of the Iroquois Confederacy at great cost to themselves. The U.S. Constitution reserves negotiation rights with Indians to the federal government. However, years after the 1794 Iroquois treaty was ratified by Congress, the state of New York imposed twenty-six further treaties on the Oneida, paring down tribal holdings from 270,000 acres to a 32-acre reservation.

What would be called an Indian rancheria at home, Anna had noted to herself.

The Oneida took their case to the U.S. Supreme Court, which in 1985 ruled in the tribe's favor. The settlement had yet to be worked out, but the Nation Representative—chief executive officer of the tribe, as few modern Indian leaders were called *chief*—promised that the Oneida had no wish to evict their 60,000 non-Indian neighbors now residing on this vast swath of upstate New York restored, at least in abstract, to them by the high court.

Apparently, the Committee for Upstate Equality wasn't convinced.

Emmett took Exit 33 into Oneida, a working-class hub of 10,000 New Yorkers, mostly white, facing an uncertain future. It looked like the few other eastern cities of its size Anna had visited: vacant brick factories, strip malls and fast food franchises challenging main street, older residential neighborhoods with tree-lined streets. Except that most of these businesses and homes rested on a gelatinous foundation of ownership that was still wobbling in the courts.

Emmett drove south along State Route 46. The countryside turned rural again.

Farmer Van Hastart's bitterness now made more sense to Anna, although she doubted he would agree that the state treaties giving him title to his farm were illegal. "Does the court have a settlement process up and running?"

"No idea." Emmett slowed to read a street sign, doubtlessly comparing the name to the address given to him last night over the phone by a detective with the tribal police department. Emmett had a nearly infallible aural memory. "Territory Road," he announced.

A carved wooden billboard proclaimed this to be the sovereign heartland of the Oneida Nation. In reality, it was the rump reservation to have survived the 26 treaties with New York. A council house drifted past Anna's window, then a cultural center, recreation hall, playground and drained swimming pool. All looked recently built and in keeping with the economic juggernaut of Oneida Nation Enterprises. But shortly beyond, the Indian Country of memory appeared as out of Anna's own past: Dented and seedy mobile homes, probably already secondhand the day they were hauled here, stood back from the road on trashy, wooded lots. Junker vehicles everywhere. Wilderness slums was how most reservations were described, and this one was little different.

Emmett located the number he was seeking on a mailbox that was punctured with bullet holes. "This is it," he said, cutting the engine, "the Two Kettles's residence."

3

THE PARTNERS FILED UP a foot-trampled path in the unplowed drive-way, Anna following. The underlying ice had been worn slick, so she had to plant every step with care. Off to the left stood a bale of moldy straw, bristling with arrows. As they drew nearer to the single-wide mobile home, she could hear children crying inside. On the front window was an official-looking notice reading C DEMNED. An attempt had been made to peel it off, obliterating the ON from what Anna assumed to be CON-DEMNED, plus the number of the tribal health and safety ordinance that had been violated.

But the noise from within said that the condemned property was very much occupied.

No tire ruts led to the ten-year-old sedan parked next to the single-wide. A sticker on the rear bumper read: IF WE GIVE 'EM BACK THEIR BEADS, WILL THEY GO HOME? Catching it, Emmett smiled over his shoulder at Anna. But less amusingly, the front bumper and grille showed the decided imprint of a tree trunk or telephone pole.

He knocked on the door, while Anna waited off to the side, weapon un-drawn but still covering him.

The knock was answered—after obvious difficulty with the knob—by a curly-headed Oneida toddler in a pink pajama jumpsuit. The opening of the door let out a blast of warm, tobacco-fouled air and more sounds of crying, including those of a grown woman. A television was also blaring, tuned to *Good Morning America.*

Anna slipped past Emmett and the toddler.

An Indian woman, late twenties, thickset and rumpled, sat on a couch covered with an ersatz Navajo blanket. Tears coursed down through the sprays of freckles on her plump cheeks. In front of her on the cigarette-scarred coffee table were a pair of pinking shears and a severed strand of hair the same dark brown as that on her head. She was sobbing big racking sobs and seemed unaware of the intrusion.

A slightly younger woman of similar appearance was at the table in the adjoining kitchen, sorting through scraps of paper she kept taking from an index card box. Her round, light brown face was also streaked with tears, but at least she had the presence of mind to ask the partners: "Who're you?"

The question hung in the air as Emmett crossed the narrow living room and flicked off the TV. That reduced the confusion to the mingled crying of the older woman, the three-year-old boy next to her on the sofa and an infant thrashing in a bassinet. Anna counted two other children present, the girl in the pink pajamas who'd let them in and a boy about the same age, quietly coloring on the gritty kitchen floor.

While Emmett explained who they were, Anna swept down the hallway to check on the bedrooms and bath. They were empty. Her overall impression of the mobile home was not one of wanton neglect, just too many people and too little income. The norm in Indian Country, but this puzzled her, given the prosperity generated by Oneida Nation Enterprises. She returned to the kitchen just as the younger woman wiped her cheeks with a paper towel and said to Emmett, "I'm Mariana Two Kettles. That's Belinda, my older sister."

Belinda suddenly glanced up as if aware of the strangers for the first time. "Who're these guys?"

"Federal cops," Mariana said.

"Indian police?" Belinda asked in a tone both wary and hopeful.

"Yeah. They're here trying to find out what happened to Mama."

Belinda abruptly stopped crying. Throwing off the blanket, she rose and confronted Emmett. "Did you see my mother's body?"

He looked her square in the eye. "Yes."

"Is it real? Do you swear this is all real?"

"Yes." The same earnest, deadpan tone.

For a split second, it seemed that Belinda would simply start crying again. But then she spun around and fumbled for the scissors in a caddy on the end of the sinkboard. It was unclear what she meant to do with them, but Emmett took no chances. He seized her by the right wrist and bent it back until the scissors dropped out of her grasp and onto the board.

"Let go of me!" Belinda wailed.

Emmett didn't, not yet.

Anna confiscated the scissors, plus the pair of shears on the coffee table, and deposited the potential weapons in a high kitchen cabinet when no one was looking.

Belinda sank to the floor, where the boy who'd been coloring carefully watched her as he bit into a crayon. Emmett let go of her wrist and patted her shoulders, if only to show the child that everything was all right. "It's okay," he murmured to Belinda. "I want you to settle down. Time to settle down. You're scaring the kids."

Mariana lit up a Marlboro, squinting through the smoke at Anna. She too had freckles, indicating a big dose of white blood in the lineage. "Bee was just going to cut off more of her hair," she said, shaking out the match. "You know what that means?"

Anna nodded. Traditional Modoc had cut off their hair and dressed their bare scalps with pine pitch and ashes as a sign of mourning. Grief somehow made human beings want to tear at their hair, and most tribes had come up with this way to minimize the damage.

Mariana gestured with her cigarette at the scraps of paper, many of which had been blown off the table by the brief tussle between Emmett and Belinda. "Mama had a chant for grief craziness, but I can't find it."

"I am not crazy!" Belinda shouted forcefully enough for Emmett to grip her wrist again. "Just tell me what happened to my mother!"

"*Hai, hai, hai,*" Mariana lapsed into a gentle singsong, an incantation. "*Anything can happen on earth . . . even insanity.*"

"Stop it, Mar!"

The infant was still shrieking. Going to the baby, Anna checked his disposable diaper. Mariana was at her side in an instant with a fresh Pampers. She undid the adhesive tape on the old one, and the release of ammonia fumes made Anna's eyes water. "I got busy going though Mama's chants," the woman said apologetically. "Bee's in AA, but when she gets this way only a drink calms her down. That's why I was looking for the chant. I'm hoping it'll quiet Bee down before she does something bad to herself." Pausing, Mariana ran an inquisitive eye over Anna's features. "Where you from?"

"A small rez on the California-Oregon border." Then, without skipping a beat, Anna asked, "What time did your mother leave the house last evening?"

"Five-ish. It'd just gotten dark."

"Where was she headed?"

Mariana bundled up the soiled diaper. "She wouldn't tell us."

"I don't understand," Anna said.

"We didn't know she was on her way to New York City 'til the tribal cops told us."

"Your mother left on a trip without telling her own family why?"

A suspicious silence was finally broken when Mariana added, "She got a phone call about four that afternoon, packed her bag and went out the door 'round five."

"Did you or your sister ask your mother what this was all about?"

"Sure we asked. She said *shush*, she'd explain later. It was better if we didn't know nothing for the time being."

"Any idea what she meant by that?"

Mariana hiked a shoulder, then scooped the squalling infant up out of the bassinet and began rocking him in her arms.

"In the days leading up to last night," Anna asked, "did she give any sign she was planning a trip?"

"Maybe. I don't know. She was a little antsy. More than usual. I really don't know."

All tribes had divisions, bands or clans that were potential sources of friction. The Oneida, according to the hotel guest book, had three clans—the Wolf, Bear and Turtle. "Which clan was your mother?"

"Turtle."

"Any trouble along those lines?"

"No, nothing like that."

Sensing resistance building against her, Anna slowed down. "Okay. I don't mean to pry. I just have to ask these kinds of questions. Cover all the bases. What kind of mood had your mother been in lately?"

"Okay, considering."

"Considering what?"

Mariana wouldn't say. She'd just caught from the corner of her eye that Emmett was listening in.

Anna put the issue aside momentarily, if only to get a cooperative rhythm going again. "What color was your mother's bag . . . an overnight bag, I'm assuming?"

"Yeah, that kind," she said, nuzzling the baby, who'd stopped crying at last. "Black."

"Purse or handbag?"

"Purse. It had sparkly black things on it."

"Sequins?"

"I guess."

"Was your mother on any medications, Mariana?"

Silence.

"Did you hear me?"

Mariana finally said, "Xanax."

"Any special reason your mother felt anxious?"

"Yeah," the woman replied sharply. "Things been tense lately with the Men's Council."

The equivalent of the tribal council, Anna surmised. "Why?"

"You really don't know?"

"No."

That was it, then. Brenda Two Kettles's daughters believed the federal authorities were in collusion with a tribal bureaucracy they distrusted. In Anna's experience, not a new suspicion among the Indian poor. "Tell me what's going on, Mariana. You're the first person I've talked to on the rez here. I want to hear your side of it."

After a sigh, Mariana said, "Most of us here on Territory Road were against the casino. All this get-rich stuff the tribal suits got going. Now the Men's Council is trying to evict us, push us off the rez so we won't have no vote in how things are run. They want Mama gone, 'specially."

"Is that why there's a condemned sticker on the front window?"

"Yeah," Mariana said, hatefully, "they're saying these old trailers aren't safe. But that has nothing to do with it. They just want us gone. Us and all our friends here on the road."

"Was that it then? Was your mother going on some sort of business trip related to the evictions?"

"I told you I don't know."

"All right." Again, Anna slowed down. "Did you overhear her making the airline reservation?"

"No."

"Is the car out front drivable?"

Mariana shook her head. "Belinda wrecked it on Thanksgiving night. She barely got home ahead of the cops before all the coolant leaked out. They still arrested her, and we don't got the money to get the car fixed."

"How'd your mother get to the airport in Syracuse?"

"She caught a ride."

"From whom?"

"We don't know."

"Did you see the car?"

"Kind of. It was dark, but I could tell it was a fancy car."

"Could you make out the driver?"

"No."

"Did you know the driver?"

"No."

"Do you know many people with fancy cars?"

Emmett interrupted, irking Anna. "What kind of shoes did your mother wear last night?"

Mariana smiled faintly as she put the baby down again. "Ruby red pumps. She said they reminded her of what Dorothy wore in *The Wizard of Oz.*"

The Kansas farm girl who'd been swept into the sky by a tornado. For a dizzying moment, Anna visualized Dorothy's house spinning into the black, howling vortex. It meant something, if only her mind struggling to make sense of Brenda's inexplicable fall.

A throaty rumble approached the mobile home. A motorcycle engine, she believed, which died as she turned for the window. She parted the venetian blinds on a chopper just as the front door swung open. A sunken-chested teenage boy entered. His hair was in a spiky pink Mohawk, which probably wasn't meant to be traditional, even though he was clearly Iroquois. He wore a black leather jacket with chrome studs and a silver chain looping down from the right epaulet. Without a word, without making eye contact with the partners, he passed through the kitchen, clasping his left forearm to his jacket. He continued down the hallway and into a bedroom. He was inside only momentarily before appearing again and making his way to a second bedroom.

"Hazen . . . ?" Mariana called after him.

The boy's answer was to slam that bedroom door.

Anna asked, "Who's he?"

"Our cousin, Hazen."

"Last name?"

"Two Kettles. My dad's brother's son." Mariana's eyes darted to a hand-tinted wedding portrait on the living room wall. A young Brenda in white beside her groom. Belinda and Mariana more resembled their father. "We raised Hazen. His folks got killed in a car wreck on the thruway."

"And your father's deceased?" Anna asked.

"Gone a long time now," Mariana said. "Cancer."

"And the fathers of these children?"

The woman grinned sheepishly. "My sister and me don't have much luck with men."

A pounding at the front door spun Anna around. An angry male voice cried, "Open up, Hazen, right now!"

She glanced down the hallway for the youth, but he failed to appear. Hazen, upon entering the trailer, had locked the front doorknob behind him, and it was now jiggling, violently.

"Open this damned door!"

When the knob stopped vibrating, briefly, Anna unlocked it and swung the door back on a young black man in a business suit. His coat was unbuttoned, and right-off she noticed his basket-weave belt, to which a police badge was attached. A gold earring glinted at his right earlobe.

Anna introduced Emmett and herself.

"Right, saw your car," the man noted, visibly calming down as he shook hands with Emmett first. A symmetrical, nicely-shaped face, but Anna didn't find it agreeable for some reason. "We talked last night on the phone. Vaughn Devereaux, detective with Oneida Nation P.D." Anna could tell by Emmett's mild look of surprise that Devereaux had not sounded black over the phone. "Hazen Two Kettles just come inside?"

"Yes," Anna said.

"Don't let him out."

At that instant, a loud wrenching noise from down the hallway made the detective shout, "Whoa!" Staying outside, he sprinted toward the back of the trailer, slipping to a knee. He scrambled back up and vanished around the corner.

Anna followed Emmett to the rear bedroom door Hazen Two Kettles had entered. Emmett threw it back against a gush of chilled air that was puffing in the curtains from the open window. Hazen was nowhere to be seen, and Anna realized that the sound had been the youth prying open the sliding window in its frozen track. Out in the tree trunks, she had a glimpse of Devereaux in foot-pursuit. His cries echoed back to the mobile home: "Stop or I'll shoot your skinny ass!"

"Keep an eye on Belinda for me," Emmett said to Anna, clambering through the window. He dropped to the ground and broke into a stiff jog through the woods.

On a hunch, Anna went to the first bedroom Hazen had entered. Brenda's bedroom, as evidenced by the queen-sized bed, although bunkbeds were pushed up against the interior wall. She peeked under the larger bed—and removed a bottle of sloe gin that had been hidden there.

Farther back in the dim and dusty space was some sort of bundle. Sliding it out, she saw that the covering was buckskin, neatly folded to enclose a mask and a rattle fashioned from a desiccated turtle. The carved wooden face of the mask leered up at her. It was framed by white hair that was brittle to the touch but still felt human. The eyes were enormous and the mouth frozen in a silent scream, suggesting that the mythical being had been caught in a moment of supreme terror. Yet, there was also something ludicrous about the look. A hysterical giddiness that defied comprehension, except when Anna thought of the earth rushing up toward Brenda Two Kettles early this morning.

She refolded the bundle and slid it back under the bed. Then she returned to the kitchen and held up the pint of sweet, reddish liqueur to both sisters.

Guilty stares.

Then Belinda dragged herself to the sofa, where she cuddled the boy still sitting there and began to weep with her cheek pressed against the top of his head. Anna followed the older sister into the living room, just to keep watch on her.

Something taped to the top of the television console drew her attention: handwritten words in English and what she assumed to be *Haudenosaunee*, the Iroquoian language—TV, picture + shadow = *Watasatalha*. She'd seen this before in other native homes, labels or flashcards penned out by a parent or grandparent in a plaintive effort to keep a dying language alive.

"Please don't let 'em go too hard on Hazen."

Anna glanced up at Mariana. "Does he have any shoplifting priors?"

"A couple. But he never steals for himself. Always for others. He likes beer, not sloe gin. He must've overheard me asking Bee if she really needed a drink on account of Mama. He must've put two and two together, and gone to get some comfort for Bee."

Anna kept an expressionless face.

Ten minutes later, Detective Devereaux and Emmett returned to the trailer with Hazen handcuffed between them. The two men had wet knees and elbows, but the youth was soaked to the waist—having tried to ford Oneida Creek, Emmett told Anna.

Devereaux thrust the confiscated bottle in Hazen's face. "Ever hear of videocams in stores, you nitwit?"

Hazen lowered his head in sullen defeat.

Anna realized that Belinda was glaring at Devereaux, her face quivering. Suddenly, she sprang up from the sofa and lunged at the detective. Emmett caught her as she stumbled over the coffee table and drove her to the carpet with another wristlock. She looked up and shouted, "What'd you do to my mother, you son of a bitch!"

4

A THIN SNOW WAS falling beyond Vaughn Devereaux's window as he scrolled through the Oneida Nation Police Department's computerized communications logs for the past three months. He was searching for any call that might help explain why late Monday afternoon Brenda Two Kettles had suddenly left her reservation trailer home for Syracuse Hancock International Airport.

Emmett watched as Devereaux studied his monitor, tapping his chin with a finger. A complaisant face. Yet Emmett had seen it turn hard with anger in the woods behind the Two Kettles's mobile home. The man didn't like being defied. Nobody did, but a veteran learned not to take defiance personally, particularly from punk kids. Devereaux's gold earring flashed in keeping with his slight body movements. It was tastefully small, but Emmett was still put off that a cop would adorn himself in this way.

He looked over the framed diplomas, certificates and commendations on the wall to his left. B.S. in Sociology from Hunter College in New York City. Same major as Anna's, he reflected, as she studied the wall with him. Devereaux had won a Case of the Year Award from International Narcotics Officers, the plaque engraved to Sergeant V. Devereaux of the New York Police Department. Quite a step-down from NYPD investigative supervisor to simple detective with a Podunk tribal outfit, unless this was a retirement

job. And Vaughn Devereaux, in his early thirties, was too young to have retired from NYPD on anything short of disability.

It was going on 11:00 A.M., and Hazen Two Kettles was being booked for
shoplifting in another part of the brand-new tribal law enforcement facility.

On the stroll from the lobby to his office, Devereaux had admitted to
Emmett and Anna that there wasn't a single Indian, let alone Iroquois, on
the thirty-officer roster. The Navajo Nation P.D., in comparison, was entirely drawn from the tribe, save one or two whites who were married to
Navajo women. But in fairness to the Oneida, there were only about 1,500
of them throughout the entire country, while the Navajo numbered over a
quarter million.

At last, Devereaux printed out a log page for Emmett and Anna, who
leaned into each other to read it. She smelled good, perfumed soap, perhaps.
"Here we go," the detective said, "this is sort of typical . . ." Using the tip of
his pen, he pointed at an entry made by a dispatcher:

12 December 2003
Arrived: 2314 hours
Cleared: 2342 hours
Type: Domestic Disturbance
RP: Brenda Two Kettles
    Territory Road

One-Paul-Two reports Brenda and Belinda at it again. Both HDB.
Advised. NFA.

HBD, of course, stood for *Had Been Drinking,* almost a requisite for a
domestic disturbance in Indian Country, where sober violence was a rarity.
NFA meant *No Further Action,* a *kiss off* in squad car parlance.

This had been the latest call to the trailer on Territory Road. There had
been three others in the same period: daughter Belinda Two Kettles nabbed for
drunk driving which resulted in a twenty-four-hour stay at the tribal detox-
ification unit; an assist by Patrol to a Madison County Sheriff's juvenile officer to shake down Hazen for a possible drug probation violation—no arrest;
and Brenda complaining of white kids on motorbikes in the woods behind
her—advised youths from the nearby non-reservation town of Sherrill.

Sitting back, Emmett looked Devereaux in the eye.

The detective slowly smiled and said, "Not much help, right? So I have no idea why Brenda headed for the Big Apple. I'm sure she had her reasons, I just don't know them."

"How many years were you with NYPD?"

"Eleven," Devereaux said after a brief pause. "Four in Patrol. Seven in Narcotics, five undercover. And those five years were *bad. Nasty.* I'm lucky to be alive." He chuckled in recollection of his street time. "You been there, Parker, I'm sure."

"Retired?"

"No, I was just ready for a change. Know what I mean?"

The conventional wisdom in law enforcement was that no cop should work undercover Narcotics for more than two years. Longer than that, his worldview—and values—began to bend to the pressures of the drug subculture. Something about Devereaux's smile said that he'd been left out on the street too long. It was a bit too tight.

Anna asked, "Are you originally from New York City?"

"No, ma'am. Connecticut. Papa was an ophthalmologist, and the principal at junior high was none other than my own dear mama. Now that was a bitch. No wonder I wound up the way I am. Suburbia did it to me."

Know what I mean?

Emmett wondered if he would feel better about the detective had the man come out of Harlem or the Bronx. In that case, the pressures and temptations of the streets would have been nothing new to him. Cops from the ghetto and off the rez often shared the same hard road to adulthood, which gave them background problems during the hiring process, like drug experimentation, petty thefts and turf-war violence. Emmett himself had been accepted only because a D.A. in Oklahoma had reduced a grand theft auto charge to joyriding.

Know what I mean?

So, as an upper-middle-class black, Devereaux had indeed been bent by the subculture of the streets, and it came out in a reflexive need to verify his cover story as if his life depended on it. He had to keep selling himself, even though the mean streets of New York were behind him. "I just had to get out of the city. It was doing things to my head, and when this job with the Oneida Nation came up I said—wow, just what the doctor ordered. I've always been intrigued with the Native American approach to life. I'm no anthropologist, but I think it opens a window on what pre-slavery life was like for my own people, know what I mean?" He gestured at the soaked knees and elbows to his suit. "Not that there aren't challenges up here in Haudenosaunee Country. Like keeping your clothes nice."

Emmett let Anna take over.

"Detective Devereaux—"

"Vaughn, please."

"Vaughn. How would you characterize Brenda Two Kettles's relationship with this department?"

"Strained." Another chuckle. "To say the least."

"In what way?"

"Have you ever worked a rez full-time, Anna?"

She shook her head. "Just lived on one."

"Well, then you still know. Nobody likes the cops. Even their own cops. Earlier this morning, you saw how things are with the Two Kettles family. Booze, drugs, thefts, bickering and fighting all the time. Naturally, Brenda never agreed with how we handled calls at her ratty old trailer."

"What about the bigger issue?"

Devereaux turned from his screen saver to face Anna. "And that?"

"Brenda Two Kettles's relationship with tribal government."

"In what context?" the detective asked off-handedly.

"The *condemned* sticker on the front window of her mobile home, for starters."

"Oh, not just her trailer. The health and safety ordinance calls for inspections of all homes on the reservation. If one's found to be beyond repair, it's condemned and the occupants are given more than fair market value of their trailers. Plus other assistance to move to new housing."

"Then why are the Two Kettleses still in their trailer?" Anna asked.

Devereaux sighed. "Because this can of worms is still before the Oneida Nation court. Might take years to resolve."

"Was Brenda Two Kettles one of the plaintiffs?"

"Yes."

"And the Nation Representative one of the defendants?"

"Yes," Devereaux replied. "Listen, this is heading way above my pay grade. I'm qualified to answer questions about this department's drug investigations, not Nation policy, know what I mean? As far as Hazen Two Kettles, I wouldn't have even been out there this morning if our patrol officer hadn't been tied up with a slot cheat at the casino. I was just filling in."

Without letting up, Anna asked, "Then who has the pay grade to talk about Two Kettles and Nation policy?"

Devereaux's right foot was now bobbing. "The special assistant to the Nation Representative."

"Who's that?"

"Christopher White Pine."

"Is he Oneida?"

"Definitely," Devereaux said as he reached for his telephone.

Emmett noticed two things about the connection that followed. One, the detective didn't clear the call through his own superiors, which was standard procedure with any agency in dealing with the branch of government that controlled it. And second, Devereaux reached White Pine by dialing a direct number, one that didn't go though a secretary. "Yes, Chris," he said into the mouthpiece, his tone casual. "Vaughn Devereaux here. I have Agents Turnipseed and Parker from the FBI and BIA in my office with me. If possible, they'd like very much to meet with you in regards to the Two Kettles incident . . ." The detective began listening attentively to White Pine.

So Devereaux had a friend in high places.

Through the BIA grapevine, Emmett was also aware of the Oneida Nation P.D.'s reputation as a kind of Praetorian Guard around the Nation Representative, suggesting that he didn't trust his own fractured society to keep the peace as he saw fit. Yet, in fairness, most tribal police departments were accused of the same thing. One reservation Emmett was presently working in Arizona, the San Carlos of the Apache, had been bitterly divided for years, with the tribal cops caught in-between the warring factions. And something had to be remembered about the Iroquois temperament—their aversion to dictators and tyrants had made its way into the U.S. Constitution.

"I understand, Chris," Devereaux finally said. "Yes, I'll be sure to show them. Good-bye." Replacing the handset in the cradle, he apologized to Anna and Emmett, "Mr. White Pine can't possibly see you two until the end of the week. He's hosting a delegation from Mexico and doesn't have a minute to spare before Friday. However, he says I'm to offer you two whatever help you need." He took one of his business cards and scribbled a number on the back before sliding it across the desk to Anna. "My home phone." She had started to rise when the detective added, "If you got a minute more to spare . . . ?"

Easing back down into her chair, Anna said, "Ms. Two Kettles's autopsy is scheduled for one o'clock, and we have to attend."

"This won't take long." Devereaux took a key ring from his pants pocket and unlocked the file drawer in his desk. "There's a letter I should show you. It's being worked by us and the Syracuse FBI office. Good man, Leo Manoukian. I mean that, sincerely."

Last evening, the young special agent had mentioned some documentary evidence having possible relevance to this case, but before he could explain he'd been pulled off the body recovery in the cornfield to assist the Utica resident agency with a bank robbery investigation.

Devereaux took a photocopy of a letter from the file drawer and handed it to Anna, who swiveled in her chair to share it with Emmett. "Not the original, just a transcription, so don't worry about touching it."

Emmett read the two paragraphs, then sat back again.

The first paragraph railed against the Oneida land claim, promising to *give and shed blood to stop it.* The second paragraph was even more ominous. *Come this January, we'll kill us an Oneida every month. Women won't be spared either. We'll also kill non-Indians who go to Oneida businesses, 'specially the Turning Stone Casino. If necessary, we will resort to suicide bombers to end the blight of gambling here in our sacred homeland what was made holy by the blood of our pioneer ancestors.*

> *God help us,*
> *The Upstate Minutemen*

Anna lingered over the letter, but Emmett had already formulated his first impression: The writer was white, modestly educated and possibly fundamentalist Christian. Or someone attempting to pose as all of the above.

Anna asked Devereaux, "Where was this sent?"

"The local newspaper here, *The Oneida Daily Dispatch.*"

"The Syracuse FBI office holds the original?"

"Last I heard. May I make you a copy off mine?"

"Appreciate it," Anna replied.

Emmett decided on a parting shot. "You haven't told us how you felt about Brenda Two Kettles."

The detective shifted uncomfortably in his chair. "Does it matter?"

Emmett remained stone-faced.

Devereaux thought a few seconds. "Strange. She was strange. I don't think I'd ever met anybody quite like her, except a couple old Haitian women in New York who practiced voodoo. She had that spooky air about her. She could give you the creeps just by looking at you."

"You saying Brenda had powers?" Emmett asked.

"There were rumors to that effect."

Emmett weighed this rumor against the unexceptional family life he and Anna had observed in the Two Kettles's mobile home. There were hidden sides to most lives, no matter how ordinary they appeared from the outside. Belief in witchcraft was relatively modern in Indian history, arising out of the reservation period. Under the stresses of dislocation and sudden poverty, people looked for scapegoats. The Navajo were the most glaring example. Ever since the Long Walk, their forcible removal in the 1860s to a reservation in eastern New Mexico, they'd been plagued by accusations and counter-accusations of witchcraft. And Handsome Lake, a Seneca prophet of the early nineteenth century who had melded traditional Iroquois belief and Christian tenets into a new religion, had actively hunted and executed suspected witches—until he was accused of eliminating political rivals this way.

Emmett knew that much. How much did Devereaux know? "How'd you hear of this rumor?"

Another wry chuckle. "How can you avoid not hearing? It's all over the rez. The Oneida are freaking over this news about Brenda, I mean to tell you, Parker."

"What specifically is freaking them?"

"How she died. Falling out of the sky. It means something to these people. Don't ask me what. I'm not one of them. But in voodoo terms, which I'm more comfortable with, Brenda's dying this way means somebody had a more powerful *juju* than she did. Her magic got turned back on her, always the danger when you're messing with that kind of shit."

"*Juju?*" Anna asked.

"Yeah, a charm or fetish. But it really means power. It all gets down to power. And what goes around comes around."

"Who are they saying had more *juju* than Brenda?"

"The Nation Representative." Then the detective grinned. "Can you believe that? They're saying the guy who turned their lives around is a witch. How's that for fucking gratitude?"

The pathologist seemed especially interested in Brenda Two Kettles's lungs.

Emmett had already watched him make the big Y-shaped incision in the woman's trunk and fold the resulting chest flap over her grotesquely misshapen head. The large skin sac of fluid caused by her impact with the ground had burst during the transportation of the body.

But the lungs were the medical examiner's concern.

Upon removing the organs of the trunk in a single, sloppy block, he immediately began slicing and probing their pinkish depths with his scalpel. Samples were carried to the illuminated magnifier on the bench across the autopsy suite, and he leaned into the eyepiece to examine them.

Emmett stared across the corpse at Anna.

She felt his stare, and her big and expressive eyes fixed on his. She'd learned the trick. To condition yourself to feel less than what you'd felt on your first case. But what was the price of these diminished feelings?

Our relationship, probably. Or maybe not. She has baggage, I have baggage. Too much baggage to journey through life together, at least on the intimate level we'd once hoped for.

The pathologist stood back from his magnifier. "Multiple interstitial or alveolar pulmonary infiltrates, especially in the right middle lobes."

"English," Emmett asked.

"I think your victim suffered from pulmonary edema."

"Antemortem?"

"Of course. Following too rapid an ascent to high altitude. But I'd like to confer with the NTSB pathologist."

Emmett considered the significance.

In the midst of all the dicing and slicing, the scraping behind fingernails for skin traces left behind by a suspect, two findings stood out in his mind. Swollen lung tissue. And something the pathologist had observed between the woman's breasts just as his scalpel was poised to begin the Y-incision: a small blister. Anna had fumbled through Brenda Two Kettles's stripped-off clothing and stockings to confirm that the burn appeared in her sweater as well. "What can burn you in the sky?" she'd asked.

Emmett had had no answer, and they wouldn't come close to understanding until they confirmed what had borne the Oneida woman up into the wintry heavens.

5

Lights to the south fanned up into the deepening dusk, marking downtown Syracuse. The brunt of the storm had blown in out of the northwest and was whitening the lanes of Airport Boulevard. Emmett and Anna were late for a 4:30 appointment at Syracuse Hancock International. Unavoidably, it was her turn to drive, and she struggled to keep her mind on the slick road surface.

Her clothes smelled faintly of this afternoon's autopsy.

She wasn't sure how other cops viewed postmortems. Non-Indian cops. Autopsies made everybody feel light-headed and a little numb, she supposed. But most tribes feared contact with human remains; the Navajo were positively phobic about being spiritually contaminated by them. Her own people were less so, although a traditional Modoc would've taken the time to bathe after coming in close contact with death, as she had in the autopsy suite.

But modern law enforcement left little time for being Indian.

Ahead, the terminal building began to materialize out of the snowfall.

Looking at Brenda's body this afternoon, she'd remembered her uncle's explanation that the life force of a human being dwelt in the heart and the breath. She'd even secretly examined the woman's scalp for the point where, at the instant of death, Brenda's breath had passed from her heart and out through the top of her head. To the Modoc, death was marked by breath becoming mere air. She hadn't feared Brenda contaminating her. Yet, the Modoc did fear the unexpected appearance of a ghost. Fright could kill, and she'd wondered during the autopsy if the spirit that had vacated this shattered and inert corpse might appear one day before her at some sudden turn.

A Modoc can't guard against horrors, just against being horrified.

Emmett interrupted her morbid thoughts with his own. "Damage to Two Kettles's lungs. *Altitude.* The woman fell from high altitude. And left a depression in the ground. Monday evening, the ground temperature here was thirty-seven degrees Fahrenheit."

"How'd you find that out?"

"I phoned the weather station here at the airport on my cell. Oneida County was even warmer, according to an automated monitoring station they got ten miles from old man Van Hastart's cornfield." Traffic was slowing for the front of the terminal, and Emmett snapped, "Get over to the right."

"Short term parking is to the left."

"We'll park out front. Time, Anna, *time.*"

"I know what time it is." Off to her side, a red maple leaf caught her eye. An Air Canada jet was climbing steeply into the snowy night.

What goes up, must come down. Often with terrifying speed.

An airport cop stepped out in front of her and waved his flashlight for her to merge left, back into the crawl of traffic. Powering down her window, Anna showed him her FBI credentials. "We're late to a meeting with Lieutenant Bellasario," she explained, blinking against the snowflakes peppering the inside of the sedan.

"Park behind me . . ." The cop shone his flashlight on his own cruiser at curbside. ". . . and leave the keys in the ignition. Our office's to the left inside, just past the Skyway Terrace."

Emmett and she half-jogged for the entrance, taking out their badge holders and hanging them from their jacket pockets.

The interior of the terminal seemed warm and stuffy after the open air. Teeming with people. Logjams everywhere created by the heightened security of the past two years.

Anna tried to see the airport through Brenda Two Kettles's eyes.

What had her frame of mind been as she passed this way Monday evening? Had the phone call leading up to this trip left her on edge? Had she expected to meet someone here, or in New York City, 185 air miles to the southeast? It was now virtually the same time of day, and the terminal was full of commuters. Had one of them meant something extraordinary to Two Kettles? Had perpetrator and victim met in one of these broad corridors, if only by accident? Or had the woman had a reason to end her own life spectacularly?

Emmett opened the airport police office door for her. He identified the two of them to the receptionist, who gestured at an opaque glass door behind her. "You're expected."

Inside the office, a man in a lieutenant's uniform rose from behind his desk and extended a soft hand. His face was equally soft, but amiable. He spoke in fast, clipped phrases. "Juan Bellasario. Ms. Turnipseed, I presume?"

"Yes, Lieutenant, nice to meet you in person."

"And Mr. Parker. Must say I've never met a detective from Indian Affairs before."

"Aren't many of us." Shaking hands, Emmett said, "Sorry we're running behind schedule. Just sat in on Brenda Two Kettles's autopsy. More to it than we expected."

"I'd imagine, given the condition of the body," Bellasario said somberly. Then, remembering himself, he glanced across the room to a rawboned man in a National Transportation Safety Board baseball cap and jacket. His Levi's and Acme boots were a departure from Eastern norms of business dress. "This is Dutch Satterlee," Bellasario went on, "air safety investigator out of NTSB's northeast regional office."

"You bring this weather with you?" Satterlee drawled with a folksy grin.

"No," she replied, "it's the only thing we're not being blamed for."

"Know how that goes." The NTSB investigator ran a slow gaze over the Indian faces before him. "My great-great-grandma was a Cherokee princess," he said.

Silence.

There had been no royalty and commoners in native North America. In fact, the democratic model of the Iroquois Confederation had inspired the framers of American liberty, who'd been sick and tired of royals.

Satterlee ended the awkward pause with a laugh. "Just joshing. No Indian blood."

His attendance was unexpected, and Emmett told him so. The man's brow wrinkled. "Excuse me for changing the subject, but God almighty—*finally*, somebody without an accent. Where you hail from, Parker?"

"Lawton, Oklahoma."

"Amarillo, Texas. Which is a long way from Parsippany, New Jersey, where I work outta now."

Emmett asked, "When'd you get in?"

"Last night and been at it ever since."

"Any progress?"

"A little." Though Satterlee didn't sound encouraged.

Glancing at his wristwatch, Bellasario said to the partners, "Dutch has kindly agreed to walk you two through the entire boarding process."

The NTSB man added, "Adirondack Airlines says a mistake may have been made somewhere along the line, but they sure as hell didn't let a passenger tumble out of one of their birds."

"Are they right?" Anna asked.

Satterlee stood. "I'll let you and Parker decide. All I know is that Flight Five-five-seven, the six-forty-five P.M. to LaGuardia, departs each night from second level, North Concourse, Gate Twenty-eight. How 'bout we head that way?"

Lieutenant Bellasario shook hands all around, unable to hide his pleasure to be rid of the Two Kettles quandary, at least for the time being.

On the way out, Anna realized something. If the woman had indeed left Syracuse on Flight 557 at 6:45 P.M., a gap of more than eight hours now existed in the timeline between that departure and the howling old man Van Hastart had heard at three in the morning.

Satterlee said, "I know the toxicology report won't be in for at least a week, but was Ms. Two Kettles on any kind of medication?"

Anna didn't want to publicize the woman's Xanax use, possibly shifting any blame from the carrier or the airport to the passenger. She wondered just how much pressure Adirondack was putting on the NTSB investigator. "Why do you ask, Dutch?"

"Oh, God only knows what a poor soul will do under the influence. You wouldn't believe the crazy stuff people do in and around airplanes. Drugs and joy juice just make them crazier."

Which meant to Anna that, after a day at it, Satterlee had no clear idea what might have happened to Brenda.

They'd come to the Adirondack Airlines ticket counter and baggage check-in. A long line wound listlessly through the ropes, but the NTSB man led Anna and Emmett behind the counter. He showed the plastic-encased NTSB identification card he wore on a string around his neck to the clerk at the nearest station. "This'll just take a sec, honey." Then he borrowed her computer terminal, typed a moment and swiveled the screen so the partners could see it over his shoulder. "Ms. Two Kettles bought her ticket here with cash at five-twenty P.M. on the sixth. She checked no luggage and was assigned seat Twenty-F."

Emmett asked, "Can we be sure it was Two Kettles?"

The clerk responded, "We now require two forms of I.D., one with photo."

Satterlee gave her arm an affectionate squeeze. "Thank you, darlin'."

So this, Anna reflected, is where the Oneida woman had entered the system, only to be expunged by it into a cornfield two counties away. "Ms. Two Kettles's daughter says she took a black overnight bag. Where's it now?"

"Possibly unclaimed baggage at LaGuardia," Satterlee answered.

"Meaning it rode the carousel until somebody noticed and pulled it?"

The NTSB man sighed. "Baggage says they can't find it. We're working on it."

Emmett frowned. "Who checked her in here?"

Satterlee consulted the screen. "Clerk Forty-one, please?" he called down the line of check-in personnel.

A frizzy brunette timidly raised her hand. Her name was Ms. Kolchek, and it immediately became apparent that Satterlee had failed to interview her.

Emmett showed Ms. Kolchek the photograph of Two Kettles they'd gotten earlier today from Devereaux. The Oneida Nation P.D. detective had penned Brenda's name and vitals on the bottom of the page. "You recall checking in this passenger on Monday evening, the sixth?"

Ms. Kolchek didn't have to rack her memory. "Sure."

"Any special reason?"

"Yes, sir. Her last name. Two Kettles. I asked her if she was Indian, and she nodded. She didn't say much, except she wanted to see the sky. She wanted a window seat. The only available one was over the wing."

Anna asked, "Did she actually say that?"

"Say what, ma'am?"

"She wanted *to see the sky.*"

"I think so. Something like it."

"Did she happen to mention why she was flying to New York City?"

"No, but she did ask me how the weather was there. I told her that if there was no delay, it was probably fine. I gave Ms. Two Kettles her boarding pass, and that was that."

Anna looked to Satterlee. "Was there a delay that night?"

"None. Flight Five-five-seven departed here on schedule and arrived on time at LaGuardia. Any further questions for Ms. Kolchek?"

"Thank you, that's all," Anna said to the clerk, then trailed Satterlee and Emmett out from behind the counter and into the crowd again.

She couldn't shake the thought—two evenings ago, this time, Brenda Two Kettles had been as alive as she. It was bad to think this way. What did the old Modoc say? *You cannot raise the sky.* It meant that you can't reverse fate. The dead dwelt in the sky, the western sky behind a great mountain that separated the two planes of existence. You cannot and should not bring them back, even in imagination.

Another long line awaited them at the metal detectors, and again Satterlee escorted them to the front. The security supervisor made doubly sure that Emmett and Anna were bona fide federal cops—in a hassle reminiscent of Anna's boarding at the airport in Las Vegas yesterday—before letting them side-step the detector with their handguns and be spared the body search with a wand.

Satterlee didn't have the inconvenience of carrying a handgun. After two years of having a telltale bulge under her clothes, that's how Anna thought of a service weapon—an inconvenience.

The NTSB man quickly determined that the same harried security crew of two swing-shifts ago was on duty this evening. He borrowed Brenda's photo from Emmett, but no one recalled the woman. Her memory had melted into the faceless, shuffling, impatient thousands that had filed through this electronic portal. Having seen or read the news accounts of the bizarre death, the examiners obviously wanted to recall Two Kettles if only to show that they were conscientious, but just couldn't.

Satterlee commented as they started down a long corridor, "So, we've got to assume that there was nothing unusual about the woman or the contents of her handbag."

Purse. With black sequins.

Last night, Emmett and she had retraced Two Kettles's possible trajectory up to the woods just beyond Van Hastart's farmhouse. They'd found nothing of interest, notably a purse or any cosmetics strewn among the corn stubble.

Or ruby red shoes.

Anna asked, "What happens to a purse found aboard after a flight, Dutch?"

"I'd imagine it's tagged with seat location by the cleaning crew and turned over to airport Lost and Found."

"Nothing was found here?"

"That's right. And I can check with the cleaning folks at LaGuardia on my way home tomorrow night."

Anna caught Emmett's frown. With no progress to report, Satterlee was already thinking of home.

The threesome filed onto the escalator.

It occurred to Anna that this upward glide had marked the first leg in Brenda's ascent, an ascent so rapid she suffered pulmonary edema. How far up had it ultimately gone? For the countless time, Anna wondered how her fall had been possible.

"North Concourse boarding room," Satterlee announced at the top. "Ms. Two Kettles probably waited for about an hour in the vicinity of Gate Twenty-eight. At the very end."

Anna glanced out the windows along the way. The jetliners outside were whitely dusted. A boom-truck was spraying the wings of a 757 that was waiting on the deice pad. The rotating yellow lights of the tow tractors and baggage trailers blinked among the planes. All in all, a well-orchestrated ballet of machines. Yet, somehow, at some juncture, Brenda Two Kettles had slipped through these cogs and wheels and plunged to her death.

They had come to the seating area at Gate 28, and Anna tried to imagine how Two Kettles had occupied her wait here. Had she read, or stood at one of the windows, pondering her summons to New York City? She sensed that if she could understand the woman's frame of mind she might grasp what had happened to her. But that might not be relevant, particularly if Brenda's death had been a bolt out of the blue, even to her.

Emmett was scrutinizing the jet idling at the gate. It had yet to be boarded. "Adirondack Airlines has old Boeing seven-twenty-seven two hundreds?"

"Mostly," Satterlee replied, "Why?"

"Can we go aboard?"

He hesitated, but then said, "Don't see why not."

As they descended the tunnel-like loading bridge to the jet, Anna asked, "Did the gate agent recall Ms. Two Kettles?"

"Nope," Satterlee said, "but the computer has a better memory than he does. The scanner picked up the bar code off her boarding pass."

Along the way, Anna reached out and jiggled the knob to a steel utility door stenciled AUTHORIZED PERSONNEL ONLY. It was locked.

"Always secured," Satterlee remarked. "There are punch code combination locks on all doors down to air-side."

"Air-side?" she asked.

"Fancy talk for getting close to the planes."

They made the right-angle turn at the end of the bridge, and Emmett examined the slight gap between the rubberized seal of the bridge and fuselage of the plane. Snowflakes whistled inside but promptly melted, dampening the edge of the ramp.

"What was Ms. Two Kettles's height and weight again?" Satterlee asked Emmett.

"Five-two, one hundred forty pounds."

The NTSB investigator drolly raised his eyebrows while looking at the gap. "Ain't likely then she squeezed through this itty-bitty crack."

"Evening," a flight attendant in a dark blue suit greeted them from just inside the small first-class cabin. Mascara had transformed her eyelashes into black butterfly wings.

"Lena, isn't it?" Satterlee ventured.

"No, Dutch," she replied somewhat indignantly, "it's Lisa. Lisa Collins."

"Sorry, darlin'. You lead attendant tonight?"

"I am." Despite the familiarity, she checked his I.D.

"These folks are feds too. They'll be taking a gander for the next few minutes."

"Please make it just a few minutes. The gate agent is already on my case to make schedule."

In a nonchalant aside, Satterlee explained that it was up to the agent to make sure each flight got off on time, otherwise the airline was surcharged by the airport for the slot rental.

Anna asked Lisa Collins, "A different attendant crew tonight from Monday evening's?"

"No, we're on the last hop of a three-day trip. Same crew."

Anna borrowed Two Kettles's photo from Emmett and showed it to Collins. "Seat Twenty-F. Remember her?" No recollection, but she'd ask the other attendant.

The cockpit door was ajar, and Anna had a peek through it at the flight deck. She could just see part of a pilot's white shirt. Emmett brushed past her and Satterlee and down the aisle toward the back of the plane. Anna followed. A cleaning crew of six glanced up from their furious vacuuming and wiping in the main cabin as the partners moved aft. Trained in recent years to respond to anything out of the ordinary, they showed slight concern at the intrusion of the large Comanche, until Emmett reassured them with an easy Southwest smile and pointed at his exposed badge. "Another useless federal bureaucrat," he said without breaking stride.

He left the last seats behind and slowed in the space between the aft galleys and lavatories, then stopped altogether at a rear door. He gave it a knowing tap with a knuckle. "Airstairs."

"What?"

A white-clad caterer—so tall, his head kept brushing the curvature of the ceiling—was wheeling a trash cart out of one of the cramped galleys. He slowed and appeared to be eavesdropping.

Emmett dropped his voice. "Seven-twenty-sevens have airstairs in their tails that can be lowered to take on or let off passengers at small airports."

Footfalls turned the partners around. The captain of the plane was approaching, with the lead attendant and Satterlee right behind. "May I help you, Officer?" the pilot asked Emmett.

"Are these airstairs functional?"

"Yes."

"The captain," Collins hastily explained, "flew this flight two nights ago. I showed him the picture."

Emmett instantly perked up. "Same plane?"

"Same plane," the pilot confirmed.

"You recall the woman?"

"Sorry."

"The other attendant doesn't either," Collins said to Anna, returning the photo.

"How are the airstairs lowered?" Emmett asked. "From the cockpit?"

"No." The captain opened the door on a dark, chilly space that was filled with the retracted stairs. He pointed out a control box attached to the bulkhead. "You lower them from right here."

"Already been down this bunny trail, Parker," Satterlee said quietly.

Ignoring the NTSB man, Emmett asked the pilot, "In the cockpit, would you know if the stairs had been lowered in flight?"

"Yes, a warning light would show on the second officer's panel, alarm too—but that assumes the stairs can be lowered, which they can't. After that D. B. Cooper business, you know—the guy back in 'seventy-one who parachuted out the airstairs with two hundred thousand in cash—Boeing installed a special vane, a locking system that keeps the stairs from being lowered when the cabin's pressurized."

Emmett asked, "Forty miles out of Syracuse, headed for LaGuardia, what'd your altitude be?"

"I don't think you're getting my point."

"I'm getting your point fine. Bear with me. Altitude forty miles out?"

"Oh, about ten thousand feet."

Emmett nodded. "Would decompression at that height get everybody's attention?"

"Not necessarily. Not like at high altitude. But let me say this, it's next to impossible to leave a pressurized seven-twenty-seven without the air crew knowing about it. Excuse me, I've got a preflight to finish."

But Emmett called after him, "Captain, would you swear in a court of law that there was no decompression incident aboard this aircraft two nights ago?"

Without turning, the pilot sarcastically raised his right hand as he continued forward.

He'd left Collins to secure the airstairs compartment. She then tested the loading door that had been opened to the elevated box of the catering truck. She had obvious difficulty with the latch. "Dammit, where are they?"

"Who?" Satterlee asked.

"The mechanics." She started back up the aisle again, as the huge caterer squeezed between Emmett and Anna to use one of the lavatories. He begged their pardon in a soft baritone, but there was a distrustful glint to his dark brown eyes. Anna had just shifted positions when she had to move again for two mechanics in tan Adirondack jumpsuits, who began examining the malfunctioning loading door. They'd just broken out their flashlights and tools when Collins asked, "How long?"

One of the mechanics, an unpleasant-looking man with a pug-nose, barked, "I don't know how fucking long. We just got here, okay?"

Glowering, the attendant turned and bumped into the big caterer, who was exiting the lavatory, the flushed toilet growling behind him. "Excuse me," he said, then greeted one of the mechanics, apparently the more even-tempered of the two. "Hey, Jason, how you doing?"

"Fine, Adrian."

In the midst of all this bustle, Anna single-mindedly asked Satterlee, "Can you think of anything on this plane that could account for a small burn on the victim's torso?"

Now, with mention of the victim, everybody was eavesdropping, including the caterer again, who was securing a beverage cart in the second aft galley.

"How small a burn?"

"A blister about a half-inch long and quarter-inch wide."

"Huh." The NTSB man rolled his tongue around the inside of his cheek for a moment. "Electric burners in the galleys, maybe."

"What else?"

"Oh, an oxygen-generating canister for the emergency breathing system. They use combustion to create oxygen, but dang if I can see how the woman could've been exposed to one of them. They're tucked way behind the overheads. I'm not even sure they use 'em on these old birds. You got me."

"I'm tempted to ride this old bird myself," Emmett muttered to Anna as he led the way forward, a few steps behind Lisa Collins. "Particularly if there's a bum door on it."

Glad to leave the crowded aft section, Anna asked the attendant, "Do you make a headcount of everybody onboard and compare that number to the passenger list?"

"Headcounts are ancient history," Collins replied. "The scanner verifies off the boarding-pass bar code that a passenger has boarded. Anything else?" Visible impatience.

"Not now, thanks." Anna found seat 20-F and sat experimentally in it, gripping the armrests. Nothing suggested that Two Kettles had left a trace of herself here. No unsettling chill. No electric snap in the air. After a moment, Anna peered out the frosted oval of the window. As indicated by the clerk, Ms. Kolchek, the only view was that of a wing, glazed now with a buildup of ice and snow. Seat 20-F was also next to one of the emergency exits. She studied the smooth surfaces of the chrome handle that would spring open the hatch to eternity.

Leaning over the back of the seat, Emmett seemed to read her thoughts: "Before departure, can we roll out a tech from the Syracuse office to dust for latents?"

A latent fingerprint was one that was invisible to the eye until dusted with black powder. Even a partial one might confirm that Brenda Two Kettles had gotten on board this 727.

Everything hinged on that.

"I can try," Anna said, slipping Emmett's cellular out of his coat pocket.

6

FLIGHT 557 WAITED ON the apron while a boom truck hosed the wings with a billowing mist of deicing solution.

Emmett checked his wristwatch: 7:46 P.M.

The Adirondack Airlines 727 had gotten no closer to New York City than the deice pad a hundred yards beyond the North Concourse at Syracuse International. At first, he'd considered the weather delay to be a stroke of good luck: It'd given the FBI Identification technician more than enough time to arrive and dust the emergency exit handle, the armrests to seats 20-F, -E and -D, the folding trays, plus anything else Brenda Two Kettles might have touched. Nothing. No prints. The cleaning crews had done their jobs well, and the tech went home empty-handed.

After that, the delay weighed on Emmett's patience.

Dutch Satterlee had long since arranged the impromptu flight to La-Guardia for the partners, then called it a day and gone back to his hotel.

Emmett was beginning to wish that he had done the same.

Anna and he had Row 20 to themselves. And then some. The plane was only a quarter-filled, but Lisa Collins, the lead attendant, had still cleared out the rows in front and behind the investigators so they'd have privacy in which to discuss the flight without alarming anybody. The inconvenienced passengers didn't complain—they were bumped up to the otherwise empty first-class cabin.

Sitting in Row 20 was Anna's idea. In fact, she'd insisted on having Brenda Two Kettles's window seat. *Whatever.* Emmett had no objection to any kind of brainstorming in search of a breakthrough. But, yawning, he noted, "We may have a bitch of a time getting a flight back to Syracuse tonight."

"No matter," she said, not convincing him.

He leaned forward and looked past her, out the window. The right engine blocked much of his view, but he could make out airport workers flitting through the storm to ready Flight 557. Gremlins out in the swirling white, disappearing and reappearing as if it were in their power to vanish and rematerialize at will. And snatch human beings from the cabin of a 727.

He shut his tired eyes. Another long day capped by no hope of sleep soon.

Anna asked, "Can a passenger get down into the baggage compartment from here?"

"I don't know." An investigation convinced you how little you know about your world, even things you'd believed to be familiar.

The plane lurched, and Emmett opened his eyes on movement.

The 727 was rolling at last. The captain announced over the speakers that he'd received permission from the tower to join the take-off line. A weak cheer from the passengers was cut short when he added that five jets were ahead of them.

Emmett heard a groan of metal somewhere above and behind him. He'd thought he had concealed his slight concern until Anna asked, "What's wrong?"

"Sounds like the stabilizer jackscrew can use a touch of grease." Not wanting to alarm her, he didn't explain that in 2000 a dry jackscrew had augured an Alaska Airlines 727 into the Pacific off Southern California. He ordinarily didn't give much thought to flying. But tonight he found himself listening to every pitch change in the engines, every shudder of the flaps.

The plane came to a complete halt again.

Minutes passed with no further movement. Emmett released his seatbelt and rose, explaining to Anna, "I want a quick look around."

Going aft, he tested the hatch to the airstairs door with a slight push—it seemed tightly shut. From inside the first galley, Lisa smiled up at him as she busily secured the space for take-off. He gave a casual shake of his head to tell her that all was well.

But was it?

Something with its beginning here had ended disastrously in an Oneida County cornfield.

What?

He liked to hit a case while it was still soft wax. He could feel this one hardening around him.

The second galley was unlit, apparently shut down due to the light passenger load. Neither galley had doors or hatches giving access to the exterior of the fuselage. Emmett checked inside the vacant left-side lavatory. Ms. Two Kettles had not flushed herself into eternity. *Christ.* He examined the right-side lavatory. *Nada.* Stepping out into the aisle again, Emmett inspected the suspect right-side loading door. Nothing indicated that it had ever been a springboard to a 10,000-foot fall.

Lisa asked him to sit down again.

He strolled forward.

"This taken?" he asked over the rising screech of the engines, startling Anna as he plopped into the seat beside her once more. Her face was a little drawn. He knew she didn't like these moments before take-off, but this seemed to be something else, something more. "What is it?" he asked.

She moistened her fingertips and ran them along the seal of the emergency exit hatch. "I think I can feel a leak. Does this seem completely shut to you?"

Emmett reached across her and gave the hatch a nudge. "Yes," he said, more confidently than he felt. The plane began building speed down the runway. "Off we go into the wild blue yonder."

The 727 bounded off the runway and began a steep climb. The storm-dimmed city lights fell away. Snow streaked past their window in continuous lines that seemed to be chalked on the Plexiglas. Beyond the whistling of the defroster loomed the sky. As a boy in boarding school, he had imagined horses in the sky. But no hoof was ever put to it. No wingless thing could transverse it. The sky was a frigid purgatory between heaven and earth which no human being, especially, could survive in the fragile body nature had given him. The sky carelessly let the living slip through its icy fingers.

Emmett sensed that Anna had been thinking something like this when he'd startled her.

What had the Adirondack clerk said about Brenda Two Kettles? *She didn't say much, except she wanted to see the sky. She wanted a window seat.*

The captain began banking into the north. Among the bleared glitter of suburban and farm lights was the definite shape of a serpent with an enormous head. "What's that?" she asked Emmett, pointing. "It looks like a snake."

"Sure does, doesn't it? Head must be Oneida Lake and the body the creek flowing into it."

Then they were in the clouds, and all was darkness outside. Even the green light on the tip of the wing vanished. Emmett thought he could feel the sky pressing against the thin aluminum skin of the plane, strumming it, vibrating it. Over this muffled roar came the captain's voice over the P.A., "You're free to move about the cabin unless the seatbelt sign comes back on . . ." But never free to move around the sky, Emmett mused. "Beverage and snack service will be available in a few minutes . . ." To inhabit the sky, you must be beyond both drink and food, beyond human needs. "La-Guardia's reporting only light rain, so we're anticipating no problems there. Enjoy your flight with Adirondack Airlines, the wings over Hiawatha Country—and soon your magic carpet to the Mexican Riviera. We're pleased to announce our merger with *Aero Mazatlan . . .*"

Emmett released his belt and waited for the crack in the system to reveal itself.

Anna rides shotgun in a sedan through the winter-barren New York countryside. It must be an FBI bucar, or bureau car, because she's seated beside Leo Manoukian. His young-old face is morose with concern, and he keeps glancing over at Anna.

The radio crackles to life. A dispatcher asks for their location, and he transmits, "Approaching Hamilton."

She has never heard of Hamilton in her entire life.

Naked woods slide past her window. Oaks, maples, elms and hickories, nearly indistinguishable without their leaves. But, somehow, she knows them by their bark. Whenever her mother had visited an unfamiliar coun-try, the first things she commented on were the trees and their possible uses. She'd admired the redwoods and eucalyptus on the UC Berkeley cam-pus, Anna's alma mater. She now realizes that that had been a very Indian thing to do, to see the world as trees.

"We're at the scene," Leo announces into the microphone with a qua-ver of dread in his voice.

Why? It's only a college, but Anna can't find the name displayed anywhere. The campus is tucked in timbered hills, an Ivy League idyll. Manoukian and she enter it along a broad street lined with handsome brick frat houses. A mostly white student body—and to think that she'd felt like an outsider even at multi-racial Berkeley. Such a tiny tribe, the Modoc, ap-pealing to the Sun and the Earth to keep them from disappearing entirely, like so many other tiny tribes.

The students appear to move in slow motion, as if having no associa-tion with crime and violence gives your life a slower tempo. And violence, especially, is like all primal human experiences, even like sex, in that it is unknowable through imagination. That is the single completely true thing she can say about her first year in the field.

Manoukian and she come to the front of a sprawling complex. A cam-pus cop stands beside his cruiser, motioning. "Leo," she hears herself say, her voice sounding hollow and far off to her own ears, "he wants us to take the athletic director's space."

Swinging into the parking slot, Manoukian says, "There's no need for you to go inside. Not after last night." Then he waits, looking at her.

"What do you mean, Leo?"

"When did you notice he was missing from the plane?"

"Who . . . ?"

When Manoukian visibly commiserates, she springs her door latch and gets out. The campus cop leads the two FBI agents toward a wing of the ath-letic center. A state trooper is posted at the entrance. He advises Manoukian that he hasn't left the scene unattended since its discovery by a main-tenance man at 10:30 this morning. Beyond is an ice rink. A peculiar whistling noise comes from inside it.

Anna drifts through the open double doors.

Wings.

The sound comes from the wings of a mourning dove as it circles around the cavernous space. A dove here in January makes no sense; it should be wintering down in Central America. The hole in the high, arched ceiling makes even less sense, until Anna tracks the beam of cold winter sunlight down to the seating area at one end of the rink. There, an impact has splintered two benches, and a circle of frosted red has spread out from a clump of something.

The campus cop and Manoukian walk past her and down an aisle to the place. She follows, listening as the cop explains, "Women's varsity played a practice game against junior varsity at five yesterday evening. They were all in the locker room by eight, and the maintenance guy was finished grooming the ice with the Zamboni machine by eight-thirty."

The dove continues to whistle round and round the chilly chasm above. Pieces of roof are littered across the ice. Manoukian, the trooper and she halt.

She screams, but no sound comes from her mouth. Tries to turn away, but can't.

After witnessing Brenda Two Kettles's autopsy, she now knows enough about freefall-impact deaths to realize that Emmett's head has been spared the traumatic brunt of the collision with the roof and then with the ice. His head angles up out of an amorphous, devastated mass of tissue and bone. Other than his face, only his upper chest is identifiable. Jutting from it is a big wooden sliver off a shattered bleacher. His facial expression is as serene as if he'd fallen asleep during his drop out of the sky, and his eyes are loosely shut—until they snap open. He declares that he loves her.

Confused, afraid, she cries . . .

Anna jolted awake.

Again, her heart raced as she searched the darkened hotel room for reality. And again it revealed itself in a narrow stripe of daylight between the drape panels. And the face of the digital clock. It read: 11:05.

She sat up in bed, reminding herself that Emmett was alive and well. Nothing untoward had occurred either on the flight to LaGuardia or their early morning return to Syracuse.

Her face was damp with sweat, and she wiped it on the bed sheet.

The only thing Emmett and she had learned from the excursion to New

York City was that Lost and Found at LaGuardia did not have Two Kettles's black overnight bag.

The Modoc knew ways to induce dreams, but she felt she had done nothing to bring this on. And, once again, she'd heard herself cry. *Not good, not good at all.* Dreams could be prophetic, but seldom in a way that was immediately comprehensible.

What does all this mean?

Turning on the lamp to drive away the night's demons, she recalled the most prophetic dream a Modoc ever had. It had come to an elder a few years before the appearance of the first white men. The elder dreamed of a luminous, curly-haired being riding on the back of a huge jackrabbit with oversized ears. A voice explained that this was a being the Modoc would soon know well. And soon they did, with the arrival of a Christian missionary. It was only then the elder understood the huge jackrabbit to be an ass and the luminous rider to be Jesus, entering Jerusalem the last week of his life.

Anna showered.

Day Three began with thoughts of coming into Jerusalem.

7

A FTER THE LUNCH HOUR, the federal investigators were given use of the airport police interviewing room at Syracuse Hancock International. The cubicle was sparsely furnished with a table and four chairs. A vertical slat of a window looked down on one of the runways. It was a bright, cold afternoon with a rare blue clarity of sky that made Emmett miss Arizona. The door swung open; Anna and Dutch Satterlee entered. Emmett had had no appetite for lunch, but she and the NTSB investigator had gone out for a bite to fortify them for the task ahead—to interview every employee on the ground at Syracuse to have had anything to do with Monday's Flight 557. Emmett felt that the air crew had already been grilled enough, for the time being.

Anna sat between the two men, a bit pasty-faced today. She seemed remote, yet considerate toward him whenever he got her attention.

Dutch squared a yellow pad in front of him on the table. "Ready for Eberhardt, Parker?"

"Let's hit it."

Dutch paused on his way out. "Where's your note pad?"

Emmett touched a finger to the side of his head. Memory relied on confidence, and writing things down eroded that confidence. It was more than a respect for the oral tradition of his people, the ear remembered better than the eye.

"Get much sleep?" Anna asked.

"Not much. How about you?"

She shook her head.

Dutch led in a man of average height with thinning, sandy-colored hair and a narrow face. Instead of a tan Adirondack Airlines jumpsuit, he wore a down vest over a flannel shirt and olive-green fatigue pants. Emmett rose to shake hands. "Jason Eberhardt?"

"Yes, sir."

"Emmett Parker, criminal investigator with the Bureau of Indian Affairs. My partner, Special Agent Turnipseed from the FBI, and Mr. Satterlee from NTSB. Sit down."

The mechanic slunk into the solitary chair across the table from the three investigators.

Over the next several minutes, Emmett drew out Eberhardt's biography: Thirty-three years old, born and raised here in Syracuse, a high school grad. He'd spent one hitch in the U.S. Air Force as a mechanic and continued to serve in the Air National Guard. He'd been employed by Adirondack Airlines for eight years. With all this out of the way, Emmett paused, then asked, "Do you recall the three of us from yesterday evening on Flight Five-five-seven?"

"Yes, sir. Before take-off, sure."

"Did you know at the time why we, as federal investigators, were on-board?"

Eberhardt licked his lips. "Sort of."

"What do you mean?"

"It came down the grapevine that the feds were in the North Concourse, looking into that Indian woman who was found dead."

Presumably, then, this rather efficient grapevine had its roots in the check-in counter and sent tendrils out as far as the mechanics in the hangars. Emmett asked, "You recall that Oneida woman from the same flight on Monday evening?"

"No," Eberhardt said too quickly, "I never got out of the hangar on Monday's swing-shift."

Dutch weighed in. "What were you and the other mechanic doing on-board last evening?"

"We got a service write-up on the hatch to the aft starboard loading door."

"Who from?" the NTSB man continued. Emmett let him—this was now heading into the technical.

Eberhardt took a moment to recall. "Second officer, I suppose. The door was sticking a little when the attendant tried to close it. She noticed the problem just before take-off in Cleveland on the morning run. It seated okay, no warning lights, so the captain must've said they could wait 'til Syracuse to fix it. Garrity and me got tagged to look into it."

"The other mechanic, you mean?"

"Yes, sir—Dan Garrity."

Emmett asked Eberhardt, "Why'd it take two of you to check the door?"

"They're tricky. They glide inward when you unlatch them, then swing out. It's like tying to touch your elbow to your nose—you know, to unlatch one and look at the hinge mechanisms at the same time."

Dutch asked, "And what'd you and Garrity discover?"

"Nothing. We couldn't make it screw up. It opened and closed as smooth as the day it left the Boeing factory. Dan told the lead attendant, who was pissed off a little, and we left."

"Did you see any indication that this loading door had recently failed?"

"Nothing. Like I said."

Dutch asked, "Any problems of late with any of the doors or emergency exits on that plane?"

"No, sir." Then Eberhardt asked hopefully, "Is that all?"

"No," Emmett said. "How do you feel about the management of Adirondack Airlines?"

"Feel . . . ?"

"Have you been treated fairly in your eight years with them?"

"There've been minor problems. But, all in all, I guess they treat me okay."

An honest equivocation, Emmett sensed—he'd probably answer much the same if asked about the BIA. "What're your feelings about Indians, Jason?"

The mechanic gave a slight shake of his head as if he had no opinion. "Just people, I guess."

The foreman of the crew that had tidied up the interior of Flight 557 Monday evening was El Salvadoran by birth. The middle-aged mestizo immediately broke into a sweat and perspired copiously throughout the interview, but Anna felt he was telling the truth in that he had no memory of Brenda Two Kettles. He and his crew were finished minutes before she would have ever boarded. His anxiety, no doubt, was related to some immigration matter that might not stand up to scrutiny. Anna wanted to reassure him that she had no intention of contacting *La Migra*. After all, only two million of the current 270,000,000 citizens of the United States weren't "aliens," legal or otherwise. Those were Indians, like herself, and certainly a Central American mestizo was as welcome in Iroquois Country as a Modoc.

But, instead of giving voice to this, she just said, "That's all, sir. Appreciate your cooperation.

Dutch heaved himself to his feet and went out to fetch the next to the last interviewee. It was going on six o'clock, and an air of disappointment hung in the cubicle. Nothing material had been developed over the past five hours, this on the heels of a long night. Emmett asked Anna, "How you holding up?"

"Fine." She didn't sound it. *Whatever.*

The door swung back, and once again Emmett was struck by the white-uniformed caterer's height. Adrian Flint was at least five inches taller than Emmett, making him about six-seven. The top of his head had brushed the galley ceiling. Flint's face was long and homely, his features bony, and his expression guarded. He hesitated in the doorway, and Dutch side-stepped around him to resume his place behind the table.

"Come on in," Emmett invited him the rest of the way inside the room.

"Whatever you say." A whispery baritone. Flint brought an unexpected scent of wood smoke in with him. He lowered his long-boned frame into the chair, which then seemed toy-like beneath him.

Emmett launched into the biographical part of the interview. Straight-off, he sensed that the caterer resented the questioning. It was like pulling teeth. He was thirty-eight years old. Born in Michigan. Spent two years at the Minneapolis College of Art and Design. Major: Studio Design. No military service. Previously employed at Minneapolis–St. Paul International with a catering service for Northwest Airlines. Three years now with Chez Sky Foods, serving Adirondack and two other regional air carriers. Most significantly, he'd loaded the galleys on Brenda's flight.

Dutch said to him, "Please take us through your loading evolution for Flight Five-five-seven on a typical night."

Flint flexed his hands on his knees. Big bony joints. "All pretty routine. I hoist the box up off my truck to the aft loading door on the starboard side, go aboard. Not much to do on these short hops. Just load a couple snack carts and take away the trash cart. Does any of this mean anything?" he asked, as if trying to hold down a slow rise of indignation.

"It might," Emmett said. "Is it routine for you to still be on the plane when passengers start boarding?"

"More so now than a couple years ago."

"Why's that?"

"The new security measures are making a mess of all the schedules."

Emmett noted, "The trash cart isn't very big, is it?"

Flint paused before answering, and when he did it was with a coy smile that said he knew where this was headed. "Not very. Certainly not big enough to carry a woman off the plane."

Emmett wanted to pursue this some more, but Dutch interrupted, "You know the two mechanics who were working on the aft door last night?"

"Eberhardt and Garrity?" the caterer said off-handedly. "Of course. See them all the time." Then a look came over Flint's face as if he'd just unconsciously accused the two mechanics of something. "I have no idea what they were doing, but they're both known to be very competent."

"How well do you know both of them?"

"Eberhardt very well. Garrity less so."

"Either of them have a chip on his shoulder?"

"What about?"

"Anything?"

"Not that I know of."

"No talk against minorities or other ethnic groups?"

"Eberhardt, never."

"What about Garrity?"

Flint stared off a moment. "I just don't know Dan well enough to comment on that." He turned his large head to focus on Emmett. "Excuse me, you're Indian, aren't you?"

Emmett found himself thinking ahead to Daniel Garrity, the other mechanic and final interviewee. Flint had gotten ahead of himself by volunteering that he hadn't whisked Brenda Two Kettles off the plane in a trash cart. But a number of employees had responded similarly.

"I'm sorry," Flint said sarcastically, "is the term *Indian* politically incorrect?"

"It's a misnomer, but one we're stuck with."

"Of course, Columbus thinking he'd arrived in India."

"Right. Most native people don't find it offensive."

"What do you find offensive?"

Emmett stared back at him. Flint was dark-eyed. He had black hair, an olive complexion and prominent cheekbones. "How about you?"

"Sir?"

"Are you Indian?"

"Not that I know of."

"Even part Indian?"

"No."

"That's all I have. Thank you, Mr. Flint."

"I was born in Oneida, raised in Chittennango, and now I live in Sherrill," Daniel Garrity said. The pug-nosed, thirty-five-year-old mechanic leaned forward in his seat and grinned at Emmett as he declared this. Proudly. As if describing the turf he would defend with his life. "I served with Army Airborne in Desert Storm, honorably discharged."

From the corner of his eye, Emmett saw Dutch make a note that Garrity had been a paratrooper. Parker then asked, "How long have you been with Adirondack Airlines?"

"Too long."

"Meaning?"

"Just that. Nine years has been too long. I start with United Airlines here the first of February, so if any of this crap fucks with my new job, you'll hear from my attorney."

Emmett ignored the threat. "What soured you on Adirondack?"

"Their chickenshit management."

"Are you active in the union?"

"Yes. Next question."

"We decide when to move on to the next question," Emmett said. "Do you have any grievances filed against the company?"

"Yeah, safety issues, mostly related to these worn-out Third World birds they got from the merger with *Aero Mazatlan*." Garrity flicked his chin at Satterlee. "If this guy's with NTSB, he knows about it."

Dutch gave Emmett a nod.

"Any of these issues involve the doors on seven-twenty-sevens?"

"Nope."

"Tell us about the problem with the door on Flight Five-five-seven," the NTSB man said.

Garrity pointed at Anna and Emmett with a twirl of his index finger. "First, you tell me what they're doing here."

"As we said, Ms. Turnipseed is an FBI agent and Mr. Parker is a federal criminal investigator—"

"—with the Bureau of Indian Affairs," the mechanic finished for him. "Indians, the two of them."

Emmett asked, "What troubles you about Special Agent Turnipseed and me being involved in this?"

"Jurisdiction."

"Mine or the FBI's?"

"No, I can buy them having a piece of this. I've seen them work with NTSB before, especially when the case goes from accident to crime. But you, Parker? The fucking Department of the Interior?" Garrity smirked, waiting for a reply.

Emmett was not about to explain that the entire investigation began with an Indian victim expiring under circumstances that were suspicious, to say the least. And he'd been further empowered to go where he pleased and ask what he pleased by the U.S. Marshal's Service, although that remained a mysterious favor. Instead, he inquired, "How do you feel about Indians?"

"Oh, I love them. The wife and I got us a three-bedroom in Sherrill. It was a fixer-upper, so we dumped a lot of money in it. Home sweet fucking home. But now the U.S. Supreme Court says the third-acre lot under our little piece of the American dream belongs to the Oneida Nation. The Department of Justice is helping them figure out how to evict us with minimum fuss. And your Department of the Interior would love to see all of

Oneida and Madison Counties go native, so they could hire more BIA bureaucrats like you to keep us white tenants in line. It's going to be a paradise when the Oneidas get all this country. Slot machines in convenience stores, school cafeterias, the blight of gambling everywhere. I can hardly wait. So yes, indeed, I'm nuts about Indians, Parker."

"Monday evening, Garrity," Dutch said insistently. "Did you have occasion to leave your maintenance facility for any reason?"

But the mechanic slammed the flat of his hand on the table and shouted, "A feeb and a criminal dick from the BIA are here because you sons of bitches think a crime was committed. I'm under suspicion. So's Eberhardt. He's as gutless as they come, but I'm not. We talk again with my lawyer present, if at all!"

With that, Garrity stormed out.

After a few seconds, Dutch scooted his chair back and planted his boots atop the table. "Looks like we hit a nerve."

"Big time," Emmett said. "So let's schedule a chat with his lawyer present. The more the merrier."

Before showering, Anna went to the closet in her hotel room and took out her carry-on bag. Once again, death was tugging at her in her dreams. *There are no logical defenses*, the Berkeley-educated rationalist within her maintained. *Law enforcement is a lottery in which you routinely gamble your health, your sanity, your life itself. You can reduce the odds against you with certain precautions, but never entirely eliminate the risk.*

However, she took a small jewelry case from inside her carry-on bag and slipped off the rubber band that held the two halves of the clamshell box together. Revealed, a clump of feathers flashed iridescently in the lamplight.

Inside was a dried hummingbird.

It had once flitted from wild blossom to blossom in the steppes and lava fields of her Modoc homeland. Until her Uncle Boston had snared it in a net. Boston was actually her granduncle. And a shaman, although the word, of Siberian origin, sounded too sinister to describe what he did. He was a practitioner of spirit power. He tried to limit the random and often senseless perils of human existence, to enlist friendly forces, called *familiars*, to oppose forces that weren't well disposed toward his clients. Boston was one of a handful still following the old road. He had the unruly white eyebrows of a traditional Modoc, and last year he had presented his grandniece with a hummingbird. At the very least, to make her feel safer, she supposed, to bring her peace of mind through an alliance with powers equal to her fear of death.

Had this been Brenda Two Kettles's tribal role as well?

If so, an old Modoc saying applied: *Few shamans die in bed.* They invariably acquire enemies. Their powers fail on occasion, and their clients become their enemies.

Anna took the hummingbird from the box and rested it in her palm. The mummified creature seemed to have no weight at all. It felt as insubstantial as her expectation that no harm would come to her here. That was the purpose of carrying this talisman. Good fortune while blundering through a maze of death.

Once again, she was exploring a death wrapped in myth.

And with that came a sudden insight.

There was a spiritual track to this investigation she was neglecting. In her determination to be the reasonable and proficient little special agent here, she'd closed herself off from that track.

The room was cold, she realized. She jacked up the thermostat, and the forced air ruffled the drapes she'd already shut on the starry evening.

To hell with a shower.

She knew she needed to rinse all the death off of her, that death might be poisoning her outlook, but she was simply too worn out.

Emmett had gone downstairs alone for dinner. She unlocked and opened the connecting door between her room and his; she wanted to be awakened by his return. No other invitation was implied by leaving the barrier open. They both seemed beyond that now, although they remained united by a thin strand of affection that refused to snap. He and she no longer knew how to test that connective thread. If it was still intact. Time and another woman might already have broken it.

Shit.

She kicked off her shoes and stretched out on top of the coverlet, folding it over her instead of crawling between the sheets in her clothes.

She would shower later. *Later.*

She rested the hummingbird beside her pillow. Hopefully, to ward off nightmares. Dreams of falling, of hearing herself cry. Dreams she could not mention before breakfast. Her days were now turned so upside-down she was no longer sure when breakfast was.

She had to sleep. Before anything more.

A little after eight, Emmett returned to his room from dinner. Switching on the light in his room, he was surprised to see that Anna had left the inner connecting door wide open.

He peered into her semi-darkened room.

She was in bed, snoring softly, which made him smile. He'd never slept with her, never even shared a room with her, so it was something of a minor revelation. Major revelations had worn him out.

His smile died.

Last December, in the wreckage of their year-long relationship, Emmett had told her he still wanted her. And she had told him that he'd have to catch her this time. Then both of them went back to their jobs, separated by the wide desert between Phoenix and Las Vegas. One busy day bled into another, and nothing more happened. Now those days of inaction seemed to weigh against them, and the scales seemed tipped against him ever catching her again.

As he turned, the floor creaked under him. He checked on her again. She didn't stir. Understandable, if she'd gone to bed even half as tired as he now felt.

Something glimmered beside her pillow.

He crept across her room to the bed, hovered over her to have a look. The hummingbird. She was back to carrying around a hummingbird to ward off her fears. With many more years in the field than she, he'd given up trying to hold his fears at bay. He accepted the inevitable that the darkness would have him one day, be it in the skies over upstate New York or along some dusty reservation road out West.

His only consolation was the promise he'd made long ago to himself that he'd go down firing.

Withdrawing from Anna's room, he closed the connecting door and stripped for a long, hot shower. The warm water did the trick, and he slipped into bed, pleasantly drowsy—except for one recollection that refused to let go of him. During the most hotheaded portion of his interview, Daniel Garrity had used the term *blight of gambling.* As had the writer of the death threat letter. Now it remained to be discovered if the mechanic had been the author or simply was a plagiarist.

When Anna awoke, the digital clock read: 9:47. She sat up and turned on the nightstand lamp. The first thing she noticed was that the connecting door was now closed. And the hummingbird still lay beside her. Perhaps it had done its work. She'd had no night terrors, but her few hours of sleep were a black, dreamless void in her memory, and there was something equally disturbing in that, a glimpse perhaps into death itself.

Immediately, she went to the hotel guest services book on the writing desk. A quick check disappointed her: The Shako:wi Cultural Center in Oneida had closed at 5:00 P.M. But, yesterday morning, while handing over his business card with his home phone scribbled on the back, Detective Devereaux had passed along the special assistant to the Nation Representative's offer to help the partners in whatever way they needed.

She now needed something—access to Oneida cosmology.

Devereaux answered on the second ring, sounding a bit less accommodating than he had the other morning. Yet, he heard Anna out, then said, "I'll have somebody meet you there."

She hung up.

Keys.

Quietly, she opened the connecting door and stole into Emmett's room. Having seen him finish dressing on a number of occasions, she knew that during the night he stored his revolver in the nightstand drawer and his keys and wallet in one of his shoes. If his hand moved for the drawer, she would announce herself, otherwise she'd simply take the keys and let him sleep.

But when the floor creaked under her, he stirred slightly. "What you doing, Ladonna?"

"Need the car keys," Anna said. "I'll be back in an hour or so."

Emmett settled back down, tossing a forearm over his eyes to block out the light spilling from her room into his.

Ladonna was the name of an ex-wife. The second one. Was it comforting to imagine himself still married to Ladonna, still tied to someone with whom he could sleep—without complication? It was the one thing she had not been able to give him.

8

A LIGHT CAUGHT ANNA'S eye as she sped westbound along the Dewey Thruway toward Oneida. The moon, waning at half, flickered through the bare woods and suggested a prayer song to her, which she first hummed and then softly sang in her people's Sahaptin dialect:

> Come to the fearful, Moon of the Sky,
> Make ready your powers, Moon of the Sky,
> Make ready to fight with death, to lose or win.

She turned onto Route 365, the moon keeping pace with her. It shone whitely through the spiky tree branches and made the ice patches on the overpasses glisten. The phases of the moon and human death were closely connected in the Modoc mind. At a cosmic council long ago, Coyote argued for a full twelve months of winter each year. But the other animals wanted no more than three months of cold, and so it was the phases of the moon were created to mark the seasons. Coyote wanted human beings to live forever, as he did. But the others saw value in death, otherwise the world would become too crowded. So the waning of the moon was like the irreversible waning of each human life.

Come to the fearful, Moon of the Sky . . .

She went left on Route 46 and kept to it for the two and a half miles to Nation territory. Still, her nap had left her groggy, and she almost missed it— the Shako:wi Cultural Center, a handsome log building. The parking lot was unlit, yet, as she pulled in, two vehicles awaited her: a Lexus sedan, possibly dark green, and a light-colored van. She had expected a tribal police cruiser, even though Detective Devereaux hadn't indicated who would meet her here.

A spotlight shone down onto the entrance, showing that the door was ajar.

She gathered up her notebook and purse, locked the FBI car and hurried toward the building.

The cold burned her ears. It could get nasty in Modoc Country, sometimes twenty below zero, but this humid eastern cold seemed to sear right through flesh. She fought a shiver. And missed home with the mixed feelings of someone who'd had a troubled childhood. *The adult is often built on the ruins of the child,* her therapist had once told her. That ruinous childhood had included sexual abuse by an alcoholic father, and the therapist had been helping her—and Emmett—work their way toward full and natural intimacy, when a month ago he and then she stumbled off that path. Perhaps for good.

A *mano* had been lodged between the door and the jamb to keep the entryway open. The Oneida probably didn't call this rolling pin-shaped grinding stone a *mano,* literally *hand* in Spanish. It would seem odd to refer to Indian tools without resorting to Spanish.

Again, Anna felt far from home.

The foyer was minimally-lit. No one awaited her behind the information desk or in the adjoining gift shop. She called out, "Hello?"

Silence.

She strolled into the first gallery beyond the foyer—and froze. A human silhouette loomed on a slight platform across from her. But it was absolutely motionless. The thing stood too still to be alive, and her racing heart settled down again.

The figure was a dummy, an exhibit of some sort.

Through a second gallery she could make out an open space beyond, a classroom perhaps. A dim light emanated from there, gleamed on the surfaces of tables. Movement passed across the light—something large—and vanished into a curtain of shadow.

Without wasting another hello on the silence, Anna strode that way. She tucked her notebook and purse under her left arm to keep her right hand free for her pistol.

Someone stepped out in front of her.

Stopping, she reached for her semi-automatic in her belt holster just as the fluorescent lights bumped on in that gallery. An unearthly face confronted her. A mashed and bushy countenance the color of straw. It seemed dead, even mummified, except for the lively brown eyes that glimmered out from two tear-shaped holes. "I apologize, Ms. Turnipseed," a voice said from the mouth slit, where a pink, animated tongue moved, "for not getting together with you sooner . . ."

Anna let go of her pistol, her hand falling to her side.

"But I've been so busy," the voice went on pleasantly. "It's the plague of modern life, one I'm sure you can relate to."

The face was a mask woven from cornhusks.

"The Husk Faces, such as the one I wear, are the messengers of the Three Sisters of Sustenance. Corn, Beans and Squash. They have the gift of prophecy. Anything you need to hear?"

"Just your name," Anna said.

A light brown hand rose to lower the mask, revealing a native man in his early sixties with a hawkish nose and thin lips. He wore a three-piece suit and a paisley tie, plus a gold Rolex watch. "Chris White Pine, special assistant to the Nation Representative."

Anna looked around.

They stood in an entire gallery of masks. Most appeared to be demonic: unruly white hair, hooked noses, skewed mouths and spikes projecting from foreheads. But none seemed as frightening as the cornhusk one had with living eyes peering out of it.

Behind the special assistant, a huge man in coveralls was retreating toward the rear of the building. "Thanks for turning on the lights, Johnny," White Pine said over his shoulder, and the figure lofted a hand in acknowledgment. "The night maintenance man," he explained to Anna. "One of those naturally innocent souls so rare these days."

Slowly, the janitor began dusting the tables in the classroom. As if listening to the conversation between White Pine and Anna. She wondered if his face was as brutish-looking as his lumbering body, but he had kept the lights off around him. Still, she felt as if she'd seen him before. In Modoc lore. One of the cannibalistic giants who dwelt in thunder and feasted on unwary children.

White Pine asked, "So what do you think of our medicine society masks?"

Anna glanced them over once again. "I don't know . . . they make me want to either scream or laugh."

"Exactly," he congratulated her. "You've hit upon something fundamentally Haudenosaunee. That which is terrifying can also be very, very funny." He shook her hand. "Welcome to *the Place of the Standing Rock.*"

She quickly disengaged herself. "Thought you didn't have a minute to spare before Friday."

"I don't. At least from eight in the morning until eight at night. But when the chance came up to help you after hours, I just couldn't resist." She searched his smile for a double meaning, but then he pivoted to return the cornhusk mask to its hook on the wall. "And forgive me for greeting you like this. It's how the Nation Rep welcomed me when I came on board three years ago. Scared the crap out of me. But when the lights came on and the mask came off, he said—*I want you to feel in the pit of your stomach how close the past is to an Oneida. Our past is always lurking around the next bend in the path, waiting to both ambush and help us, depending on the mood of the Forest People.*" White Pine faced her again. "Those, Anna, are the spirits we honor with most of these masks. And, as you probably know, the spirits aren't necessarily friendly to human beings. Given the choice, the beggars prefer to screw with us. Okay if I call you Anna?"

She nodded.

"And you must call me Chris. By the way, Detective Devereaux asked me to tell you that Hazen Two Kettles was released this morning."

"Good," she said, despite a hopeless feeling that the youth would be back in detention before long. The odds were against him, particularly with his aunt gone.

The janitor was now unabashedly eavesdropping. He'd quit dusting. She could tell he wore glasses from the reflective glints.

White Pine was eyeing her notebook. "You're here tonight because you think it'd be useful to understand the Oneida past, correct?"

"Correct," she admitted, "if it's not too much trouble."

"None at all." White Pine examined her face for a moment, then declared, "You're Modoc."

"Yes." At last, somebody had gotten the name of her tribe right.

"I've met a few Modoc-Klamaths. National Indian Gaming Association meetings. But I've never met one who professes to being just a Modoc."

"I'm one of the few."

"Then how'd your Modoc ancestors avoid repeated intermarriage with the Klamath on the rez you shared with them?" Before she could reply, White Pine added, "Unless a substantial portion of your family was isolated on the Oklahoma reservation. Ah yes, that's it—you're a product of the Modoc diaspora."

"What do you know about it?" she asked evenly, although she didn't like being referred to as a *product*.

"Let's see. Kintpuash, known to white settlers as Captain Jack, fought relocation to the reservation with the Klamaths. The resulting war was the costliest per capita in U.S. history. About a hundred and fifty Modocs, including women and children, inflicted more than that number of casualties on the U.S. Army, fending them off from their refuge in the lava fields near Tule Lake for six months. But, in the end, the rebellion was put down and Kintpuash . . ." White Pine paused. "Ancestor?"

"Great-great-grandfather."

"Kintpuash was hanged," the man said remorsefully. "His family and closest followers were shipped off to a small rez in northeast Oklahoma. Forgive my pedantry, but I'm something of an expert on the scatterings of tribes."

She hid her surprise by reminding herself that White Pine had simply done his homework, this sort of tribal history was available in any Native American encyclopedia. The bigger question was why he had bothered. "Odd specialty," she said.

"Not really. See, after New York stole our lands in the eighteen-twenties, there was a lot of pressure to kick the Oneida out of the state. Bad for public morale to keep tripping over the ragged waifs you just dispossessed. Some Oneida went to Canada. Others wound up in Wisconsin. My own band bought land from the Sault Sainte Marie tribe of the Chippewa in Michigan and rebuilt the Oneida world there in isolation. They kept apart even from their Chippewa neighbors. I'm probably more full-blood than any of the Oneida here in the New York, who intermarried with other Iroquois. And I certainly speak Haudenosaunee better than most. But some people around here think I need to be reminded what it means to be an Oneida. Sound familiar?"

Anna finally smiled back at him. "It would've been to my father. He heard stories about the Modoc homeland all the time he was growing up in Oklahoma. Like it was some kind of paradise. He moved out to California in his twenties. But he never did fit in. I don't think the homeland quite lived up to his expectations."

"Not easy being the prodigal son, believe me. I take it your father's deceased?"

"Yes."

"Sorry," he said. "But he returned to the homeland. That took guts, Anna. He faced down his own dreams and went after his destiny." White Pine guided her back into the main gallery off the foyer. "Forgive the Disneyland atmospherics, but Grandmother does help us get our message out to the public. Who can hate a kindly-looking old woman?"

He was referring to the figure on the platform, a manikin of a female elder with long white hair and outfitted in a beaded dress. Her most lifelilke feature was her pair of warm, brown eyes. *But, apparently, somebody doesn't care for Oneida grandmothers,* Anna thought to herself, remembering Brenda Two Kettles's broken corpse.

White Pine pressed a button on the edge of the platform, and the manikin proved to be an automaton when she suddenly gave two broad blinks and smiled. *"Sheko:li,"* her recorded voice said, *"That is our word for Greetings . . . !"*

He sat on one of the benches arrayed before the platform and patted the place to his right for Anna to do the same. She sank down beside him as Grandmother gave the name the Oneida had for themselves, the *Onyotaa:ka, the People of the Standing Rock.* Right off, she pointed out the ancestral lands the Oneida had lost.

White Pine checked for Anna's reaction, but she was careful to show none. She didn't like to be monitored for reactions.

"In the beginning," Grandmother continued, "all was darkness and water. In the heavens above, the Father Spirit looked down on this world and was not pleased with it. It was not complete. So he uprooted a white pine, which is sacred to us, creating a hole in the heavens . . . he spoke to his daughter, whom he loved very much. He told her to go below into the world of darkness and water—"

"Forgive this Chamber of Commerce version of the origin story," White Pine whispered. "In the traditional view, Sky Woman was expelled from the heavens for varying transgressions."

Anna looked sharply at him. The phrase *Sky Woman* had leaped out at her. "What'd you just say?"

"Shush," he gently chided her. "Listen."

"This woman," Grandmother continued, "who would be called Sky Woman by all the water creatures below, began falling. As she fell, the animals gazed up in wonder and fear. Far above them they saw a radiant light that was Sky Woman. Gradually, they overcame their fear and began to worry about what would happen to her when she struck the water. There would be no land to receive her, and she would drown. Beaver said she needed some dry land, so he swam deep under the water to find some earth. He failed—"

"And perished in the attempt," White Pine murmured. "But we decided that a dead beaver would be a bit much for the kiddies."

Anna scarcely heard him. She was watching Grandmother's mechanically-driven lips:

"Loon tried, and he too failed. Finally, Muskrat managed to find some land at the bottom of the waters. He brought it to the surface in his claws and patted it on the back of Turtle to make North America, as we know it today. We and Sky Woman are forever indebted to Muskrat and Turtle . . ."

At the end of the presentation, Grandmother went still again.

Anna was almost as still. She felt as if she'd just heard Brenda Two Kettles's story, except that there'd been no Muskrat and Turtle to cushion her fall.

"Forgive the oversimplifications," White Pine said, "but that's how, in the traditional view, the modern era began. The plane of woe to which we've all been sentenced by the Father Spirit."

She turned toward him. "You say those two things a lot."

"What things?"

"*Forgive* and *in the traditional view.*" She indicated the mute automaton. "Is this your view as well?"

"No," White Pine said, "although there are some notable similarities with *Genesis. The earth was without form and void, and darkness was upon the face of the deep, and the Spirit of God was moving over the face of the waters. And God said, 'Let there be light.'*" He stood. "It's natural for me to refer to forgiveness. I'm a Christian by faith and a clinical psychologist by vocation. The former needs no explanation, but the latter is in the business of getting people to forgive themselves." His gaze probed hers. "Does this make sense to you, Anna?"

It did, with the uncomfortable feeling that he was reading her past in her eyes.

"As for tradition," he went on in a lighter tone, "the ninety dispossessed Oneida who went to Michigan did so in the hope of creating an Indian Christian community free of a nontraditional influence that had come hand-in-hand with the reservation era—witchcraft."

"Are you aware of the rumors that Brenda had powers?" she asked.

"Who told you that?"

"Detective Devereaux. He compared her to voodoo priestesses he'd known in New York."

"Well, I wish he hadn't." Starting for the entrance, he looked genuinely exasperated. Anna followed. "Rumors and accusations of that sort absolutely fractured Oneida society back in the nineteenth century. Covet a man's wife, brand him a witch and see him murdered. Lust for power, plant an innuendo or two that your political foes are practicing the dark arts. It nearly destroyed us as a people. It could still do it today, so I'm going to have a word with Vaughn about careless talk."

"He was simply responding to Mr. Parker's question. And . . ."

"And what?" White Pine asked, filling the pause.

"Brenda Two Kettles did fall out of the sky with no explanation so far."

"Well, I'm sure she didn't get up there on a broomstick, aren't you?" White Pine drolly said. "I know what you're getting at, Anna, but I can't say what's happening here. Ms. Two Kettles—did the poor woman die in some kind of bizarre parody of our creation story? Is there some cosmic conformity at work here? If I thought that, I'd believe the myth per se. And I don't. Even though it fascinates me. But no, the earth we stand upon came into being because God commanded a firmament in the midst of the waters, not because Muskrat and Turtle got together to give Sky Woman a landing pad."

"Then you don't believe in native myth at all?"

He drew Anna to a halt in the middle of the gift shop. "At the risk of putting the anal in analyzed, I believe in the *power* of myth in the same sense that I believe in the power of psychology—as a tool to mold and influence productive human beings. And yes, you're quite right—Brenda's death could be a mockery of the creation story. And, despite my Christian faith, I'd take offense to that. It disrespects a past I do indeed value. More than you might realize."

"Are you the Nation Representative's therapist?"

White Pine laughed out loud. "He'd get a big kick out of that. No, no—I'm more like his chief of staff. Though I'd say that psychology enters into most everything we talk about. In the end, every issue is ultimately a behavioral one."

He was searching through the bookshelves when Anna asked, "How does behaviorism enter into the controversy over the mobile homes on Territory Road?"

He frowned. "Unfortunately, the question is before the tribal judiciary, which has issued a gag order. So I can't publicly comment. Can you keep a confidence?"

She didn't believe in gag orders on reservations. Occasionally, free speech was the first casualty of tribal sovereignty, which sometimes meant those in power trying to retain that power at all costs. Yet, she had no evidence so far that that was the case here among the Oneida. "I can keep any confidence until I'm under oath."

"Fair enough. You saw the Two Kettles's trailer," White Pine said, his voice rising. "It's a firetrap. All the old ones are, and an Oneida family of four's dead to prove my point. We can't hope to govern ourselves unless we function like real governments all over the world, and health and safety are a primary function of government anywhere. But that has little to do with what's going down here."

"What do you mean?"

"In all struggles, Anna, defining symbols emerge. Sooner or later, a symbol comes to define the cause. Here, that symbol happens to be a collection of rattletrap trailers."

"And how do you see the struggle?" Anna asked.

"The usual one in Indian Country. Progressives versus traditionalists. Those who want to put their tribes on an equal footing with the dominant society against those who will deny us the use of anything modern in our efforts to survive as united native peoples."

"Such as?"

"Gambling. I've got no affection for gaming. Too highly addictive. However, it was the catalyst for the Oneida economic miracle that now includes textiles, coffee importation, the largest Indian newspaper in the country and a production studio. Without gaming, the Nation would still be down to those thirty-two acres on which the old trailers rust, and I'd still be in Minnesota, where I had my practice after giving up trying to make a living on the rez—largely a practice of bored white housewives and pimply delinquents." Crouching, White Pine ran a finger along the spines of books stacked on the lowest row of the shelf. "But the traditionalists say gambling is un-Oneida, even though the Haudenosaunee bet on anything and everything centuries before Columbus showed up south of here."

"The plaintiffs claim that their homes have been condemned so they can be banished, moved off the rez and away from the mainstream of tribal life."

White Pine's sparse lips tightened over his teeth, before he chuckled once more. *"Banished,"* he echoed, *"Off the rez.* That's the mentality they're all stuck in—"

"Including Brenda Two Kettles, before her death?"

"Especially Brenda." He began searching the shelves again. "She saw those lousy thirty-two acres as the navel of the Oneida world. You want to feel banished? Try Wisconsin or Ontario or upper peninsula Michigan." He looked up at Anna. "The Nation's recovering its former territory in two ways. The first is the land claim, which has been decided in our favor but not administrated by the federal courts. Two settlement attempts with the white community have failed. In the meantime, we're not waiting for the courts to give us what we're owed. We're buying up our ancestral lands whenever they become available on the real estate market. It's to those re-acquired lands this handful of traditionalists will be *banished,* as you put it. Banished into brand new, up-to-the-code single-family residences subsidized by the Nation. This will not be off the rez, as they maintain. They're ignoring the fact that a federal judge has ruled repurchased Oneida property to be Indian Country, with full sovereign status. Ah, here we go." He plucked a boxed book from the shelf and stood erect to present it to Anna. "A gift to you from the Nation, Anna."

"Regs won't let me accept—"

"Then a gift to the federal government," White Pine interrupted. "The Good Lord knows we've made a number of valuable gifts to that government, including its independence from England."

"The whites around here don't seem to remember that."

"Oh, they did when the Oneida were flat on their backs. That's what the Nation Rep tells me. The whites were far more appreciative when the Nation was down to thirty-two squalid acres and Indians cut firewood or cleaned motel rooms for a hand-to-mouth living."

"What happened then?"

"Nothing breeds resentment like success," White Pine said.

Anna slid the tome out of its simulated leather case—*The Oneida Creation Story*, with a gold embossed sticker indicating that the limited edition was personally autographed by the translator—Dr. Christopher White Pine. She smirked at him. "You like to spring little traps, don't you?"

He smiled back at her. "Just little ones, Anna."

She studied the cover art. The painting, suggestive of the American primitive style, portrayed heaven, a sunlit meadow dotted with Iroquois longhouses, hovering above a brooding sky and dark, wind-chafed waters. Plunging headfirst through a hole created in the meadow by the uprooting of a pine was a black-haired woman.

Plunging as if to her death.

9

T HE SYRACUSE SATELLITE OFFICE of the FBI cooperated fully with Emmett's plans, which surprised him. Anna and he arrived shortly after
lunch. She immediately closeted herself with the special agent in
charge in his glass-partitioned office, presumably to assure him that she and
her BIA partner weren't co-opting any of his ongoing investigations. Fred
Cochran, the SAC, was a typical feeb stuffed-shirt with a compact mustache
and a habitual, meaningless smile.

Emmett, meanwhile, buttonholed Leo Manoukian.

Tuesday evening in the cornfield, the young special agent had referred
to the death threat letter but not explained it before he was called away on
a bank robbery investigation. Privately, Emmett had every intention of co-
opting this case from the FBI if the interrogation of Adirondack Airlines
mechanic Daniel Garrity, scheduled for two this afternoon, hit pay-dirt.

Manoukian had collected the letter from the op-ed cubicle at *The
Oneida Daily Dispatch* on December 15th of last year. Emmett didn't ask
Leo how long he'd been out of the academy, but he did inquire how and by
whom the Upstate Minutemen document had been handled. No use starting down this path if the evidence had already been contaminated. It might
verify a suspicion, but a verified suspicion wasn't necessarily proof, let alone
a quantum of proof.

"The editor at the *Dispatch* was on the ball," Manoukian eagerly replied. "She recognized the criminal intent right off, locked the letter and envelope in her desk, and called us."

"And how'd you handle the evidence?"

"With kid gloves," the agent explained. "I carefully put each article in a separate plastic sheet protector."

The correct drill for preserving document evidence. Emmett said, "Anna and I were shown a transcribed copy of the letter at Oneida Nation P.D., but not the envelope."

Manoukian took a photocopy from the file he'd spread open atop his desk and handed it to Emmett. The number-ten envelope was addressed in twelve-point type to the editor at the *Dispatch*. There was no return address. However, the December 14th postmark was the Sherrill, New York, Post Office, which quickened Emmett's pulse. This was where Daniel Garrity resided. But would the mechanic have mailed the letter from his own hometown?

It takes a stupid bird to shit in his own nest. Or maybe just a cocky one.

"Any type impressions on the original, Leo?" Emmett asked.

"None that I could make out. I think it was done by a laser printer."

"Was the letter run by the newspaper?"

"Not on the op-ed page," Manoukian said. "It was quoted by the *Dispatch* in a news story that was page one on December sixteenth and picked up by *USA Today* the next morning."

So Garrity had had multiple opportunities to read and appropriate the *blight of gambling* phrase. "I hope the entire letter wasn't quoted."

"No way." Manoukian smiled in self-congratulation. "I had the media hold back the line that came after the one about killing whites who patronize Oneida businesses—*for they are traitors who aren't worth our sympathy.* You know, in case we get somebody who confesses, to tell if we've got the real writer."

Emmett shot the young agent an approving look. "Postal inspector involved?"

"Yes, but nothing from his end yet on where the letter was dropped."

Manoukian's desk was in the middle of an open bullpen. Through the glass partition at the far end of this common area, Emmett had a view of Anna chatting with SAC Cochran. Their exchange, although inaudible, appeared pleasant enough, but she looked tired. Emmett had slept eleven hours, a rarity for him no matter how used up, and only over breakfast this morning had he learned from Anna that she'd left the hotel last night and met the special assistant to the Nation Representative at the tribal cultural center. Christopher White Pine had done his homework on her background, something that disconcerted her a little, and in parting he'd begged her to restore peace of mind to the Nation by finding Brenda's killer or killers. He was justifiably afraid of witchcraft rumors and counter-rumors getting out of hand.

Emmett found it extremely disconcerting to learn that Anna had fetched and returned the car keys to his shoe at bedside without awakening him.

He'd always trusted in his own vigilance.

Despite her fatigue, Anna had spent much of the remainder of the night reading *The Oneida Creation Story*, on the assumption that some form of copycatting might be occurring, patterned after an Oneida culture hero named Sky Woman.

Emmett wasn't prepared to take on Haudenosaunee culture heroes. His hands were already full with airline employees.

He turned to Manoukian again. "What's your lab in D.C. have to report?"

"They're backlogged up to the eyeballs. But the techie I talked with promised to use the latest chemical process to try to develop latent prints off the letter and envelope. Naturally, I fingerprinted the editor at the *Dispatch* and sent the exemplar card to Washington, even though she says she only touched the envelope and the margins of the letter itself."

Latest chemical process—what was cop work coming to? Time was when taking fingerprints off paper was impossible. Now technicians could even lift latents off human skin. One by one, the old kiss-offs for not taking evidence at a crime scene were vanishing. "You did well," Emmett said.

The agent's soulful eyes brightened, leaving Emmett to try to recall when compliments had meant something to him. The only memory that sprang to mind was the defining moment when his field training officer at Oklahoma City P.D. had stopped calling him *shit-for-brains*.

From the corner of his eye, he caught the NTSB investigator entering the bullpen. Today, Dutch Satterlee wore a ten-gallon Stetson, a fleece-lined rawhide jacket and snake-skin boots. An ensemble which drew smiles from the FBI agents. He hastened over to Emmett and said urgently, "We need a place to talk."

Manoukian offered, "I think the conference room is already empty for your two o'clock interrogation."

Emmett checked his wristwatch: It was ten minutes 'til.

Anna had also noticed Satterlee's entrance, and Emmett now waved for her to join them as they filed toward the conference room. Inside, he took the chair at the center on the home-team side of the long table. A high window revealed another socked-in, iron-colored sky. Yesterday's vaulting blue had been too good, too reminiscent of the West to last.

Satterlee unfolded some kind of chart on the table, just as, simultaneously, Anna came into the room and Emmett's cellular rang from his jacket pocket. "Parker here."

"*Emm-uht.*" Identification on the other end was unnecessary. The two breathy grunts that had passed for *Emmett* were unquestionably from his supervisor at the BIA office in Phoenix, a Mescalero Apache of few words. Emmett's far-flung temporary assignments with Turnipseed had kept them apart for most of the past year. "Marshal's Service faxed me a copy of an authorization deputizing your sorry ass."

"How about that."

"*Why?*"

"I don't have a clue." Emmett glanced up at Satterlee, who was waiting impatiently to share whatever significance his chart had.

"They talking about the trust funds with you?" his supervisor went on. That was his concern, then. The billions of dollars belonging to the tribes that had been held in trust by the BIA and were now missing. The in-house fear was investigation by an outside agency, like the FBI or Marshal's Service.

"You maybe thinking of transferring to them?"

"And miss out on scintillating conversations like this one? Good-bye." Emmett disconnected.

Dutch pointed at the chart. Emphatically. "*Look.*"

"What am I looking at?"

"The radar tracking plot for Adirondack Flight Five-five-seven on the evening of January sixth along the flight path to LaGuardia," the NTSB man said. "We just got it from the FAA . . ." Dutch marked a spot in Oneida County with a red pen. "That's the cornfield where Two Kettles's body was found. You all see . . . ?"

Finally, Emmett did. As did Anna—her eyes got bigger.

At its nearest point, 557's flight path Monday night had been miles—around fifteen miles by a quick check of the scale at the bottom of the chart—to the southwest of Van Hastart's cornfield. As indicated by a dotted string of boxed coordinates on the map, the 727 had been heading southeast along the prescribed air route toward New York City.

"This town of Hamilton . . ." Anna had touched the tip of a fingernail to it. ". . . is there a college there?"

Dutch said, "I don't know. Could be—"

"Yes." Manoukian had entered the conference room to oblige Satterlee with a cup of coffee. "Colgate University."

"Do they have hockey, Leo?"

"Sure, Division One."

"Women's hockey too?"

"You bet." Manoukian withdrew back into the bullpen, leaving Anna looking utterly baffled. Something in Dutch's briefing had gotten her attention.

Whatever was preoccupying her, Emmett had the sense she didn't care to discuss it in front of Dutch. "How accurate is this plot?"

"Fairly," Dutch said.

"Within a margin of error of fifteen miles, you mean?"

"No, no, within a mile or two."

"What about the winds on the night of the sixth?" Emmett asked.

"I'm not sure. Why?"

"Simple—could a human body, freefalling from ten thousand feet, sail fifteen miles before hitting the ground?"

Dutch paused thoughtfully before saying, "I doubt it, but Christ if I really know. You'd have to ask a parachutist."

Daniel Garrity had been a paratrooper, Emmett recalled.

Manoukian stuck his head inside the room. "Subject's here. And his attorney."

"Show them in, Leo," Emmett said.

Anna sat on his right to operate the tape recorder, and Satterlee to his left, hopefully to translate any aeronautical jargon. Emmett whispered to him, "Do me a favor, Dutch, and keep hammering away on the fuselage doors issue."

"Whatever blows up your skirt."

Barreling into the room, Garrity stopped abruptly behind the center chair on the visiting-team side of the table. He wore an out-of-fashion corduroy suit and a clip-on tie. His hands were fisted. He looked hard at Emmett and then Anna. Dutch was ignored. Three seconds later, an imperious-looking redhead with a briefcase quick-stepped inside and offered her pale white hand across the tabletop to Emmett, who rose to accept it. Her skin, Emmett decided on second sight, was less pale than flawlessly white, completely untouched by the sun. As if she'd spent her entire life indoors. She also had striking violet eyes. "I'm Portia Nelson, counsel for Mr. Garrity. I already know Mr. Satterlee, of course."

Emmett introduced Anna and himself, and all sat again.

Garrity seemed more subdued than he had been yesterday afternoon in the interviewing room at the airport. That meant he'd been settled down and coached by his attorney. Emmett would have preferred him to be his usual volatile self.

Anna punched a button on the tape machine and identified the participants for the record.

"Well," Portia began warily, "I must say I'm confused by the exact nature of this proceeding."

"And how's that?" Emmett asked after a beat, having made up his mind not to let her establish the tempo.

"As Mr. Satterlee knows, I'm a member of the NTSB Bar Association and can practice before the NTSB, FAA and the Department of Transportation. With the FBI and criminal investigation of the BIA present and obviously in the driver's seat, this does not strike me as being a normal accident hearing."

"It isn't, Portia," Satterlee confessed.

"Thank you." Portia smiled expectantly at Emmett, perhaps waiting for him to deny that he and Anna were in control. "Do you intend to Mirandize my client?" Before he could answer, she inclined her head at a portrait of the current FBI director on the wall and said, "If your purpose was simply to explain a possible aviation mishap, you could have held this at the airport, as you did yesterday. Instead, my client finds himself in the incommunicado atmosphere of a police facility—"

"Incommunicado?" Anna repeated, shaking off her abstracted funk.

"Yes, Special Agent Turnipseed, *without means of communication, in confinement.*"

"I know what the word means. Your client is neither confined nor lacking means of communication. You seem to be communicating quite nicely for him."

Portia seemed to take Anna's measure again. Before, probably because Turnipseed had operated the recorder, the attorney might have mistaken her for the clerical help. "Are you going to Mirandize Mr. Garrity?" Needlessly.

The mechanic was visibly getting a kick out of all this.

In a rapid monotone, Anna recited his rights to him, changing the line about his right to an attorney present to a pointed declaration that his counsel was indeed present. When she asked Garrity if he understood his rights, he said under his breath, "I suppose."

Portia whispered something in his ear.

"Okay, let's talk," he amended. "Let's get this over with. I've got nothing to hide. Nothing to do with what happened."

Presumably meaning Brenda Two Kettles's plunge to her death.

As requested, Dutch walked Garrity through the process by which he'd been notified of the problem with the loading door on Flight 557. Although far more sullen than his fellow mechanic, Eberhardt, had been yesterday, Garrity essentially told the same story. The service write-up had come from after the door stuck during preflight in Cleveland. Using his blunt, grease-stained fingers, Garrity counted off all the checks he and Eberhardt had made on the door. With each check, his voice became a bit more strident, so that by the end of his lengthy answer, Portia appeared close to cautioning him. Emmett smiled at her quandary: There was no way for her to do this without drawing even more attention to her client's hot temper on the tape.

Garrity, he trusted, would show even bigger cracks under increased pressure.

Doing just that with a rapid-fire series of questions, Dutch asked Garrity about things like actuating cylinders, struts, control cables, cams and control rods. The mechanic seemed taken aback by the attention to detail and paused to scratch his reddening neck with a nervous hand.

Portia tried to buy him time to regain his balance: "I believe my client has fully answered your concerns about that door."

Dutch glanced to Emmett, who nodded and then asked Garrity, "On an average shift, how much freedom do you have to move around the airport?"

"That's left up to my supervisor."

"Can you leave the maintenance facility on lunch or other breaks?"

"I'm not on anybody's tribal dole, so I brownbag it."

Good, Emmett thought, *he's headed in the direction I want.* "Usually or always?"

"Always."

"But you are at liberty to leave, right?"

"I suppose."

"Did you have occasion to leave the facility at any time during your shift on Monday, January sixth?"

Garrity exhaled. "Yes."

"And where'd you go?" Sitting back, Emmett focused on Garrity's voice, listening for stress. This would be different from the strident anger he'd previously shown; that had flared from what was probably genuine emotion. This would be an almost imperceptible catch in the voice caused by the tension of mounting a deception. Unlike the truth, lies were high maintenance.

The mechanic hesitated, momentarily. "The other side of the airport."

"The vicinity of the North Concourse?"

"Yeah."

"And the gate where Flight Five-five-seven was waiting for passengers?"

"It was nothing," Garrity replied indirectly, both skipping ahead and needlessly elaborating. "The captain wanted to discuss some work I'd done on the accessory gear box to the port engine on that three-holer."

"Three-holer?"

"A seven-twenty-seven."

"The captain of Flight Five-five-seven, you mean?"

Garrity let out a thunderous breath. "I still don't understand why this isn't going down at the airport," he complained, "or even at a goddamned NTSB office."

Portia put a hand on Garrity's wrist as Dutch said, "Our closest office is one hundred and fifty miles away in Parsippany, New Jersey."

Emmett asked, "You said you were an Army paratrooper, correct?"

Garrity just glared at him, even though Portia's fingertips were now pressing into the back of his hand. "Answer him, Dan," she cautioned.

"Yeah, yeah—I was Airborne. But what's that got to do with shit?"

"Probably nothing," Emmett went on, "but I'd appreciate use of your expertise in that area."

"How?" Garrity asked suspiciously.

"Let me give you a hypothetical, Dan. A human body is dropped from a certain point over land from an altitude of ten thousand feet. Given the aerodynamic properties of any falling body, will it sail some miles distant from that given point?"

Garrity considered the question, his smallish eyes turning even more narrow. "Not much. When a body burns in—"

"*Burns in?*" Emmett interrupted to clarify.

"Freefalls into the ground. When a body burns in, there's a little angle to the fall. But not much."

"Enough for someone on the ground to believe that body angled over his house?"

"Fuck this." Garrity slid his chair back but didn't rise. "You think I'm a nitwit?"

Emmett shrugged at Portia. "Counsel knows I'm not qualified to pass judgment on mental capacity."

"You don't think I know where this is going!" the mechanic shouted.

Emmett said nothing and sat very still. Peripherally, he saw Anna do the same. When a cop worked traffic, sometimes he wanted a certain driver to bolt. He just knew that driver was dirty for something big. If he ran, an arrest could be made on a charge of recklessness. So, with clear country roads ahead on a warm Oklahoma night, the patrolman hung back from the suspect's vehicle as he hit the lights and siren, encouraging the driver with the hope he could escape if he put the pedal to the metal. That's what he was now trying to do with Daniel Garrity.

Hang back and let him run.

But at that second Manoukian crept apologetically into the room. Garrity flinched as if he was about to be handcuffed. Instead, the agent passed around him and handed Emmett a folded slip of paper across the table.

"Sorry," Manoukian said, retreating again, and Emmett scanned the note:

From document div. lab mgr.—

1. *Envelope and letter printed by Hewlett*
   Packard LaserJet 1100.
2. *Partial latent fingerprint on letter. Not editor's.*

3. *No saliva envelope seal.*
4. *Fiber evidence present, green synthetic.*

Leo

Unexpectedly, the agent's interruption had had a calming effect on Garrity, and Portia motioned for him to scoot his chair back up to the table. He did so and seemed in control of himself again until Emmett said airily, "We were discussing falling bodies."

Garrity rocketed up from his chair, knocking it over, and bawled, "You know, smart ass, if I'd wanted to kill that woman with nobody being the wiser I would've brought down the plane with a catastrophic decompression!" He ignored Portia, who was tugging sharply on his corduroy coat, and bared his teeth spitefully. "That seven-twenty-seven would never be seen again, then good luck trying to put your neat little puzzles together!"

Dutch tried to settle him down. "Listen up, Garrity, nobody's accusing you of—"

"Let's see you put your bullshit theories together with a three-holer twelve thousand feet under the fucking ocean!"

Emmett didn't want to settle Garrity down. Things were just getting fun. "Does that turn you on, Garrity?"

"What!"

"The thought of all the evidence under thousands of feet of water?"

The mechanic reeled on Portia. "What's this Indian cop doing here?" He pointed at Anna. "Two Indians, by the looks of her. What right do they got to be here?"

"Calm down, Daniel," the attorney said severely.

"The federal government sent them here to make an example of me!"

"In what way?" Emmett interjected.

"I've got shit to say to you, Tonto. The government's got no right to sic you on me or any other white, patriotic American!" So, Garrity was a true believer in his own prejudices, and like most true believers he found it galling that he had to justify the truth to anybody who failed to share his views. "I'm saying nothing to nobody, unless it's at a bona fide NTSB accident hearing in New Jersey or wherever!"

Emmett smiled up at the tremulous-faced mechanic. "Mr. Satterlee is a bona fide NTSB air safety investigator."

Garrity pointed at Dutch. "I don't care if he dresses like John Wayne, this white son of bitch is a traitor. Traitors aren't worth our sympathy. Wait and see!"

Then he stepped over his overturned chair and left the conference room.

Emmett had to conceal his delight behind a mask of indifference.

Portia rose to follow her client, presumably to persuade him to return to the table. "We've got to talk, Parker," she said on her way to the door.

"No, we don't," Emmett said after she'd gone. "Not now, sister."

10

A FEW MINUTES AFTER sundown, the Oneida County deputy sheriff stopped beside an old spur line of the New York Central. He let down his side window, shut off his engine and listened for the rumble of a diesel locomotive. Tiny droplets of fog sifted inside the car and tickled the side of his face. But there was no sound. He radioed his dispatcher, "Is the reporting party a train engineer?"

"That's unknown," she responded. "Call was routed through railroad police. Stand by, I'll re-contact."

But then the fog shifted on the breeze, and the deputy could make out a yellow pinprick blinking down the line. "Never mind," he transmitted. "I think I've got a visual on him. I'll be out of the unit and on my Handie-Talkie."

The deputy restarted his engine and parked well off the tracks. Grabbing his flashlight and radio pack set, he got out and buttoned his jacket against the clammy cold. There was a grayness of wet woods to both sides of him, and no view through them of Bridgewater Flats beyond.

He started on foot down the middle of the rusted rails.

An engine purred somewhere out ahead of him.

He expected to find a train, a caboose at the end and a locomotive at the front. Instead a track inspection vehicle materialized out of the murk, a three-quarter-ton pickup with railcar wheels. Its spotlight bore a laser-like hole through the fog but barely lit up the iron trusses of the bridge over Hardscrabble Creek.

Near the span, a flashlight beam slanted down toward the water. The deputy couldn't see the holder, but as he approached the light a male voice called out, "Watch where you step!"

The deputy stopped dead.

A shadow moved toward him, footfalls crunching over the gravel between the ties. A human form took shape. A stout man. His parka was open at the front, showing pin-striped coveralls and a watch fob, just like in the movies. "You almost stepped on it."

The deputy didn't like the sound of that. "On what?"

The railroad man swung his flashlight around on an object that lay between the rails less than two feet in front of the deputy. He joined his own beam to the railroad man's.

A shoe.

Specifically, a woman's pump, candy red in color. Had it been shucked off on a forlorn dash to the bridge? Seeing it, the deputy understood why the track inspector had called in a possible suicide.

The shoe was coated with frost, as if it had lain there for some time. He decided not to touch it for the minute, in case this got turned over to Homicide. Their chronic bitch was that Patrol always screwed up evidence.

He gazed down the optical illusion of the rails narrowing toward the bridge. "When's the last time you inspected this line?"

"Three months ago," the track inspector answered.

"Anybody else been along here?"

"Nobody from the railroad."

Rising, the deputy followed the track to the bridge, but instead of venturing out onto the span he side-stepped down the embankment to the edge of the creek. It was encrusted with dirty ice. The water shone inky black in the stingy throw of his flashlight. Impossible to see bottom. He swept his beam across the surface, passing over any low-hanging willow boughs and stands of rushes that might have ensnared a floating body. January was a treacherous month to search a creek, with muddy ice and mats of dead branches often hiding the true edges of waterways.

But maybe he wouldn't have to search the banks.

The deputy recalled something he'd left inside his cruiser, a flyer from the local FBI.

He started back through the fog for his car, pausing only long enough to pick up the shoe.

Portia Nelson did not return to the conference room in the Syracuse FBI office to talk. But then, Anna felt that Emmett hadn't given the attorney much time for any damage control on behalf of her hotheaded client. Within minutes after Garrity had bolted, Emmett hunt-and-pecked out a search warrant affidavit and scooped up the tape of the second Garrity interrogation, plus a complete copy of the original threatening letter to *The Oneida Daily Dispatch*.

"Find us a black robe," he told Leo Manoukian.

They found the on-call federal judge in the walnut-paneled smoking room of a country club on the monied outskirts of Syracuse, a martini in his hand and the fireplace crackling behind him. He showed annoyance at being interrupted by Anna, Emmett and Manoukian, and Leo stammered through the necessity of seeing him after hours. The judge perused the affidavit, then the copy of the threatening letter with greater care, before telling Manoukian to play the recording of the interrogation on the tape machine he'd brought along.

"Skip ahead," he interrupted at one point, "this is all in the affidavit."

The judge paid special attention to the linkage between the phrase in the letter that had been withheld from the public, *traitors who aren't worth our sympathy*, and Garrity's outburst this afternoon.

After minutes of silent waiting, Emmett cleared his throat.

The judge frowned up at him from his throne-like wingback chair. "This land claim situation is more complicated than you can imagine, Mr. Parker," he said condescendingly. "We're all groping our way toward the light an inch at a time. So I'll ask you to exercise care and restraint during your visit to our part of New York."

Anna thought Emmett was going to snap back at him, but then coolness prevailed—he wanted the search warrant, badly. Manoukian saw an opportunity to help Emmett out, so, without being prompted, he summarized what the FBI lab manager had reported on the envelope and the letter.

The judge accepted the information with an indifferent nod, then asked the young agent to replay the potentially incriminating portion of Garrity's verbal explosion.

At last, he signed the warrant form, but only after making a few notations on it. "Here you go, Mr. Parker," the judge said in parting. "Again, be circumspect."

Something in the notated warrant made Emmett's jaws tighten, but he said nothing until Anna, Manoukian and he were passing through the clubhouse lobby on the way to the front door. "Son of a bitch," he swore. "It's not endorsed for night service."

That meant they had only until 10:00 P.M. to get things rolling, otherwise they had to wait until six the next morning before hitting Garrity's residence. Anna thought there had been a territorial ring to the judge's declaration, *our part of New York*. Driving them back to the FBI office downtown, Manoukian remarked that this magistrate was a native of the Syracuse area and had taken personal offense to a white outcry that the federal judiciary was in the Oneida Nation's pocket. "So," Leo concluded, "no Gestapo knock-knock in the middle of the night on anything even remotely related to the claim."

An hour later, Anna held her penlite to a topographical map she'd spread over her lap. Sherrill lay less than two miles from the Oneida Reservation, although the communities were separated by the swampy woodland along a creek and the Madison-Oneida County line. The most direct route to Sherrill from Syracuse was through Oneida's central business district, but Emmett had chosen a rural back way into the suburban town of 3,000. Thus, he reduced the chance of someone spreading the alarm about the three-vehicle convoy that had left the FBI's Syracuse office thirty-five minutes ago and was closing in on Daniel Garrity's residence through scattered patches of fog.

She checked her dash clock: 8:59.

Emmett had braked for another thick, blinding pall, but now accelerated again. He was following the tail-lights of another bucar, containing Manoukian and a burly special agent with a crew-cut named Marvin Roth, who served on the critical incident team, the office's SWAT unit. Behind Anna and Emmett was a van driven by a technician who would process any evidence seized.

During the stopover at the FBI office, Anna had phoned the campus police at Colgate University, fibbed that she needed to corroborate something
said in an interview. She wasn't trying to confirm an interview statement.
She was trying to confirm a dream, trying to ratify what it meant to be
Modoc—"Do you have an ice rink?" *Yes, ma'am, Starr Rink in the south
wing of Reid Athletic Center.* "So you have a large athletic complex?" *Oh
yes.* "If women's varsity played a practice game against junior varsity at five
in the evening, about what time would maintenance finish grooming the
ice?" *About eight-thirty, I'd say.* "Thank you," she said as she hung up, a
chill corkscrewing up her spine. She had dreamed all of these things with
faith-shattering reality. Faith in reason. In modernity.

Why?

She already knew what her Uncle Boston would say about this experience: It was easy to miss the point of a dream. As with the old Modoc who'd
foreseen a luminous, curly-headed Jesus riding on the back of a huge
jackrabbit, only time would reveal the meaning. This was no comfort to her,
for whatever remained murky about that dream—Emmett's involvement
was not.

A sign pointed right to Sherrill, and Manoukian turned.

Emmett followed.

Over the radio, Leo told the FBI dispatcher, "Make the notification." He
didn't say what the notification was for, but prior to leaving the office he'd
explained that many local deputies were convinced the titles to their own
homes were in jeopardy because of the court decision on the land claim. So
Manoukian was notifying the Oneida County Sheriff's Department of the
federal warrant service at the last minute, if only to prevent a misunder-
standing that could lead to an exchange of friendly fire.

She looked out on a neighborhood of two-story frame houses. There
were signs of hard-earned prosperity in a few of the side yards: RVs and
boats, cocooned for the winter. She sensed this was the kind of working-
class enclave that believed Indians were the lazy beneficiaries of a runaway
welfare system, instead of the recipients of payments that had been agreed
to by the U.S. government in exchange for vast tracts of native lands. These
payments were mistaken for welfare only because the American public had
long forgotten the nation-to-nation treaties that obligated the government
to pay up. Yet, splotches of festive color brightened the misty night, strings

of Christmas lights that had yet to come down. Like a spirit of reconciliation that refused to die. Despite five centuries of racial conflict, the hope that, one day, all of this might be fairly settled without further bloodshed.

The sound of Manoukian's voice brought her back to the moment. He radioed his office that the warrant service detail had arrived—and made sure the dispatcher recorded the time: 9:12 P.M. Then he parked across the street from Garrity's house, should his car unexpectedly become the team's fall-back position. Emmett swung into the driveway, blocking a decade-old Ford Bronco from backing out. Garrity's vehicles were excluded from the search.

Anna felt through her FBI jacket to make sure that her pistol was snugly in her belt holster. It was no longer an inconvenience.

Bailing out of the sedan with Emmett, she saw nothing that set the Garrity's residence apart from those flanking it, nothing that would make it the incubator for what had happened in the skies Monday night, nothing to indicate that it was a nest of racial hatred.

She twirled the squelch button on the Handie-Talkie Manoukian had loaned her, making sure the battery was charged. It was. The radio went in a jacket pocket.

Roth jogged past Anna and Emmett and through a side gate to cover the back of the house. The technician remained in his van several houses down the block.

She scanned the residence for movement.

Lights shone from three windows, one of them the pebbled glass of an upstairs bathroom. The porch light was not on.

Emmett took the front door. She stood slightly below and to the right of the cement stoop, right hand on her pistol grips. Manoukian waited on the lawn to the left of the stoop, giving himself a clear angle past Anna on the entry. Despite the cold, the scents of the night filled her head, especially the straw-like smell from the dormant grass their shoes had just stirred and the car fumes from her own convoy still lingering in the air.

Emmett ignored the bell button and pounded on the door.

Three seconds later, the porch light came on, flooding the yard with yellow.

Anna flinched when the door jerked open about ten inches. A glassy-eyed Daniel Garrity gawked at Emmett and then shifted slightly on the balls of his feet to take in Manoukian on the lawn. Booze-breath, cigarette smoke and a Patsy Cline song drifted out to Anna.

"What are the charges?" the mechanic asked, squaring his fists on his hips.

Declaring the warrant, Emmett entered and pushed Garrity back into the house. Not violently, but forcibly. He rested one hand on the mechanic's forearm, ready to restrain him if the need arose. But Garrity backed up with little more than a few mild protests—into the kitchen. She and Manoukian were close on Emmett's heels as he again identified his purpose and ordered three people—two women, one in her mid-thirties and the other in her sixties, and a sixtyish man with a shaved head—to stay seated at the kitchen table. The tabletop was littered with filled ashtrays, highball glasses, an almost empty bottle of Seagram's V.O. and numerous cans of Sprite and Coke. Emmett frisked Garrity—there wasn't much to search, he was wearing only a sleeveless T-shirt and sweat-pants. Then he asked the others, "Any of you have any weapons?"

Murmurs, all in the negative.

"Any guns in the house?"

Garrity mentioned a shotgun in the basement.

"Go ahead," Emmett said over his shoulder.

Manoukian and Anna fanned out into the rest of the house. Upstairs, she was reaching for the knob when the door swung back into a steamy bathroom. An adolescent girl, pink and flushed, cowered in shock before Anna. Maybe fifteen years old, she was clad in a terrycloth robe with a towel turbaned around her wet hair.

"It's all right," Anna said. "FBI."

"*FBI?*" she asked incredulously.

"Yes. Are there any more children in the house?"

"No."

"Step out and let's join your folks in the kitchen."

The girl started for the stairwell, but twisted her upper body away when Anna tried to pat her robe down.

"Stand still," Anna said. The girl froze theatrically, and Anna completed the cursory search. "Okay, let's go."

"I cannot believe this shit." Then the girl's whine turned into a loud wail. "Mom . . . !"

"It's all right, baby," a female voice consoled from the kitchen. "Your daddy told you this would happen someday."

Manoukian had let Roth in through the back, and together they were clearing the den and living room. Patsy Cline was cut off mid-measure with a scratch, and Anna heard Leo transmitting from the living room—*Code Four*, all was well for the moment.

She delivered the girl to the kitchen. Garrity was now seated at the table with the others, heat building in his whiskey-damp eyes. The mechanic asked if he was under arrest or not. Emmett refused to answer.

"Come here, Janis," the younger of the two women said to the girl. There were no more chairs, so Janis languished on the woman's lap. They twined their arms around each other and watched Emmett's every move.

Quietly, Emmett explained to Anna that the younger woman was Garrity's wife, Veda, and the elderly couple were neighbors, Jake and Louise Cutler, whom he'd like to kick loose as soon as he felt everything had simmered down.

"What's going on, Daddy?" Janis asked.

"It's all right, sugar. Don't worry. This has nothing to do with you." Garrity said this with enough fatherly concern for Anna to sympathize with him. She knew what it was like to have authority burst inside your dwelling. In her family's case, that authority had been all white, often justified, but still resented for the shock of the intrusion, the sense of personal violation.

But then she remembered Brenda Two Kettles on that autopsy table. That had been genuine violation.

Jake Cutler cocked his gleaming head and winked at Garrity. "They're playing hardball now, Danny." Age had turned his eyes the color of faded blue jeans, but there was still a bright hardness to them. The big arteries in his neck were pumped up with excitement.

Emmett turned to Anna again. "Leo can bring the tech in. Have him videotape everything."

She went to Manoukian in the living room and passed on Emmett's request. He slipped out to fetch the technician from the van, leaving the front door open. Through it, Anna saw a sheriff's car drive by: The deputy didn't wave at Manoukian as he continued down the street at patrol speed.

The young agent had been riffling through a simulated oak secretary, probably from Wal-Mart. The bookshelf portion was jammed with Jim Beam Bourbon commemorative porcelain bottles, the usual panoply of white icons—Kennedy, Elvis, Reagan. The pigeonholes in the desk portion were jammed with bills. Most were stamped *second notice* or *overdue*. Just before she'd interrupted him, Manoukian had been examining a business letter. Daniel and Veda Garrity, it appeared, were going to lose their home for non-payment to Upstate Mortgage Company long before the Oneida land claim ever got down to evictions.

There was no sign of either a computer or a printer in the living room or the den, and she'd seen none in the kitchen.

A tapping sound drew her up the stairs in search of Roth.

She found him in a bedroom frilly enough to be the girl's. He'd fired up a vintage Apple II-C, and the daisywheel printer finished tapping out a page. Like Anna, he was in possession of a copy of the original threatening letter and now compared it to one of Janis's homework assignments he'd just printed in the same approximate font.

"Nope," Roth said, "but we'll take it and have our forensic computer geek have a look."

"Daisywheel leaves a strike impression, laser printer doesn't," she noted. And according to Manoukian, the lab in Washington had been firm about the make and model of the printer used: a Hewlett Packard LaserJet 1100. Apparently, the HP had a distinctive way of proportionate-spacing— small *a*'s crowded the letters preceding them, ever so slightly.

She climbed the stairs once again.

There was little hope of finding computer equipment in the master bedroom, but she turned to the closet just as a scorching light zeroed in on her—the technician had arrived and was videotaping under a flood attachment. "Say cheese," he said as he moved on, leaving Anna to sort through Garrity's wardrobe in the comparative dimness of the ceiling fixture. Anything green got tossed in a pile on the bed, including a forest green U.S. Army uniform with a paratrooper's badge over the right breast pocket and sergeant's chevrons.

Manoukian soon relieved her of the chore of bagging and tagging the clothes pile, so she could go down to the basement. Reaching the hall on the first floor, she could hear the mechanic's anger spilling from the kitchen. He was snarling that only the county sheriff had the lawful authority to exercise a search warrant in the home of a private citizen. Jake Cutler heartily added that all true constitutional power rested with the county, not a bunch of parasitic federal bureaucracies.

Emmett let them all go on venting.

Flipping a light switch, she descended the wooden steps into the basement. It smelled of moldy laundry, explained by the clothes piled on the cement floor beside the vintage Kenmore washer and dryer. Shoved against a cinderblock wall was a NordicTrack. It was partly buried under storage boxes and stacks of outdoor magazines. The task of looking through so much junk was daunting, but Anna began rummaging for computer components and an HP printer.

She came across the shotgun, but the case was too coated with dust to have been opened recently.

Garrity had said during his tirade at the airport: *The wife and I got us a three-bedroom in Sherrill. It was a fixer-upper, so we dumped a lot of money in it. Home sweet fucking home.*

Still a fixer-upper, Anna thought to herself as she surveyed the termite-pitted floor joists above her. She was in the dungeon of a man's castle. It was odd to her, how whites put such pride in possession of a wooden box on a rectilinear piece of deeded land. Most Indians had a wider sense of home, an expanse of country that bled indistinctly into the lands of neighboring peoples (there had been no Indian surveyors). The extent of this expanse dwarfed the importance of an individual family's dwelling, even to this day. Home reached in every direction and up to the sky.

There was no computer or printer in the basement, and she returned to the kitchen.

The tech had entrusted his fingerprint-rolling kit to Emmett, and he was inking the pad on the sinkboard. Taking him aside, she told him in soft undertones about the daisywheel machine in Janis's room, the only printer in the house. He didn't bother to hide his disappointment, and from the corner of her eye Anna caught Garrity smiling confidently at his wife.

He was finally getting it through his dense skull that his arrest wasn't imminent.

Emmett ordered him to stand and approach the sinkboard. Rising somewhat unsteadily, Garrity said, "You can tell your bosses at the BIA they're going to start a revolution with this kind of horseshit."

Emmett seized his right hand, began inking and rolling his fingertips. "You mean the violent overthrow of the government?"

In spite of his intoxication, the mechanic knew where that could lead him. "When Americans get mad, they get serious mad," he waffled, wisely avoiding a direct answer. "We'll burn our houses and salt the earth before we give it to you Indians."

"I don't want your sorry-ass house and third acre of suburban bliss," Emmett responded.

"You ain't Oneida," Louise Cutler said as she swept her glass up to her mouth. She held an ice cube on her tongue, then began crunching it between her molars.

Anna could barely breathe, the smoke was so thick in the kitchen.

Emmett finished with Garrity and gave him a pre-moistened swipe that came with the kit. He sat again, wiping the ink off his hands, and Parker motioned Veda that she was next. She looked dumbstruck. *"Me?"*

"Do every ridiculous, illegal thing they tell us to do, sweetheart," Garrity said. "That'll only help our case when we sue their asses off in court. C.U.E. is going to love this."

The Committee for Upstate Equality, Anna realized, although this might be a lunatic fringe even C.U.E. wouldn't want to claim.

Janis jumped off her lap, and Veda slunk over to Emmett's side. Anna stood close by, in case the woman got combative. Short and stubby, Garrity's wife leered up at Emmett as he took hold of her right hand. "You honestly think a thousand whites round here are going to let sixty thousand Oneidas take away everything they ever worked for?"

Louise Cutler let out with a nicotine cackle. "You got it backwards, lovie. There's sixty thousand of us and only a thousand Oneidas."

The table exploded into laughter. Even Emmett smiled.

But Veda looked embarrassed. "I'm pissed off, okay?" she said to her neighbor. "Really pissed off. The Oneidas are using their gambling dollars to buy up both counties. Ten thousand acres so far, which the courts say they don't have to pay taxes on." She glanced to her daughter. "What'll it mean to these kids' generation when there's no tax base left? Hell, there won't be any sheriff's departments, just the Oneida Nation P.D. to stick the boot to whitey. So I'm really pissed off. I'm being personally sued by the Great Oneida Nation and this guy's honchos, the Justice Department, for everything I ever earned down at the beauty shop."

"I don't work for Justice." Emmett handed her a swipe and gestured for her to sit again. "I work for Interior. You know, Jellystone Park and all that?"

Veda Garrity saw no humor in his remark.

Emmett crooked a finger for Janis to come to him. Her parents froze, then Veda squawked, "What you messing with her for?"

"We need fingerprint cards for everybody who resides in this house."

"Do what he says." But then Garrity patted her daughter's cheek. "You just remember this night, baby girl. In the long fight that's coming, you remember everything about this night."

"Amen," Louise intoned.

Janis obeyed. While printing her, Emmett asked the two men over his shoulder, "Both of you were Airborne?"

Garrity had gone silent and sullen, but Jake said proudly, "Yessir, same division, though separated by twenty-five years and two different wars. I was with the Eighty-second Airborne in Nam and Danny was with it in Desert Storm. I was an Intelligence officer."

"At what level?"

Jake lit a fresh cigarette, an unfiltered Lucky Strike. "You in the military?"

"No, I was a cop at twenty-one," Emmett replied. "Getting shot at with all the comforts of home. Intel at what level?"

Jake spat a flake of tobacco off the tip of his tongue. "I was the G-Two at Regiment. Fascinating work. Real glimpses into human character. You really get a handle on what makes a man squirm."

Emmett said, "And what makes a man squirm?"

"Lack of hope. A man can stand up to most anything as long as he can talk himself into having a little hope. So that's what you deprive him of. You show him there's no hope."

Manoukian appeared in the doorway from the hallway. He lifted his chin for Emmett to approach, then showed him two sheets of white paper. One, Anna believed, was the copy of the threatening letter. Emmett drew Manoukian farther out into the hallway and tersely whispered something to the agent. After several seconds, he came back into the kitchen, staying only long enough to ask Anna to complete printing Janis Garrity and take control of the scene in his absence.

"Why?" she demanded.

"No time to explain." Emmett backed out of the kitchen on a coy shrug, then turned for the front door.

Daniel Garrity tracked Emmett's departure with worry in his face for the first time.

11

EMMETT WAS TAKING THE Airport Boulevard exit when his cellular finally rang. It was the judge, who—without so much as a hello—asked if the printer in question was airline property.

"Undoubtedly, sir," Emmett replied.

While searching one of the smaller bedrooms in Daniel Garrity's house, Leo Manoukian had come across a cardboard box labeled WORK. In it were bulletins, memos and forms issued by the Syracuse maintenance operation of Adirondack Airlines, and the first one Leo pried from the collection—a directive about sick leave abuse—had been printed in what appeared to be the same twelve-point font used for the Minutemen letter to *The Oneida Daily Dispatch*. At least, to Emmett's eye. Close enough for him to ask Manoukian to get the ball rolling by phoning in a request for an expanded search while he himself sped into Syracuse. In addition to seizing the printer for forensic comparison to the death threat letter, Emmett wanted a look inside Garrity's locker.

"What do you think you'll find, Mr. Parker?" the judge asked.

"Maybe the source of the fiber evidence left in the envelope."

"*Maybe?*"

"It's called probable cause, Judge, not certain cause."

"And a good faith fuck-up is still a fuck-up." The magistrate paused.

"All right, I'll expedite a new warrant to airport police first thing in the morning."

"Tonight, sir—please. I'm pulling into Syracuse International right now. So far, I've got nothing to hold Garrity on. If I wait 'til tomorrow for the search, he'll sanitize his work spaces long before I ever get to them."

A petulant sigh followed, but then the judge said, "I'll phone the airport chief at home and notify him of the search. You and one of his officers must jointly execute the warrant."

Less than a ringing endorsement for the BIA, even with a Marshal's Service deputization, but Emmett didn't argue. "Thanks," he signed off.

Security was conducting an impromptu trunk search of all vehicles approaching the front of the terminal, so Emmett was delayed ten minutes in the logjam. But the judge was as good as his word: Emmett identified himself to the first airport cop he saw, and the officer used his Handie-Talkie to point. "Lieutenant Bellasario's expecting you—take that fire lane up to the gate."

He waited another ten minutes at the chain-link gate. Jets were taking off, which meant it was no more than a ground fog and the runway lights were visible from above. But at eye-level, the shifting pall was thick. Finally, an airport police cruiser drove up, amber flashers going. Bellasario got out, unlocked the gate and rolled it open. He waved for Emmett to drive inside the restricted area, then secured the gate behind Parker. "Follow me," he said, getting back inside his car and leading the way.

Emmett stuck to Bellasario's rear bumper.

A jetliner lifted off, too close for comfort. He estimated the near edge of the runway to be fifty feet from him. He had to trust that the lieutenant intimately knew the access roads threading between and around the runways. A hangar appeared off to the left; the huge door open to the night, an Air National Guard cargo plane and helicopter within, looming above the fluffy layer of gray.

Bellasario drove on to a second hangar, where he stopped and exited his vehicle. Emmett left his parking lights on and joined the lieutenant outside.

"This way, Mr. Parker," he said, sounding less affable than he had two nights ago. The investigation kept zeroing in on the airport. His airport.

The pavement was icy in spots, but deicing pellets had been spread over the concrete steps they bounded up. The Syracuse maintenance facility for Adirondack Airlines, according to the sign on the door. The office seemed overheated and the fluorescent lights glaring after the dank night. One entire wall consisted of floor-to-ceiling glass panels that overlooked the interior of the hangar itself. The space was so vaulting and expansive the older model 757 parked on the floor seemed small. The logos still read AERO MAZATLAN, but the exterior of the plane was obviously being prepped for the paint shop.

A big-bellied man in a white shirt and skinny tie rose from a desk, on which he'd spread out his lunch, and ambled over to the counter. "Help you, Lieutenant?"

Bellasario introduced Emmett to the manager, then described the purpose and scope of the search. "Judge promised to send us the warrant by late morning. I'll run a copy over so you can attach it to the paperwork for your bosses. That's about it."

The manager nodded, visibly calculating the possible consequences to himself. Apparently, one of his mechanics was bringing federal attention down on the entire operation, and that was never good. He lifted a drawbridge-like extension of the countertop to let Emmett and the lieutenant pass into the employees-only section of the office.

Instantly, Emmett's eyes riveted on the computer work stations in carrels at the back of the room. In addition to two sets of monitors, computers and keyboards, there were a pair of printers. As the manager led them closer, Emmett had to keep a smile off his face—both printers were Hewlett Packard LaserJet 1100s. "Mechanics have access to these computers?" he asked.

"They're for them." As the manager said this, Emmett noticed that the keyboards were grease-smudged. "This is where the mechanics do their service reports."

"Daniel Garrity definitely had access to both of these?"

"Yes."

"Access to any other computer stations?"

"No, just these."

"What about your own computer?"

"For me alone, protected by a password."

Emmett gestured at the work stations. "I have to take both printers."

"No big problem. I've got a spare."

"But an FBI technician will have to look at the computer hard drives. You have backups for them?"

The manager winced. "At our Buffalo facility. But we'd be in a bind until we get new drives from them."

"We'll work with you on that," Emmett said. "Next I need to see Garrity's locker."

He had the manager lock all the doors to the office during his temporary lapse in custody of the two printers. Then the three of them filed out onto the floor of the hangar. Emmett indicated the *Aero Mazatlan* plane. "This from the merger?"

"Yeah," the manager carped, "twenty-year-old seven-fifty-sevens. Just what we needed, more antiques to maintain." He added on a sudden thought, "I don't have access to Garrity's locker. A concession to the union."

"What kind of lock?"

"Combination, I think."

Passing an open tool box, Emmett grabbed a ball-peen hammer and long-handled screwdriver. "Mind if I borrow these for a few minutes?" Emmett asked the mechanic working at a nearby work-bench.

"Be my guest."

He and the other mechanics inside the hangar took no special notice—"suits" strolling in and out were probably a common occurrence—until it was clear that Emmett, the manager and the lieutenant were headed for their locker room. At that point, a hush fell over the hangar.

Garrity's combination lock was a high school–quality cheapo, more a privacy than a security device, and one blow of the hammer and screwdriver popped the shackle out of the case. Emmett opened the locker door less than an inch, then shone his penlite through the crack. He was looking for wires, pressure switches, anything indicative of an improvised explosive device. Garrity might've already killed.

There were no apparent triggering devices, no bombs.

Emmett fully opened the door. Garrity's tan jumpsuit formed a drape from the top shelf to the base.

"Dan always seemed like a pretty good guy to me," the manager quietly offered. He felt the need to defend Garrity, if only tepidly. The same syndrome that made the neighbors of a serial killer describe him as a friendly sort who always waved good morning.

"Uh-huh," Emmett murmured, thinking—*You know damned well Garrity's an asshole.* He removed the jumpsuit. The pockets were empty.

Numerous grease and oil spatters on the outside, but none of visible blood. He set the uniform on the bench behind him. A hard hat was stored on the top shelf. Emmett glanced inside the webbing: a photograph of Veda and Janis. He was sliding the hat back onto the shelf when a wad of olive drab at the very back of the space caught his eye. Olive drab was a uniquely military shade of green. Bundled together was a pair of gloves this color. The smooth material felt like rayon or nylon. Manoukian's hasty note on the lab report had indicated only green and synthetic.

Close enough for government work.

Before the raid on Garrity's house, Emmett had grabbed several paper and plastic evidence bags at the FBI office. He now deposited the gloves in a paper sack. A plastic bag created its own little hothouse, and the heat could destroy traces of blood as evidence. Emmett wanted to preserve everything inside the locker for blood analysis in the hope it could be established irrefutably that Garrity's and Brenda Two Kettles's paths had crossed here at the airport Monday evening.

Nothing was as irrefutable as blood.

Emmett noted the date, time and case number on the bag, then pocketed the gloves. Examination of the larger items inside the locker, and of the metal cubicle itself, for minute traces of blood would be left to an FBI technician.

Something in the paper trash on the floor of the locker caught his eye. A syringe. Emmett picked it up by carefully clasping the edges of the plunger's top between his fingernails. Empty and apparently never used.

"Dan's no doper," the manager asserted.

Unwittingly, he had just incriminated Garrity more than he realized. Emmett could imagine other uses for a syringe, such as incapacitating an Oneida woman. He bagged the syringe, then flipped open his cellular. But the screen showed low signal strength inside this huge steel box. "Mind standing by the locker a few minutes?" he asked Bellasario.

The lieutenant said he didn't.

But the manager asked, "May I get back to my office?"

"Not quite yet," Emmett said. "Give me a few minutes to round up some technical support." Distractions, such as employees itching to get back to work, were invariably exploited by a defense attorney, and Emmett had no intention of letting Portia Nelson imply that evidence had been mishandled or contaminated.

He strode out into the hangar again.

The mechanics looked up from their jobs at him, eyes resentful—all but a junior mechanic, who offered an insipid grin as Parker passed by on his way to the personnel door.

The fog outside felt doubly cold.

He halted several yards beyond the hangar and illuminated his phone screen for another signal check. The strength was good, and he paused a moment to recall Manoukian's cell number. He hoped that the technician working Garrity's residence was close to wrapping up. While dialing, he caught movement passing in front of the parking lights to his car. He thought he heard shoes on the icy pavement, but at that instant a jet went to full throttle on take-off, and all other sound was lost.

He switched off his phone and started following on foot. Following what, he wasn't sure. He wanted to check his sedan for tampering but knew he couldn't delay.

The fog enfolded him, and he searched through it for another flicker of movement.

Figure.

Had he actually glimpsed a human figure, or might it have been an airport vehicle or some sort of animal? His sense was that it had been large. He'd had no reason to take a headcount of the mechanics, but now guessed that one of them was outside, walking away from the hangar and deeper into the fog. Emmett had caught him screwing with his car, and the man wouldn't slink back to work until the coast was clear. A union brother was being threatened, pack mentality was setting in, and most of the mechanics could be expected to rally around even a black sheep like Daniel Garrity.

Emmett continued to sense movement out in front of him, although the ground fog was so dense he couldn't pick out the terminal. His internal compass told him that the big building was directly across the runway from him. Off to his left, a line of blue dots intersected a line of brighter dots: taxiway lights merging into high-intensity runway lights. Against which the upper body of a male appeared and disappeared in the blink of an eye, leaving Emmett with the impression that a dark-haired man had just ventured out onto the runway.

After a stretch of winter-blanched grass, Emmett felt pavement beneath his shoes again. Grooved but still slick asphalt. He continued at a trot, looking for the figure. But the fog was like a wall.

He stopped to listen.

A faint whistling spun him around. In the distance, another jet was getting ready to take off. This was stupid: He was being lured out into a dangerous and alien environment. He wouldn't fall for it. He'd go back to the hangar and wait for the mechanic to return. One of Garrity's friends. He admired loyalty, but only as long as that friend knew it had a cost. The wrath of Emmett Parker was definitely a cost.

He backtracked across the runway and believed he was close to the expanse of grass he'd already crossed—when the fog turned to glittering diamond dust all around him. He threw up his right hand to shade his eyes against the glare. There was no sound, but he felt a deep vibration in his chest, and the instinct was so strong that he was about to be crushed under a massive weight he flung himself to the asphalt. Something struck close to him, making a noise like a chirp—except that it was deafening. It moved on, leaving the stench of burnt rubber in his nostrils. He raised his head to look but was buffeted by a blast of hot kerosene fumes. He pressed his face into his left shoulder until the howling winds abated around him. The jetliner parted the fog into two curls of white mist and smoke as it braked. Its anti-collision light vanished into the murk, but the roar of the engines were still in Emmett's ears as he staggered to his feet and started running for the hangar.

Swinging through the kitchen while carrying another armload of evidence out to his car, Leo Manoukian told Anna in a whisper what he'd found in the spare bedroom: printed material from Adirondack Airlines in just the font they were looking for. She congratulated her fellow agent as he hurried out, but she wanted nothing more than to smack Emmett Parker in the face as soon as she caught up with him. Once again, he had left her with the house-keeping chores while he himself had bounded off after the most promising lead.

She realized that Daniel Garrity had witnessed her whispered exchange with Manoukian. In stone-faced silence.

About fifteen minutes ago, she'd let Jake and Louise Cutler leave, presumably for their home down the street. Garrity had barely responded to the couple's warm promises of support. He continued to slug down V.O. and Seven but seemed no more intoxicated than he had when Emmett had shoved him from the front door to the kitchen. In fact, he almost appeared sober in his distracted state, leaving Veda to spew anti-Oneida bile at the FBI team as they wrapped up the search. Janis either dozed or pretended to doze in the chair vacated by Louise Cutler.

A cell phone rang out in the living room. Manoukian answered, paused, then said, "Yes, Emmett . . ."

Garrity had jumped at the first ring and now stared through the doorway toward the living room, hanging on every word.

"Okay," the agent said to Emmett, "then that's where we'll leave it— finish up here and meet you at the airport." A second pause, longer. "Well, we can kick him loose right now, if that helps." Garrity morosely ran a fingertip around the lip of his highball glass, making a moaning sound. "Right, Emmett—see you in about an hour." Manoukian called the tech in from another room and told him to go on ahead to the Adirondack maintenance hangar. That presumed Leo, Roth and Anna would follow.

Something had paid off at Syracuse International.

Veda Garrity had also continued to drink, but unlike her husband her words were now slurred as she obsessed on Anna. "Why'd you join the FBI? So you Indians can take over the government and then the whole goddamn world? You all figure after so many hundreds of years it's your turn to be on top again?"

The Bureau, which had ultimate jurisdiction on most reservations, was a powerful symbol of authority to Indians, whether they liked the FBI or not. Unconsciously perhaps, Anna had wanted some of that power to rescue her passive mother from an alcoholic and abusive father. At least, that's what her therapist had suggested. But, as for now, she'd learned early not to argue with a drunk.

Surprisingly, Garrity came to her aid. "Leave the woman alone," he snapped at Veda.

"I was only trying to make conversation," she complained.

"Turnipseed," the mechanic asked, "okay if I make a phone call from here first?" That meant he believed he still might be arrested and booked, thus entitled to a second opportunity to call.

"Go ahead," Anna said.

Garrity stood, rocked slightly on his feet and went to the wall phone. He punched in a number he knew from memory. Still standing, Anna shifted her stance to protect herself in the event he came at her. Some knives were stored in a wooden block, but completely across the kitchen from him. He frowned as the seconds ticked on, then said in the slightly stilted tone people use with an answering machine, "Portia, this is Danny. Phone me at home right away. FBI's here, ransacking the place. I think they're trying to pin this Indian woman thing on me on account of my support for C.U.E." He said all of this with an odd flatness to his voice. If anything, he'd sounded defeated and afraid.

Veda pointed, "She's not handling C.U.E. business no more."

"But her partner is." Disconnecting, Garrity turned to the side of the refrigerator, which had notices and photos attached to it with decorative magnets. "Where the fuck's the phone list?"

"Watch your mouth, Daniel Patrick," Veda said in a rasp she then tried to wash away with a drink.

Anna had seen Manoukian take the list, earlier.

Garrity yanked open a cabinet drawer that was overstuffed with saving coupons clipped from magazines. "And now where's the phone book?"

Janis opened her sleepy eyes. "I got it in my room." The girl started to rise, but her father ordered her to sit again. He dialed information and asked for the law firm of Katz and Nelson in Vernon.

"Katz is a wuss," Veda observed sarcastically.

Garrity flashed a palm for her to shut up.

Manoukian returned to the kitchen, making Garrity back up two steps as he reattached the phone list to the fridge with a ladybug magnet. The mechanic was so intent on leaving a second message he paid no attention to the agent. "Mr. Katz, this is Dan Garrity. Call me as soon as you can, no matter what time it is. My number is . . ."

"Finished," Manoukian said to Anna. "How about you?"

She nodded.

Garrity lowered the receiver from his ear, eyes fixed on the pair of handcuffs Manoukian wore looped over his belt. But the agent politely motioned for Anna to lead the way out.

The night air had a new consistency, half fog and half mist. All the neighbors in the vicinity had turned on their porch lights, and the street scene had a surreal pointillist effect. She realized for the first time that this had been the consistency of the air inside the ice rink she'd dreamed. *Starr Rink . . . it has a name, has a reality. Emmett fell into it, yet most often when I dream, it's me falling. What am I falling toward?*

The technician and his van were already gone, and Anna was cutting across the mechanic's lawn toward Manoukian's sedan when a car turned the nearest corner and thundered toward her. It was an old Chrysler New Yorker with primer spots, tinted windows and mufflers so comically noisy she was reminded of the cars on her rez. The driver hit his high-beams, which made her hang back on the curb just as she prepared to cross the street. The passenger-side, rear window was cranked halfway down, and from that opening a boisterous war whoop rose above the engine noise.

"Get back, Anna," Manoukian said nervously from behind.

She did—and saw that Roth had stepped out of the bucar and was trying to shine his flashlight through the tinted windows of the Chrysler for a look inside. Anna believed that there were several occupants, all sitting low.

Then there was a loud blast.

It thumped through the heavy air and made Anna pull her head down into her shoulders. She knew that she hadn't been hit, but her heart went wild. There was the squeal of peeling tires as the driver of the New Yorker stomped on the accelerator and took off down the street. She couldn't recall having drawn her pistol, but it was out of her holster and trained on the fleeing Chrysler. No target. She had no real target, and the vehicle was speeding past a backdrop of houses, all filled with people at this hour of the night.

Manoukian ran through her sight picture on his way to the sedan.

Rising, Anna pointed her muzzle safely skyward and looked for Roth. He came loping back up the street, handgun held down at his side. Obviously, he'd gone in foot pursuit of the Chrysler and quickly seen the futility in it.

Manoukian gunned his engine to life and pulled forward for Anna. She took the front passenger bucket seat, and Roth flew into the back. He started to say something but then realized that Manoukian was transmitting: "Control, possible shot just fired at this unit . . ." The acceleration pressed all of them back in their seats. "In pursuit of a blue Chrysler, westbound on Harmony Street in Sherrill. Partial New York plate of Sam Victor Henry, no further."

The dispatcher acknowledged, then hit an alert tone and rebroadcast the information on the mutual aid frequency.

Anna took the shotgun down from its roof rack and made sure a shell wasn't already chambered. She left the chamber empty and the safety on, for the moment. A shotgun discharge—that's what the blast from the Chrysler had sounded like. She had seen the big, ragged holes buckshot left in flesh, but tried to drive the images from her mind.

The tail-lights of the Chrysler were tiny in the distance ahead, but Manoukian was gaining on them.

Emmett lined up all the mechanics in the middle of the hangar. Their manager stood awkwardly off to one side of the formation. The front of Emmett's suit was dusted white from deicing granules spread over the runway, and there was a rip in his right pant leg just below the knee. He felt no need to explain his appearance. He had kept a grip on his anger while he checked the loaner car for tampering—none was apparent—and then phoned Manoukian to get the Identification technician rolling here. But now, confronting the hush-mouthed mechanics, he knew that he was losing that grip. The tense, unsmiling expressions on their faces told him so.

"Who's missing?" he demanded.

The mechanics said nothing, but the manager was beginning to stir just when the personnel opening in the big hangar door creaked open.

A uniformed Adirondack mechanic entered, but halted when he saw Emmett and the others.

It was Jason Eberhardt, who with Garrity had attempted to find the problem with the loading door on Flight 557. The man's normally nervous face was positively stricken-looking as he swept his fur-lined cap off his thinning hair. That hangdog look gave Emmett unexpected hope. "Come on in," he invited the mechanic, "join the party."

Eberhardt walked over to the formation and tried to melt into it by joining the center. The manager sprang to his defense: "About an hour ago, I sent Jason to a plane parked at the terminal to check an auxiliary power unit."

"Get it fixed?" Emmett asked pleasantly.

"Yeah," Eberhardt replied, "piece of cake."

An hour ago. Emmett noticed the portable radio on the man's utility belt. He had been gone from the hangar an hour, long before Emmett and the lieutenant had arrived, but could have been advised of the search by any of the others. He smiled at the assembly, "Well, everybody's got an asshole, and yours is named Dan Garrity . . ."

A few of the men sniggered.

"But he's being treated fairly. His attorney was present when he was questioned this afternoon. So, as a federal cop, I will take exceptional offense if any of you fail to treat me fairly. Do I make myself clear?"

As the mechanics stared off into space or at the cement floor, Emmett's cellular rang.

It was the FBI technician, who in a single breath advised that Manoukian had given him Emmett's number in case there was any difficulty locating him at the airport, that he'd left Garrity's residence and was presently halfway to Syracuse on the thruway. Emmett wasn't certain why he was being told all this, until the tech sucked in a quick gasp of air and added, "Something's coming over the radio. Shots fired on Harmony Street, and there's a pursuit."

Choking down a spasm of panic, Emmett asked the technician, "Any of our people hit?"

"I don't think so."

"Was Garrity the shooter, is he fleeing?"

"I don't . . ." The tech paused, and on the other end of the connection Emmett could hear an upswelling of radio traffic inside the evidence van, loud but garbled, a static-ridden voice that vaguely resembled Manoukian's normal talking one. He thought he'd made it clear to the young agent that it was too soon to collar Garrity, but had this been misunderstood somehow? "I don't know who did what," the tech finished. "I'd already left the house when this went down."

"Where's the pursuit now?"

"Tending down into Madison County. You want me to keep rolling to the airport?"

"Yes, keep coming . . ." Emmett looked for Bellasario, then recalled that the lieutenant was still guarding Garrity's locker. He told the tech, "Get an airport cop to escort you to Adirondack's maintenance hangar."

"I'll see you in about ten," the tech said.

"Not me, the lieutenant here. He'll maintain control of the evidence until you arrive." Emmett pocketed his cellular and saw that Eberhardt had stepped up to him, his hands buried in his jumpsuit pockets.

"Go ahead and take me downtown," the mechanic said. "I got nothing to hide."

Judging from his evasive eyes, he had a lot to hide, so Emmett decided to take him up on the offer, even though he had no intention of returning to the FBI office anytime soon. Besides, Eberhardt could help him safely negotiate the fog-bound access roads. "Okay," he said, "let's go. You got a key to the gate?"

"I do," the mechanic answered with an odd tone of formality. As if he were already on the stand.

A red aircraft-maintenance truck was now parked outside the door. "You just drive this?" Emmett asked Eberhardt.

"I did."

Emmett felt the pickup's hood as he passed by. It was warm, warm enough on this cold night to make him doubt that the engine had been shut down for the minutes Emmett had been tracking the figure out onto the runway.

"Hang on a second, Jason." Emmett frisked him, finding only a spanner wrench in a hip pocket. "Not going to try to brain me with this, are you?"

Eberhardt remained silent.

Emmett kept the wrench and unlocked the passenger-side front door for the man. The mechanic had to move Anna's topographical map off the seat.

Getting in behind the wheel, Emmett flipped through the radio channels until he located the unmistakable traffic of a hot pursuit. A new voice, not Manoukian's, was reporting the progress of the chase into Madison County, the latest reference point being someplace called Munnsville.

Emmett started his engine and sped for the terminal. He said nothing as he drove, just occasionally checked on the mechanic, who was sitting ramrod-rigid and staring through the windshield.

12

Leo Manoukian had just transmitted that they were almost to Munnsville when the tail-lights to the Chrysler New Yorker went out and darkness fell over the highway ahead. The section of country road was straight, and there had been no red flash to tell that the driver had slowed prior to turning. "Suspect driver is now—" The agent dropped the microphone and slammed on his brakes as a dog darted in front of them. Anna braced for a sickening thump, and Manoukian swerved, but then released the steering wheel to let the car straighten out on its own. That kept them on the road, and the dog slunk off into the brush, uninjured.

"Shit," Marvin Roth said from the backseat.

Manoukian fumbled around his shoes for the mike. Anna picked it up and slapped it into his palm. "Driver's now running without lights," he broadcast. "Advise oncoming units."

The dispatcher relayed the warning to any cruisers closing in out of the south.

The moon was no longer bright enough to cast tree shadows on the forest floor and across the roads, as it had earlier in the week, and Anna realized that the driver of the Chrysler really had to know these byways to run them without headlights. The *yelp, yelp, yelp* of the siren reverberating inside the car made her head ache. Nor did she care for the dull hypnotic way the grille-mounted emergency light strobed against the paddle-markers whooshing by.

Munnsville streaked past, and she caught flashes of window lights, frosted-over cars and mailboxes.

Manoukian kept racing into patches of fog, and the sudden white pressing against the car windows made her feel as if the world had been turned on edge and she was plunging through a cloud.

> *Down and down she falls,*
> *And as she is enveloped by darkness,*
> *She keeps falling down and down . . .*

The Oneida Creation Story, which she'd read in its entirety last night, kept coming back to her, as did the notion that she was dreaming all this. To a Modoc, a dream was an authentic experience, not an illusion. You were either warned or promised something by a familiar, a spirit in animal form that had taken an interest in you. Was hers Hummingbird? Was her mummified bird trying to tell her something?

Stay focused on the moment.

Manoukian set the microphone on his knee so he could steer with both hands. The mike dropped to the floor, and Anna retrieved it for him once again. She raised her voice over the scream of the engine. "This is silly, Leo."

He checked his speedometer—ninety-five miles an hour. "What's silly?"

"I don't have a clue where we are." She turned to Roth in the back. "Let's switch."

"Fine with me."

She rested the Remington in the space between the seats, muzzle pointing forward. "Shotgun chamber's empty, safety on." Unlatching her seat, she reclined the backrest as far down as it would go and clambered over into the rear. Roth, a large man, had a harder time getting over than she, and the heel of his shoe clipped Manoukian in the ear as he clumsily swung his legs around.

"Sorry, Leo." Finally, in place, Roth took over the radio. "Control, we just cleared Munnsville, still southbound on Thirty-five." His thumb lifted off the mike button. "You guys see that?"

Anna could see virtually nothing. As in most new cars, the rear seat was too low and the windows in the back too small.

"See what?" Manoukian asked.

"*Right*, turn right at the stop," Roth said excitedly. "I just caught some chrome shining on Forty-six." He keyed the microphone again. "Control, believe suspect vehicle just turned north on Highway Forty-six." Anna shifted so she could see between the front seats: A highway branched off to the right and cut through a low hill beyond the creek they'd been following.

Manoukian slowed for the turn, but just barely, and almost stood the sedan on its left-side wheels. He then fishtailed on the icy bridge over the creek.

Anna felt for her seatbelt, only to realize that she'd failed to strap herself in. She buckled up with trembling fingers, then clenched her hands to steady them.

"Now confirming," Roth transmitted, "suspect vehicle is northbound on Forty-six." He leaned over to see the speedometer. "We're pushing a hundred, Control."

Anna finally saw the Chrysler again, this time a black dot on the highway far ahead of them. Without warning, its brake-lamps blinked twice. After the darkness of the last several minutes, the flashes seemed like fireworks.

"Control, he's turning westbound on Williams Road. What kind of help do we have to the west and north of us?"

A flurry of call signs and positions came back at Roth over the airwaves. Presumably they were sheriff's and state police units, but Anna recognized only one voice—that of Vaughn Devereaux, the detective with the Oneida Nation P.D.: "Units, use extreme caution. We had several reports of shots fired on the rez earlier tonight—all linked to a vehicle of your description."

Ten miles beyond Syracuse, Jason Eberhardt observed timidly, "We're not going downtown, are we?"

"No." Emmett split his attention between the mechanic and terse chatter coming over the radio. "I want to check on a hot pursuit down in Madison County first."

"Then you want to get off the Dewey Thruway and drop south along U.S. Twenty."

"Appreciate it, Jason." Emmett followed his directions and took the next off-ramp. "Now tell me what you're not hiding."

"Pardon?"

"You told me you're not hiding anything."

"I'm not. Honest. I want to cooperate."

Emmett swung out into the left lane and made a tight pass on a curve. A truck horn blatted at him.

Eberhardt stiffened in the high beams of the semi, then yanked his shoulder belt to make sure it was functioning. "Ask me your questions, and you'll see I'm cooperating. You sure you need to drive this fast?"

"Yes. What time did you finish checking that power unit on the plane tonight at the terminal?"

"Ten-thirty-six," Eberhardt said without hesitation.

"How can you be so exact?"

"I kept checking my watch."

"Why?"

"Departure got delayed, and the lead attendant was on my ass because the gate agent was on her ass. That's Adirondack for you—everybody on somebody else's ass."

"Sounds cozy. Think the attendant could confirm what time you were done?"

"Probably."

Emmett made a few calculations, then ordered, "Light up your watch face—show me." The mechanic obeyed, and Emmett compared the time to his own. Only a minute's difference. An alibi was rearing its ugly head: Eberhardt may indeed not have had enough minutes to drive back from the terminal and then lead Emmett on foot out onto the runway. Another mechanic, then? Or somebody else entirely?

Emmett punched the gas pedal again. He'd let up, and the reports on the pursuit were still coming over the radio fast and furious. The chase had left Williams Road and gone north on Brown Road, wherever the hell they were.

Eberhardt asked if he could smoke.

Emmett said no. It was already misty enough outside without smudging up the interior of the car.

The mechanic sulked for a bit, then got over it and said knowingly, "You didn't come to the hangar looking for me, did you?"

"Then why did I come?"

"Dan Garrity."

"So?"

Silence.

Emmett looked at the thin-faced mechanic again. Why this hesitancy now after volunteering to go downtown? Was it fear of Garrity or self-loathing at the prospect of ratting on a union brother? He was finding it hard to read the man.

Roth reported that the Chrysler was on Highway 46 again, northbound. Emmett asked Eberhardt, "You hear that?"

"Yeah."

"Give me a shortcut north, fast."

The mechanic took his bearings. "Uh, this is Morrisville. Take a left at the second light."

Laying on his horn to freeze the traffic in the intersections, Emmett blew a stoplight, then another as he turned left. The town lights faded in his rearview mirror.

"You sure I can't smoke?"

"Positive," Emmett said. "What am I looking for next?"

"Rocks Road, about a mile. Make a right there."

"Tell me about Garrity."

Eberhardt ran a hand over his sparse hair. "Dan . . . Dan . . . Dan. He's like totally Airborne."

"Gung-ho?"

"Right. He's always ragging on me for being in the Air National Guard unit at the airport. Says we're one of the non-military services." Eberhardt hunched forward for a look. "This is Rocks Road."

Emmett turned. The new road narrowed as it twisted through ravines and scrub woods. "What's his being Airborne have to do with anything?"

"He's really gung-ho against this land claim thing. It's all he talks about—stopping the Indians before they drive us off the land. He says we'll wind up like wandering Jews or gypsies, with no place to rest our heads. The whole damn country."

"The whole country?" Emmett asked skeptically.

"Yeah, this claim thing will snowball. The courts will say all the old treaties are bogus, and not a single white guy in the country will have a valid deed to his property. Dan says the Old World won't have us back, and the New World will be run by Indians. We'll be like black people used to be in the South, always getting the boot and afraid to do anything about it."

Emmett carefully monitored the radio traffic again. Names of unfamiliar byways and streets were broadcast, but the general direction of the chase seemed to continue north, and Eberhardt suggested that he might want to take the next left. "I want to keep heading northwest, Jason?"

"Yeah."

"How do you feel about the Oneida claim?"

"I don't know."

"You own a home in the affected area?"

"Right in the heart of it, Vernon." Eberhardt slipped a pack of Camel filters from the breast pocket of his jumpsuit, but then remembered himself and put the cigarettes back. "I got this buddy at the airport. Real smart guy. Educated, unlike me. He makes things clear for me, even though sometimes it's like he's arguing with himself."

"A fellow mechanic?"

"No, he's in food service."

"A caterer, you mean."

"Right."

"What's his name?"

"Adrian Flint."

The towering caterer with the attitude. "Go on," Emmett said, interested.

"Adrian says white people round here are finally feeling what Indians felt two hundred years ago. You know, the threat of losing everything with nobody powerful on your side. You asked me how I feel about the claim, well maybe I don't like the way the federal government's taking the Oneida side in this. Even if New York is forced to make a cash settlement to the tribe, I don't like it. As a taxpayer, I just don't like it. If this is Streeter Road, take it."

It was. "Is Adrian Indian?" Emmett asked, regaining speed. Flint had denied this during the interview, but Parker still had a suspicion. There was nothing unusual in an Indian denying his blood, particularly in a region where it wasn't popular to be one.

"Naw. Sometimes he sounds like he doesn't even care for Indians. But he sees things from a lot of different angles." Eberhardt chuckled. "He says he's everything and everybody all wrapped up in one body."

"What's that mean?" Emmett asked.

"I'm not sure. Maybe just that he sees stuff from a lot of different ways. All I can say, he sure helped us out when my old lady and me were having some troubles. Helped me see her side of it."

"Sounds like Adrian went through troubles of his own."

"Oh, he admits that up front. Says he was in therapy for years and years."

"He say for what?"

"Not really. My old lady thinks he had a shitty childhood."

"Why?"

"He never mentions it. She even asked him once, but he wouldn't talk about it."

The traffic over the airwaves had gone silent, which churned the acid in Emmett's stomach. He hoped that it was nothing more serious than the FBI chase car having lost contact with the Chrysler. "So you and Garrity knew why the federal investigators came aboard Flight Five-five-seven Wednesday night."

"Right," the mechanic repeated. "We got a heads-up through the grapevine that you feds were coming."

"How'd you get the word?"

"Over our radios."

"Who specifically told you?"

"A buddy in security."

"And this security guy told you we were looking into the Oneida woman who'd been found dead?"

"No, that's not quite it."

"That's pretty much what you said when we interviewed you."

"I know," Eberhardt admitted. "It was Garrity. He told me you guys were there to find out what happened to *the Indian bitch*. Those were his words, not mine. He acted like he knew what'd happened to her, even though the rest of us have been scratching our heads ever since we heard about it."

"Did he explain what happened to her?"

"No, never. And I'm not accusing him of nothing, Parker."

"Understood. How do you think it might have happened?"

"The woman falling?"

Emmett nodded.

The mechanic's answer was slow in coming. "All I can figure is this— she got stuffed into the nose-wheel well, maybe strapped in somehow. The second officer missed her on his preflight inspection. It's dark up inside the well, and he doesn't have much of a flashlight. The three-holer took off, and she was dropped out just before the landing gear was retracted over Oneida County."

"What do you mean—*dropped out*?"

"I don't know," Eberhardt said evasively. "Mechanically released somehow. There's ways to do it."

Emmett had one major problem with this theory. Eight hours had elapsed between the take-off of Flight 557 and Van Hastart's hearing Brenda Two Kettles's corpse plummet out of the sky. Unless the farmer had been mistaken about the time of the strange howling over his house. Still, he asked, "Who would've arranged to have her stuffed in the wheel well?"

"Their big muckety-mucky—the Nation Rep. Everybody's saying he was behind it."

Anna noticed that a cruiser was following them about a mile behind, flashers going. Its siren was barely audible over the pounding of their own. "Leo, backup behind us."

Manoukian's eyes darted to his rearview mirror, and Roth radioed, "Unit behind—identify."

A slightly breathless voice said, "Madison County S.O. You still got the Chrysler in sight?"

"He's rabbiting without lights," Roth explained, "but has to hit his brakes on some of the curves."

"You catch the full license plate?"

"Negative."

Anna realized that, at last, the moon was down. About two miles ahead, the Chrysler's running lights came on. The driver had no choice. It was just too dark for him to continue blacked out.

The dispatcher advised that state police were setting up puncture strips at Five Chimneys Corner. Strips of jagged metal that could shred automobile tires like tissue paper. Acknowledging with two mike clicks, Roth explained to Anna, "We're not going to let this go back into congested areas. It's only—"

Then all three of them saw that the Madison County cruiser was speeding alongside. *"Jesus Christ,"* Manoukian blurted in confusion. He pressed his accelerator to the floor, but the sheriff's car inched ahead.

"What the hell you doing?" Roth fumed over the air.

Incredibly, the deputy didn't respond. He didn't even reach for his microphone, which remained clipped to the dashboard. Nor did he glance over at the FBI agents.

Both vehicles came to a hairpin curve, and Manoukian had to fall back or risk a head-on with any oncoming traffic. The sheriff's cruiser veered back into the right lane. And slowed, ever so slightly.

"What are you doing!" Roth repeated, more angrily.

"Slow down a little," the deputy finally replied. "Deer area."

"Pass him, Leo," Roth said.

Manoukian tried, but as he signaled his intention with his high beams, the deputy accelerated again.

A road sign whisked past Anna's window. She thought it had said Oneida Indian Reservation four miles and the city of Oneida six miles. The highway started up an incline, along which the cruiser steadily gained on the tail-lights of the Chrysler.

"Turn off your siren," Anna asked.

"Why?" Manoukian said, decelerating.

"Please just do it." As he killed his siren, she tried to power down her side window, but the switch had been disabled for prisoner security. "Roth, let down your window."

The blast of cold air hit her full in the face, but she clearly heard what she thought she had—the deputy had turned off his yelp and was hollering over his public address speaker, shouting something above the New Yorker's muffler noise.

Roth shook his head. "Is he actually *talking* to the driver of the Chrysler?"

The deputy's unit and the New Yorker vanished over the crest at the top of the grade. By the time the agents reached the same place, the two other vehicles were out of sight. Fog had settled over the hollow beyond, masking even the faintest glimpse of car lights.

Blinded, Manoukian had to brake again.

"How far to Five Chimneys Corner, Roth?" Anna asked.

"A mile at most."

"Don't worry," Manoukian said hopefully, "we've got the Chrysler hemmed in."

It hurt Anna's eyes to peer into the reflected glare of Manoukian's beams. She sat back and looked out her window. Her view was limited to a feeble glow from the right headlamp that rippled along the shoulder of the highway.

Then something registered.

Something she had seen back some yards.

"Turn the car around, Leo," she urged. Both agents glanced back at her, questioningly. "I'm serious—hurry!" Manoukian made a U-turn, and she told him to drive slowly the way they'd just come. "Stop. See them?"

Manoukian let down his window and shone a flashlight on two different sets of tire impressions, cookie-cutter distinct, in the viscid mud of a dirt turn-off. Eagerly now, he drove down the rutted track into a thicket of small trees. The trunks were fluorescent with orange and green lichens. She was scanning for human figures when Manoukian stopped, hard, and killed the engine.

Fog sifted across the headlights, but Anna could make out words on the trunk of the vehicle: MADISON COUNTY SHERIFF. Roth seized the shotgun, and the two agents bailed out, leaving their doors wide open. They went forward into the mist, leaving Anna to jiggle her disconnected door handle. She whistled for their attention, but neither of them returned, so she crawled over the front seat.

Outside, she drew her pistol and listened. Nothing broke above the stillness, not even footfalls. The deputy had extinguished all the lights on his vehicle, plus his motor, and the FBI car's headlamps penetrated only twenty or so feet before they were dissolved by the restless gray.

She inched forward.

Grunts and scuffling noises drifted to her. She picked up her pace. Figures, some standing and some kneeling, flitted in the confines of a cramped space. Drawing closer, she saw that the space was between the hood of the sheriff's cruiser and the rear bumper of the Chrysler. Manoukian was pitching empty beer cans out of the interior of the New Yorker, which appeared to be unoccupied. Roth was clasping his flashlight to the shotgun and aiming both at a prostrated figure, who had already been handcuffed by the deputy. The suspect wore a leather jacket with chrome studs. His hair had been trained into a spiky pink Mohawk.

The county cop was winded. "Got the son of a bitch. And I thought that partial license was familiar. My family car. This son of a bitch stole my own goddamned car!" The nameplate on his green jacket read: CHUCK KETCHUM.

She wanted to ask the deputy why he hadn't radioed the change in direction of the pursuit, but at that instant he and Roth hoisted the captive to his feet.

She was confronted by Hazen Two Kettles, who had a fresh bruise on his forehead. His dazed eyes widened as he appeared to recognize Anna, but he held his tongue. She holstered her semi-automatic.

"Just one kid?" Manoukian was holding a twelve-pack carton. "Lot of beer cans for just one kid."

"Just him," Deputy Ketchum answered. "What's that you have there?"

"Half-empty box of M-Eighty Explosive Simulators."

The deputy laughed. "Those are nothing more than military firecrackers. That explains the *shots fired*."

Manoukian offered, "I'll call in our location and set some flares out to mark this road for assisting units to find us."

"Let me," Anna volunteered. She relieved him of the box of simulators and carried it to the FBI car. First, she radioed dispatch that the chase had ended on an unmarked dirt lane short of the Five Chimneys Corner roadblock. "All's code four." No immediate danger. "But continue to roll assisting units."

"Copy," the dispatcher said.

Anna popped the trunk, deposited the box inside, grabbed three emergency flares, then closed the lid and set out on foot for the highway. Her penlite was so weak against the night she put it away and relied on the tunnel that had been cut through the trees for the road. Fog was condensing on the branches, dripping off with a noise like rain. The night was warming, slightly.

One kid.

And it had to be Hazen Two Kettles. Having run from federal officers would be his least worry. Grand theft auto off the reservation was a state offense, and Madison County would be less inclined than the Oneida Nation to release Hazen to the custody of his cousins, pending his juvenile hearing. Indians saw incarceration as cruel and unusual punishment. Freedom of movement meant life itself.

Despite the Chrysler's tinted windows, she'd had the impression on Harmony Street back in Sherrill that there'd been more occupants than just the driver. And the war whoop that had flown from the halfway-down rear window seemed out of character for the shy Oneida boy.

Anna sensed the highway opening out before her, and she'd just stepped on asphalt when off to her left branches crunched under pressure. She thought she could hear a tense whisper.

Then it was undeniable.

Something was crashing through the barren undergrowth.

She half-expected a deer or other large animal. Instead, three human silhouettes, boyishly lean, crossed the highway no more than thirty feet from her. She could smell beer on them. Her penlite wasn't worth slipping from her jacket pocket, so she twisted the cap off one of the road flares and used the striker-surface to ignite the incendiary device. The flame festered to life, dripping sparks.

Quickly, she hurled it toward the figures.

The flare bounced among them. Their startled expressions were caught in the sputtering glare. As if of one mind, they turned and ran.

"Hold it!" Anna cried, following.

Something about the varsity jackets and athletic shoes kept her from leveling her pistol on the three boys. But she ran after them, holding her weapon down at her side.

"You got somebody standing in the road, Parker," Jason Eberhardt noted.

Emmett jerked the steering wheel and braked, and still narrowly avoided Leo Manoukian. The agent had fixated on a solitary flare burning on the highway shoulder. He virtually ignored Emmett's car and gaped into the fog all around.

Emmett powered down his window and asked, "Where's the traffic stop?"

Manoukian flapped an arm toward the apron to a dirt road. "Turnipseed came out here to lay down some flares."

"And?"

"I thought I heard her shout something."

Emmett jammed the shifter into park and got out. "You haven't seen her since?"

"No."

"How long ago?"

"Maybe three minutes ago. I came right out to the highway."

"Park my car for me," Emmett ordered, taking Manoukian's flashlight from him without asking.

Getting inside the sedan, the agent asked Eberhardt, "You a prisoner?"

Emmett heard the mechanic answer, "I'm not sure."

Manoukian drove down the unpaved lane just as headlights appeared out of the north. A state trooper, who stopped and stepped out.

"Do me a favor," Emmett said, his heart in his throat. "My FBI partner just shouted something from the highway here. We can't find her. Her name's Turnipseed. How about working this stretch with your spotlight?"

"You got it." Slamming his door shut, the trooper started south, his spot probing the shrouded woods.

Another cruiser materialized out of the pall, this one with Oneida County Sheriff's Department decals. The deputy asked Emmett if he was FBI.

"BIA. But I'm looking for my partner, who is FBI."

"Listen," the deputy said urgently, "I've got to show you something. It was found on the railroad tracks in Bridgewater Flats this afternoon."

Emmett could think of nothing more important than locating Turnipseed. "Stow it. How about lighting up the woods to the north of here?"

"But—"

"No buts. I can't find my partner. I need your help."

Reluctantly, the deputy got back in his car, flipped a U-turn and did as asked.

Emmett walked over to the far shoulder, where the flare continued to burn. Shoe tracks appeared under the flashlight beam in the half-frozen earth—and continued off into the stunted trees. He was not relieved to see that there were several sets of tracks, most from athletic shoes. Sizes tens and elevens, judging from his own elevens. The smallest pattern—Anna's—overlaid the others, meaning that she had been in pursuit. At a hurried stride. Three subjects, he counted, probably male.

Emmett followed the tracks down a slope to a frozen creek, then across and up the far slope to a rocky ridge line. Icy drips rained off the overhanging boughs, and most seemed to find the back of his collar and trickle down his neck.

A spot of fiery red appeared down in the next drainage.

Emmett jogged for it.

He batted branches away from his face with his left forearm while taking out his .357 magnum revolver with his right hand.

The spot of red got brighter, revealed itself to be a highway flare. It was jammed in the crotch of an oak tree, illuminating a circle perhaps fifteen feet in diameter on the forest floor. Anna crouched in the middle of that circle, wrenching something in both hands.

Emmett skidded down the last yards to her on his heels.

She was restraining someone by applying a wristlock. The male subject, a teenager—judging by his varsity jacket—was grunting in pain, although he had yet to learn to lie still for he tried to buck Anna off. She cranked on more pressure, and he growled as his pimply face was driven back into the mud.

Emmett gave Anna his cuffs, and she put them on the boy. A big boy, maybe six feet tall, wearing size eleven Nike basketball shoes. With wet and blackened oak leaves pasted to his face as he looked up again.

"Who the fuck do you think you are?" he crowed at her.

"FBI."

"You can bite my ass, FBI."

Emmett seized him by the forelock and shone the light into his beer-reddened eyes. "Shut up before I *kick* your ass." For the first time, he looked off-balance, perhaps not having known that Anna had a back-up.

Meanwhile, she had finished a cursory search and come up with a knife and a wallet. It was a six-inch butterfly knife, capable of being opened with a snap of the wrist. No doubt illegal in New York, as in most other states.

Brushing the hair out of her eyes with the back of her hand, she explained, "There were two others. They got away."

"How'd you bag this one?" Emmett asked.

"Tackled him."

She said this so matter-of-factly, Emmett laughed. All 105 pounds of her had brought down a 170-pound youth in a varsity football jacket. He wished he'd seen it.

"What's so humorous?"

Still smiling, he reached out and touched his left hand to her cheek. He meant only to soften the look on her face, to apologize for the slip that he'd been surprised by her physical prowess. But then she clasped her palm to the back of his hand. Ever so briefly, but in that instant her eyes moistened, although she couldn't seem to bring herself to look at Emmett.

Then he let go of her, and the moment was gone. They were back to their unspoken truce to stay clear of the intimate.

She holstered her pistol, which she'd rested on the ground beside her, and went through the youth's wallet. Holding what appeared to be a driver's license to the light of the flare, she suddenly cried, "Dammit!"

"What's wrong?"

Anna seized the chain between the handcuff rings and pried the teenager's arms back, forcing him to stand. "All right, Charles Ketchum, Jr.," she exclaimed, "let's see if we can book the father-son cell at county jail for daddy and you!"

With that, she gave him a shove toward the highway.

13

GRANDMOTHER BLINKED TWICE, AND the smile wrinkled her brown latex cheeks. *"Sheko:li!"* she said to Johnny Skyholder, who had left his janitor's cart in the back of the main gallery of the Shako:wi Cultural Center and sunk onto the bench closest to her. "By now," she went on, "you've learned that this is Haudenosaunee for *Greetings!* The last time we visited, I told you about Sky Woman's fall from the heavens. I told you how a flock of swans flew up at the last moment and gently rested Sky Woman on the new earth that had just been formed on Turtle's back. Well, my children, a short time after she arrived in this world, Sky Woman gave birth to twins. The first twin was an easy birth, and he became known as the Good Spirit. But the second twin gave his mother so much pain delivering him, she died. The Good Spirit bore her radiant head up into the sky and scattered it into lights that became the sun, stars and moon. He buried the remainder of her body, and so it is that all good and nurturing things spring from Mother Earth . . ."

Johnny slowly frowned. Mention of swans reminded him of Goose, and his mind's sight drifted back to the past, where Goose and his terrible beak were locked away most of the time. But only most of the time, for Goose had taught him that you can be hated without reason in this world.

Listen, you foolish boy!

Johnny was astounded to see that Grandmother had become Oneida Nana, with her wrinkle-mouthed scowl and bloodshot eyes. It had happened before, things switching in the blink of an eye, but each time the transformation was a shock.

He hung his head.

Every damn time you come back from that white biddy, you go on and on about her goose. Sit still and listen. You heard nothing I been saying. Listen to me, now!

"Yes, Grandmother," he said obediently, the smell of gin wafting down to him.

He looked up at her, attentively.

"While the Good Spirit was busy making light," she went on, her face pretty and kind again, "his brother, the Evil Spirit, created darkness. The Good Spirit went about making good and pleasing things, but his bad brother countered each with something evil or poisonous. The Good Spirit made Deer and Bear; the Evil Spirit loosed serpents and spiders on the land. The Good Spirit created the stately oak, the sacred white pine and trees with sweet fruit, but his brother brought gnarled bushes into being, gave them thorns to tear flesh and bitter fruits to poison us . . ."

Johnny struggled to keep his mind on the words, but he kept seeing the face of the Evil Spirit. Big and sneering. Taunting him.

"One brother made broad rivers, the other churning rapids. Finally, the Good Spirit fashioned Man and Woman from red clay, but the Evil Spirit spun demons out of sea foam to haunt humanity. So it was that everything good was countered by something evil. This is how the world, as we know it, came into being." As Grandmother paused, her kindly look faded until her clear, fox-brown eyes were bloodshot again—and riveted angrily on his.

You heard nothing I been saying.

"Yes, I have, Nana. I heard everything."

No, you were off in lala land again. Every time you stay with that woman, you come back all lala and stubborn. Every time you come back, I got to beat the white out of you, don't I? It's your white blood that makes you this way. I got to whip you!

"No, no, Nana," Johnny moaned. "Please."

You're no good. Not like the other.

The untruth of that stung Johnny. As painfully as the lash of the willow switch he awaited with clenched eyelids. The Oneida did not beat their children, yet Oneida Nana beat him.

Why? Was he truly that bad?

As he sat cowering on the bench, his fear was replaced by outrage. A hard kernel of hate suddenly sprouted within him. When he gazed up again, Grandmother had gone still and silent on her platform.

I'm good. Better than the other.

Rising, he went into the office off the gift shop. He sat down at a desk. His long fingers closed around the telephone receiver, but he didn't pick it up. He waited anxiously for the phone to ring of its own accord. For the Voice to remind him that he was weak and could do nothing on his own. But the phone did not ring, and, emboldened, Johnny whispered, "I am the Good Spirit, the Good Spirit, protector of mankind."

Then he clasped the receiver in the crook of his neck and pulled out the writing slide to the desk, which had the Oneida Nation phone directory Scotch-taped to it. He resolutely dialed the Turning Stone Resort. *I am good, I am good.*

"Front desk," a clerk answered.

Johnny didn't know her, and the voice suggested that she was a white lady. "I need to talk to somebody."

"Who, son?"

Johnny ignored the intimation that he was much younger than his thirty-eight years. It happened all the time. "I think her name's Turnipseed, or something like that."

"One minute, please."

The number rang and rang and rang. Johnny was ready to hang up when the clerk came back on the line. "Want me to connect you to her voicemail?"

"What's that?"

"It's like a message machine. You can leave a message for her."

Johnny sucked on his lower lip. "Okay."

After a few seconds, a male voice told him to talk after the beep.

The beep made him jump a little.

"I got to talk to Turnipseed," he said, frightened now the Voice would come on the line and scold him for trying to tattle. The Voice that could contact him at any hour and control him. But he was still mad over what Oneida

Nana had said about him. "We got to stop somebody from doing evil things," he went on to the voicemail. "I'm doing my best, but I need some help. I'll call again later. Good-bye for now."

Hazen Two Kettles startled as something gave his shoulder two sharp taps.

He looked up at the bearded detention officer looming over him. His heart sank as he realized where he was. The air had the all too familiar institutional smells of disinfectant and floor wax. His black leather jacket, Levi's and boots were gone, replaced by a tangerine-colored jumpsuit and faggy slip-on shoes. He'd slept in these jail clothes on top of the cot.

"Time to get up," the officer said, handing Hazen a plastic bag containing a toothbrush and a small tube of Crest. "I'll get you something to eat, but then you got to talk to the cops."

Hazen hadn't had enough sleep, but sudden stabs of pain killed off any lingering drowsiness. His head hurt, as did much of his left side; left hand, elbow and lower leg were all skinned up. "They find my bike?"

"Who?"

"The Indian cops."

"You'll have to ask them."

Anna hoped that the open air might revive her after the sleepless night. So, she left the stuffy lobby and went out to the front of the Madison County juvenile detention facility. It was in Wampsville, the county seat five miles southwest of the city of Oneida. The pale gold light of early morning was being scattered by a band of clouds low on the horizon, and despite the brisk temperature the air felt too dank and heavy to be refreshing.

Still, she paced the topmost step, trying stay awake.

Minutes ago, she'd phoned the Two Kettles's residence and advised Mariana that her cousin, Hazen, was back in detention. No surprise on the woman's part, just a weary resignation. She didn't even ask what the charges were, even though Anna had been prepared to explain that the boy might be blameless and he was more in protective custody than anything else at this point. She wanted that to be clear, before the juvenile hall advised Mariana as well.

Soles scuffed wet cement.

A skinny, black-haired woman bounded energetically up the steps toward Anna. She might have been pretty, except that her features were crowded on a small face. Shifting her briefcase to her left hand, she shook with Anna. "Linda Freccia—you must be Special Agent Turnipseed."

"Yes—call me Anna. Thanks for being on time."

"I bet you're dead on your feet."

"Close."

Freccia was the juvenile detective with Madison County. She led Anna back into the lobby and rang the buzzer on the counter. Waiting for a staff member to respond, the woman shed her fawn-colored trench coat, draped it over her forearm and smiled. "Well."

Anna broke the awkward quiet that followed. "Any news on the other two juveniles?" The two who had gotten away while she was busy apprehending Charles Ketchum, Jr.

"Search and Rescue has been out since four, but nothing yet. Daylight will help."

"Any leads on their identities?"

"Young Ketchum isn't talking, and no missing reports."

The temps had dipped into the low twenties toward dawn. Had someone contacted the parents or guardians of the two boys, persuading them not to report their failure to return home last night, despite the dangers of the January night? Also, Anna wondered if the juvenile detective knew the names of young Ketchum's two friends and was sitting on that information for the time being. Would her cooperation completely dry up if the FBI rode roughshod over Deputy Chuck Ketchum? In fairness to Freccia, Madison County S.O. was her home turf, for better or for worse, and she had to live here. "Where's Ketchum now?"

"Home, I suppose," Freccia replied with a hint of distaste, reassuring Anna that she didn't care for what Ketchum had done last night. "He's suspended, pending investigation. Meets with IA at one o'clock this afternoon. I understand he'll be accompanied by our association's attorney."

Ketchum was facing his own Internal Affairs bureau, no doubt after both Leo Manoukian and Fred Cochran, the special agent in charge of the Syracuse FBI office, had harangued the sheriff over the phone earlier this morning to act. Turns out, it had been Leo's first actual high-speed pursuit, a rite of passage for most cops, and Ketchum had stolen it from him.

Anna had offered to remain in Wampsville to help question Hazen Two Kettles, letting Manoukian and Roth swing by their homes for a few hours' sleep before they finished wrapping up all the loose ends left by the execution of the search warrant and the pursuit.

"Here we go," Freccia said.

Finally, a detention officer opened the door for them. Anna and Freccia deposited their pistols in the gun lockups, then followed the bearded man through a security door and down the freshly-waxed corridor to one more cramped interviewing room in a numbing chain of them. For an instant, Anna felt disoriented, not quite knowing where precisely in America's sprawling penal system she was—until her eyes fastened on the detective again. Dark-haired, Italian, New York—the level of hell she was presently visiting was also known as upstate New York. But it could have been Portland or Albuquerque.

The detention officer promised to be back in a few minutes.

Anna yawned.

Freccia found the sight infectious, and together they sat, stifling yawns. "How long you been with the FBI, Anna?"

"Two years."

"Out of Washington, D.C.?"

"No, the Las Vegas field office, though there's been talk of moving me to the Indian Desk in D.C. My partner and I are sent wherever there's some mess in Indian Country nobody wants to touch."

"Why you two?"

"Assumption at Justice is that natives will relate to natives, though I knew nothing about the Haudenosaunee until this week."

"What kind of Indian are you, if you don't mind?"

"I don't mind. You've never heard of us—Modoc from Oregon-California."

"How do other Indians react to you?"

"Like anybody else who isn't from their tribe. Until they need something and figure they can play the Indian card with us."

Freccia's small face broke into another sympathetic smile. Anna was beginning to think she was nice. "Know what you mean," the detective said, touching her fingers to the back of Anna's hand in a very Mediterranean gesture. "The sheriff's office had me work organized crime at first. Hated it. Every Sicilian sleazeball I met called me *sister*."

Hazen Two Kettles was escorted into the room. His ordinarily spiky pink Mohawk lay flat against his scalp this morning, and the bruise on his forehead had left the skin around his eyes puffy. The detention officer shot the boy the obligatory warning glance to behave, then withdrew, leaving Hazen to slump in the only chair provided for the interviewee. It was bolted to the floor.

Freccia gave Hazen the Miranda advisory, and he waived his rights quite literally: by waving his left hand. The blade of that hand was abraded and stained with iodine. The detective asked him how he felt, how his bruises and scrapes were, what kind of treatment he'd gotten from the nurse.

Hazen muttered soft, indifferent replies, but his state of mind seemed all right for questioning, that he wasn't prone to undue suggestibility.

Last night, he had frantically begged Roth for the two *Indian cops* to transport him. So Emmett and she had driven him from the dirt lane near Five Chimneys Corner to the facility here. Handcuffed and placed in the backseat, he had almost immediately fallen into an exhausted sleep, seemingly relieved to be out of Deputy Ketchum's clutches. As they were entering Wampsville, he was roused by the town lights flickering across his face. "Find my bike," he said hoarsely to the partners. "It's in some brush on Forest Avenue. That's near the rez. Find my Harley, and you'll see."

Emmett then tried to get more out of Hazen, but the boy clammed up—they had arrived at juvenile hall and the white world closed around him again. The partners decided that trying to question a sleepless youth at two-thirty in the morning could be construed as torture.

Now, Detective Freccia asked, "How much did you have to drink yesterday, Hazen?"

After booking, blood had been drawn, but the toxicology report from the lab would be some days in coming.

He thought something over, the blood test perhaps. "Nothing."

"Not even a single beer, Hazen?"

"Nothing."

"What about drugs?"

Hesitating again, he glanced to Anna. She dipped her head for him to go on, but he stared keenly at her for several long seconds. Then, astonishingly, he confessed, "I smoked a little weed around four in the afternoon."

So, Hazen was savvy enough to understand that a lie inevitably exposed by a blood test would do him no good in his current fix. Still, there would be consequences for this admission; he was on both tribal and county probation. Obviously, something weightier was on his mind, something bigger than marijuana use, and he needed the trust of his two interrogators.

"All right, Hazen," Freccia said without sounding judgmental, "tell me what happened right after you smoked that joint." She too probably sensed that Hazen wanted to tell the truth, and by skipping over the joint she relieved him of squealing on any of his buddies.

His palms were wet, for he wiped them on the pant legs of his jumpsuit.

He began to talk in a monotone about his night.

Emmett asked, "Where's Forest Avenue?"

"This is it coming up," Vaughn Devereaux replied, slowing for the turn off Territory Road.

The sun had just broken through low clouds, and the flat rays spread across a field overgrown with berry vines. Emmett disliked this country. It was densely overgrown and lacked open vistas even in winter. Matted tangles of roots and tendrils seemed to squeeze the breath out of the land. And he was bleary-eyed from another long night with the complimentary mint still waiting on the pillow in his hotel room. "Are these tribal lands?"

"No, private," Devereaux said.

Devereaux had shown up at the traffic stop on the unpaved road just before Anna and Emmett transported Hazen Two Kettles. He had shaken his head with apparent sadness at the Oneida youth's involvement in his second scrape of the week, advising him that the Nation's public defender probably wouldn't help him with this one. It was a county matter. Hazen made no response, other than to try to burn a hole in the tribal cop with his eyes. Then, Devereaux departed, and Hazen was transported to juvenile, along the way telling the partners about his Harley. Emmett phoned the detective, who'd just gotten to bed after doing him a favor by transporting Jason Eberhardt back to the airport, and asked for his help in locating the bike. Devereaux had met him at a donut shop in Oneida at 5:00 A.M.

The detective now slowed along Forest Avenue. The pavement was hemmed in on both sides by sloughs choked with ten-foot-high willows. Again, a land teeming with vegetation. "How'd the search go at Garrity's house?"

Emmett sifted through his fatigue, trying to recall if he'd informed the Oneida Nation P.D. about the search warrant. No, he decided, but then he realized that Eberhardt had probably told Devereaux all about the heat coming down on Garrity. "Search went all right."

"Mind telling me what slant you're working on him?"

"Slant?"

"You figure Garrity had something to do with Brenda Two Kettles's death? Or is it something else entirely?"

Doubtlessly, the cat was already out of the bag in regards to the confiscation of the computer hard drives and printers, so Emmett saw no harm in pretending to confide. "Keep this under your hat—Garrity might be good for the death threat letter that was sent to the *Dispatch*."

"Really?"

Emmett nodded, scanning all around for a sign of Hazen's motorcycle.

Devereaux grinned. "Excellent. I'd heard good things about you, Parker, but this is really excellent. You make shit happen. The Nation Rep is going to love you." There it was again: the reflex to turn all strangers into allies that came from extended undercover work.

"Pull over," Emmett said.

Devereaux stopped, and Emmett got out of the detective's unit, still holding his cup of coffee from the donut shop. He had noticed two recent scars in the asphalt, both about four feet long. The distance between them approximated that between the tips of a handlebar and footrest. And off to the right side of the road was a gap where the willows had been bent over.

Taking a sip of tepid coffee, Emmett peered down into the ditch. There lay a Harley-Davidson. It had come to rest up-ended, and the handlebars were frozen into the muddy ice. The rear fork and shock absorbers showed collision damage. Emmett noted the shoe tracks on the shoulder of the road, suggesting that the chopper had been dragged off the road and manually tossed into the slough. Athletic soles, three individual sets, all sizes tens and elevens. Like last night in the woods.

Devereaux had come to Emmett's side. "Well, that puts a different spin on things."

Emmett poured out the last of his coffee and crushed the cup in his fist. "That's why we're going to do this crime scene ourselves. Even though it's off the rez. Mind rolling your I.D. tech?"

"Not at all." Devereaux went back to the car to radio his station.

Emmett knelt to examine the impressions from an oblique angle. Shoes. That reminded him how last night, in all the confusion, an Oneida County deputy sheriff had pressed an evidence bag on him. In it was a woman's left shoe—casual-wear, red in color, size six. A railroad worker had found it on Bridgewater Flats near a bridge over Hardscrabble Creek. The deputy had shown Emmett the spot on a map. It was about two miles northwest of old man Van Hastart's cornfield, and fourteen miles east of the path used by Flight 557 on Monday night.

There was no question in Emmett's mind that the red shoe had belonged to Brenda Two Kettles. Once he got some sleep, maybe everything would come together, everything would become clear.

Devereaux returned from the car. "I.D. is rolling."

"Thanks."

The detective chuckled under his breath. "Man, you sure scared the crap out of that mechanic."

"Who, Eberhardt?"

"Yeah."

"I went easy on him," Emmett said.

"No doubt. It's your face, know what I mean? No offense, Parker, but I would've loved unleashing your face on New York City. It's the way you don't show anything. Least of all pity. Hell, you make *me* feel like confessing, and I haven't done anything."

"Runs in my family," Emmett said, heading back to the warmth of the car's interior.

"Things been really bad at home since Aunt Brenda got killed," Hazen began, "so I didn't feel like going back from the tribe rec hall right away. My probation officer with the Nation says I got to be home by seven at night, but it was only five-thirty, or so. It'd just got dark."

"That's okay." Detective Freccia smiled at the boy's pains to be precise.

Anna could understand his reluctance to go back to that overcrowded, dilapidated mobile home. Years ago, she'd often dreaded returning to her own reservation home at the close of day. Where secret, fumbling touches awaited her. "Excuse me, Hazen," she interjected before he went on, "but tell me a little about your aunt."

"Strong," he answered after a lull. "People get on your case, she'd back 'em off."

"Meaning, people were afraid of her?"

"Kind of."

"Oneida or white people?"

"Mostly Oneida."

"Why were they afraid of her?"

Hazen visibly struggled with his answer. "She was just *strong*." That was it. He had nothing more to say about Brenda.

"Sorry," Anna apologized to Freccia for having broken her momentum. "Go on, Hazen. You left the rec hall."

"Then I rode out on Forest Avenue. There was fog, but not much, and I opened it up. I going pretty fast when I saw headlights right on my ass . . ." He paused to gauge their reaction to his choice of language. Neither Anna nor Freccia said anything. When he continued, he was less self-conscious. "I mean *right* on my ass, a big old Chrysler. I pulled over to the right to let him pass, and this guy went right too. I went left, he went left. I slowed down, he slowed down. It was like that for a ways—then he slammed me. Pow!" He slapped his palms together to simulate the collision. "I went down on my left side, messing up my elbow and leg here." Gingerly, he touched the side of his lower left leg. "I was pinned under my Harley, trying to get if off me, when they came up."

"Who?" Freccia interrupted.

"At first, I couldn't tell on account of the headlights. But then I saw it was Charley Ketchum who got out behind the wheel. Next I saw Jerrold Webster, laughing. The third guy, all I know is—they call him Doc, on account he always has pills in his daypack."

"What kind of pills?" the Madison detective asked.

"Anything you want, but mostly ecstasy." Hazen's eyes turned worried. "I know Charley's in here, but what about Jerrold and Doc when you catch 'em? Will they be locked up too?"

"Most likely," the juvenile detective promised.

Anna asked, "How do you know Ketchum and Webster?"

"We all go to high school in Oneida. I think Doc goes to Sherrill High, so I only seen him a couple times, like at the movies."

"Excuse me a moment," Freccia said, rising and taking her cell phone from her trench coat pocket. She stepped out into the hall, presumably to advise her department of the identities of the two missing boys.

As soon as the detective shut the door, Hazen said to Anna, "You got to help me get away from here."

"From county detention?" Anna asked, surprised.

"Yeah."

"You know I can't. And you're probably safer inside."

"No," he said obstinately, "that's not so."

"Why not, Hazen?"

"I'll wind up like my aunt in here."

"What makes you think that?"

He ignored the question. "Find my bike yet?"

"Not yet. My partner went out to look for it."

Freccia re-entered and sat again. "Continue, Hazen."

He gave Anna one last pleading look. "Well, Jerrold and Doc lifted the bike off me, and I thought maybe they were all going to help me, but then Ketchum kicked me in the head. After that, I kind of lost track of time for a while."

"Meaning, you were unconscious for a period?" Anna asked, wanting nothing more to diminish his capacity as a witness to recall exactly what had happened. His admitted marijuana use already opened the door for a defense attorney to discredit his testimony.

"I guess. In and out. Anyways, I kind of remember them carrying me over to Ketchum's Chrysler and throwing me in the back. I woke up in the backseat, between Jerrold and Doc, with them holding on to my arms."

The detective asked, "As best you can remember, did they say anything to you while they put you in the car?"

"Like what?"

"*Like—we're going to get you to a hospital, or drive you home?*" Good,

Freccia was trying to nail this down as a kidnapping by eliminating any other possibilities.

Hazen chuckled sourly at both notions. "No, no—they never said nothing nice the whole time. It was all like *you blanket-ass* or *you Oneida nigger*. Every time one of 'em said this last thing, Doc yanked on my Mohawk hard."

Anna asked, "Where were you when you became fully aware of your situation again?"

"I guess when Ketchum was driving us around the rez in the dark. Chuck would get out now and again and blow up a mailbox with these big firecrackers he had in a box. I kept hoping the tribe cops would hear and do something."

"But they never appeared?"

Hazen shook his head. "So I decided to try to get away. I started fighting, but Ketchum reached over the seat with this forty-four magnum revolver and put it right here." He touched the indentation between his eyes.

Anna felt a chill at this first mention of a handgun. "How'd you know it was forty-four magnum?"

"Jerrold told me that's what it was. The most powerful handgun in the world. What Dirty Harry uses."

"Do you know if the revolver belonged to Ketchum's dad?"

"No."

"You don't know?"

"It didn't belong to Ketchum or his dad at all. Doc said it belonged to his granddad, and the old man let him have it sometimes to go out and shoot cans—Afri-*cans*, Puerto Ri-*cans*, and Mohi-*cans*. I told 'em I was Oneida, not Mohican, but that only made em laugh again."

"What happened to the revolver?" Freccia asked.

"Doc gave it to Ketchum's dad after he stopped the car out in the trees."

The detective frowned, made a note on her pad, underscored it with two bold lines, but then said, "Let's not get ahead of ourselves."

And Anna was left wondering if the blast she'd heard on Harmony Lane had been the bark of a forty-four—aimed at her or one of the other agents. Death could brush past so unexpectedly, and when it did you were left feeling fragile instead of lucky. Luck was a bank account, and it didn't take you long in this business to figure out when you were overdrawn. *Maybe that's Emmett's problem, lately.*

Freccia finished taking notes for the moment. "What time did you all finally get to Sherrill, Hazen?"

"I don't know. Late. Seemed like Ketchum been driving us around forever. All over the rez, then out to Canastota and back again."

"An hour? Two?"

"More like two."

"What was said during this time?"

"Lots of stuff."

"Such as?"

"Some of it what guys say when cruising around." Hazen began to smile, but then stopped. "Some of it was pretty bad. They had beer, and Doc, 'specially, got wasted. We was leaving Canastota, and he asked Ketchum for his knife."

"Describe it," Freccia said.

"Oh, longer than a pocket knife. And Doc could open it by doing just this." Hazen flicked his wrist, extending a forefinger which he then held alongside his neck. "He put the blade up to my throat and started talking real soft and fast . . ." Anna rubbed the backs of her arms through her jacket sleeves. "Doc told me the whole Oneida Nation is going to get ours. Soon, too. There are like hundreds of these white guys called the Minutemen. He said they're in every kind of business you can name. Teachers, bus drivers, plumbers, doctors, cops. He said lots of cops are Minutemen with nobody knowing—deputies, city cops and state troopers. Judges too. The thing that makes them hang together is their houses and land. They aren't going to hand their property over to *a bunch of lazy blanket-asses.* All the leader of the Minutemen has to do is snap his fingers—and they'll snuff an Oneida for him."

Freccia had been listening, transfixed. "Who's their leader?"

He paused, his look far-off. "Doc never said. All he told me is that the Minutemen have started the killing."

Quietly, Anna asked, "Did you believe him, Hazen?"

"Of course."

"Why?"

"Aunt Brenda's gone."

Freccia frowned again. "Did Doc say that the Minutemen killed your aunt?" •

"Kind of," he said. "He told me she was the first, and there'd be one a month from here on out. It was no good for me or anybody else to go to the cops, because the cops would cover everything up. Doc said—*Watch, nobody'll ever go down for your aunt. No arrests. Nobody will ever even figure out how it was done.*"

"Did he indicate what he and the others meant to do with you?"

"Not Doc, but Ketchum said they hadn't made up their mind if they wanted to kill me too, or let me go back to the rez and tell everybody what was coming for them."

"Did you believe you were about to die, Hazen?" Freccia asked.

"I figured it could happen."

"How?"

"The whole ride felt like other times out on the rez to me. Some things start half-joking, you know, but then they get out of hand. I thought Ketchum, Jerrold and Doc could get out of hand, even if they didn't mean to at first."

Anna realized that this boy, who was probably only marginally literate, had just defined the nature of most youth crime in America.

"We're getting ahead of ourselves again," Freccia pointed out. "If you know, why did Ketchum drive into Sherrill and down Harmony Lane?"

"I'm not sure, but right before Doc got a call on his cell. I couldn't hear the guy's voice—"

"You think the caller was a male?"

"Maybe. But Doc acted like it was somebody older than him. An older guy. And whatever the guy said, it got Doc all riled up. After the call, he told Charley Ketchum and Jerrold that the feds were hassling Dan Garrity and God only knows who was next. Jerrold said he had to get home, but Doc wanted to go by Harmony Lane and see what was happening."

Now, Anna knew that Madison County Search and Rescue was searching empty woods and fields. If Doc had had a cellular phone, he and Jerrold Webster had arranged to be picked up hours ago.

"What happened on Harmony Lane?" Freccia prompted.

"Right before Ketchum turned down the street, he took his knife back from Doc and gave Jerrold the forty-four. I guess he figured Doc was too drunk by now to handle any weapons. Ketchum told Jerrold to shoot me if I made a peep, so he stuck the gun in my ribs. I couldn't see much, but I saw you on the lawn . . ."

Hazen met Anna's gaze.

As before with the intense portions of interviews, she stopped hearing words and instead saw the event unfolding, all the more vividly because she herself had been there:

The tense silence in the car was suddenly broken by Doc, who let out with an Indian war whoop. Then came the blast. For a second, Hazen thought he'd been shot, he even felt a phantom flow of blood down his ribs. Ketchum stomped on the accelerator, screaming, *"What happened? What happened!"* Doc laughed maniacally through the sulfur smell of the match he'd lit and touched to the fuse of an M-80 blast simulator in the space beneath the rear seat. He told the others what he'd done, and Ketchum shouted, *"You stupid dick-head, what'd you do that for!"* Doc had responded with an *Ooo-wah!*, a cry with no meaning to Hazen. Jerrold begged hysterically to be let out of the speeding Chrysler, but by then the FBI car was closing on them and the countryside was too open for anybody to get away on foot.

Ketchum headed south, back into Madison County, knowing that his father was on duty in the Stockbridge beat, the area in which most of the pursuit had occurred. Eventually, a new set of emergency lights appeared behind the Chrysler, and Ketchum's father broadcast over his speaker: *"Charley, this is Dad. Old logging road coming on the right. Turn off. There's a roadblock ahead—turn off!"*

At this point, after telling how Charley Ketchum had followed his father's instructions and turned off on the logging road, Hazen fell silent.

"What's wrong?" Freccia asked him.

Anna knew what was wrong. Hazen could sense the danger: He was on the brink of accusing a white adult, a peace officer. And he might not be believed.

"I'm not going to let anything happen to you," Anna said, drawing a brief stare from the juvenile detective. "Whatever comes of this, no one will harm you."

His eyes moistened. "Charley's dad got us all out of the Chrysler."

"How'd you know the deputy was Charley's father?" Freccia asked.

"Him and me had some run-ins before over my chopper being street-legal. He never liked me. Anyways, we could hear another siren coming—"

Again, Anna had to interrupt. "Why do you say *we*? Did the others react to the sound as well?"

"Yeah. Charley's dad looked real shook up. He took the forty-four away from Jerrold, then went back to his police car to turn off all the lights."

The detective obviously knew that this point would be the smoking gun to this afternoon's Internal Affairs hearing, for she clarified, "You mean—as the siren got closer, Deputy Ketchum purposely turned off all his vehicle lights, including the emergency flashers?"

"That's right," Hazen replied.

"Go on."

"I was thinking maybe everything was over and I was okay finally, mostly on account I could see the lights from another cop car coming." The bucar, in which she'd been, Anna realized. "But then Charley's dad put the cuffs on me and knocked me to the ground. He told me nobody steals his car and gets away with it. I said I didn't know what he was talking about, but then he hit me on the forehead. The same place Charley kicked me."

Freccia grimaced—not in disbelief, Anna felt, but in shame. "What happened next?"

"He told Charley and the other guys to run into the woods. He said to meet him later."

"Where?"

"I'm not sure," Hazen told the detective. "He just said *the field where we use to hunt rabbits*. He was going to give Charley his cell phone, but Doc told him he already had one. So the guys started running. A minute later, the FBI pulled up."

"How'd you know it was the FBI?"

Hazen lifted his chin at Anna. "I seen her before at my trailer house."

"Tell me," Anna said, "why didn't you let me know what had happened to you right away? Why'd you wait until now?"

"I'm not even sure I should've said something now," Hazen replied fatalistically. "But I have. So that's that. See, Charley's dad said if I ever told what really happened, I'd wind up dead. Just like my aunt."

14

THE CASINO COFFEE SHOP was just beginning to fill up with the lunch crowd, but Emmett still had most of an entire section to himself. He sat in a booth, trying to ignore the cartoonish melodies spewed out by the video slot machines. He drank decaffeinated Olmec Gold coffee, even though he'd been awake so many hours now he felt as if he might never sleep again. Maybe sleeplessness was a path to immortality.

Olmec Gold.

A cooperative effort between the Oneida Nation and the Indians of southern Mexico, a brochure on the table explained. He couldn't say that he liked or disliked the blend; his stomach was too sour for him to enjoy anything.

Purple. Subliminal touches here and there, he observed.

Casinos splashed up their decor with plenty of purple, reportedly a color that made people want to gamble. Purple just made him want to puke.

That is what he was thinking as Portia Nelson sat down across the table from him. She wore a pink V-neck sweater and jeans, reminding him that it was Saturday for the rest of the universe.

"Ms. Nelson," he said. At least his confused brain thought she was the same redheaded attorney with violet eyes he'd last seen at Daniel Garrity's interrogation—how many days ago? Didn't matter. While purple made him want to puke, violet made him want to do something else. Even to the counselor for Garrity with apparent ties to the Committee for Upstate Equality. Anna had told him that the mechanic had left a message for her last night, blaming the search on his support for C.U.E. She, apparently, had represented the committee in the past.

"Two federal investigators of Indian ancestry staying in an Indian-owned hotel," Portia said, rolling her eyes to indicate the Turning Stone Resort, "are bound to make a wider community wonder how impartial they really are."

"We tried another place," Emmett said, covering a yawn with his hand. "But the cavalry bugles in the parking lot kept us up all night."

She leaned toward him. "Seriously, Mr. Parker, you're sending a message by staying here."

"Seriously, Ms. Nelson, as you well know from your work with the NTSB, my office contracts with a local travel agency in Phoenix to make reservations for us based on price, quality and convenience of locality. Given those criteria, Turning Stone popped up on the computer screen. I could give a rat's ass where I stay. I'm sick of being on the road."

"Married?"

"Once."

"Married once, or married once upon a time?"

"Married thrice," he said, "once upon a time."

Smiling, she eased back into a beam of stronger light projecting down from the ceiling. Her skin was truly flawless, especially at her throat. Milky, unblemished, suggesting more softness that was hidden from him.

He asked, "You married?"

"I'm sure you know all about that," she curtly answered. Issue closed. He racked his fuzzy brains for what she might be referring to, but came up empty. Before he could ask her, she said, all business, "My partner, Sherwin Katz, is asking for a meeting with the Assistant U.S. Attorney here right away. This afternoon. He has no objection if you and Ms. Turnipseed are present. In fact, it'd probably expedite the process if you could answer any questions the prosecutor might have then and there. Frankly, you two would make useful allies in this."

"What makes you think we want to be allies?"

"You will. First, Daniel Garrity is willing to plead *nolo contendere* to writing the threatening letter to the *Dispatch* . . ." Emmett kept a poker face, but his mind raced to keep up. *Nolo Contendere* was essentially a guilty plea, but it afforded the defendant some protection against civil suits arising out of the criminal act, like every Oneida in upstate New York suing the mechanic because his letter had robbed them of sleep and put them off their food. "Secondly, my client is willing to submit to a polygraph examination given by a qualified examiner agreed upon by him and the U.S. Attorney—"

"Hold up," Emmett interrupted. "You won't attend the meeting?"

She took a sip from his water glass without asking. Using her left hand, he noted. "No."

Anna had also told Emmett that, according to Veda Garrity, Portia was no longer handling C.U.E. business. "Why not?"

"I'm sick and tired of anything even remotely related to the land claim. It's taken over our lives here in upstate, especially mine. I'd like to stand back and get a new perspective on it. I think there can be a resolution if—"

"Excuse me, Ms. Nelson." A uniformed security guard stood over the table. A second guard, also white and the first's equal in thick-necked burliness, waited slightly behind. "We got to ask you to leave."

Portia's answer was a brash laugh that was loud enough to turn heads throughout the coffee shop.

"What's the problem here?" Emmett asked the first guard.

"We reserve the right to refuse service to anybody, and Ms. Nelson knows she's not welcome here." The guard lowered his voice and assumed a *let's-be-a-good-girl* tone with her. "That's what my supervisor says, so come along, ma'am. We'll walk you to your car."

"You have got to be kidding," she said with a tight grin.

"No, ma'am. Nothing personal."

"It is personal. I don't see you asking any other white people to leave."

"You can tell your supervisor this," Emmett said. "I'm a registered guest and law enforcement officer with the Bureau of Indian Affairs. I'm conducting federal business right now. If I am prevented from doing so by the management, I will make damn sure no employee of the U.S. Government ever stays at Turning Stone Resort ever again."

After a brittle second, the guard turned, lips moving as he tried to commit Emmett's words to memory, and lumbered down the aisle between the tables. His partner gave Parker an apologetic shrug, then followed.

Emmett smirked at Portia. "Aren't you glad now I'm a registered guest of the Turning Stone Resort and Casino?"

She laughed. A sexy laugh that hinted at an appealing crack in her professional persona. But then she got down to business again. "Where were we? Oh yes, the polygraph."

"Back up a tad."

"How far?"

"This letter Garrity allegedly wrote. It's a cheap plea. Sending a threatening letter through the mails, even if the government tacks on a Civil Rights charge, is like jaywalking compared to murdering Two Kettles."

"Mr. Garrity is *not*—"

"How can I be sure old Dan even wrote the letter? I got an unkind suspicion he can't even write his name with a stick in the mud."

Portia looked as if she'd been waiting for this. "A line in the original doesn't appear in the version printed in the newspapers."

"Congratulations. But you'd know that just being familiar with investigative techniques."

"Would familiarity with investigative technique tell me the exact words that follow the line *We'll also kill non-Indians who go to Oneida businesses, 'specially the Turning Stone Casino?* For the record, they are: *for they are traitors who aren't worth our sympathy.*" She paused. "Do I have you hook, line and sinker, Mr. Parker?"

Emmett glanced out over the casino. "Let's say you might have lipped me with the hook. If Garrity can prove authorship, what's he need the lie box for?"

"To absolve himself of any and all involvement in Two Kettles's death. You should discuss this with Mr. Katz."

"If you're so sick and tired of the land claim quandary, why'd you sit in the Garrity interview?"

"I thought the concerns were NTSB-based. I wasn't aware at the time that Mr. Garrity had authored the letter."

"Now that you've recused yourself, what do you think of the letter? Off the record, of course."

"I think it's excretory. But it doesn't mean Garrity killed that decent woman."

Emmett's eyebrows went up. "You knew Two Kettles?"

Portia paused, glancing to the left. "Only by reputation."

She'd just revealed an evasive tic: Usually, left-handed people look to the left when they tell an untruth.

He let it slide for the time being. "You originally from around here?"

"No, Manhattan."

The waitress appeared, but Portia declined to order anything and Emmett waved off another pour of Olmec Gold. "So, Counselor, I must confess I'm not sure what we're dealing with here."

"We're dealing with the truth, Mr. Parker."

"That'd be refreshing." He swept his gaze over the casino again. "How'd you find me?"

Her eyes were riveted on him, an unblinking violet. "I phoned your room from the front desk. No answer, but the clerk remembered just seeing you. So I hunted around."

"You hunt well," Emmett said.

She rose. "Thanks for sticking up for me with Tweedledum and Tweedledee."

"Anytime."

As she made her way toward the front entrance, Emmett scanned the spaces among the velvet tables and slots for another glimpse of William Jordan. Three times during his conversation with Portia he'd glimpsed the chief deputy marshal at varying locations out in the casino. He'd apparently returned from Louisiana. If he'd ever left upstate New York.

And now that the attorney was gone, he was gone too.

Only when Anna closed the drapes in her noon-bright room at Turning Stone did she notice the phone message light blinking. She turned on a lamp and dialed the message center, then glanced through the open connecting door into Emmett's room. Arriving back minutes ago, she'd been surprised not to find him asleep. If he'd ever returned to his room, the coverlet on the bed was still smooth. She herself had had brunch with Linda Freccia, confident now that she had at least one friendly contact with local law enforcement.

An automated voice advised her that the following message had been received at 12:05 last night: *I got to talk to Turnipseed,* a juvenile-sounding but fairly deep male voice said. Perhaps a retarded adult. *We got to stop*

*somebody from doing evil things. I'm doing my best, but I need some help.
I'll call again later. Good-bye for now.*

She massaged her forehead with one end of the receiver. Anonymous
calls like this always came in during an emotionally-charged investigation.
Notoriously violent cases triggered something in fragile or twisted personalities. Most often, these expressions of knowledge or even guilt had nothing to do with the crime at hand. They were cries for help the FBI was not
equipped to answer.

The automated voice told her that she could save the message by pressing one or delete it by pressing two. Her finger was poised over the two key
when she opted to save the message. Then she phoned security and asked
the supervisor to make her a cassette copy of the message in her voicemail.

Finally, after thirty hours filled with interrogations, a search and a pursuit, she collapsed across her bed. The lamp on the nightstand was still on, but
it was all she could do to flip off her shoes and bury her face into the pillow.

Sunday morning dawned before Hazen Two Kettles could doze off. And
then his cousins made so much noise beyond the wafer-thin walls of the
bedroom he shared with two of the toddlers, his sleep was shallow and
crawling with fresh memories. He relived being released from juvenile hall
yesterday just before supper. Once again, Charley Ketchum, who was being
processed out at the same time, glared at Hazen through the glass door that
separated them, sneering at him in a way that made him dread school come
Monday morning. Through the grapevine, he learned that Jerrold Webster
and Doc had been arrested, booked and then immediately handed back to
their parents, without ever having to give up their own clothes. Once again,
Cousin Mariana picked Hazen up in a neighbor's car, and on the unhappy
drive home told him that Deputy Ketchum had not been arrested at all. It
was all over the rez how the kidnapping was being swept under the rug.

Nobody ever seemed to get punished—except him. He was afraid, so
afraid. Talking to the cops was the stupidest thing he could have done. He
had gambled and lost again.

I should've known an Indian cop can't get nothing done.

He'd spent the whole night wide awake, nerves twitching with the expectation that a Madison County Sheriff's car or the old Chrysler would cruise

past the trailer on Territory Road at that slow, cool speed a shooter needs to take aim at a window. He himself had no gun, and none of his friends would loan him one now, for fear they'd be drawn into the growing mess.

Hazen sat up in bed as something crashed out in the living room. Glassware.

The two women started arguing, their voices loud. Belinda had never gone to sleep either, although she had spent the night drinking sloe gin and crying, convinced that the Minutemen would come next for her and her kids. She believed that the Evil Spirit had sided with the Minutemen and was zeroing in on the family. First Aunt Brenda had been taken and now the rest of them would follow one by one. No use trying to convince her otherwise, for Hazen feared the same thing. As Jerrold Webster had said, there are lots of white people waiting for the chance to kill an Oneida.

The door creaked open, and one of his little cousins peeked inside the room. "Shut the door, Kathy. I'm trying to sleep!" Hazen flopped prone again.

But he knew he wouldn't be able to close his eyes now. Kathy had left the door ajar, and the sounds of the mobile home flood inside his room. Mariana was yelling at Belinda to help her put away the food. A constant stream of sad-faced relatives and friends had dropped off casserole dishes, Tupperware bowls full of hulled-corn soup and Jell-O desserts. Now, most of it was beginning to spoil. Mariana and Belinda hadn't even started on the plans for the funeral.

Nothing ever gets done here, Hazen thought. *Nothing ever gets right.*

He missed Aunt Brenda, hated to think what his life would be like without her. At times, she had made things seem close to right. At least she tried.

Getting out of bed, he stepped into his Levi's and pulled them up. Then he put on his boots and leather jacket, which made Mariana ask as he whisked through the kitchen, "Where you think you're going?"

"For a walk—and you're not my mother," he said, slamming the door behind him on the smells of stale food. Not a long walk, for the ground squished underfoot. He went no farther than the bale of straw he used as a backstop for bow-and-arrow practice. Drizzle was sifting down out of low clouds, and he hooded his jacket over his head to keep his Mohawk spiky. He checked to make sure Mariana wasn't snooping out a window and then scanned all around to make sure that the wet woods were empty of neighbors.

Only after taking these precautions did he kneel behind the bale and rake aside some loose, damp straw with his fingers. A cavity was revealed. From this he took a Folger's Coffee can and pried the lid off. Inside were a pipe, matches and a Baggie of dark green-brown marijuana. He was filling the bowl of the pipe when the sizzle of tires on the wet pavement made him glance around the edge of the bale.

Shit.

A cop car had parked out front.

Quickly, he jammed the pipe and Baggie back in the coffee can, stuffed the container in the hole and kicked straw over the opening.

Standing, he thought to run down to the creek and melt into the swamp that separated the reservation from Sherrill's outer ring of houses, to lie still and silent until moss grew on his backside. But then he realized that it was a tribal police cruiser, not a sheriff's unit. Devereaux was behind the wheel, and the black cop could run fast, fast enough to have caught Hazen earlier in the week just before he reached the sanctuary of the swamp.

Dropping his jacket down off his head, Hazen held his ground. For the moment.

Devereaux waved, but Hazen ignored him.

A passenger sat beside the detective, and he got out, alone. Hazen had never spoken to the well-dressed Oneida man, but knew him by sight. Christopher White Pine had a prominent nose and, seemingly, almost no lips at all. He was one of the tribal *suits,* a bigwig who had been distrusted by Aunt Brenda. His shoes were shiny, and he took a few ginger steps across the soupy road shoulder. "Hazen, come here," he said, smiling.

The youth hesitated.

"We're not going to arrest you," White Pine added with a soft laugh. "Come on. Please."

Hazen strolled over to him, and White Pine offered his hand. He shook firmly, like a white guy. Aunt Brenda had said he was from Michigan, and all the Oneida who'd gone there many years ago were Christians. They'd been brainwashed and bribed by the missionaries into thinking the sacred beliefs of the *Onyotaa:ka* were superstitious garbage. They were not to be trusted.

Yet, Hazen's own parents had been Methodists, so all of this was a confused jumble to him. He didn't know what to show, so he showed nothing.

"Mind if we sit out of the rain?" White Pine asked.

Hazen shrugged a shoulder, and the man opened a back door on the caged area of the unit. The boy knew that the rear doors in patrol cars only opened from the outside. When he balked at entering the vehicle, White Pine said, "Honest, we're only here to help. You can keep the door open. And you can walk back inside your house anytime you want, okay?"

Hazen slid into the backseat, but used the toe of his boot to keep the door ajar.

"Hey, Haze," Devereaux said, "how's it going?"

"Fine," he lied.

Both men turned around in their seats and stared at him through the mesh of the screen. The drizzle was now so light the windshield wipers shuddered over the glass. One of the two smelled of men's perfume; Hazen suspected it was White Pine, who then said, "We're here to let you know that, despite past differences with your family, the tribal offices are on your side. You were kidnapped. Nothing less. And we can't let that happen to one of our people. That's what the Oneida do, Hazen—they rally together when they're attacked. They support one another. Now, I just talked to the Nation Representative about you."

The boy hid his surprise.

"The Representative is very disturbed about what happened to you Friday night," White Pine continued. "He's ordered extra patrol for your home. You and your family are to phone the police department if anything concerns you. *Anything at all.*"

Hazen glanced at the trailer. The faces of two of the kids and Mariana were glued to the front window, their breaths misting it up.

White Pine said, "We'll make every effort to see that those white delinquents and the deputy are prosecuted to the fullest extent of the law. But . . ." His thin mouth skewed to one side. ". . . there are problems with that, Hazen. It'll be a state case. The same state that stole our lands from us."

"White man's law, babe." Devereaux finally turned off the wipers. "It wasn't passed with you and me in mind."

"So we're asking you to be patient, Hazen. Don't do anything rash, anything the white community can use against our people. The entire Nation will help you see this through. If you have problems at school, or anywhere, you are to contact the detective here. Immediately."

Devereaux slid a business card through the slot beneath the screen to

Hazen. "Day or night. You got all my numbers there. You are to take no shit off any white kids. Phone me, and I'll end it right now. No shit off Madison or Oneida County deputies, know what I mean? Let me deal with them. Understand?"

Hazen nodded that he did. Still, this all felt odd to him. Devereaux had never been on his side before, and somebody as important as White Pine had never even given him the time of day. "Finally, we're going to make things right around here," the special assistant went on, sounding just like Hazen's family and their neighbors who weren't happy with how the tribe was being run. "Have you heard the good news?"

"What?"

"It was on the radio this morning, Hazen. The two federal investigators, the Indian cops, have made an arrest in the death threat letter. The suspect has already admitted to writing it, which only means he was involved in worse things."

"Who is he?"

"A mechanic who works for Adirondack Airlines," Devereaux explained. "His name is Garrity. The FBI was searching his house in Sherrill when the car chase began the other night. The pursuit you got caught up in."

Hazen's head was buzzing, just like it had when he'd been told that his parents had died in a wreck on the Dewey Thruway. "Did this Garrity guy kill my aunt?"

"We don't know for sure," White Pine said. "But I'm sleeping better knowing that he's behind bars. Be patient. Let the law do its thing."

"The judge isn't going to O.R. Garrity, is he?"

Devereaux chuckled. "No, babe, Garrity ain't getting kicked loose on his *own recognizance*. Bail's set at two hundred thousand, and that's a lot more than a piece of poor white trash can come up with by his lonesome."

Hazen tried to digest it all. A mechanic for Adirondack Airlines. Aunt Brenda took that airline from Syracuse, then tumbled to her death. The inside of the boy's head began buzzing even more fiercely.

"Another thing . . ." White Pine said. "We want you to cooperate with the two Indian investigators in whatever way you can," the special assistant went on. "Turnipseed and Parker are here to help us. All of us. Tell them everything you know."

"Like what?"

"Why your Aunt Brenda was flying to New York. Do you know why?"

Hazen calculated. *Careful, careful.* If these two men thought he wasn't going to be helpful, they might not order the extra patrol for his family. He didn't know where his aunt had been headed, but he replied, "Maybe."

"Why?" White Pine asked, quietly.

Headlights filled the interior of the cruiser: A tow truck pulled up behind the police car.

Devereaux was staring at him, waiting. "You honestly know where your auntie was going, babe?"

Hazen knew there were things his cousins hadn't told Turnipseed and Parker about Aunt Brenda, and they'd warned him not to trust them. They just might be getting information to help the tribal bigwigs with the trailer evictions. But now Devereaux and White Pine appeared to be on his side. Hazen didn't know what to do. So he changed the subject. "What's with the tow truck?"

"A surprise for you," White Pine said, getting out.

Hazen walked with him to the rear of the truck. There, strapped to the tilt bed, was his Harley. Right off, he saw that the rear fork, shock absorbers and wheel had been replaced. "You fixed it," he said.

"The Nation replaced the damaged parts for you—the old parts are being stored as evidence for the kidnapping trial."

The tow driver lowered the back end of the bed, so Hazen could walk his chopper off. But before he started to retrieve his bike, White Pine gently restrained him by the arm. "I know it isn't easy growing up. Truth is, I wouldn't want to be your age again. All the choices. The pressures. I appreciate how hard it is. The loneliness." Like Devereaux, the special assistant handed him a card with a phone number penned on the back. "Do you know what a therapist is, Hazen?"

"Yeah," he grumbled, "the county made me go see one first time I was on probation."

"He or she?"

"A woman."

"Oneida?"

"No, white lady."

"Well, I'm not just an official for the tribe, Hazen. I'm also a licensed therapist. An Oneida therapist, who knows firsthand what it was like to grow up on a rez. I'd like you to drop by my office anytime you like."

"Why?" Hazen asked.

"To talk," White Pine said, warmly. "Sometimes it helps just to talk."

15

ANNA AND EMMETT STOOD under the roof overhang to the Seneca Gun Club outside Sherrill, waiting. The closed sign had been put up in the office window, and theirs was the only car in the parking lot. "You sure he said to meet him here?" she asked.

Emmett's breath curled up like white smoke into the entryway light. "He didn't say. I talked to his wife. She said we could find him here."

The day-long drizzle had let up, but the overcast lingered. Rain smelled different here in the East. On the high steppes along the California-Oregon border, rain unleashed the aroma of wet sage, so much so she couldn't distinguish the scents in her mind. Rain was sage. Here, the rain left a fetid smell.

Emmett pivoted and retraced the path the two of them had just taken, down along the side of the building to a stretch of chain-link that offered a view of the skeet and trap ranges. Ten minutes ago, they had been floodlit but unused. They were still unoccupied, for Emmett came ambling back to her, looking disgruntled. He rapped on the office door for what must have been the dozenth time.

Again, no response.

Inside, the phone rang twice before either the caller gave up or the ringing was answered at an extension.

Anna cupped her hands around her eyes to block out the glare of the exterior spotlight and looked inside. No one, although a faint glow shone up a plunging staircase.

Emmett checked his wristwatch. "You want to wait inside the car?"

"No, I'll nod off." She would too, having only gotten a brief nap yesterday afternoon and then three hours of tossing and turning last night.

"Sometime . . ." Emmett began, then stopped, his unfinished sentence evaporating into mist.

She had an inkling his *sometime* had had something to do with them. Personally. A future *sometime* that would never be. Inevitably, one of them would reveal that conviction, however innocently, however unintentionally. Yet, her hope endured that *sometime* they would return to therapy together, to put to rest their resentments once and for all—his for her being untouchable and hers for his having touched another in the midst of his frustrated wait. *Don't go there.* She decided to keep either of them from straying into the personal, and nothing quite filled the growing gulf between them like the job. "Why is Garrity so willing to cop this plea and go on the box?"

Emmett glanced at her, then away.

Garrity's new attorney, Sherwin Katz, and the U.S. Attorney General in Syracuse had agreed upon a polygraph examiner, who'd fly in from Washington tomorrow and administer the test first thing Tuesday morning. He was retired FBI but had a clientele largely composed of defense attorneys. Anna didn't fully trust the polygraph. Increasingly under attack by the scientific community, the lie box measured a subject's galvanic skin response, raw emotional reaction to a question and not any specific degree of deception. The polygraph was too blinded by false positives to be the eye of God.

Sadly, Emmett seemed relieved that she'd steered the conversation back to the professional. "So is Garrity sacrificing himself to protect a conspiracy, something he believes to be greater than himself?" he mused out loud. "Or is Katz—and Portia, for I'd guess she's still running the legal show behind the scenes—pouring on the smoke because they know damn well Garrity offed Two Kettles?"

Since their admitted tête-à-tête yesterday in the coffee shop at Turning Stone, Emmett had taken to referring to the attorney by her first name instead of her last. Anna told herself that the shift in address was probably meaningless. But it annoyed her. Keeping an even tone, she asked, "How does Nelson fit in all this?"

"What do you mean?" Emmett said snidely. "She's a lawyer. She'd represent Beelzebub, if he could write a check without the paper bursting into flames."

"Yes but, why C.U.E.? It's a lightning-rod job. Is she a long-time local with no love for the Oneida? Does she stand to lose real estate if and when the claim's settled?"

"Not that I know of," Emmett replied. "Bigger questions to me are—why'd she quit representing the committee . . . ?" He paused. "And why is a chief deputy marshal shadowing her?"

He'd already told her about sighting Jordan in the casino, but now for the first time Anna ventured a guess. "The Attorney General has parallel investigations going, one by us and one by the Marshal's Service."

"So the A.G. has more than one dog in the hunt?"

"Yes."

"And how's that make you feel?"

"Pissed off," she admitted.

A jingle of keys spun them both around.

From inside the office, Jake Cutler unlocked and swung back the door. The smell of gun-smoke clung to his military-style fatigues. "Sorry," he apologized without bothering to sound sincere, "I was in the underground pistol range and didn't hear you. My wife just called, said the FBI was on the way again."

Not *just called*, Anna suspected, for the phone had rung in the office at least five minutes ago. How had Cutler used those minutes?

"You want to come in or not?" the man asked, holding the door open with one of his spit-shined paratrooper boots. She recognized the glossy depths of a spit shine from her days at the academy. Obsessive grooming even for a retired soldier.

Emmett led the way. "You the range-master here?"

"Only part-time. In exchange for use of the facilities whenever I want. Come on, we can talk while I shoot."

They trailed Cutler through the office and outside to the stations on the skeet range. Bullet-headed and shoulders back despite his age, he seemed to be unfazed by the second appearance of federal officers in his life over the past forty-eight hours. Usually this follow-up intrusion rattled even the most unflappable people.

Cutler took a shotgun from a plush-lined case on top of the trap machine. It had not lain there for long; no beads of drizzle coated the lid. "I fire fifty pistol rounds and fifty shotgun rounds a day." He fed birdshot cartridges into the magazine of the shotgun without looking at his hands. Just as FBI agents were taught so as not to have to break visual contact with an armed suspect. "I also try to walk wherever I go. I'm not in the condition I was in the Army. But close."

"Expecting a war?" Emmett asked.

"Never know." Cutler hit the foot pedal that launched a clay pigeon from the trap machine. The bird whirred out into the dense air. His tracking motion was liquid-smooth and his squeeze of the trigger gentle. But he missed the clay, only to lower the shotgun from his shoulder and act as if it meant nothing to him. "You shoot, Parker?"

Emmett's right hand was perched on his hip, casually but not far from his revolver. "Never for sport."

"But you do shoot?"

"Yes," Emmett said with just the right tone to indicate that he wouldn't be screwed with.

"And you, young lady?"

"Whenever the Bureau gives me the ammunition." She stepped farther away from Emmett, spreading out Cutler's targets in the unlikely event he decided to do the unthinkable.

The man tapped the pedal for another black disc. Again, he missed. Again, apathy.

Anna asked, "Why is your grandson, Maurice, called Doc, Mr. Cutler?"

The man faced down-range. She thought he was smiling as the machine spit another clay into the sky. This time, Cutler failed to raise the shotgun to shoulder level. He fired nonchalantly from the hip, and the disc disintegrated into black confetti. The bird's angle had been low, difficult to pick up in daylight, let alone under artificial floods. "I'm to blame for that."

"Oh?" Anna said.

Cutler reloaded. "I used to do that Bugs Bunny thing—*What's up, Doc?* Maurice got such a big kick out of it when he was a little guy, I started calling him Doc. And I don't think he ever took to the name *Maurice* any more than I did. His mother had musical ambitions for him."

Emmett asked, "What'd he learn to play, other than your Colt forty-four magnum?"

Cutler fired from the hip once more. Another clay fell to the ground in pieces, and the ejected shell bounced between Anna's shoes. "You bet it's my forty-four. And you got that info from the unconstitutional gun registration laws this government jams down our throats. But I will deny Doc fired it Friday night. I can prove it."

"How?"

"The I.D. man with Madison County S.O. swabbed my grandson's hands. No powder residue. Nor did he find any evidence whatsoever that the weapon had been fired lately."

The partners had not been informed of these tests, although Detective Freccia had been forthcoming in relaying registration information on the seized .44 magnum to Anna—that's why Emmett and she were here.

"But the revolver was still used as a weapon," she pointed out to Cutler.

"In what way, young lady?"

"To keep Hazen Two Kettles from trying to flee the car."

"I'm sure that's how the Indian boy tells it. Doc and his friends—all good students and athletes, by the way—will swear on a stack of Bibles that gun never came out from under the front seat. That Oneida mope is the biggest hophead and drug salesman on campus. Ask anybody." At last, Cutler was too agitated to shoot. He put the shotgun back in its case. "You are not going to railroad my grandson on the word of an Indian hophead, believe me."

Anna asked, "Why'd you phone Doc on his cellular Friday night?"

A forked artery stood out on his brow.

"No crime in calling your grandson, Mr. Cutler," she pressed. "I'd just like to know why you phoned him as soon as you left Dan Garrity's house?"

"The big bust," he explained grudgingly.

"Meaning?"

"For years, we've been waiting for the big bust."

"Who—C.U.E.?"

"No. C.U.E.'s increasingly irrelevant."

"The Minutemen?"

"Minutemen don't exist. They're just the pipe dream of a lot of frustrated people. No, I'm talking about all the normal, solid folks who are resisting the land claim. We all know the night's coming, our *Kristallnacht*, so to speak."

The evening in 1936 when broken glass glittered in German streets like crystal. But Anna couldn't see the correlation between the Nazi attack on synagogues and Jewish business and anything the U.S. federal government might conceivably do to enforce the court order on the Oneida land claim. She sensed that the gap between how she and Jake Cutler saw the world might never be bridged. "You think we're Nazis?"

Cutler shrugged. "Ask Dan Garrity and his family."

"I'm asking you, sir."

The man leveled his faded blue eyes on her. "I sure as hell don't think you're in the justice business anymore."

Emmett leaned his head toward the parking lot. Obviously, he wanted to go.

"I can live with that, Mr. Cutler," Anna said. Then she added with a glower, "But I don't know what I'd do if you called me a Nazi."

"Be interesting to find out, young lady."

Her blood was up, and she wasn't finished with Cutler, but Emmett became even more insistent with a sharp tilt of his head toward the lot.

"Evening, Mr. Cutler," he said, and she followed him out.

As soon as they were in their car, she asked why the rush to leave. Emmett started to say something, but a pickup truck had turned off the highway. It crept slowly along the driveway that snaked up to the gun club.

Starting down the same lane, Emmett lowered his side window, unholstered his revolver and held it behind his right thigh. Anna drew her pistol as well and kept it out of sight.

Three middle-aged white men were jammed shoulder-to-shoulder in the front seat of the pickup. The rack behind their heads held two long guns. They looked over Anna and Emmett, their eyes shining in the dash lights, but the driver continued past and on up to the range office.

She now knew how Jake Cutler had spent those five minutes between his wife's call and his opening the door for Emmett and her.

They put away their weapons, and Emmett joined the highway. He said, "Don't flush a bird from cover until you're ready to drop it."

* * *

Emmett and Anna were almost back to the Turning Stone Resort when he noticed two police cruisers, with flashers going, pulled up to the SavOn gas station. SavOn was tribally-owned, and Oneida Nation P.D. officers were questioning some white picketers. Among them stood Vaughn Devereaux, hands buried in his topcoat pockets against the cold.

As Emmett flipped a U-turn, Anna asked, "Does it look like they need back-up?"

"No, but I got a question for Devereaux."

"What?"

"Yesterday in the coffee shop, when I asked Portia if she was married, she said, *I'm sure you know all about that.*"

"Do you?"

"Not a thing, so it's funny she put it that way."

"Why'd you ask her if she was married?"

Emmett could tell that she instantly regretted asking. "She asked me first," he replied, feeling a bit lame. He knew that a few months ago this would have been occasion for a tart little squabble. But somehow they were beyond that now, and in a way that disappointed him. He let down his window to speak to Devereaux. "What's up?"

"Oh," the detective said, "these protesters know they're not supposed to cross onto Nation property. They did so to use the john. No biggie. But we've got to draw the line someplace, or they'll be picketing inside the casino . . ." One of the white men was holding a sign that showed at least a glimmer of humor: TAKE NO MORE GAS OFF THE ONEIDA. "What've you two been up to?"

"This and that," Emmett said. "Anything new?"

After a moment, Devereaux said, "Nothing worth passing along. Just the same old fight for love and glory." But then he shifted to say to Anna, as if suggesting she had more concern for the boy than Emmett, "We're giving Hazen and his family extra patrol around the clock."

"Good," she said.

"Portia Nelson isn't from upstate, is she?" Emmett asked, testing his hunch that the former NYPD detective might know about her.

"No. She's from the city. Moved up here five years ago."

"Why'd she do that?"

Devereaux knelt, so he and Emmett were eye-to-eye, then lowered his voice. "You ready for this?"

"Ready for what?"

"She *shot* her husband to death."

From the corner of his eye, Emmett caught Anna doing a double-take. "You help work that case, Vaughn?" he asked.

"No, but everybody on the department knew about it."

"She murdered her hubby?" Anna blurted.

"Justifiable homicide, not murder. And all because of love, sweet love. Know what I mean?" Devereaux took his right hand from his pocket and blew into it. "She represented an airline pilot when the FAA tried to yank his license. Seems he flew with an elevated blood alcohol on a run from Buffalo to LaGuardia. Missed the approach twice, and his co-pilot had to take over. He lost his license on appeal, but Portia and he fell in love, married and then fell out of love when he started slapping her around. She convinced a jury he was on the verge of beating her to death in bed when she shot him."

Emmett asked, "She have great bodily damage—medical reports, photos of obvious physical trauma to show the jury?"

"None." Devereaux laughed suggestively. "Portia is a very good attorney. Know what I mean?"

Emmett waited for the detective to volunteer more, but he didn't. "What airline did her husband work for?"

"Adirondack," Devereaux replied.

16

EVERYBODY AT ONEIDA HIGH School knew what had happened to Hazen Two Kettles Friday night. He was sure of it. And, even if they didn't, Charley Ketchum and Jerrold Webster were roaming the hallways to tell them. He relived the humiliation of his abduction in every mocking smile, every whisper, every joke that was cracked just out of earshot. Charley and Jerrold ignored him in two chance encounters, one near the snack bar and one among the lockers. Looking buff in their varsity football jackets, they breezed past Hazen both times as if he didn't exist, which gave him a sick feeling to realize that, had anything gone differently Friday, he wouldn't exist.

He'd be gone like Aunt Brenda.

He expected something to happen. Sooner or later, something bad would happen either to him or his cousins. And the worry he had for his family was much worse than that he felt for himself. It clotted inside his chest until it was hard to breathe.

The lunch hour came, but he had no appetite. Would he ever be hungry again?

"Haze!" It was Tommy Burr, a half-Seneca kid. He came jogging up, his long reddish-brown hair bouncing around his shoulders. "You hear?"

After the past week, Hazen didn't like conversations that began this way. "What?"

"Dan Garrity bailed out of jail."

In a white-hot flash, the buzzing inside Hazen's head was back. Yet, he believed Tommy had it wrong. Garrity had admitted writing the hate letter, and it only stood to reason that the mechanic had killed Aunt Brenda as well. She'd fallen out of the sky, and Garrity worked on airplanes. He worked for the very airline that auntie had taken last Monday night. *It was a federal case, for godsake.* "Where'd you hear that?"

"It was on the radio," Tommy replied. "The noon news. White folks raised the two hundred thousand dollar bail for Garrity last night, and he walked free!" Burr's excitement turned to indignation. "Isn't that the way? Kill an Indian and nobody does fucking shit."

Hazen tried to think, but Tommy went on distracting him, his eyes excited. "My grandpa says a real Haudenosaunee don't count on the law."

"Why not?"

"He says in the old days, if somebody wasted one of your relatives, you had to at least try to kill the murderer. It was expected."

"You telling me I got no balls?"

"No, Haze," Tommy backtracked. "It was just something my grandpa said."

There were pay phones outside the administrative offices, but he wanted no whites to overhear him. Tommy and he shared a remedial English class after lunch. "Tell the teacher I'm sick," he said, starting for the parking lot.

He was sick. Sick with fear. More bad news would follow. It always did. His legs pumped out strides, but he really couldn't feel them moving under him.

"Where you going?" Tommy called from behind.

Hazen didn't tell him. He couldn't explain that, despite what Tommy's grandfather had said, he was about to turn to the Oneida Nation P.D., which had done nothing but hassle him for years. Always watching him. Pulling him over on his chopper for chickenshit reasons. But now he needed the tribal department, bad.

Firing up his Harley, he throttled out into the bright, cold day. The wind burned his face. He realized this, but only the thinnest possible thread seemed to connect his mind to his body. It was strange how bad things could happen on a beautiful day. He could not remember a winter afternoon so beautiful.

He pulled in to the nearest convenience store.

Taking Devereaux's business card from the pocket of his leather jacket, Hazen dialed the detective at work. A lady answered, and he asked to talk to him. But she said, "I'm sorry, Detective Devereaux had a meeting in Wampsville. He should be back soon. May I take a message?"

"Yeah, have him phone Hazen Two Kettles at home."

"May I say what this concerns?"

"He'll know. Just have him phone me right away."

Then Hazen got back on his motorcycle and sped for the mobile home.

Anna, Vaughn Devereaux and Linda Freccia awaited the Madison County district attorney in his conference room. The D.A.'s secretary had ducked inside twenty minutes ago to apologize to the trinity of federal, tribal and county investigators that he was still tied up. It was now pushing one o'clock, and their meeting—requested with little advance notice and no regard for lunch—had been scheduled for noon.

At seven this morning, Anna had put Emmett aboard a United commuter flight to Washington, D.C. Emmett expected to have his business concluded in the capital by five and be back in Syracuse at nine-thirty tonight. He'd declined to explain that business, which still irked her. However, things were different from what they'd been only a few short months ago, and now they each had zones of privacy the other didn't violate. He was the one who had cheated, a one-night stand in North Carolina, yet she was the one now being denied trust.

Screw Emmett Parker.

The D.A. finally came through the door, a natty man in his sixties. "Lord, what a day." He shifted a file folder from his right hand to his left to shake. "You must be Special Agent Turnipseed."

"Yes, sir."

"Call me Harry," he said with just the right tone to suggest he didn't like being called Harry by low-level investigators. He greeted Devereaux and Freccia, and everyone sat again. Fortunately, the D.A. was too far behind schedule to waste time in small talk. "Look it," he said, "I'd really like to prosecute the Hazen Two Kettles case. I think it's absolutely disgusting what happened to this kid the other night . . ." His gaze shifted to Devereaux, whose face had gone very still. "But we're going to have big problems with Two Kettles on the stand, and we positively must do that to have any hope of convicting the three youths."

"Oh, man," Devereaux protested, "don't tell me. I don't want to hear this. Just don't want to." But that was all the normally talkative detective had to say for the moment. His gold earring glinted as he shook his head, dejectedly.

It was left to Freccia to ask, "What kind of problems, sir? Two Kettles copped to smoking a joint the day of the abduction. So what? We've put juveniles on the stand who've had a couple beers at the time they witnessed offenses—and nobody sacked their credibility."

The D.A. turned to Devereaux again. "How many priors does he have with the tribal judiciary?"

"A lot," the detective admitted. "But he's not a hard-ass. Not yet."

"I'm not so sure." The D.A. slid the file across the table to the three investigators, who crowded together to have a look. Freccia flipped open the cover on a toxicological report. Hazen Two Kettles's. His elevated THC levels—the psychoactive ingredient in marijuana—were no surprise. But Anna winced as she saw the proof that Two Kettles used methamphetamine prior to being kidnapped.

"How unlucky for the prosecution," she said.

The D.A. responded to her sarcasm with a practiced smile. "Ms. Turnipseed?"

"Had Hazen been the victim of homicide, and not just kidnapping, we wouldn't have to worry about his credibility, would we?"

"But we do," the D.A. argued. "You know what the defense can do with this—the kid was whacked out on meth. He hallucinated the whole thing under the stress of his aunt's death. If not that, the entire event can be painted as a drug deal gone wrong. The waters are muddied, Ms. Turnipseed, and I'll be damned if I can think of a way to clarify them."

"Life is muddy," Anna said. "I'd still take it to trial, sir. Even if it meant a change of venue to a county outside the land claim area."

Ignoring her insinuation that the claim had colored his decision, the

D.A. turned to Devereaux and Freccia. "What are we talking here, both tribal and county probation violations vis-à-vis controlled substance abuse?"

The two investigators answered yes.

"I'm assuming Two Kettles is at school," the D.A. went on to Freccia. "I'd appreciate it if you picked him up and delivered him to juvenile."

"And if he isn't at the high school, sir?"

Devereaux stood. "The Great Nation of the Oneida People will snatch him off its sovereign territory and hand him over." He gave the D.A. a sigh. "The last thing, sir, I'd ever say is that you're bowing to political pressure from the white community. But you've got to know that this, plus Garrity's release on bond, is going to blow the lid off the rez in the coming days."

The D.A. gathered up the file again. "The law's the law, Vaughn, and I trust in the common sense of both communities to see it that way."

Emmett declined an invitation to view the repaired section of the Pentagon, sensing that the BIA's liaison with the U.S. Army's Criminal Investigation Division wanted more time to learn how deep retired Lieutenant Colonel Jacob Cutler was in trouble. Fairly deep, Emmett felt, although that was more intuition than hard information at this point. He hadn't even wanted to share that intuition with Anna, should she point out the holes in it. "Did you pull his file for me?" he asked.

His CID contact leaned back in his swivel chair. The gray depths of a court-yard filled the window to his back. "This might be related to the Indian woman who fell into that field out of a clear blue sky?"

"Clear *black* sky. Can I see the file?"

Infuriatingly, the man wouldn't commit, and Emmett didn't want to have to resort to subpeona. Subpoenaing the Defense Department was like whistling for a buffalo to come. "So this is how it's going to be?"

"For now," the CID man said, meaning that for the time being this discussion about Jake Cutler was occurring beneath the bureaucratic radar screen. Cutler might have friends in high places, and this meeting could be denied if there was no paper trail.

"All right," Emmett said, "Cutler didn't leave the Army on disability, correct?"

"Correct."

"But he was passed over for full colonel and forced out as a consequence."

"Right."

"Attitude?"

"Everybody in Airborne has an attitude. It's part of being a paratrooper. Parker, you know how I hate to divulge material from investigations that were closed as unsubstantiated."

"Disclaimer duly noted."

At last, his conscience salved, the man leaned forward in a confiding hunch. "The Hue-Phu Bai area of I Corps, Republic of Vietnam, 1968. Cutler was the battalion G-Two . . ." The intelligence officer, as Garrity's friend and neighbor had already admitted about himself. "Elements of the Eighty-second Airborne and South Vietnamese army hit a Viet Cong tunnel complex. Prisoners were taken. Two were high-ranking. Cutler personally took them in his commanding officer's chopper. One prisoner was missing when the Huey landed at the fire base, and the other V.C. developed diarrhea of the mouth in the weeks that followed."

Helicopter.

Emmett resisted the impulse to bolt up out of his chair.

The possibility of a chopper had occurred to him, explaining how Brenda Two Kettles might have plunged to earth fifteen miles off the flight path to LaGuardia. Certainly, helicopters were available at Syracuse International. But he was only a week into this case, and loose ends flitted all around him, teasing, tickling and often shredding to pieces as soon as he grabbed for them. He realized that he was getting ahead of himself by focusing on a chopper. "How'd Cutler explain his missing prisoner?"

"The gook was a V.C. colonel. In fact, he was Cutler's counterpart in intelligence, so he knew damned well he couldn't be taken alive and tortured by the South Viets. So, at five thousand feet over triple-canopy jungle, he jumped out while Cutler was preoccupied with the other captive."

"Says who?"

"The crew-chief. He parroted Cutler's story to a tee."

"And the other prisoner?"

"He wouldn't say one way or another. When the interrogator brought the subject up, he just broke into tears." The CID man stood. "So, does that help?"

"Yes," Emmett said.
"I was afraid so."

The soles of Hazen's boots pattered over the mud as he coasted his motorcycle up to the front door of the trailer. An image had been replaying inside
his mind like a bad horror movie ever since he'd sped away from the convenience store in Oneida. Even the chronic murmuring of the TV from inside the mobile home now failed to reassure him. He saw bodies inside his
head. Familiar bodies made unfamiliar by death. Corpses sprawling all over
the place.

Standing on the stoop, he forced himself to look all around for the danger that may have already hit his home. He drew in sharp breaths. He could
feel them pass down his throat, but the air didn't seem to reach his lungs.
His blood pounded for want of oxygen.

Through the stark winter woods, he spotted a yellow van parked down
Territory Road. But it was close enough to a neighbor's place to account for
its presence.

He went through the door.

Belinda was quietly drinking on the couch, one of the toddlers dozing in
her lap. Mariana was at the sink, cleaning up after lunch. More casserole
dishes than he remembered crowded the sinkboard—friends and relations
kept dropping them off as if dumping food into the hole left by Aunt
Brenda.

He shut his eyes for a few seconds.

"What you doing home from school?" Mariana demanded, detergent
suds dripping off her elbows.

"Not now, Mar." Hazen slipped the bottle of sloe gin from Belinda's languid grasp and took a swig. On the coffee table before her was the front page
of the *Dispatch* with Garrity's photo on it. The airline mechanic had a flat
nose and beady eyes that made him look like a killer. Anybody would know
he was a killer, just looking at him.

Belinda roused from a soap opera to retrieve her bottle. "Hey, that's mine."

Hazen asked Mariana, "Anybody call?"

"Why, who's going to call on you, the school?"

Hazen's head felt like it was going to explode. Irritation was spoiling his sense of relief that everybody was all right. He was starting for his bedroom when the phone rang. He grabbed it before Mariana could. "Hello."

"Hazen?"

"Yeah."

"This is Detective Devereaux." The connection was full of static.

"Where are you? I called already."

"Just checked my messages. I'm on the thruway coming into Oneida. Listen, I want you to stay where you are. Stay at home. I'm less than ten minutes away."

A cop was telling him to stay put, and cops said that only when they wanted to snatch you up.

"You hear me, babe?" Devereaux repeated.

Hazen felt the receiver trembling against the side of his skull. "What's happened?" he asked suspiciously.

After a pause, Devereaux said, "Your blood test came back heavy on meth. I've got to take you in. Nothing personal, know what I mean? The Madison juvenile detective has gone to the high school, looking for you. I think it's better if I drive you to juvie."

Hazen couldn't believe it. "They let all those white guys go—Garrity, Charley, Jerrold, Doc, all of 'em—and they're putting me back in the hall!"

"Settle down. Sometimes we just have to bite the bullet. Go with the flow until things correct themselves."

"They let Garrity go, and he killed my aunt!" Hazen saw that Mariana and Belinda were at his side, looking scared.

"We can't be sure Garrity killed her," Devereaux said as if none of this really mattered to him now. "You've got to control—"

But Hazen had slammed down the receiver. His hand was shaking so bad he missed the phone cradle on the first try. But then, bucking himself up, he faced his cousins. "Nobody's going to hurt you." He shoved his way past Mariana and flung open the kitchen drawer filled with knives.

Anna waited inside her car in the high school parking lot while Linda Freccia and a uniformed deputy went inside to grab Hazen Two Kettles out of class. She wanted to talk to him after he was readmitted to the hall, although she had no idea how to soften the blow of what was obviously a raw deal.

If I see it that way, how will a teenage boy react?

And another thing. Why had Hazen's toxicological report been so fast in coming while his aunt's was still being processed?

The deputy exited the school, alone. He drove off without waving to Anna, even though they'd been introduced. Freccia appeared a few minutes later, looking down at the mouth, and gestured for Anna to join her inside her sedan.

"Hazen ditched fourth period," she said, switching frequencies on her radio and reaching for her microphone. She raised Devereaux and advised, "Subject's no longer at school. Left about an hour ago. Ball's in your court."

"Copy," Devereaux responded. "I phoned his residence a while ago. Nobody's seen him since he left for school. I'll swing by and take a look for myself."

"Ten-four." Freccia hung up the mike and smiled unhappily at Anna. "After all this, have enough stomach left for lunch?"

The cold jacked Hazen up as he turned down Harmony Lane. He stood on the footrests of his motorcycle, searching the right side of the street for the house on whose lawn he'd seen the lady FBI agent Friday night.

He recognized it, but in the same instant a blue Bronco started to back out of its driveway. A pug-nosed man was behind the wheel.

Garrity.

He braked for Hazen, who swerved wide of him and continued down the lane at the same speed. A peek over his shoulder told him that the Bronco was following.

He made the first right turn and let Garrity drive past. A woman sat next to him. She glanced Hazen's way, but Garrity paid no attention as he accelerated toward downtown Sherrill.

As soon as the Bronco was out of sight, Hazen made a U-turn and rejoined Harmony Lane. He let Garrity get far enough ahead for other cars to begin to fill the distance between them. The pale sun was quickly lowering in the west. It reflected off the roof of the Bronco more brightly than any of the other vehicles, as if the sky were fingering Garrity for him.

There was something special about the daylight. Slightly unreal. It made him feel as if he were in a movie. And beautiful. Maybe this was how your last day on earth was. Achingly beautiful.

Garrity's right blinker came on, and the Bronco turned up State Street.

Hazen hung back. The wind billowed under the cuffs of his Levi's and chilled the foot-long butcher knife he had put down his boot. Even through his sock, the blade felt like an icicle. He'd never been cut, not seriously, and he wondered if the knife would feel cold going in. An older guy on the rez he knew had served time for assault with a deadly weapon, and he'd said that stabbing a human body felt like stabbing a pillow. No more than that.

Hazen back off the throttle.

The Garritys had parked in the lot of P & C Foods.

Veering over to the curb, Hazen watched the mechanic and his old lady—they had joined hands like a couple—stroll toward the entrance to the supermarket. They seemed happy, almost playful. He knew better than most what it felt like to be released from detention. Fresh freedom gave a rush, like a drug. He didn't want Garrity to be high. The mechanic didn't deserve to feel good.

Hazen parked his bike, rear wheel to the curb so a cop wouldn't hassle him at this moment. Pocketing his gloves, he set out for the entrance. The knife flopped around inside his boot. Passing the registers, he picked up a hand-basket and began filling it with stuff he didn't want. He felt strong and alive. He roamed the aisles looking for Garrity, sure that the thumping of his heart could be heard over the Muzak on the store's P.A. It amused him to think that his heart was the most powerful thing inside the store.

He found his aunt's killer in the frozen foods section.

Garrity had separated from his old lady, which was all right with Hazen. There had to be limits to this thing, otherwise it could all spin off into madness. He had only one thing to accomplish here.

But now, as he got close to doing it, that thing seemed harder than he'd ever imagined. He hadn't visualized drawing the knife and rushing Garrity. Maybe he should have prepared himself better, because, as he stood watching the mechanic down the length of the aisle, Hazen could not quite bend over and force his hand inside his boot to take hold of the knife handle.

Instead, he reached into the compartment for some Tater Tots and dumped the limp plastic bag into the basket. He liked Tater Tots, but right now he couldn't recall what they tasted like. His saliva had a bitter rusty tang to it, and bile was burning the back of his throat.

Garrity leaned over the edge of the freezer case to get something at the very back. As his coat rode up, a revolver was revealed. Garrity was packing heat in the waistband of his trousers. The hem of the coat lowered back down over the grips, and the man tossed a half gallon of ice cream in his shopping cart.

Then he turned and narrowed his eyes at Hazen.

The boy grabbed another bag of Tater Tots, put them in his basket and rounded the end of the aisle into the produce section. Each step he took away from Garrity was more hurried than the one before, until he was nearly running as he dumped his basket of unwanted groceries in the grapefruit bin.

He burst out the automatic doors, the air icy on his hot face. He failed to notice a car, and the driver laid on his horn. He viciously wagged his middle finger at the face behind the windshield, but all he really felt was disappointment. In himself. As much as he tried, he couldn't turn around and go back inside the store after Garrity.

By the time he reached his bike, his eyes were tearing up and his heart didn't seem to be beating at all.

He slumped on the seat and rested his forehead against the handlebars.

Tommy's voice dogged him: . . . *in the old days, if somebody wasted one of your relatives, you had to at least try to kill the murderer. It was expected.*

Hazen kick-started his engine and rode down State Street. He was cold, so deeply cold. At the first red stoplight, he buttoned his leather jacket to the throat and put on his gloves, but still he was shivering. An old white man in a Pontiac was waiting beside him for the green light. He gave Hazen an ugly look and then pretended to ignore him.

He felt it coming. Like a sneeze. Irresistible like a sneeze. An impulse he couldn't resist. Before he had really thought, his left boot flashed out to the side and put a dent in the driver's door on the Pontiac. The dent put him back on top of things. In control. The signal light had yet to change, but he made a U-turn in the middle of the intersection and throttled back for the store.

The Garritys were coming out the entrance as he angled into the lot. They were headed for their Bronco, bags of groceries in their arms. Hazen started to reach for the knife again, but then sensed that Garrity would hear the bike coming and simply lean back from the passing swipe of the blade.

Hazen needed something bigger, something harder to dodge.

An empty shopping cart caught his eye.

He snatched it on the fly just before he clutched and built speed, the small wheels rattling over the pavement. It was difficult to hold the cart straight and steady, but he leaned into the task. All the while he kept Garrity squarely between his crooked-neck handle-bars, using the bars as a sight. The mechanic startled at the sound of the approaching motorcycle. By then, it was too late for him to do anything except drop his bags and push his wife out of the way.

Hazen peeled off, releasing the cart with a flip. It tumbled and careened, then bounced up into the mechanic's head with such ferocity he became a blur of arms and legs. Strings of saliva flew out of his mouth and hung curved in the air as his revolver skidded under the Bronco.

His wife's scream trailed off behind Hazen.

17

ANNA STOOD AT THE Gate 22 windows, watching the sky over Syracuse. Each pair of landing lights to wink on in final approach made her pulse quicken. She wanted those lights to be Emmett's United flight from Washington, D.C. She *willed* them to be his flight, even though the arrival board had told her that his plane was delayed fifteen minutes.

She no longer trusted the sky.

Each experience as an investigator seemed to make you leery of something new. Dark roads. Anonymous reports. Going first through doorways. Now, the heavens themselves were suspect, and the sky, where the Modoc dead dwelt, shrieked and howled with dangers. It was from the sky, in her dream, that Emmett had plunged to his death.

Nor was heaven as innocent as she'd imagined.

Two nights ago at the Shako:wi Cultural Center, Christopher White Pine had been correct in saying that the automaton Grandmother's version of the Oneida creation story was watered down for public consumption. The more authoritative written version he'd given her—and personally translated—hinted that Sky Father had had an incestuous relationship with his daughter, Sky Woman. Sadly, something Anna could relate to, something she could never fully put behind her, no matter how hard she tried. Filled with sexual jealousy when his daughter gave water to a sweaty lacrosse player, Sky Father had strong men uproot a white pine and hurl her down the hole.

So Sky Woman was not a gift to this world. She was an exile.

Anna caught two reflections on the window glass. One was her own: small, indistinct. The other was a man in a Stetson and Western clothes. Dutch Satterlee. She'd lost track of the NTSB investigator. Just as she'd now lost track of how many days she and Emmett had been on the case.

"You're still here," she said, turning.

"Yes," he drawled, "but I've gone and come back."

"Home?"

"Not long enough to warm up my bed. Flew down to—" The arrival of Emmett's flight was announced over the P.A. "I flew down to Florida."

"Why?"

"There was another passenger sitting in Row Twenty on Two Kettles's flight," he replied. "A clothing salesman."

"Did he recall Brenda?"

"No. He swore he had the row to himself the whole flight to LaGuardia. A motor-mouth, so I think he missed having any company."

That was it then. The Oneida woman never got onboard.

"Here they come," Dutch said, indicating the tired-looking passengers filing off the loading bridge.

Satterlee's presence at the airport tonight confused her. "You just fly in?"

"No, got here this morning. Emmett phoned me on his cell from the air, asked me to meet him."

"Did he say why?"

"Nope."

Good. She now took it less personally that he'd not told her why he'd gone to Washington today.

Emmett came loping up the bridge, a head taller than the others, impatiently bypassing those slower than him. The trip seemed to have energized him. "Hello all," he greeted Anna and Dutch. A bit impersonally, she thought.

Satterlee asked, "How was your flight?"

"Tolerable, Dutch. Had a bitch of a time, though, getting past Dulles security, even without my gun. Must have been my swarthy good looks." Emmett caught Anna's eye. "You still got my piece?"

Carrying a weapon onboard a commercial plane for a day trip simply wasn't worth the hassle, so she had locked his revolver in the trunk of their FBI loaner. "No, I pawned it."

"Evening," another voice said. Anna looked behind. Juan Bellasario, the airport police lieutenant, had joined them out of the crowd. "Ready, Mr. Parker?"

"Ready," Emmett said. "No bags." As they started down the loading bridge, he leaned into Anna. "Apologize for not explaining myself this morning. I just didn't want to have to justify my hunch too soon." That came from having worked mostly solo until paired with her, something he no doubt still considered to be an imposition. Yet, he also had what amounted to a Puritan work ethic toward leads: If you didn't have to work for it, the lead was worthless at best, bogus at worst.

The lieutenant led the three investigators to a security door. He tapped in the lock code and swung the door open on a night raucous with jet noise. You couldn't even hear yourself scream, and roiling kerosene fumes made it hard to see. They followed the lieutenant down a flight of metal stairs. A police cruiser was parked at the bottom.

"What hunch?" she asked Emmett as they got in.

His answer was lost in the whine of a 737 taxiing past. He tried again, but gave up. Then they were shut up in the overheated car with Dutch and Bellasario, who drove away from the terminal. The lieutenant dodged through a shifting maze of airport vehicles. She turned to Emmett, who'd taken the backseat with Dutch. "How'd you rate this limo service?"

Bellasario chuckled politely.

"I phoned the good lieutenant here from the air," Emmett explained. "He was kind enough to offer to get us across these goddamned runways in one piece."

"No problem," the man said.

"Easy for you to say." Emmett yawned. "Had me a productive day in D.C. How about yours, Dutch?"

The NTSB man reported what he had learned from the only apparent passenger in Row 20 on Brenda's flight. "And everything's set up for you on the ground here."

Emmett took this all in without reaction, then asked Anna with a concerned look, "How're you doing?"

She wasn't up to talking about what had happened today. Not yet. "Okay."

Bellasario wound around the runway on a series of access roads. He made one last dogleg, and ahead lay a civilian helicopter on a pad before a small hanger. A light shone from a window in the office adjacent to the hangar, and the lieutenant stopped in its spill. Opening his door and resting one shoe on the pavement, Emmett said to him, "Don't want to tie you up any more than I have to. Can you return, say, in thirty minutes?"

"Fine."

Anna got out, and Bellasario drove back toward the terminal. Emmett then said to Satterlee, "Dutch, go on ahead and tell these folks the posse is coming. We'll be along in a minute."

Obviously, Dutch thought Emmett wanted some privacy for a personal exchange. So did Anna. She waited as Satterlee strode for the office, his snakeskin boots clipping over the pavement.

The night was cold but silent of rumbling aircraft engines for the moment.

He and she were finally alone, and he avoided her inquisitive gaze. "Jake Cutler," he began, "pulled a caper in Nam worth noting. He chucked a Viet Cong prisoner out of a chopper from five thousand feet. There never was enough to take the case to court martial, but—" He stopped and studied her. "What's wrong, Anna?"

"Hazen Two Kettles killed Garrity this afternoon."

She gave Emmett a moment. "Jesus Christ," he finally said. "Where'd this go down?"

"A grocery store parking lot in Sherrill."

"How?"

"Hazen was on his motorcycle. He grabbed a shopping cart, accelerated and let it go like a missile. Garrity died an hour later on the operating table from head injuries."

"Where's Hazen now?"

"Missing. Presumed drowned."

"How do we get to *drowned*?" Emmett asked, his voice cracking. A young death affected him like no other. His brother had died young, a suicide.

"Hazen must have lain low until well after dark. Around seven, an Oneida County deputy spotted him, went in pursuit. Southbound out of Sherrill. I think Hazen was trying to get back to the rez. Oneida and Madison County units hemmed him in. State police set up a roadblock. Hazen ran his bike off a bridge and into the lake to avoid it. Everybody searched. But . . ." Anna had nothing to complete the sentence, except: "I cleared the scene about eight o'clock. Still nothing then."

"They always head back to the rez," Emmett said grimly. "Like god-damned lemmings." Then he headed for the office of Cayuga Helicopter Service.

So what happened?

What honestly happened?

The thrill of flight, then a splash, breathtaking-cold. Frigid blackness all around, and bubbles crinkled in his ears. He hadn't known which way was up and which way was down, and he would never have known had it not been for the beams of light that flitted over him. He broke back up into the night and tried to take a breath. But his lungs were already packed with a frothy mix of air and lake water. His racking coughs and heaves were so loud he was sure the spotlights would zero in on him. Yet, they roved over the water, still searching.

His sodden leather jacket and boots made it impossible for him to swim. But he was moving. Something was pushing him along. It was the pull of the creek, gathering strength at the outlet to the lake. There were stretches where his toes touched bottom, but mostly there was nothing but water beneath him, forcing him to kick off his boots and church his feet to stay afloat.

Within seconds, his muscles grew thick and numb from the cold. He knew he had to shed his jacket, somehow. But his mind kept putting off this task and focusing on the need to keep his mouth above the surface of the water.

Cat tongues began licking his face.

Bulrushes.

The current was carrying him through a thicket of reeds, dragging the sandpapery outer skins of the stalks across his face. He grasped at a passing clump of rushes, hoping to support himself long enough to wrestle out of his jacket. But the roots to the clump came loose from the bottom, and he still had to tread water.

He wanted to cry out for help.

But he had no help. Never again could he rely on anyone except himself.

The shorelines tapered into him. He realized that he had left the lake and was being swept down Oneida Creek, under the bridge.

His feet struck bottom again. He braced his legs against the heavy flow, and a pillow of water formed behind his neck. Grunting, he strained to pull his jacket off his right shoulder and pry the sleeve off his arm. Yet, this partial removal only ballooned his jacket into a sail and bore him downstream at even faster speeds. A spurt of anger—against the cold, the day, life itself—helped him thrash toward the nearest bank. But then the cold completely humbled him, and when the current spread out over shallows he could do no more than drag his unfeeling toes over the rocky bed of the creek, feebly trying to slow himself.

His face had dropped into the water, perhaps for the last time, when a hand seized him by the scruff and rolled his body over.

He expected a cop.

But the voice was too gentle, too sympathetic to belong to any cop he'd ever known. "You're lucky it's my day off," the silhouette said with that muted, husky lilt that was instantly recognizable as being Indian. Yet, he also sounded young. Too young for his size. The massive man gripped him under the arms and hauled him like a rag doll toward the bank. The man's legs splashed and then tinkled through the fringe of skim ice just before reaching dry land.

In a final cruel illusion, the cold had deceived his brain into believing that his chilled, viscous blood was flowing like warm maple syrup through his veins, spreading comfort throughout his entire body. He felt so very, very good. Druggie good.

Then he started shuddering again. His spastic hands projected like claws from the cuffs of his leather jacket.

"Just a second more," the silhouette said, lowering him onto a hard patch of snow.

The creak of a vehicle door opening, the sudden glow of a dome light falling dimly over him, doing no good to bring things into clarity, his vision was so blurred. Yet, a halo of fuzzy golden light appeared to have attached itself to the head of the figure as he spread open a sleeping bag in the back of a van. The sight of the haloed figure was so beautiful, so unworldly he began to wonder if he was dead. "No time to get you out of your wet clothes right now," the man said quietly, lifting him off the ground. "You killed that guy in Sherrill."

Then mindless black slowly came on the wings of this rising sensation, and one by one the stars blinked out as he ascended toward them.

Hazen awakened, not sure where he was. When this usually happened, that meant he was in juvenile hall. But the air smelled of wood smoke, not disinfectant and floor wax. The room was almost blacked out, yet the atmosphere within it had that dusty, muffled quality that comes from clutter. The walls in juvie echoed with sterile concrete emptiness.

He eased up on his elbows.

Sweat-damp cloth clung to his skin. He was lying nude in a sleeping bag. His hands and feet tingled as if they were ant farms. A voice remembered from a first-aid class told him that this kind of pain following exposure to cold was good.

This is good. This is life.

He knew he wasn't alone, even though he could hear nobody else in the stillness. He sensed eyes on him. Unblinking eyes. However, no human shapes broke the pools of shadow in the room. A few red lines were etched in the air, suspended there as if somebody had drawn them on the darkness. They made no sense until there was an explosive pop of pitch.

A wood stove.

And by then, Hazen's pupils had enlarged to take in more of the firelight escaping from the seams in the stove.

He made out a huge man sitting across from him. Sitting almost perfectly still.

"Where am I?" Hazen asked.

The man rose from a chair that continued to rock behind him. He knelt before the wood stove and opened the door several inches. A sliver of light flickered over him. He was tall, as tall as Hazen even when on his knees. He had a long face that was homely but mild-looking, and his eyeglasses captured the firelight in red glints that hid his pupils. Picking the fire poker up off the brick hearth, he stabbed at the burning log inside the stove, stirring a torrent of sparks that crackled like strings of miniature firecrackers. Some arced into his brown hair but quickly went out. He smiled at Hazen. "You're at my place. Not far from the the rez. Not far. Don't worry."

"What time is it?"

"About four in the morning."

Time was almost as good as distance when it came to eluding the cops. Hazen figured they were eight hours behind him, now.

The man was still smiling at him.

His gaunt expression was a bit spooky, but so far Hazen felt no alarm. Just lucky. Had this man not waded the shallows, Hazen saw himself floating dead all the way down into Oneida Lake by now.

He noticed his leather jacket. It was hung on the wall behind the stove like a turkey buzzard spreading its night-damp wings to the warmth of the sun. His Levi's and underwear were neatly folded over a wire hanger beneath the jacket. The room was enclosed by rough plywood walls. Junk everywhere, books and magazines, a sagging sofa, a padded rocker on which the man had been sitting.

Hazen saw that he himself was in a filthy sleeping bag atop a canvas camp cot. "I know you, don't I?" he asked.

"Maybe." The man reached out, offering his hand. Hazen felt his own fist vanished into a veritable catcher's mitt made of bone and gristle. "I'm Johnny Skyholder." Johnny shyly withdrew his hand. "I'm a janitor at the Shako:wi Cultural Center. Tonight's my night off. Lucky for you."

Hazen didn't say that he'd never been to the center. It frosted him how people stared at him in most tribal facilities. Outside his cousins' trailer, he kept to the recreation hall, where mostly kids went. "You part Indian?" he asked. Something about his sunken cheekbones and massively-boned body made him seem white. Even though he talked Indian.

"*Full-blooded* Oneida," Johnny insisted with a hurt look.

Hazen hid his skepticism, but still prodded, "How come I never seen you around?" Less than a thousand Oneida remained in the area, and this peculiar member of the tribe would have stood out. Unless he had a gift for making himself scarce, as did some ex-cons Hazen knew.

"I just came—" Johnny cut himself short as he looked sharply toward the only window in the room. Holding his breath, he listened to the dark morning outside. He seemed very tense, almost afraid. The seconds ticked by, and nothing happened. Finally, he faced Hazen again, holding his cigar-sized forefinger across his lips. When he spoke again, it was in a hush. "Tawiskalu is coming back any minute."

Hazen lowered his voice too. "Who's—"

"Tawiskalu," Johnny repeated, sounding displeased, like one of Hazen's teachers. "This is a duplex, and he lives next door."

Hazen knew what a double-wide was, but not a duplex. Was he in some kind of apartment building? The neighborhood beyond these walls seemed too dark and silent to be inside any of the cities in the surrounding counties.

Johnny went on in the same strident whisper, "Tawiskalu must never hear you. Promise me that. He must never become aware of you as long as you stay here. This is for your own protection. You got to understand I'm do-ing my best, but I'm not strong enough to do everything. Do you promise?"

Hazen nodded once, firmly. He was a fugitive, a murderer, and he had nowhere else to go, no means to get there even if he knew of such a safe haven.

The promise seemed to relax Johnny. "I'm not from round here," he continued in a more conversational tone. "So many of us Oneida got scat-tered to the winds long ago." He fluttered his big fingers, mimicking leaves scurrying along. "I wound up far away. But my Oneida Nana told me about the homeland. Always the homeland. She said if I got up early enough on this certain morning in winter to see the sun rise above the earth, it'd point to the exact place where the homeland was. Finally, I headed for the rising sun, Hazen."

The boy froze.

"What's wrong?" Johnny asked.

All of a sudden, Hazen missed the butcher knife that he'd shoved down his boot and lost in the lake. He had nothing, not even the fire poker, which lay at Skyholder's muddy boots.

"You're scared, Hazen. Don't be scared."

It was a trick of his never to introduce himself. That way, if strangers knew his name, he was tipped off. Nobody learned your name unless they wanted something from you or meant you harm.

He could feel the silence build in the room.

Yet, Johnny wasn't flustered. "I know all about you, Hazen Two Kettles. Your poor, poor auntie too."

"How?"

"It's a small rez. Everybody knows everything about everybody else."

Except about you, Hazen thought, wondering if his clothes were dry yet but not wanting to slip naked out of the sleeping bag.

Beep . . . beep . . . beep . . .

Johnny swept his left wrist up into the firelight and silenced his watch alarm. "Time for my medicine," he said. He rose with an almost robotic single-mindedness and made directly for an alcove. He flipped on a light switch, and the alcove was revealed to be a kitchenette with dirty dishes, cans and cracker packages piled high on the sinkboard. The bright light from the fixture accentuated the mean smallness of the place. Whatever a duplex was, it wasn't much. Less than his cousins' condemned mobile home.

The faucet made a shuddery sound, as if the pipes were bad, while he rinsed out a jelly glass and filled it. Next, he reached into one of the deep pockets in his coveralls and came out with a plastic prescription container. He shook some capsules out into his palm and swallowed them by downing the full glass of water, his Adam's apple bobbing like a piston.

Wiping his lips on his sleeve, he turned toward Hazen. "You want some medicine too?" he asked, holding the pill container between his large forefinger and thumb. "It'll help you rest. You're going to need to rest."

"What is it?"

"Seconal."

Barbs would be nice. A soft, sleepy cushion for the crash he knew was coming. As his numbness wore off, reality awaited him like a cement wall. Yesterday had divided his life into day and night, and there was no going back to the daylit half ever again. Sooner than later, that would sink in. Then he would desperately need that silken twilight sleep that existed midway between day and night. As uncertain as he felt about this man, this place, he could not be choosy about his friends and havens from now on. Sleep would be nice.

"Sure," Hazen said at last.

Johnny obliged him with two capsules and handed him a fresh glass of water.

Hazen was very thirsty, even though his throat was raw from the lake water he'd gulped down. He slurped as he drank, which made Johnny laugh. "Easy, easy."

Hazen lay back down, waiting for the intoxicating drowsiness that would wipe away the consequences of yesterday with a sweet nocturnal confusion in which nothing really mattered. Nothing did matter, and that, he sensed, was the only peace that was left to him.

Johnny was lumbering back into the kitchen when a cell phone rang. He took his cellular out of the same deep pocket from which the Seconal had come. "Hello," he answered. A pause in which Johnny switched off the kitchenette light and returned to the rocker. "Yes, took my medicine just a minute ago," he told the person on the other end of the connection. "I am sitting and I'm comfortable." He began rocking. "Warm, safe and relaxed, just like you say." A long lull followed in which Johnny, lit only by the fire again, rocked with the phone against his ear, eyelids shut, his thick lower jaw cocked to one side, his body rocking slower and slower as if the tempo of his heart was slowing too. "Okay, okay," he said with a faint weariness that almost bordered on surliness. "Time. It's time." Rising, he disconnected and slid the phone down into his pocket again.

He knelt beside the cot, his face close to Hazen's. He smelled like smoke and sweat. "I've got to go now. Don't make a sound. Otherwise Tawiskalu will hear. I can't be responsible for what he does. So whatever you do, don't let him hear you. Okay?"

"Okay."

Then Johnny went out.

Drowsiness came to Hazen in a sweet wave, but he struggled to stay awake long enough to hear the engine to the van being fired up. He waited and waited, but it never came. Nor did he hear anything from the apartment next door. Finally, he murmured, "Fuck Tawiskalu."

Saying that, he recalled who Tawiskalu was.

Aunt Brenda had told him.

Tawiskalu was the Evil Spirit, the Bad Twin, the hateful son of Sky Woman who'd burst from her womb, killing her.

Emmett had been interviewed about high-profile cases several times during his career, but it still always amazed him how a television studio consisted of chaos and semi-darkness, except where the lights shone. There serenity and order prevailed. Standing on the news set beside a blank blue screen was an attractive woman with a meticulous coiffure, pointing out cold and warm fronts that materialized only on the monitors. "So, Syracuse, that's your daybreak weather. Have a terrific day."

As the anchor went on with some soft news, the station manager whispered to Emmett, "Any chance we can get an interview with you two about the recent developments?"

"We'll check back with you as soon as we discuss those developments with our superiors," Emmett replied. He had no intention of doing anything of the sort. He and Anna had come here to interview, not to be interviewed. Let the Syracuse office of the FBI handle the public relations.

As the weatherwoman stepped off the set, the manager motioned her over. She smiled pleasantly and shook hands with the partners, although introductions weren't made until the foursome had passed through double doors and were out in the corridor. Her name was Madeleine Allen. "Mr. Parker and Ms. Turnipseed are federal agents working the Oneida cases," the manager explained. "They need some weather background on the region for their investigation."

"My pleasure," Ms. Allen said, although somewhat tentatively. "Step into my weather station."

Relieved of his burdens, the manager peeled off, and the partners followed the woman inside a cramped office. There was no place for Emmett and Anna to sit, so Ms. Allen didn't use her own chair. She began gathering up computer printouts. "The weather of the past month has been pretty typical for this time of year, meaning if you don't like it wait an hour—" Then, catching the partners' expressions, she interrupted herself, put down the charts, shut the door and asked, "This isn't just about the weather, is it?"

"No, it involves Cayuga Helicopter Service," Emmett said, watching carefully for her reaction. She rolled a corner of her lower lip between her front teeth. Waited.

Last night, the owner-pilot of Cayuga had admitted having been airborne in his chopper in the hour Monday evening after Adirondack Flight 557 had departed. He also admitted to having a passing acquaintanceship with Jake Cutler, having taken the retired lieutenant colonel up for sightseeing flights in the past. When Emmett pressed to know if he had taken Cutler up last Monday evening, the pilot turned evasive. Under continued pressure, he confessed that he had taken a female friend up for what amounted to a joyride. He and the female were married. Not to each other. They'd had a fling a couple years ago while doing "weather and traffic together" for the station. Found out, both had promised their mates on pain of divorce not to meet again.

That female was Ms. Allen, who was now doing weather without traffic.

Emmett now asked her if what the pilot had said about her going on the flight with him was true.

She nodded.

Emmett showed her a military ID photo of a younger Jake Cutler. It was the most current he had from CID. "Did this man go on the flight with you two?"

The weather woman's forehead creased in confusion. "No. No one else went along. Just Chip and me. Flight wasn't long either. Just over the city lights and back to the airport. For old times' sake."

"Do you know this man?" Emmett asked, continuing to hold up the photo.

"Of course. He's Jake Cutler. Active in C.U.E. Either he or Portia Nelson gets the counter-point reaction interview every time the Oneida Nation Rep speaks."

Anna asked, "That chopper has a cabin behind the pilots' seats, right?"

"Yes."

"Is it possible somebody could have stowed away in the cabin?"

"No," Ms. Allen said. "As soon as he touched down, Chip and I went back there." Her blush returned, blossomed around her throat.

From that Emmett surmised that *old times' sake* had involved more than viewing the lights of downtown Syracuse.

"Is there anything Chip asked you not to discuss?" Anna quickly clarified: "About the flight?"

The woman suffered several more seconds of visible embarrassment, then gave a shaky smile, as if she were about to burst out laughing or cry. "No need."

"Pardon?"

"There was no need for Chip to ask me anything like that. He has as much to lose as I do."

18

A SHERIFF'S SEARCH AND Rescue boat was dragging the bottom of Sunset Lake with grappling hooks. Anna stood beside Emmett on shore, watching the small craft stitch back and forth, listening to the burble of its outboard motor. The air smelled of murky water, punctuated by whiffs of boat exhaust. A wan sun stood midway to noon, laying a ribbon of spangles across the surface of the lake.

It'd been simple enough to recover the motorcycle. The Harley-Davidson had crashed through the shelf of skim ice that encrusted the entire shoreline, except at the lake's outlet, and settled to the bottom at a depth of twenty feet. Corpses didn't cling to the bottom, like motorcycles. They drifted, even rose again on the gasses of putrefaction and floated away, although that was presently unlikely, given the frigid water temperatures that had held the sheriff's divers to no more than fifteen minutes of immersion. Temperatures Hazen Two Kettles was not likely to have survived, although a ground search had widened into the surrounding countryside.

Anna checked on Emmett again.

The flat rays of the sun in his face had brought out his squint lines. She sensed that he wasn't seeing a lake that was hiding a boy's body. His eyes had turned inward, perhaps back to his mother's kitchen in Lawton, Oklahoma. Blood and gore-splattered. Another boy, another death. His younger brother had shot himself at the table in that kitchen.

Despite seeming invigorated on his return from D.C. last night, Emmett's mood had plummeted earlier this morning after he'd tried to contact William Jordan at the phone number the chief deputy marshal had provided on his business card. An automated AT&T voice answered. A subsequent call to the A.G.'s office in Washington, demanding to know what the hell was going on, had yet to be returned.

Emmett then confided in Anna that somebody powerful wasn't playing square with them. And he wanted out.

Say something. Anything. Before he sinks deeper into this funk— and this entire investigation coughs and dies. "What're you thinking, Em?"

It'd been a while since she'd called him that, and he smiled, as if a little amused. "Nothing."

She wasn't about to let him off that easy. They needed to talk. "Sometimes it seems so futile, doesn't it?"

"Wait 'til it feels that way all the time."

"It's that way for you?"

He went on tracking the boat. "You accomplish so little in this job. The dead stay dead. You just try to figure out who had a reason to kill them. One day, after enough killings, it hits you that you might be the only thing in the whole damned universe keeping track. And you're so powerless. Even the smartest cop in the world is powerless. You can't make things right again. Can't resurrect the dead, let alone punish the guilty." Finally, he looked at her. "But you go on."

"Why?"

"Momentum sweeps you along. Maybe this futility thing is like a wall, and one day you realize you've passed through it, somehow. Futility's behind you, and you just deal with the moment." He stopped watching the search boat and surprised her with a soft, penetrating look. "Everything lately has been a waste of time . . . except you."

She tensed, waiting for him to comment on the wreckage of their relationship. Perhaps ironically.

But then he further surprised her. "I can look back on one thing with a little satisfaction. You're up and running as an investigator. I taught you all I know. But that didn't take long, did it?"

She reached for his hand, a bit clumsily if only because their last physical contact had been weeks ago. "You sound like you're leaving."

Still smiling, he sighed. "An Indian can't really go home. Not after he's been gone as many years as I have."

"Why not?" she asked, even though she didn't like him suddenly talking about home.

Emmett began gently rubbing his thumb over the back of her hand as he stared off at the search boat. It was blaze-orange. Strange how such a striking, cheerful color could come to represent death. "I was just a rookie with Oklahoma City P.D." he went on. "Got a domestic dispute call, this old Shawnee woman wanted to kick her alcoholic son out. He wasn't combative, just hungover and sad that it'd come to this. He asked me what tribe I was, where I hailed from. I stood by in his room to keep the peace while he packed his stuff. That stuff included an Army major's uniform and the Medal of Honor with its blue ribbon under picture glass. I'll never forget how his boozy eyes settled on me as he dumped that framed medal into a pasteboard box with his dirty socks and underwear. He told me—*Never try to go back to Lawton, Parker. You'll wind up just like me.*" He released her hand and started up the beach for their sedan. "Let's go. Let's keep moving, though I'm getting the feeling we'll never have a gold-plated answer to this goddamned mess."

She followed. "Then why are we here, Em?"

"Somebody needed a little native window-dressing. As usual."

An hour or so after nightfall, Hazen thought he heard a vehicle approaching the duplex. He'd had the whole of the day to explore his new world but had stirred no more than necessary from the cot, twice to Johnny Skyholder's grimy bathroom and once to his kitchenette for water and some stale Saltine crackers. Each time he moved, no matter how carefully, the flimsy, plywood floor creaked. When he turned on the tap, the faucet moaned and the drain gurgled. After each of these noises, he stood as still as he could and listened for Tawiskalu to rouse next door.

Nobody came.

Still, he never sneaked outside. The window was his only opening on the neighborhood, and upon awakening mid-morning he saw that it was no neighborhood at all, just a meadow of brown weeds dotted with rusting cars, ringed by the same kind of woods along Territory Road.

The distant engine noise got louder. Unmistakably, a car was coming.

Hazen rose from the cot and went to the window. Through the fly-speckled panes, he saw lights wash over a distant rise, a humped hill he found vaguely familiar. He hoped that Johnny was returning at long last in his van. Even strange company was to be preferred over no company at all. Hazen was hungry and bored after the long day of lying low. Plus cold. The fire had burned out, and he'd not rekindled it, afraid that Tawiskalu would notice the smoke while Johnny was known to be gone.

Headlights crested the rise and slanted down through the pines. They were headed for the duplex. No question now.

He had not seen Johnny's van, except in the haziest way while being loaded into its back last night. The vehicle that was coming was boxy, like a van, but the pines and the trunks of the oaks were too thick to tell for certain. This morning, while in the grip of a heavy-lidded Seconal sleep, he thought he'd heard the van started up and driven off. This was hours and hours after Johnny had gone out the door.

The vehicle sped from the woods into the meadow. Something glinted on the roof. An emergency light bar. Unlit, but obviously a light bar.

Hazen jerked his face away from the window.

It was a sheriff's four-by-four cruiser.

Creeping over to the door, he made sure it was locked. The window was without curtains, but he couldn't risk throwing a blanket or a towel over it now. And at that instant, a spotlight blazed through the panes and illuminated Hazen's leather jacket, which was still spread against the wall behind the wood stove. He'd put on his underwear and Levi's earlier, but the jacket had still been damp.

The spotlight went out.

Two car doors slammed—that meant two deputies.

Hazen darted low across the room and took down his jacket. He fumbled into it. The leather was stiff but dry. He crept back to the outer wall and pressed himself against it, staying as far from the window as he could.

His boots and socks were at the bottom of Sunset Lake. Johnny had left a pair of worn-out tennis shoes in the clutter, but Hazen would have looked like a clown in the size fifteens, and running in them was out of the question.

Pounding on the door made him jump, even though he'd known it was coming.

"Sheriff's department! Anybody there?"

Another voice asked the same question while knocking on Tawiskalu's door.

Would the deputies come inside? What would he do if they did? He had killed a man yesterday. The fact did not seem real today, but the arrival of deputies took big bites out of that sense of unreality. A flashlight beam shot through the window and probed the room. The brass gleam of the fire poker caught Hazen's eye. Last night, Johnny had left it on the hearth. It was out of reach for as long as the deputy ran his beam over the interior of the place. Hazen realized that he should have grabbed the poker along with his jacket.

Could he ever kill a cop?

Yes, he decided. He had the right to get away, just as he'd had the right to take out Daniel Garrity to protect his family.

The waiting became so unbearable Hazen shut his eyes. *Go away . . . go away . . . go away.* Already, he imagined himself racing out into the woods, the icy ground chafing at his bare feet, his back arched, waiting for the smack of a bullet. Part of him wanted to run. The other part of him wanted whatever was coming to be over, no matter the cost.

"County sheriff!" the deputy cried. "Anybody there?"

Hazen bit into the back of his hand to keep from making a sound. A groan, a shout, a scream—he wasn't sure which—was bubbling up his throat, and he had to cut it off. He felt as if his skin was crawling right off the muscles. His skin was leaving without him. His skin knew what to do.

Hazen opened his eyes.

The flashlight beam was reaching for him. Sliding prone, he squeezed under Johnny's bed. Something obstructed him, a cloth bag of some sort. Quietly, he shoved it aside so he could crawl completely under. His hand fell through the open zipper, coming to rest on a piece of silken material.

The flashlight went out.

After an eternity, two car doors slammed again.

Hazen held his breath, listening over his heartbeats. The engine revved, and the headlights shone across the duplex as the driver turned the cruiser around. Then the darkness returned shade by shade, and the sound of the motor faded away.

Minutes passed before Hazen could make himself rise and peek out the window. The red tail-lamps of the four-by glittered through the trees. Then they were gone altogether.

His first instinct was to run. Escape from this place before the cops returned in even greater numbers. Flee into the woods and swamps, shoes or no shoes. Put Oneida territory miles and miles behind. But a calmer voice told him that the deputies had left the duplex satisfied nobody was here. Otherwise, they would have kicked in the door. If he left, Hazen might walk into a trap. They wanted him to be on the move. People would sight him that way.

Weariness weighed him down. He sank onto Johnny's bed, flopped on his left side and tried to calculate. He didn't feel comfortable staying here with Skyholder. The man was just too weird. He would rest, then leave. He'd never imagined life beyond this place, except Florida. Disney World. Maybe he could make it to Florida. He was too nervous to sleep, but he dreamed of palm trees and roller coasters for a while, comforted by the imagined warmth of the tropical winter.

He'd dangled his arm over the side of the bed, and once again his fingers brushed the silky cloth. He grabbed it and went to the windowless bathroom, the only place he felt safe to turn on a light. Closing the door, he examined the material. It was a woman's slip, white. He grinned as he imagined Johnny playing with women's things. Maybe Skyholder got off putting on these things, and that's what made him so strange.

Then Hazen remembered the bag under the bed.

He retrieved it and went back to the bathroom. The light over the sink showed it to be an overnight bag. He took hold of a baggage tag and slowly turned it, his neck hair tingling as he read:

Adirondack Airlines—Wings over Hiawatha Country
Name: B. Two Kettles
Address: Territory Road
Oneida, NY 13421

Inside were the clothing and toiletries Aunt Brenda had packed for her flight last Monday night. And her sparkly black purse. The very one she'd taken out the door with her.

The bag tumbled out of Hazen's hands as he reached for the switch and killed the light. He stood in the darkness, his head buzzing worse than ever before. Roaring like Niagara Falls. He needed to run, but his legs felt like jelly. He tried to think, but he was close to throwing up. He wanted to splash cold water over his face, but he was afraid of the sound the tap would make.

Maybe Johnny had nothing to do with the overnight bag. Maybe Tawiskalu had brought it—and Aunt Brenda—here. The deputies had not raised Tawiskalu either, so the Evil Spirit wasn't inside his half of the duplex. For the time being.

Hazen froze.

Another vehicle was coming through the woods. Maybe the same cruiser. Maybe an entire line of cop cars. Suddenly, he thought of the police with feelings of hope. They would help him sort this all out. Maybe Detective Devereaux was with the deputies, and he would make good on his promise to help Hazen.

This hope was swiftly crushed by the realization that Daniel Garrity's death made it impossible for him to go to the cops.

Socks.

Aunt Brenda always packed a pair of thick woolen socks. Her feet got cold.

Hazen riffled through the bag until he found them, then sat on the toilet seat and pulled them on. He could bear the cold ground this way, at least for a while.

Headlights showed through the window, closing fast. Only one car. But he was also surprised to see that the night had turned misty while he'd rested. As if the sky had descended to earth, bringing all its strange horrors. He went to the hearth and seized the fire poker, before creeping back to the window. A van pulled up before the duplex. He couldn't tell the make or the color, but he believed it was Johnny Skyholder's.

The engine died, and the running lights went out.

Hazen ran to the bathroom for Aunt Brenda's overnight bag. He stuffed it back under Johnny's bed. In case he needed time to get away from here, in case he needed Skyholder to be none the wiser.

When he went to the window again, the driver was still seated behind the wheel, a large and brooding silhouette, refusing to budge, as if he sensed something was out of the ordinary.

Moistening his lips, Hazen recalled that a yellow van had been parked down Territory Road from the Two Kettles's single-wide yesterday when he'd returned from school.

The driver's door swung open, and the man clambered out. Johnny seemed to be staring right at Hazen, although his eyes didn't show in his shadowy face. Again, Hazen licked his dry lips, wondering if it was best to pretend nothing had happened. Not even mention that the deputies had come and gone. He was trying to think of some casual way to greet Johnny when the figure walked toward the other half of the duplex.

Something was wrong.

The figure was tall and big-boned like Johnny, but he didn't move like Skyholder. His hands were in fists, and his stride was angry.

Tawiskalu!

Hazen realized that he had screwed up. Two vans. The two residents of this duplex each owned a van. Johnny had seemed genuinely scared that Tawiskalu would discover Hazen, and now it was clear—Johnny knew what his duplex-mate had done to Aunt Brenda. That was the source of his fear. He didn't want Hazen to wind up like his aunt. He'd saved the boy from the creek, hadn't he?

Tawiskalu didn't go through his own door. There was no sound of a door opening and closing. Instead, he disappeared around the far side of the building.

His vanishing, however temporarily, freed Hazen to act. He padded across the thin floor in his aunt's socks and grabbed the fire poker, then stood with his back pressed to the kitchenette wall. One hand grasped the heavy fire tool, and the other was poised on the light switch.

Waiting, his mind skimmed from thing to thing. Could he make his way out to the van? Had the keys been left in the ignition? Could a single blow from the poker bring down a man that gigantic?

A new noise made Hazen jump again.

A rattle. It fell silent, only to be repeated several seconds later.

Hazen knew what it was. He'd played with Aunt Brenda's mud turtle rattle often enough to know the sound the cherry pits inside made. He knew that Tawiskalu was shaking it to frighten him, but he felt no less scared for knowing.

The rattle now came from directly out front.

Hazen braced for the door to be bashed down. He didn't move, waiting for Tawiskalu to storm inside.

But nothing happened.

His fingers trembled weakly on the switch, but he let the darkness be. He would use the darkness. His eyes were better adjusted to it than Tawiskalu's.

His skin felt sticky with sweat, despite the cold. He rested the tip of the heavy poker against the floor, and it was through this brass shaft that he felt a nudge from below. It was followed by a spine-tingling screech from the nails surrendering their hold on floor joists. An entire panel of plywood flew up. Hazen side-stepped but kept his hand on the switch as Tawiskalu burst out of the black square he'd just created and hurled the panel out into the living room.

Hazen flicked on the switch.

No ceiling light came on. And in the continuing darkness, Tawiskalu threw a forearm around Hazen's lower legs and pulled. Falling, Hazen brought down the poker as hard as he could. It fell short of the man and thudded against the lip of the hole in the floor. Hazen landed on his back and flung a heel toward the man's eyes. Tawiskalu rolled his face into his shoulder, and the kick glanced off the side of his head. Hazen knew that contact had not been violent enough to cause real harm, but the man screamed in rage, "You filthy little redskin!"

The voice was guttural, pitched from the back of the throat, pitiless. And it didn't sound dumb, like Johnny's.

Hazen strained to make out the man's face, but couldn't. He stank of perspiration and wood smoke.

His going behind the duplex was now explained by the darkness: He'd cut the electricity at the breaker box.

Hazen thrashed a leg free and kicked again. This blow was solid. Tawiskalu recoiled, and as he did Hazen scuttled back before his legs were grabbed again. He extended the poker like a sword to fend the man off. A mistake. Tawiskalu yanked the poker out of his grasp and heaved it into a far corner.

"You pathetic little redskin!" he bellowed.

A thought swirled through Hazen's confusion and fear. Tawiskalu had not seen him in full light, yet he knew the boy was Indian. Had Johnny told this terrible creature about his guest?

Hazen reared up from the waist and drove his fist against the man's large, bony skull. A fist came right back at him, but whooshed through the air wide of Hazen's ear. Tawiskalu leaned back out of Hazen's range, but went on clasping his legs.

"How long have you been here?" he demanded.

Hazen saw no reason to answer.

"Who said you could stay here? Answer me—did Thaluhyawaku say you could stay!"

This was too much to figure out. And there was no time, for at that instant Tawiskalu let go of Hazen's shin only to glom on to his belt. The boy unhitched his Levi's and squirmed out of them. He was nearly to the door when he tripped over a leg to the cot and was sent sprawling. By the time he got on his feet again, Tawiskalu had swung back the door but was blocking the opening. "You want to run? Run!"

Hazen lunged headlong under one of his long arms, flinging himself toward the misty dark of the night, the possibility of freedom beyond—but Tawiskalu pinched the boy's neck between that arm and his ribcage. Hazen pummeled the man's belly with his fists, but that only tightened the vise. His ears began to ring, and the spaces inside his head gradually turned as gray and indistinct as the waiting night. Blood was no longer flowing to his brain.

"Thaluhyawaku knew better than to bring you here," he said as if he were very, very sorry about this. His pity was just as terrifying as his rage.

Then he hurled Hazen out the door.

The ground came up at him as total blackness.

When he came to, he was flat on his back. Dead leaves had become trapped in his Mohawk and crackled as he moved his head to peer woozily around. A porch light was shining over him. He couldn't make out the closest trees, but had a vague idea where they jutted out into the meadow. He might be safe in the woods, just past a row of junker cars. Getting ready to crawl that way, he tried to swing his left arm around so he could roll over onto his stomach. But his left arm was stuck to his side. And he couldn't separate his right arm from his right side. He bent his hands inward to explore his restraints. They felt like straps.

There was no time to deal with them. He was alone for the moment, but he knew that wouldn't last, and the safety of the trees beckoned.

He tried to snake toward them on his side, but it was like jogging in place. Flopping onto his belly, he was able to move like an inchworm, doubling at the waist and the gliding forward on his forehead.

He had not gone far when a kick sent him sprawling.

A big shadow knelt beside him, the porch light to its back. "Did your Nana ever tell you, *We should've knocked you in the head and saved the milk!*" A cruel laugh broke from the darkened face. "Did she ever say that, redskin?"

"No," Hazen croaked, yet hoping that there was some way to appease the man. "I never knew my Nanas. They died before I was born."

"You're lucky."

The light was broken by movement again, and Hazen realized that Tawiskalu had risen. Immediately, the boy began inching like a caterpillar toward the woods again. The chances of reaching them were slight, and he expected another kick any second, but he had to try. He could feel the paralysis of fear setting up like cement in his limbs. Once he stopped trying to move, he might not be able to move ever again.

He reached the taller, rougher grass of the meadow. It was long-dead and rustled loudly as he crawled through it. But he was almost beyond the throw of the light and into the old cars. A blessed wall of darkness awaited him. Not far off, he believed.

Another kick flattened him against the frozen earth.

"I'm giving you one chance, Hazen," Tawiskalu said. He knew his name. Maybe that was good.

The boy wheezed and wept. "What? *What!*"

"Where was your aunt going?"

"New York City."

"No," Tawiskalu said with a chilling finality. "Not good enough."

19

"**T**HANKS FOR COMING," ANNA said. Yesterday, she'd taken it upon herself to try to weave together some loose ends over the phone. The result of that effort was that she found herself lead investigator this morning. Special Agent in Charge Cochran had given her use of his conference room, but then found an excuse to skip the roundtable meeting. And disassociate himself from a downward spiral of cases that were now drawing hard questions from the national media and Washington. "So here we are . . ."

Emmett sat on her right, staring out the window on another sky with the consistency of wet ashes. Even under the best of circumstances, he didn't believe in the corporate approach to solving cases. And over the past twenty-four hours, he'd closed within himself, staring out on the world with a sullen obstinacy he refused to explain—a periodic trait in male Comanches, she suspected.

Leo Manoukian had left his phone ringing off the hook out in the bullpen. A normal morning in an FBI office. He'd taken the chair next to Linda Freccia with obvious pleasure, the color in his alternately young-old face deepening as he tried not to look at the Madison County S.O. juvenile detective too intently. Over lunch yesterday, Freccia had confided in Anna that she and Leo were dating, and Anna had drummed up an encouraging smile. Another star-crossed law enforcement affair off and running.

Vaughn Devereaux made a point of checking his wristwatch.

"Dutch," Anna said to the NTSB investigator, "you mind kicking things off?"

Satterlee paused before speaking. Anna had advertised this as a brainstorming session, but apparently he wasn't going to take that as an invitation to carelessness. "I've now gone through the boarding evolution for Flight Five-five-seven a hundred times. I don't feel I'm any closer this week than I was last week to explaining how Ms. Two Kettles wound up like she did. Something crazy happened before, during or even after that boarding process last Monday evening. Something that's never happened in the history of fatal aircraft incidents. One of our techs went through the nose-wheel well on that bird with a fine-toothed comb, looking for any signs the woman had been stuffed up there, like that mechanic suggested to Parker. Nothing. I wish I could offer you more. I can't. How about you, Emmett?"

He roused, slightly. "Two Kettles probably never got airborne on the seven-twenty-seven."

"You still thinking about a chopper?" Satterlee asked.

Emmett shrugged as if he didn't want the investigation to go down that path, even though the owner-pilot of Cayuga Helicopter Service had taken Jake Cutler up for sight-seeing a few times.

"Anything to add, Juan?" Anna asked Lieutenant Bellasario of the airport police.

"I tend to agree with Parker. The woman never got on the plane. Other than that, I can't explain what happened to her between the ticket counter and the loading bridge. But what do we do? Widen the scope of the interviews to include every living soul in the airport at that time who might've crossed paths with Ms. Two Kettles? That'd mean going through every passenger list for every flight."

Devereaux shook his head. "A lot of feet to hold to the flames, and it still wouldn't account for somebody in the terminal who just walked up, stuck a concealed gun in her ribs and told her to accompany him out."

Anna asked the tribal detective, "Any buzz on the rez that she might have been stalked by Garrity or somebody else in the days or weeks prior to the flight?"

"Nothing. And thanks to Garrity's death threat letter, the presence of white folks has been duly noted and reported to our P.D. Yesterday our patrolmen jacked up two Mormon missionaries who made the mistake of spreading the good word on Territory Road. White boys in suits. Lucky they weren't shot by our locals, know what I mean?"

Satterlee asked, "Emmett, what was the name of the other mechanic— not Garrity?"

"Jason Eberhardt."

"What'd he say about getting a heads-up regarding feds in the terminal?"

Anna hid a smile behind her finger. So Satterlee was learning to rely on Emmett's phenomenal memory. It could become a crutch to those who worked with him.

Emmett didn't miss a beat. "Eberhardt said: *It came down the grapevine that the feds were in the North Concourse, looking into that Indian woman who was found dead.*" He seemingly took no pleasure in his own prowess. Something was deeply wrong, and she could think of no way to draw it out of him. Early this morning in the hotel, she'd heard the TV going in his room, something so infrequent she noted the time: 3:00.

Satterlee sat back.

"Anything else?" Anna asked him.

"No. Except we should find out each and every person who made up that grapevine at the airport."

"No need," Emmett said. "Eberhardt told me in private that a buddy in security radioed Garrity and him we were on the way. Juan interviewed him."

The lieutenant held up his palms. "*Nada*. It was a bonehead thing to do, but his intentions were innocent."

Devereaux consulted his watch again, so Anna asked him, "Did you get the copies of our reports all right, Vaughn?"

"Yeah, sure. Appreciate it." Then the detective chuckled sardonically. "Hope nobody takes offense at this, but aren't we beating a dead horse here?"

It was obvious from her look that Freccia didn't care much for Devereaux. "Why?" she asked.

"Well, Daniel Garrity wanted to get back at Adirondack Airlines. He was fed up enough with the company to give notice. He also wanted to kill Oneidas. He confessed to writing a letter that promised as much. We may never really know how he learned Brenda Two Kettles was going to board that flight. But, sure as hell, the man did. I see last Monday night's events transpiring where these two motives intersected, know what I mean?"

Anna didn't. "How'd Garrity get back at the airline by making Two Kettles disappear?"

Sudden irritation showed that Devereaux didn't want to put too fine a point on this. "I'm just saying Garrity meets all the criteria for wanting what happened to happen. But okay, fine, let's go on flogging this pony 'til Kingdom Come. Had Hazen Two Kettles not taken justice into his own hands, Garrity would've flunked that polygraph exam—and you'd see what I'm saying is true."

Gloom settled over the room as, once again, the realization sank in that Hazen might have shut down their most promising lead with a shopping cart in the parking lot of a Sherrill supermarket.

"We're not saying it's untrue, Vaughn," Anna said. "Any rumors that Hazen might be hiding out somewhere on the rez?"

Devereaux took a moment. He'd know that she'd grown up on a small reservation, a self-contained island with its secrets and codes of silence. He finally said. "Some folks believe he survived that cold water and made for Mexico. I think that's bullshit. He's stuck in the mud at the bottom of Sunset Lake."

"Why Mexico?" Anna pressed.

"What do you mean?"

"Why would it occur to Hazen to go to Mexico?"

"I don't know," Devereaux said offhandedly. "The Nation has a lot of enterprises going with Mexican interests. Maybe he ran across some Mexican Indians at the rec hall or something, and they fed him a line of shit about how nice it is down there in Margaritaville. That Mexico talk is just wishful thinking on the part of his family and friends."

"But what if Hazen isn't dead or isn't in Mexico? Are you working that too?"

"We have the Two Kettles's single-wide under surveillance. We've had somebody on it for a week now."

Anna looked across the table at Freccia. "What does the sheriff's office believe happened to the boy?"

"It's a small lake. Search and Rescue believes they should have located the body by now, unless it washed all the way down the creek to Oneida Lake . . ."

Unless . . . unless . . . unless . . . Anna thought she was going to im-
plode from sheer exasperation.

"Water this time of year will kill you in minutes . . ." Freccia let her lack
of a conclusion hang in the air. "But our deputies have been going from
house to house along the drainage. Nothing so far."

The room went quiet again. Then Devereaux said, "When the water
heats up this summer, he'll bob to the surface of Oneida Lake. Wait and see."

Freccia nodded that this scenario was probable.

Anna had already dropped by the Two Kettles's mobile home yesterday
evening to see how Mariana and Belinda were doing. Not well. Too much
had fallen on them too quickly for an already fractured family. She now felt
relief that she and Emmett would be long gone if and when Hazen's remains
reappeared, a relief laced with guilt. She too was beginning to want out.

An errant thought crossed her mind—last evening during that visit,
she'd had no sense or sign that the trailer was under surveillance by the
Oneida Nation P.D. But Devereaux had just insisted that it was.

Emmett's turn to report. But, given his present mood, she skipped over
him to Manoukian. "Leo?"

The agent took a single sheet of steno pad paper from the inner pocket
of his blue blazer and unfolded it. "I wanted to have more for this meeting,"
he apologized, "but I've been tied up on a series of burgs at the airport.
Every time I turn around, something new winds up missing, so they keep
calling me back. Anyway, toxicology protocol on Ms. Two Kettles isn't finished yet, but I bugged the lab for a quick verbal on the findings. The head
toxicologist—"

"Who are *they*?" Emmett interrupted.

Manoukian glanced up from his solitary green page, faintly intimi-
dated. "Pardon?"

"Who got hit at the airport?"

"The Air National Guard Search and Rescue wing," the agent replied.
He referred to his steno page again. "Ms. Two Kettles had a significant
amount of alprazolam in her bloodstream." He noted to Anna, "That's the
Xanax, the anti-anxiety medicine you mention in your report. What her
daughter says she was taking on account of her troubles with the Men's
Council." He then asked Devereaux, "What's that about?"

"Same old story. The ratty trailers flap."

The agent nodded, referred to his page once more. "She also had keta-mine in her system."

"One of the date rape drugs," Freccia said quietly.

"Yeah," Manoukian went on, blushing again, "though the autopsy came up with no indication of sexual violation. Still, ketamine is a fast-acting and powerful sedative. The effects of five cc's of Special K last about an hour, and she hadn't completely metabolized it out of her system at the time of death."

Bellasario slapped the table and grinned at Emmett. "There's the reason for the syringe we found in Garrity's locker!"

"Possibly, though that one was apparently unused," Parker said with little interest, as if he'd already made the assumption that drugs figured in Brenda's abduction.

"Nothing else came up on the blood panel," Manoukian said. "But this is kind of interesting regarding some residue collected during the post-mortem. The tiny burn the victim sustained, you know, the blister between her breasts? Well, the source was hot enough to have scorched her sweater, melting the fibers and leaving trace amounts of black powder."

"Like gunpowder?" Satterlee asked.

"Yeah, but not the modern smokeless kind used in most ammunition," Leo replied. "The tech could think of nothing onboard a commercial plane that could have caused that."

"Me neither," the NTSB man admitted. "But I'll check with Boeing."

Emmett interrupted the roundtable's growing momentum. "What was taken from the Air Guard center?"

Manoukian visibly gathered his thoughts about the burglaries. "Uh, a spool of nylon webbing—"

"What's this have to do with anything?" Devereaux asked.

Emmett held up a hand for him to hush.

"Some switches," Manoukian went on. "I forget what they're called. Chief master sergeant with the unit thinks the burgs are drug-related, kids who'd take anything not nailed down and try to fence it in town. The spool was laid out on a big table, ready for the airmen to make some harnesses."

Emmett sat forward in his chair. "How many burgs?"

"Three."

"When'd the burgs occur?"

"Over the last couple months." Leo paused. "Okay to go on with the rest?"

"Go," Devereaux urged impatiently.

Emmett seemed preoccupied as Manoukian brightly announced some largely useless news, now, that the lab had extracted Garrity's death threat letter from the hard drive of one of the computers confiscated from the Adirondack Airlines maintenance hangar.

Devereaux sat up and clapped the agent on the back in congratulation.

But Garrity was now old business.

And Anna suspected that some new business would fill the remainder of Emmett's and her day. She considered slipping him a note, advising him that she'd kick his ass if he tried to exclude her from that business.

It was the job of the timber cruiser to tramp the forests of Maine on foot and mark trees suitable for harvesting with a splash of orange spray paint. Often he worked on snowshoes, but after a recent thaw the drifts had refrozen solid enough for him to walk on them without breaking through the crust. The day was overcast, and the soft blue snow was easy on his eyes.

He suddenly halted—something had caught his attention. Something high on the slope above him. He was familiar with all the shades of natural green in the woods, and this object was none of them.

He started climbing that way.

He liked to find things, other than trees suitable for cutting. Twice he'd found radio-transmitting collars attached to the necks of deer carcasses and returned them to the Maine Department of Fish and Game. Both times, the department had sent him back a real nice letter, thanking him for taking the trouble. And last winter, a shred of red plastic had caught his eye in a low tree branch. A thin yellow ribbon attached the shred to a note encased in plastic. It said that a third grade class in Cairo, Illinois, was studying the weather and wind currents. They had launched this and twenty-nine other helium-filled toy balloons and would appreciate hearing from the people who found them. When he got home that night, the timber cruiser was amazed to learn from his atlas that the third-graders' balloon had ridden the winds for 1,015 miles. Naturally, he notified them, and they wrote back, every last kid in the class, thanking him. The balloon he'd found had traveled farther than any other that had been located so far. The story was even written up in the local paper.

So, eagerly now, the cruiser dog-trotted the last yards up to the object.

It proved to be tangle of nylon webbing, a shade of green he recognized as being military. A green unlike that of any conifer in the woods.

He tried to pry it out of the drift, but something more was buried underneath. He scooped the snow away with his gloved hands, and the tangle of straps finally came free. Three black-rubber scraps were tethered to a single rope, and that to a ring on the assembly of straps. Dang if he could identify the contraption's purpose. Crimped around one loose end of webbing was a metal cylinder about the size of a D-cell battery. The other end appeared to have been cut as clean as a whistle.

None of this made sense to the cruiser, but it all appeared to be very military to him. Maybe something hush-hush out of an Air Force base. Something the government would like to have back.

At the very least, he expected a nice letter in return.

20

Leo Manoukian met the partners at the Air National Guard center at 4:35. Sunset backlit the hangar, a glow in a drapery of snow clouds that spit flakes now and again. Emmett noted that the Adirondack Airlines maintenance facility stood on the same side of the nearest runway, a few hundred yards distant.

The man-sized personnel door in the Guard hangar swung open. A lank Air Force chief master sergeant wearing a maroon beret strolled out to the chain-link gate and rolled it open. Manoukian had already explained that this non-commissioned officer was on full-time duty here with the reserve unit. And it was apparent that, after a string of unsolved burglaries, he was on familiar terms with Leo. "How you doing, hotshot?"

"Fine, Chief Riley." He introduced the partners.

"Glad to meet you," the non-com said. "Come on in."

Emmett delayed the young FBI agent a moment. "Any sign of forced entry on your burgs?"

"None."

"You have your tech examine the locks for brass shavings?" Evidence that the tumbler pins had been raked with a picklock.

"Every time," Manoukian replied. "Nothing."

Nothing, nothing, nothing. Most cases seemed to yield nothing significant until that sudden crux when the floodgates burst open, and you were swimming in leads with scarcely enough breath to follow up on them. Just once, Emmett wanted an investigation to unfold at a steady, sensible pace.

Anna followed Manoukian inside the hangar, letting Emmett know with a glance that she was worried about him.

Perhaps with reason.

Sometime before three this morning, he'd opened his eyes on a figure standing at the foot of his bed. Not the first time for him; imagined phantoms were the mind's way of sorting out the terrors of a cop's day. And, years ago, Emmett had given his wife at the time, Ladonna, a nasty shin bruise by kicking out at one such specter looming at the foot of their bed. Last night, it'd been his younger brother Malcolm, dead by suicide nearly a decade now. The visitation had been brief, wordless and shocking. Did he believe the experience? *Who knows what you believe at two in the morning.* Emmett then watched old movies until dawn, hoping for sleep that never came again.

Dreams of deceased relatives hummed with *puha*, spiritual power. They were usually warnings, although he felt he was already too exhausted to heap new precautions on those he normally took.

Inside the hangar, Anna was standing between a Pavehawk helicopter and a HC-130 cargo plane. Emmett came to her side just as she asked Chief Riley, "May I see the flight logs for Monday, January sixth?"

"I don't think our birds were airborne that day, ma'am."

"I'd still like to see them," she insisted.

As the chief went off to retrieve them, Anna gestured at the two aircraft and asked, "Are these the reason we're here, Em?"

"I'm not sure," he admitted. "Just had the feeling I needed to check this place out."

She treated him to a playful smile. "Are you having any other feelings I should know about?" Precisely the same tone she'd used last December when she said, *You'll have to catch me this time, Em.* The same questioning, wistful, almost teasing look that had disappointed him before. Yet, it was he who had disappointed her. One night of infidelity. A mere moment. Not a moment of weakness, but rather a moment of impatience with the interminable months, even years, a sexual abuse survivor needs to recover, to embrace intimacy without fear. Still, he was disgusted with himself. And fed up with her endless mixed signals while both of them groped for a solution.

Manoukian was nearby, listening in with interest.

Thankfully, at that moment the chief returned with two log books. "Just like I said, ma'am," he said, standing between the partners to show them the pages, "neither aircraft was up on the sixth of this month."

"What about the seventh?" Anna asked.

"No flights at all until this last Saturday, the eleventh. Our HC-One-thirty was taken up on a profile mission following a phase inspection."

"What's that mean?"

"A flight check after maintenance."

Emmett's forefinger darted to the name that appeared on a page of the transport's log. "This man was the mechanic?"

"That's correct, sir."

The check-offs were signed by S/A J. Eberhardt. *Senior Airman Jason Eberhardt.*

Faking a disinterested calm, Emmett took a second to recall the mechanic and weekend-warrior's schedule. Swing-shift at the Adirondack maintenance operation had already begun, and it was time to talk to Jason again. "Leo, you mind driving over to the Adirondack hangar and borrowing Eberhardt for a few minutes from his supervisor?"

"Okay, but what do I say?"

Emmett lowered his voice. "Nothing. Just haul him over here. Put Eberhardt in the backseat."

He wanted the mechanic to stew in silence.

As Manoukian scurried out, Chief Riley asked Emmett, "Is there some problem?"

"We just need to clarify a couple things," Emmett hedged. Then he asked the chief to show Anna and him where the stolen nylon webbing had been stored.

"That'd be inside our parachute shop." Riley led them into a side room. A large table stood at its center, and against the far wall there was a heavy-duty sewing machine. The chief took a sample of green webbing off the table, flexed it between his hands. "The material comes in long rolls. We cut strips, sew them together with buckles and clips to make parachute harnesses. Right now, we're making cargo webbing for practice supply drops out of our cargo plane next month."

Emmett asked, "And you've been burglarized three times in the last several months?"

"Yes, sir. Ain't it a bitch? We could really use an alarm system, but command says we're not high-tech enough here to warrant it. You know the military."

"What else was taken?"

"Snips, utility knives, and the like. Also a box full of cutters, though I'll be damned if I can figure out what use they'd have out in the civilian world."

"Like knives?"

"No, let me show you." The chief unlocked a metal cabinet and removed a cardboard box. He opened the lid on a dozen metallic cylinders. "These, in particular, are used to sever cargo harness. Smaller ones to cut shroud lines, so a pilot won't get tangled up in his parachute after a water landing."

The personnel door opened, and through the shop doorway Emmett watched Jason Eberhardt and Manoukian enter the hangar. He went out to meet them, trailed by Anna and the chief.

Confronted by the threesome, the mechanic stopped dead. Just as he had last Friday evening in the Adirondack hangar when he found Emmett dressing down the swing-shift crew.

"Come on in," Emmett said to him, his voice purposely cold, even though Eberhardt had been cooperative at their last meeting.

The mechanic slowly advanced, his narrow face losing more color with each step—until it was a dull yellowish white by the time he stood before Emmett. He swiped his lips with a dry tongue, but didn't try to speak.

Manoukian waited behind him, unsmiling.

Emmett let a long silence cut into Eberhardt's last bit of nerve, eyes boring into him, his look nullifying everything the Miranda warning promised. *You will talk,* it said.

Finally, the mechanic cleared his throat and spoke. "How long you been watching me?"

"A while," Emmett lied.

Eberhardt nodded dismally. "Then you know where to look in the birds."

Emmett paused. Now was not the time to admit that he had no idea what *it* was, so he said, "Yeah, save us all some time and narrow things down for us."

"You know," he said bitterly, again revealing a belief that he had been under surveillance. The power of paranoia.

The fastest way to douse this with cold water was to profess ignorance. The case had zigged just when Emmett had expected it to zag. "All right, Jason," he said, "you can help yourself in this fix. Or not. The choice is yours, and I can't think of a bigger one you'll ever make."

"This is all I got to say right now."

"You positive? We're trying to help you here."

"Yeah. Nothing more 'til I got my lawyer present."

"Who's that?"

"Portia Nelson."

Naturally.

Riley looked baffled, although it was clear that his protective instincts for one of his men had been stirred. "What's going on?"

"Hang tight a few minutes, Chief." Emmett then indicated with a nod for Anna to watch Eberhardt while he took Manoukian aside.

The young agent whispered, "What *is* going on, Emmett?"

"Christ Almighty if I know, Leo. And I won't have a clue until we have a look inside any Adirondack or *Aero Mazatlan* planes coming through here. Where do you hold federal prisoners pre-arraignment?"

"Onondaga County Jail."

"Take your time transporting Eberhardt there. And have the deputies drag their feet booking him."

"Keep Eberhardt from calling his attorney for as long as possible?"

"You got it. Make the charge generic but strong enough to let us take direct action in the coming hours."

"Investigation of murder?"

"That has a solid ring to it. You already pat him down?"

Manoukian looked stung by the inference that he might have been sloppy. "Before I ever let him inside my car."

"Good, but do it again after you cuff him. No shame in being overly careful. Watch him every minute, Leo—he may be trying to confess to homicide."

The two men returned to the others. While Manoukian cuffed and re-frisked Eberhardt, Emmett advised Riley, "Tomorrow, Chief, I'll meet with you and your commanding officer. Everything I know, you'll know, but I can't say anything until then without getting my ass in a sling. Fair enough?"

"Fair enough." The chief walked toward the office, turning once to watch as Manoukian ushered a stricken-looking Eberhardt out by the cuffs.

The door slammed shut behind them.

Emmett approached Anna. The search had to begin with any planes inside the Adirondack hangar. Immediately. But before he could say a word, Anna said, "I hope you're not thinking about making a warrantless search."

"Things seem to be moving along just dandy without one. Airplanes have a bad habit of suddenly leaving the ground. I could argue that, plus press the dangerous nature of the crime possibly involved."

"Plus, you don't have a clue what we're searching for," she added caustically. "That won't look good on the affidavit."

"Don't know how I could've gotten along without you this last year," he griped.

"Wish you'd never met me, Em?"

"No. Never that." The emotion in his own voice took him aback. It completely ambushed him, moistened his eyes and overpowered him with the sense that this was the last time he'd ever work with her. *Change the goddamned subject.* "Okay," he pretended to relent, "we go warrant. I'll let you get hold of the judge and explain that we're on to instrumentality used in the Two Kettles's homicide, slant Eberhardt's voluntary admissions toward that." He recited the magistrate's number from memory.

"Thank you."

"We've got to move fast. God only knows who else around the airport might be involved. I'd like to have some idea of what's going on before the *next* suspect cracks."

She borrowed his cell phone and was dialing the federal judge when Emmett heard something. He believed it was coming from the personnel door. He stepped closer. Scratching. It sounded like a dog or a cat wanting inside.

He opened the door. Night had fallen, and it was snowing moderately. Looking straight out, he saw headlights, stationary, glimmering on the mesh of the cyclone fence. Taxi-way and runway lights dotted the darkness beyond. Then something gripped the cuff of his right pant leg and yanked.

Emmett looked down.

Leo Manoukian lay at his feet, eyes shining brassily in the light from inside the hangar. His clinging fist was coated with black. Trying to raise himself up, the agent revealed his shirt front. It too was covered with black, most of it around his belly.

"Anna!" Emmett cried as he seized Manoukian under the arms and dragged him inside. "Anna, quick!" In stronger light, the black liquid became arterial red. Rolling the agent onto his back, Emmett found the five-inch-long slash in his shirt front through which something sharp had savaged Manoukian's abdomen. His weapon was still in his holster. Both his coat and shirt sleeves had been slashed, exposing defensive wounds to his forearms.

He was gasping, possibly convulsing, but tried to say something to Anna, who had fallen on her knees beside him. Nothing but air escaped his gaping mouth.

Drawing his revolver, Emmett ordered, "Direct pressure to his belly."

"I know, I know." She clasped her hands to the bloody shirt. "Leo, did you see—?"

Manoukian gave a fierce shake of his head.

Emmett said to Anna, "Put out the call if I don't come back right away."

Then he went through the door into the night.

Chief Riley took a big compress from a first aid kit and ripped open the package with his teeth. Anna pulled back her hands, and he applied the sterile wad to Manoukian's belly wound. "Got it?" she asked.

"Got it," the chief said.

Emmett had not come back right away.

Running, Anna drew her semi-automatic pistol. Her hands were slippery with Manoukian's blood. Outside, she stood to the side of the open doorway, sweeping her gun sights over the tarmac. She was so afraid of accidentally drawing down on Emmett she kept her forefinger out of the trigger guard.

Steam curled up from her hands—from Leo's blood, still warm.

Clear. No movement except a jet taking off, its thunder blotting out all other noises except her heart.

Manoukian's sedan.

It lay just outside the fence, headlights on. She jogged through the gate, keeping to the vague shadow of the hangar. Halted. Scoured the scene with her pistol. The driver's door faced her. It was wide open, and the dome light revealed the red-splashed bucket seat and floor mat. No blood on the door latch, suggesting that Manoukian had not opened it. His attacker had sprung it for him.

Eberhardt?

He appeared to be gone.

Cautiously, she worked her way around the back of the FBI car. The rear left passenger door was also wide open. Jason Eberhardt had not stabbed Leo. The mechanic—belted in, his wrists still cuffed together behind him— had toppled halfway out of the backseat and come to rest with the top of his head almost touching the pavement. Blood had pooled beneath him and continued to drip out of his sandy-colored hair.

His throat had been slashed.

His eyes were wide, but so glassy Anna felt no need to check for a pulse. Instead, she looked for Emmett's and her loaner car.

It was parked where they'd left it, which meant Parker was on foot.

She sat behind the wheel but kept the door ajar in case she had to return fire. Switching off the dome light, she watched for movement out on the runways. Manoukian's blood was making her hands sticky. She set down her gun and clenched them into fists, to try to stop their shaking, then took hold of the microphone.

Slow. Slow. Fear garbled your words over the air, made your voice sound as if you'd just inhaled helium.

She identified herself. Put out the 10-99. Officer down. Location. Air Guard hangar. Ambulance needed, plus surgical team and technicians on standby at the local hospital. Contact the tower. Shut down flight operations immediately. BIA investigator possibly in foot pursuit on runways. Advise airport police and all backing agencies. "Break," Anna said, pausing so the dispatcher could re-broadcast the emergency traffic.

What have I forgotten?

To keep an eye out.

Still clasping the mike, she stepped from the car and scanned all around with her weapon. Again, no movement.

The dispatcher asked her if she had suspect information.

"Negative," Anna said, irritated, sitting inside again. Had she had such information, she would have said so. "Make sure the hospital has Manoukian's blood type. Severe loss of blood."

"Copy. Be advised, airport ambulance already responding."

And to confirm this, flashing lights started moving from the airport fire station toward Anna along an access road. The microphone and her semi-auto now felt as if they were glued to her hands. She wanted to wipe the congealing blood off them, but had nothing to use.

Snowflakes melted on her cheeks.

Something terrible had not registered until now, although she'd seen it minutes ago. Something ugly. A scenario written in blood. She'd seen from a wavering trail of splatters, pools and smears how Manoukian had staggered from his car, collapsed on the tarmac and finally crawled toward help.

A jetliner blazed down out of the sky and landed on the runway right in front of her.

"Control," Anna transmitted, "you contact the tower yet?"

"We contacted airport police, who promised to do it for us."

"*You* do it—*now.* Planes are still coming in!"

When Emmett first ran out of the hangar and caught sight of the tiny figure loping directly across the runway toward the terminal, he believed that it was Eberhardt. That belief was swiftly dispelled when he looked inside Manoukian's car and saw the mechanic in no condition to do anything. Ever again.

Was he chasing the same figure of a week ago? Unlike last Friday night, there was no ground fog, and the sparse snow did little to dampen visibility.

Still, Emmett watched the skies.

This paid off when, from the corner of his eye, he saw landing lights descending toward him. He expected the pilot to veer away. By now, Anna must have alerted the tower to abort all landings. But the lights got brighter by the second, and the engines became audible. Emmett tried to guess which runway the pilot would use. Possibly the one he was trotting across. No portable radio. He and Anna left their borrowed H.T. off at the Syracuse FBI office to be recharged overnight. He picked up his pace, alternating glances

at the approaching jet and the dark figure that continued to appear inter-
mittently out in front of him.

The jet turned slightly, and Emmett stopped.

Clearly now, the pilot meant to use the runway Emmett was nearing.
Down, down, the United 737 smoothly came, landing lights transforming
the tire-scuffed runway to day. The pilot had almost touched down when
the pitch of the engines rose to a frantic scream and the big bird lumbered
skyward again, banking over Oneida Lake.

Emmett thought he'd seen what the pilot must have. The figure flatten-
ing himself against the runway. Definitely human, possibly male, but nothing else had been apparent about it, except maybe that the runner was fast.
He sprang up and sprinted on toward the terminal.

Emmett followed again.

If this were the same man who'd lured him out onto the runway Friday
night, he'd just enjoyed his own taste of pavement. Whoever he was, whatever he was, he beat Emmett to the crisscrossing airport vehicles. Jet refuel-
ers, electrical power units, lavatory trucks, catering vehicles—all seemed to
be pulling back to the two concourses as if on a single signal. He became
aware of their motor noise as, one by one, the jets idling in their slots were
shut down.

He trotted past a ground controller, who tried to stop Emmett by waving his twin red flashlights. "What're you doing here!"

"Federal police," Emmett shouted in the same split second the controller noticed his drawn revolver. "You see anybody on foot in the last couple minutes?"

"No."

"Any employees run past you?"

"Nobody except you."

Emmett spun completely around, searching. Thankfully, the ambulance
had arrived at the Air Guard hangar across the runway. Closer, a few terminal doors had been flung open, but these were guarded by airport cops who
were checking the IDs of employees streaming in off the tarmacs. A complete evacuation must have been issued. Emmett saw no sign of the runner.
Did that mean he had an identification allowing him to pass through one of
the guarded doors? Emmett had to make a choice quick. If the runner was
an employee, he might have already melted back into the exodus of other

workers. But if his uniform was splattered with Manoukian's and Eberhardt's blood, he couldn't be seen like that.

How, then, might he have gotten inside the terminal to make his way to the street or parking garages beyond?

A tractor towing two baggage trailers sped in front of Emmett. He fell in behind it. The driver entered the baggage processing facility beneath the north concourse. Emmett chased it inside. Hearing his footfalls, the driver stared back at him, scared. Emmett showed him his credentials, motioned for him to stay where he was. Then he approached the last trailer. He shoved aside the weather cover—on luggage. Crouching, he worked the length of the trailer with his revolver, kicking bags aside.

Just luggage.

He searched the second trailer while the driver watched, petrified with fear. A supervisor-type whistled for their attention. "Get out!" he hollered over the whine of the conveyer, which was still going. "Whole terminal is being evacuated to the street!"

Emmett jogged over to him, flashing his creds again.

"You're not the airport police, are you?" the supervisor asked.

"No, federal. You see anybody tear through here?"

"Yeah, some nut case ran up the belt."

"How long ago?"

"Just now. I haven't had time to report it."

Backing up toward the conveyer, Emmett asked, "Get a look at him?"

"Just his legs as he crawled into the baggage claim area."

Emmett climbed onto the belt and dropped to a knee to steady his aim as he trained his revolver on the slatted black skirts at the top of the conveyer. It was his first chance to catch his breath. But the pause was brief. He broke through the rubberized skirting and into the brightness of the baggage claim area. Immediately, he rolled off the carousel onto the floor.

The hall before him was entirely empty. Luggage rode the carousel with nobody to claim it.

Emmett ran for the exit.

Turning the corner, he entered a long corridor. Employees and passengers trooped along it. Their backs were to him, but one figure was unmistakable. The Chez Sky Foods caterer, Adrian Flint, ambled slightly behind the others, his height and white uniform making him stand out.

Emmett holstered his weapon and closed on the fleeing throng. He glanced over the others—and recognized none of them. Except the enormous Flint, who, according to Jason Eberhardt, had been the mechanic's friend, *who sees things from a lot of different angles, who never mentions his childhood.* In short, Jason and he had been connected.

Hearing Emmett, the caterer pivoted and stopped. "Mr. Parker," he said, sounding surprised but also unperturbed. "Any idea what all this is about?"

Emmett glanced over the white uniform. Nothing. Not even a single fleck of red. There had been too much vicious slashing outside the Air Guard center for the attacker to go unspotted. Could Flint have shed a bloodied uniform and put on another?

Emmett had no time for niceties. "Fold your hands behind your neck and interlace your fingers."

Seemingly confused now, the caterer nevertheless complied. "Have I done something wrong?"

Patting him down, Emmett felt an object at waist height under the coveralls. He unzipped the front and found a cell phone clipped to the man's belt. Flint's body was warm, but not warm enough to have just run across half the airport.

"Is there a reason I'm being singled out?" Flint sounded indignant now. His uniform smelled of wood smoke, something Emmett remembered from their previous meeting. So he heated his home with wood, nothing unusual in this country.

"Go ahead and put your hands down," Emmett said.

"Thank you," Flint said sarcastically.

"Where were you when the call to evacuate came down?"

"Backing my truck up to an Adirondack flight to Boston. Am I being accused of something? Are you going to *peck* away at me, Mr. Parker, like you did last week—until I confess to something?"

Emmett was kept from answering by the evacuation announcement over the P.A.

Leaving Flint, he rushed ahead to catch up with the others. Had he missed someone on his first glance-over? Someone flush-faced and breathless?

Where the corridor intersected another, Juan Bellasario had taken up a post between the merging streams of humanity, motioning for the crowd to keep moving. Beside the airport police lieutenant stood Vaughn Devereaux. "Here he is," the tribal detective said, eyes worried. "Parker, is Leo okay?"

Emmett looked to Bellasario. "Got an update from the ambulance?"

"No." The lieutenant raised his pack set to his mouth. "Control," he radioed his dispatch, "you have a status report from the EMTs on the scene?"

"Negative," the dispatcher responded. "Want me to raise them?"

Emmett shook his head, and Bellasario transmitted, "Negative, let them do their work." He hitched his radio to his Sam Browne belt again. "See anything outside, Parker?"

"Yeah. Somebody making for the terminal."

"Did he reach it?"

Emmett's gaze fell on Devereaux again. "What're you doing here?"

"I was waiting for a flight when all hell broke loose. Saw the good lieutenant and thought he might use some more manpower. Know what I mean?"

After his exertions and the cold of the night, the interior of the terminal felt very warm to Emmett. The warmth, perhaps, accounted for the sheen of sweat on Devereaux's upper lip.

"Where were you headed?" Emmett asked.

"Mexican Riviera. Making it a long weekend. Time for a little R&R. But I'll stay now. After what's happened to Leo, you bet I'll stay." The right cuff to his jacket was pulled low over his hand, half-concealing the fingers that held an American Airlines ticket envelope. He had no overcoat, but then again he said he was bound for Mexico.

"What time's your flight?" Keeping his motion natural and fluid, Emmett slipped the envelope out of Devereaux's grasp. It was empty. No tickets. Still, the detective tried to snatch it back, raising his right arm and showing a spot of red on his white shirt cuff that was just beginning to brown from exposure to the air.

Devereaux grinned, as if putting on a show of nonchalance, but then his mouth twisted into a scowl as he studied Emmett's face for what was coming next.

"Stand still, Vaughn," Emmett said calmly. He was reaching out with his left hand to check Devereaux's midriff for a weapon when the detective proved that he had none by jerking Bellasario's pistol from his holster. The lieutenant reacted. Wrongly. He instinctively clasped his own hammerless weapon but didn't deflect the barrel away from his body. The pistol discharged with a deafening blast in the tiled confines of the corridor.

Screams pierced the echoes.

Emmett drew his revolver, but Bellasario slumped across his sight picture, collapsing into his legs and nearly tackling him.

By the time Emmett could stand and raise his handgun again, Devereaux had darted into a cluster of evacuees who, confused by the overlapping echoes, didn't know which way to flee. No safe shot. He bowled through the throng, shouting, "Hit the floor! Everybody hit the floor!" Few obeyed, and he tripped over a briefcase. From the floor he glanced back at Bellasario, who was clasping his side, grimacing, but gestured with his H.T. for Parker to go on.

Devereaux emerged from the far side of the group, half-shuffling as he hung on to a hostage around the neck, a United Airlines captain. He kept the pilot squarely between himself and Emmett's gun. They vanished behind the turn up the corridor to the north concourse.

Emmett rose, jogged to the corner, but went prone again before peeking around its edge at floor level.

Still, Devereaux fired a round at him. It glanced off the wall above Emmett with a wicked-sounding ricochet and crunched into an air-conditioning vent behind him. "Where do you think you can go, Devereaux!"

The man's shout reverberated to Emmett. "It's a bigger world than you think, Parker—if you know how to use it!"

Emmett ventured another glance around the corner. This time Devereaux was preoccupied badgering the pilot up the escalator. The captain wasn't exactly resisting, but he wasn't cooperating either. As soon as the two of them ascended out of view, Emmett got up and gave chase again. He kept to the middle of the corridor—bullets striking a hard surface tend to travel along it. How many firefights now in his career? *Luck is a bank account, and I'm already overdrawn.*

He scrambled up the down-escalator, legs churning beneath him, then lunged onto the floor, landing on his stomach, arms extended and hands tight on his revolver grips.

The pilot's cap lay upturned about ten feet in front of him.

A rhythmic thudding sound at the far end of the boarding room made Emmett rise. *What?* He ran to a flight insurance machine and dropped behind it. Slowly, he peered over the top, past an advertisement that asked— *Are you sure you have all the bases covered?* The thudding was coming from the last gate, where Devereaux was kicking the locked door to the loading bridge while keeping the pilot pinned to the wall at gunpoint.

Gate 22.

Emmett checked a flight info monitor, then his wristwatch. Gate 22, a United flight to Baltimore, scheduled to have departed ten minutes ago. That meant the plane had been ready to leave when evacuated.

Devereaux was looking to the skies for his escape. With the help of a pilot whose body language told Emmett that he wouldn't go easily. At some point, he would fight back.

Emmett had to be there for him when he finally rebelled against his abductor.

Devereaux stopped kicking and rested a moment, bracing his free hand on a thigh and staring out over the boarding room. He was thinking. He had more than enough experience to think under pressure.

Emmett slid down out of sight again.

The sudden absence of a whining noise told Emmett that somebody had found a way to shut down the escalators. Seconds later, the drumming of shoes on the now motionless stairs and the jingling of keys told him that the airport cops were advancing. Before he got shot from behind, Emmett crawled into the seating area at the nearest gate and started closing on Devereaux by wriggling under the banks of connected plastic chairs.

A pistol blast was punctuated by a loud *thunk!* Splinters of orange plastic flew above Emmett. It'd been a blind shot from Devereaux, one Emmett saw no need to answer. He slid quietly over the linoleum on his belly, only to abruptly stop and listen. More shoe and key noise. Why did most cops insist on dangling a wad of tinkling keys off their Sam Browne belts? Might as well wear a cow bell. He sensed that several cops were slipping into the room behind him. This was confirmed by two more shots from Devereaux's direction.

All went silent to Emmett's back.

There was a tinkling crash of glass ahead of him, followed by the clatter of shoes over the shards. He reared up, no more than enough to peek over the tops of the chairs—Devereaux had somehow broken out most of a floor-to-ceiling window and was pushing the pilot through a saw-toothed opening. Snow flew inside, swirling around the tribal detective, parting his jacket to reveal the blood dappling his shirtfront. Manoukian's blood, no doubt.

At last, Emmett had a clear shot, however brief.

He rocketed upright and squeezed his trigger twice.

Catching sight of Emmett, Devereaux was reeling to return fire when at least one of the .357 slugs hit their mark. He tumbled back against the window frame, arms flailing open. But he held on to Bellasario's pistol. He also managed to stay on his feet before hurling himself through the jagged hole in the window.

To let Emmett know that he wasn't finished, he reached around a broken edge of glass and pumped three shots into the boarding room.

They came nowhere near Emmett, who held up his left hand toward the cops behind him to stay where they were. From behind a newspaper rack, one of Bellasario's sergeants waved that he was more than willing to do so.

Taking two deep breaths, Emmett ran for the shattered window.

He couldn't believe that Devereaux and the pilot had leaped fifteen feet to the tarmac. Blinking against the snowfall, he leaned outside, first craning all around for a sign of the two men. Not seeing them, he glanced down at the pallet loader an employee had parked just below the window, giving Devereaux a platform as long as the loading bridge itself. At the crookneck on its far end, the detective had wrenched back the rubberized seal that joined the bridge to the fuselage of a United 737. No doubt gaining access to the plane's passenger-loading door.

Emmett dropped the five feet down to the bed of the pallet loader and inched toward the aircraft. The windows of the 737 were lit, a string of amber beads through which he looked for Devereaux and the pilot.

He took stock of his ammunition. Four rounds remaining in his cylinder. A speed loader with six more cartridges in the flap pocket to his coat. Bellasario's pistol had looked like a 9mm. Most had fourteen-round magazines. Devereaux had expended about half of that.

Emmett thought he could see an elbow through the forward-most window. But by the time he got to the weather seal, the glimpse of one of the two men was gone. He wedged himself through the space between the fuselage and the seal. As expected, the door was secured against him, the handle smudged with bloody prints. From the other side came a commotion, shouting. Emmett held his left palm to the cold skin of the plane, feeling movement within. The door was being jarred from inside.

The pilot had made his move.

Gritting his teeth, Emmett pounded his fist on the door.

The pucker of a bullet erupted from the metal skin. It sprouted a few inches away from his face with a sound like a BB hitting a tin can. Emmett held his spot, although he stooped slightly. Waiting for another bullet. It came a second later. Precisely where Emmett had anticipated: to the right of the door. Devereaux was a cop. He knew that cops stood to the side of a door when expecting gunplay.

Suddenly, the door parted a crack. Before it might shut again, Emmett pocketed his revolver, thrust his fingers into the narrow opening and pried. The door began to give toward him, grudgingly. He peered inside on a chaotic view. A struggle over something with a red handle. Devereaux was waving the pistol around but obviously had no intention of punching a hole in his only ticket out of Syracuse—the pilot, who was being pushed up against the door while grappling with the detective for control of a fire axe. Both men were slipping like novice ice-skaters on the deck, which was awash with blood. Devereaux looked punch-drunk, which made sense when Emmett noticed the red flowing over his shoe and onto the deck.

But the wounded cop was still deadly.

Where the hell were the airport cops?

Emmett pried on the door with both hands. Finally, it jerked open enough for him to thrust his upper body inside—just as Devereaux ripped the axe out of the pilot's hands. He won the axe but dropped the pistol in the process. The captain ducked out of sight to retrieve it. Emmett fumbled for his revolver and was awkwardly jamming the muzzle through the opening when he saw the axe blade swinging at him.

Time slowed. Still, there wasn't enough of it to get out of the way. Emmett was pinned by the door, his left arm tangled uselessly behind him. But there was just enough time to avenge himself before the blade bit into his chest. He got off two shots—in Devereaux's face—before he felt the blow. The impact was without pain. But an acute loneliness cut through the shock. Never had he felt so alone. It would have been intolerable, except for the blackness that swiftly followed.

21

EACH BANGING SOUND SEEMED to burst a little pocket in Hazen's brain, leaving a blank stickiness that blocked thoughts before he could finish them. His skull was packed with half-finished images, like confetti. Aunt Brenda. His stash under the straw bale. Daniel Garrity. The chase in the old Chrysler through the foggy night. Charley, Jerrold and Doc. All jumbled together in ways that made no sense. Auntie smoking a joint as she fell through the sky. Charley Ketchum, dressed like a Haudenosaunee warrior, cooking a rabbit over an open fire in the Two Kettles's trailer. Garrity being splattered, not by the shopping cart but by the Chrysler speeding through the fog.

Light penetrated Hazen's eyelids. He wanted to crook his elbow over them so he might fall asleep again, but he couldn't lift his arms. Something was pinning them against his sides. The light slowly roused him to a consciousness he didn't want.

The banging stopped, replaced by sounds like somebody sawing wet wood. Hazen realized that the sounds were his own breaths flowing over his swollen lips, and each inhalation also reminded him that he had broken ribs. Exploring his teeth with the tip of his tongue, he found that some of them were loose. Others were chipped and left with razor-sharp edges.

He suspected that he might be back in juvie. But, the truth was, they never beat you there. Another kid might, but fights in the hall didn't last long enough to leave you as wasted as Hazen felt. And afraid.

He struggled to open his eyes. The lashes felt as if they'd been Krazy Glued together. But at last he looked out on a world that fluttered like a broken film. Hazy, flickering shapes teased him, but gradually a large man in coveralls came into focus. He was stooped over the floor, a claw hammer in his fist.

Johnny Skyholder.

Relief washed over Hazen until he remembered that Tawiskalu, who'd beaten him within inches of his life, lived next door in the duplex. Running was out of the question. He couldn't even lift his head off the pillow. Glancing downward, he saw that he was not in the filthy sleeping bag atop the cot. He was strapped to Johnny's bed.

"Sorry for the noise," Skyholder said, taking a nail from the corner of his mouth. "But I want to fix the floor before I go to work . . ." The sheet of plywood Tawiskalu had burst up through. How many nights ago? Hazen had no sense of time. Leastways, normal time. He'd already been in Johnny's place forever. Normal time was for people who hadn't murdered anybody.

"They let me miss work sometimes." Johnny came to the side of the bed on his knees. "They're real nice that way." He took a cloth from a bowl of water on the floor. His hammy fist wrung most of the water out of it, then gently applied the wet coolness to Hazen's face. The boy flinched, but after a moment the cloth felt good.

"Poor guy," Johnny cooed, the dull sweetness in his eyes blurred by his horn-rimmed glasses. "But I told you, didn't I? Told you not to let Tawiskalu know you were here."

"I didn't, Johnny," Hazen croaked.

"Who did then?"

"You did."

Skyholder lowered the cloth from Hazen's face. "I didn't want to. But you can't keep secrets from him. He pecks away at you until you just got to tell. But I also told him not to hurt you."

"He called you something. I can't say it right. Aunt Brenda tried to teach me, but my tongue never got it right."

"Thaluhyawaku," Johnny said flawlessly, just like Aunt Brenda had.

"Yeah."

"That's my Oneida name."

"The Good Twin." Hazen paused, thinking. "Is Tawiskalu your twin brother then, Johnny?"

The man nodded.

"But he called me a redskin. He doesn't like Indians."

"Because he's not."

Hazen's head ached with confusion again. "You told me you're full-blood Oneida."

"I am." The woodstove ticked as it began to cool down, and Johnny swung around to feed another log into it. "Tawiskalu says oil and water can come from the same well, but they never mix. Same way with good and bad blood. One twin gets all the good blood and one twin gets all the bad blood—that's just how it goes sometimes, okay? Even if the papa's Indian and the mama's white, one twin can get the Indian blood and the other twin can get the white blood. Same way one brother gets blond hair and one gets brown."

Hazen had never heard anything even remotely like this, but Johnny seemed so sure about it. "Nobody's all good or all bad."

Johnny looked taken aback. "Who told you that?"

"Therapist. White lady probation sent me to."

Skyholder's homely face brightened. "I go to therapy too. Been going for years and years. Stopped me from fighting. I used to fight a lot in bars, get in trouble." To prove this, Johnny popped out his front teeth and showed the dental bridge to Hazen before reinserting it in his mouth with a click. "I don't drink no more. Fight neither."

"See what I mean?" Hazen pointed out.

"What?"

"You're not all good. You used to fight and drink. Even if you quit, you used to do bad things."

Hazen could tell that his words weren't making a dent. He couldn't understand how something so obvious could fail to register on a brain that, judging from the size of Johnny's long skull, was sizable. But there were more pressing things to worry about. "Where's Tawiskalu now?"

"Sleeping," Johnny replied indifferently. But then he added with emphasis, as if it were vital for Hazen to understand, "I was born first, you know. I got the paper to prove it. Born seven minutes before Tawiskalu busted right out of Mama and killed her."

All this pointless chatter made Hazen squirm. He tested the straps. There were two sets, one tight around his chest and arms and one around his ankles. But they wouldn't give. "Get me out of here, Johnny," he begged, his voice breaking like he was thirteen again. "Take me away in your van."

"Oh, nothing doing. Tawiskalu won't let me."

"Why not? What's he care about me?"

Johnny drove another nail into the floor, making Hazen's head throb with each blow of the hammer. "He says you need to tell him something before he lets you free."

"Like what?"

"He wouldn't say. He's that way sometimes. Stubborn. Me, I'm not stubborn." Johnny stood, towering over the bed. "Did he ask you something before he hit you?"

Frantically, Hazen glanced around the shabby room, trying to remember. His head felt empty and dry, like a gourd. "My aunt," he abruptly said. "He wanted to know where Aunt Brenda was going when she fell out of the sky. I told him New York City, but that wasn't good enough for him."

"Where'bouts in the city was she going?"

"I don't know, Johnny. She didn't say."

The man nodded reflectively. "Did she take lots of trips?"

"Not lots, but some."

"How many?"

"Two trips before this one, both for a couple of days."

"And didn't say where she was going those times too?"

"Never," Hazen replied. "It was kind of weird. I mean, usually she'd tell us even if she was just going to the market."

"How'd she get to the airport?"

"What do you mean?"

"Well, Belinda smashed up your car Thanksgiving night."

The boy knew he should feel suspicious. Perhaps he should even shut up. But he sensed that Johnny genuinely wanted to help him deal with Tawiskalu. "How d'you know so much about us, Johnny?" he asked, sounding more disappointed than distrustful.

"I don't. I just heard about the cops chasing your cousin that night."

Hazen pressed the tip of his tongue to a chipped tooth—it hurt with each breath he took. "Somebody picked Aunt Brenda up in a gold Beemer."

Johnny had sunk into his chair and was quietly rocking. "You see who?"

Hazen probed his memory, but it was as dark as both those winter evenings. Yet, there was the distant flaring of a dome light as Aunt Brenda put her overnight bag in the backseat and sat up front, revealing a red-headed white lady behind the wheel. "A white woman," he finally answered.

"You know her name?"

"No. But she had red hair."

Johnny stopped rocking. "You think maybe she was a witch too?"

"My aunt wasn't no witch."

"It's all over the rez—she was."

"Says who, Johnny?"

"I'm sorry, but that's what I hear. She put a spell on her husband to get him to marry her, on account she wasn't much to look at. And she was witching the Nation Rep when her power got turned back on her. That happens sometimes. Your evil comes back on you—that's what I always try to tell Tawiskalu. Your auntie got caught up in some terrible evil. How else you explain her falling out of the sky? She had to do something real bad to die like that."

"Auntie liked the old ways," Hazen cried, "but she was no witch!" His own shout left him hurting all over. And dizzy.

"Okay, okay," Johnny said. "Don't go upsetting yourself. I'm just saying women can do mean things. Like my Nanas. They did mean things all the time. I loved 'em both, but they did lots of mean things to me. But in the end I loved 'em. I loved white Nana so much I even touched her in her coffin, like they asked me. They made me kiss my fingers and touch 'em to white Nana's face. The skin was all hard. Like a plastic doll. But I did it."

Tawiskalu had said something about his Nanas, too, but the inside of Hazen's head was now a fiery mess. "Can I have some water?"

"Oh sure." Johnny got up for the kitchenette, and the rocker went on rocking as if occupied by a ghost.

Hazen would rest a little, then get out of here. He'd figure out a way to deal with the straps and put this creepy duplex far behind.

"Have some more barbs." Johnny returned with a jelly jar of water, and

Hazen willingly extended his tongue. The man placed two pills on it, and the boy swallowed them with water.

And instantly regretted taking them.

Pills were now a habit. Aunt Brenda had warned him this would happen. Now he would be groveling and helpless when Tawiskalu awoke.

But, after a while, he felt so good. So very, very good. Like nothing could ever hurt him again.

Anna was standing in the Intensive Care Unit waiting room at Community General Hospital in Syracuse when a far door opened and a tiny, hunched woman came out on the arm of an orderly. She moved arthritically, but smiled as she chatted with the young black man. Emmett Parker's mother gave no sign that she had just left a son who was existing on mechanical ventilation and deeply submerged will. The axe blade had collapsed his left lung and bruised his heart. He had lost a great deal of blood.

But the little Comanche woman from Lawton, Oklahoma, went on chatting to the orderly. The Comanche were big on face. Maintaining it, never losing it. Almost oriental in how they valued it. Celia Parker thanked the orderly, let go of him and reached for Anna's hand. Her grasp, despite the curved fingers and swollen knuckles, was firm. Wrapped around her palm and wrist was a rosary: Anna could feel the warm beads. "You must be Anna," she said.

"Yes, Mrs. Parker." She hoped her numbness of the past eighteen hours would not be construed as indifference. She had not cried, slept, eaten or drunk in all that time, just floated through an endless series of investigative chores, waiting for the other shoe to drop. The first shoe had been Leo Manoukian. His injuries were so massive, direct pressure would never have been enough. He bled out and died on the way to the hospital. The paramedics who transported Emmett had been no more optimistic about his chances. The doctors still weren't. Lieutenant Bellasario was the luckiest of the three to have run afoul of Vaughn Devereaux: The bullet had missed his spine and only nicked his gall bladder. But now all her dreams of late made perfect, undeniable sense—Emmett had wound up on the brink of death with an axe stuck in his chest like a splinter off the shattered benches in the college ice rink.

It was all too unnerving to really think about, but now she was close to accepting the fact she had a new investigative tool. A horrible one she would never share with her white supervisors or coworkers, one that might make her dread sleep in the coming years. She now had *dreams*.

Celia Parker said with the same, unwavering smile, "Let's sit."

They sat. The old woman continued to grasp her hand, sharing the rosary with her. "That nice young man I was talking to was in the Army at Fort Sill . . ." The orderly, she meant. "Emmett and Malcolm started out at the Fort Sill Indian School just outside the post. But they were a handful, and the BIA kicked them both out for running away all the time and other things. Did you know that?"

"No," Anna said.

"Oh yes. They'd shimmy down a drain pipe. Like little monkeys, the two of them. And go into town all night. I was lucky to get them in the Indian mission on the other side of the fort. Near Anadarko. I knew the priest. He wasn't so sure about taking them. Word got around. But in the end Father Gerhart was very fond of Emmett. He even wanted him to become a priest."

Anna was comforted by all this. She'd never been sure how much, if anything really, Emmett had told his mother about her. She was afraid he'd said too much, especially lately when things had not been going well. But the old woman was treating her as a confidante, and Anna felt her numbness start to melt away. But was she ready for that on no sleep?

"I could never keep my boys," Mrs. Parker went on. Months in their relationship had passed before Emmett had told Anna his parents had divorced when he was young, and his father was deceased. "I was a housekeeper for some well-to-do folks in Lawton, and the boys could stay with me only once in a great while. And then I had to keep them quiet in the big house. It was such a long bus ride up to Anadarko in those days . . ." She let go of Anna's hand and went through the rosary, first in Latin, then in what was possibly Comanche. Anna let the old woman withdraw for a while. For the first time, Celia Parker was radiating anxiety, and Anna feared being infected by it. So much to do. Emmett would expect her to carry on.

Through the tinted windows behind them, the sun was going down. Strange how, with a precious life hanging in the balance, you wondered every minute if it was the last sun to set or rise on that life. You truly understood time, time passing, no time at all. The sun loomed, menaced.

While Mrs. Parker droned on in the sacred tongue of Rome, Anna sang to herself in her own language:

> *Come to the fearful, Sun of the Sky,*
> *Make ready your powers, Sun of the Sky,*
> *Make ready to fight with death, to lose or win.*

If he died now, she would be dogged with a sense of failure for as long as she lived. She would have failed at her first attempt at love, failed to manage adversity in an affair of the heart. She'd always assumed there'd be time to repair the damage to their relationship both of them had caused. Time would heal their love wounds. And now this.

Mrs. Parker put on her smile again. "I never really had my Emmett with me. Malcolm, at the end. But never Emmett. See, Anna, when he was a baby, I got tuberculosis. That's when my husband began to lose interest, I think . . ." Another moment of visible pain, again put aside. "My mother raised Emmett at first . . ." She laughed. "Oh, so old-fashioned, my mama. She carried him round in a cradleboard for three years. That's why he learned to talk late, I think. And when you talk late, you read late. But in the end, he turned out smart. Both boys did, like their papa."

Anna saw a younger Celia riding the bus to Anadarko to visit her sons, whom divorce and racial bureaucracy had removed from her. It was too much for Anna. Too evocative of her own mother's burdens. Her numbness was crumbling into heartache. "I've got to go, Mother Parker. Visit the girlfriend of the FBI agent who was killed."

"Tell her I'll pray for her. And don't be too sad, Anna. I'm going to have my boy home again. You come down to Lawton if you like, and we'll all be together."

Anna kissed her. She had not come to see Emmett. After the horrors of last night, she'd vowed not to see him until he awakened from his sedation. If he never awakened, she knew he wouldn't want to be remembered in his present state.

Face.

22

A SLIVER OF WINTER-WHITE moon hung over the roof of the Iroquois longhouse. It was the final thin crescent of the lunar cycle. Here, a quarter mile back from Territory Road, masked from prying eyes by willow thickets, stood the last stronghold of Oneida spirituality. The clapboard building reminded Anna of both a steeple-less country church and a railroad box car. It looked old. The roof was sway-backed and the paint was curling off the walls. Orange light flickered through windows as she parked beside a Cadillac Seville. Inside it, a uniformed tribal cop sat up out of a bored slouch and motioned for her to go on into the longhouse.

There was risk in responding alone to this late night invitation to the Oneida Nation. Risk to Anna's career. While careerism was the last thing on her mind right now, she had a sense that this might not be true in the coming months—when she might have nothing left but the job. In moments now, she found herself peeking over the horizon into a world without Emmett Parker.

Cochran, the Syracuse SAC, had assumed the reins, promising to take an ultrasound to the investigation. And possibly killing the baby in the process, she felt. He wasn't aware that she'd driven onto the reservation tonight. And there was even talk of a manager from D.C. flying in to direct the circle of cases that began with the death of Brenda Two Kettles and had widened to include a half dozen casualties, including Emmett. That manager would tolerate no freelance activities from lowly field agents.

But she had decided to come.

Inside the longhouse, a stocky man in a graphite-colored business suit knelt at the hearth, adding chunks of split wood to a blazing pile of kindling. There were two fireplaces, one at each end of the single room, and the only illumination came from the one he'd lit.

This man had asked her to come alone.

And she had because Emmett had convinced her of the need to take career risks.

Hearing Anna cross the wooden floor, the man turned and rose, light on his feet. "Anna," he said with a quiet smile, "thanks for coming on such short notice." Everything he did and said was smooth. Not unctuous, but smooth. That was to be expected of the CEO of what might eventually become a Fortune 500 company, especially if the land claim was enforced instead of settled. With an MBA in business from Harvard and a law degree from Yale, the Nation Representative was anything but a backwater rez politico.

He gave her a quick, unaffected embrace.

"Hello, sir."

"How's Emmett?"

That gave her pause. Not from his using the first name of a man he'd never met. She thought she was going to relive the impact of seeing Emmett torn and unconscious in the back of an airport ambulance. That's all it really was so far—an impact, a fiery blow that had cauterized any gush of emotion. "Not well."

The Representative looked genuinely distressed to hear it. "And the airport police lieutenant?"

"Better. He'll recover."

He checked on his fire, the light reflecting off his broad face. "Mice chewed through the wiring, shorting everything out. I hadn't realized the place was in this kind of shape. Breaks my heart. I'll get some people out here to make things right." He glanced around the room. "When I was a boy, this was the center of our world. It'd shrunk down to this, Anna. The new moon is just a couple of days away. Back then, that was the signal for all of us to gather in this old longhouse for a week . . ." He gestured at the dusty benches along all the walls. "Women and children there. Men there and there. The middle of the room was left open for dancing. New moon brings in our Midwinter ceremony. Your people have something like that?"

"Something," she muttered, distracted. A shiver had just gone through her, making her suddenly wonder if Emmett had passed. But she'd made up her mind that phoning the hospital each time she had an errant chill was out of the question. Wittingly or not, Emmett and she had said their good-byes the other morning on Sunset Lake, while a Search and Rescue boat dragged the bottom for Hazen's body.

"We gathered here to renew our dreams," the Representative went on. "And it amazes me how far we've come since those days. We were on the ropes by the mid-seventies. Down to thirty-two acres and an unbreakable cycle of poverty. Waiting to vanish. How very, very far we've come since the low point." But his expression was anything but gratified. "Yet, tonight, I feel as if, after all the effort, all the pulling ourselves up by our own bootstraps, we've lost sight of our dreams. And some of those dreams have turned into nightmares."

Anna said nothing. She was still waiting for him to reveal the purpose of this summons.

"Vaughn Devereaux," he said simply, then watched her.

Emmett had taught her to show nothing; silence had a purgative effect on most people.

"We took him in, Anna, trusted him to protect us and our interests. We expected him to do this legally and honorably. We—" He cut himself off in sudden consternation. "Are you absolutely convinced he murdered your fellow agent and that mechanic?"

"Yes." Then she offered no more than what the FBI public affairs officer would release in the morning. "DNA test results aren't in yet, but Manoukian's and Eberhardt's blood types were found on Devereaux's shirt, slacks and shoes." His personal car had been found in a long-term parking lot not far from the Air National Guard center, his service weapon in the glove box, probably so security wouldn't hassle him after the hit as he moved through the airport, trying to get back to his car by a roundabout route.

"And the murder weapon?" the Representative asked.

"Technicians found a knife . . ." They had retraced Devereaux's probable path across the airport with a metal detector. A switchblade had been
thrust into the ground of a grassy area between the Guard center and the
runway. "There were traces of blood on it, plus a partial of Devereaux's
palm print."

Staring into the fire, he compressed his lips. "What was he doing? Was
he out of his mind?"

No, Anna thought to herself, *the tribal detective was carefully guarding something.* Although a search of each and every Adirondack and *Aero
Mazatlan* aircraft in the U.S. had yet to reveal that *something.* "He met with
us yesterday at the Syracuse FBI office," she explained. "Leo Manoukian
brought up the burglaries at the Guard facility. Later, Devereaux was obviously in the area when Manoukian transported the mechanic from Adirondack's hangar to us."

"Meaning, he felt something important to him at the airport was being
jeopardized?"

"So it'd appear," she said.

"Narcotics?"

"We just don't know. The sniffer dogs with Customs didn't come up
with any."

"Are you aware that we worked like crazy to save our regional airline?"

"No."

"Well, we did. We brokered the merger between *Aero Mazatlan* and
Adirondack. More than a business deal. We're trying to reestablish the ancient trade route between us and the indigenous peoples of Mexico. Just
thought you should know. And it infuriates me, Anna, to think that route
might be criminally abused." The Representative inhaled deeply, eyes shut.
"The U.S. Attorney General held out a hand of friendship to me and the Nation by sending two native cops to help defuse this mess." He looked
steadily at Anna again. "That forged a covenant chain between us, Anna,
and I have no intention of breaking it."

A covenant chain, she'd read, was a beaded wampum belt signifying an
alliance.

The headlights of an approaching car passed over the windows. A sedan
swung around to park away from the other two cars. The lights went out,

and a trim figure hurried from the Lexus and across the frozen mud of the lot toward the entrance to the longhouse.

Moments later, Christopher White Pine entered.

"Chris," the Representative said. His tone was polite but also ambiguous, enough so Anna had no idea if his special assistant was about to be white-washed or made a scapegoat.

"Good evening, sir," White Pine said, although his stare never left Anna, letting her know that she was a surprise. He waited for the Representative to explain her presence.

He didn't. "Come closer to the fire, Chris." More pointed ambiguity? "You look chilled."

"Thank you." Along the way, White Pine halted beside Anna and said quietly, "So saddened to hear about Leo. Was he married?"

"No." And Linda Freccia had gone to her parents in Rhode Island for a few days before the funeral.

"How's Emmett doing?"

"Still critical," she replied emotionlessly.

White Pine continued on to the hearth, and the Nation Rep rested a hand on his shoulder. Why these after-hours summonses to the longhouse? White Pine had already told her that his boss liked to frame his chats in traditional settings. He also had a flair for the dramatic. "Chris, I'm the last guy to Monday-morning quarterback. Hindsight can't be confused with foresight. Still, we've got to explain why the devil we ever hired Devereaux."

"Of course."

"And I can't very well hurl the selection committee's recommendation back in their faces. Both you and I acted on it."

"Yes, sir, we did."

"So, where'd the process fail us?"

"I've been asking myself that nonstop for the past twenty-four hours. And I don't have an answer. We contracted with one of the best backgrounding agencies in the East—"

"Which one?" Anna interrupted.

"Mid-Atlantic Investigations in Albany," White Pine said without batting an eye. "They did the whole nine yards, everything you could ask for in a comprehensive background check—polygraph, on-site interviews with former employers, teachers, pals, even Vaughn's high school girlfriends."

"And the consensus?" the Representative asked.

"Vaughn had a history consistent with that of a detective who'd worked undercover Narcotics for a considerable period of time. We were cautioned to expect some background problems." White Pine's gaze shifted to her again. "As you know, Anna, undercover work is dirty business. Full of moral compromises. But it was Mid-Atlantic's opinion that nothing in Vaughn's past precluded us from hiring him. And we were bringing him onboard to work the drug problem on the rez, plus for his expertise in investigating money-laundering schemes—always a big worry when you run a casino. We weren't looking for a Boy Scout, sir."

"Understood, Chris."

Anna began to sense that she'd made a mistake in coming. This might be dog-and-pony show, rehearsed earlier and meant to sidetrack an unflinching FBI look into how Devereaux had wound up a detective with the Oneida Nation P.D.

"I'll admit I never went through the full hiring report," the Representative said. "We've got thousands of employees."

"Thousands," White Pine parroted.

"But damned if I recall anything about a DEA investigation, do you?"

"Sir?"

"Yeah, Chris. DEA investigated Devereaux for sales of unreported drug seizures while he was with NYPD. Were you aware of this?"

White Pine had stopped blinking. "I was, sir. No secret about that. It was one of those undercover issues we had to take a hard look at. A white detective, already convicted of drug trafficking, trying to reduce his sentence by sucking up to the DEA, accused Vaughn of this. No arrest was ever made, and even my DEA contact admitted the accusation might've been racially motivated." The fire was finally roaring, and White Pine took a step back from the hearth. "You sure all this wasn't in my memo to you, sir?"

"I'm sure. Anna, tell your superiors I'm opening all the tribal offices to them. Examine and audit what you want—without subpoena. Together, we'll find out what Devereaux was up to. All I ask in return is that you personally oversee the process. It'll be easier on the feelings of my people if a native investigator heads up the effort."

"That'd be up to my bosses," she said.

"Understood. Still, it isn't much for them to give in exchange for our complete cooperation."

White Pine ended a moment in which he'd seemed deeply distracted. "Sir, I agree completely with a spirit of openness, but—"

"Good, Chris," the Representative cut him off. "I need a united front on this." He turned to Anna. "I'm reminded of a news story I saw on TV—how the FBI could've been spared all the grief that special agent who was a Soviet mole gave them by just administering more polygraph exams in-house."

"That's true, sir."

"Then I think an across-the-board polygraph is in order. In the spirit of complete openness, I think you and I should go first, don't you, Chris?"

"Whatever you say, sir," White Pine relented. "I have no problem with that."

Morning came, and Johnny Skyholder awoke to find himself still in his rocking chair. His back and shoulders were a little sore, otherwise he felt okay after spending much of the night sitting up. How much of the night he didn't know. He never quite knew. There were inexplicable gaps in the fabric of his time, and his mind grew fuzzy when he tried to think about them. He vaguely remembered calling in sick to work, although it was Hazen Two Kettles who was sick, too sick to be left alone.

The room was cold, but Johnny didn't want to disturb the boy with the noise of building a fire.

Hazen was still asleep, strapped to the bed, his swollen lips parted and his pink Mohawk limp against the brown stubble sprouting on the rest of his scalp. The boy was sweating. He'd sweated heavily last night, but maybe now his fever was breaking, and he'd feel better.

It hurt to look at the boy, so thin and sick-looking, his face lumpy and purple.

Gladly, Johnny would let Hazen go, except that he was afraid of Tawiskalu. He'd always been afraid of his brother, even when they were little and being bounced from one Nana to the other because nobody really wanted the two of them, with their mother dead at childbirth and God only knew where their papa was, maybe all shacked up drunk with that Ojibwa woman again, slowly dying of drink.

Hazen moaned, dreaming.

He looked so unhappy Johnny decided there'd be no harm in awakening him. Stiffly, he rose from the rocker, crumpled some newspaper and stuffed it in the fire box along with a couple of pine cones. The fire was soon crackling and popping.

The boy moaned again. This time it was more like a scared whimper.

There was no reason to treat Hazen this way. No way to treat any child, Indian or otherwise. His eyes began burning with anger, and he wanted to hit Tawiskalu, drive him to the floor and keep hitting and hitting him until he died.

His hands fumbling with rage, Johnny dug the cellular out of his coverall pocket and grabbed the phone book atop the pile of old magazines beside him. He looked up the number for the Turning Stone Resort and dialed. "Miss Turnipseed," he whispered, so Hazen wouldn't hear. Tawiskalu too. He despised the Indian woman, railed against her every chance he got: *She'll be the death of us unless we put her out of commission.*

Again the clerk put him through to the agent's room, and again there was no answer except a mechanical voice telling him how to use the voicemail.

"Listen, lady," Johnny said, hushed, "it's me again. You got to understand I'm the good one. He killed our mama coming out of her, and I took her head up into the sky and turned it into the sun and stars and moon. I put the lights up in the sky. I don't make poisonous things. I make nice things. Pretty things. We're night and day, him and me . . ." Johnny ground his yellowed teeth together in the urgency to make it clear as glass that he and Tawiskalu were nothing alike. As different as day and night. "He's got the Two Kettles boy. I'd let him go, but I'm scared. I'm doing my best, but I need some help. I want to stop him, but he's so mean. Next time, *be there* when I call. I'll call after work tomorrow morning, and maybe we can figure out what to do. Good-bye for now."

Disconnecting, Johnny saw that Hazen was staring at him. "Who you talking to?" His voice sounded old, as old as his Oneida Nana's voice the howling night she died.

Johnny didn't think he'd had been awake to hear his mention of Turnipseed. He didn't want Hazen to know, in case Tawiskalu beat the boy for information again. "My girl," Johnny finally said, smiling at his own joke. He had no need of a girlfriend. His plumbing was no good, the doctor in Michigan had said. It'd never be good.

Beep . . . beep . . . beep.

Johnny turned off his wristwatch alarm. "Time for my medicine. You want some too, Hazen?"

"I . . ." The boy shook his head, drunkenly. "I don't know."

"It'll help you rest," Johnny said on the way to the kitchenette, digging the pill container out of his pocket. "That's what you need. Rest." He filled a jelly glass with water, then swallowed the capsules. Returning to the bed, he offered two reds to Hazen. The boy's mouth opened like a baby bird's, and he accepted them on his tongue.

After he'd washed the capsules down, Hazen said pathetically, "I messed myself again, Johnny."

He stroked the boy's damp forehead with a hand. "That's okay, Hazen. I'll clean you up. No big thing. That's what I do for a living. Clean things up."

"But it *smells.*"

"Not so bad."

Johnny had no sooner finished with Hazen than his cell phone rang. For a confused second, he thought it might be Turnipseed calling, but then he recalled that he'd been told never to give his cell number out. "Hello."

"Did you take your medicine, Thaluhyawaku?" the Voice asked.

"Yes, just a minute ago."

"Are you sitting?"

Johnny eased down into the rocker. "Yes."

"Are you comfortable?"

"Yes, I'm comfortable."

"Warm, safe and relaxed?"

"Uh-huh." Strange, how swiftly the Voice could make Johnny drowsy. He could feel his heart, which had been going fast on account of Tawiskalu treating Hazen so mean, begin to beat slow and steady.

"Are you warm and comfortable?"

"Yes," Johnny muttered, the lids drooping down over his eyeballs.

"Go back home to Michigan."

"Which home?"

"White Nana's house. Can you go back there?"

"Don't want to," Johnny said, jerking his head from side to side like an angry toddler.

"Of course you do. It's summer. Nice birch trees all around so nobody can see into the backyard. Sunshine. Butterflies. Your play pool is filled with nice cool water that sparkles in the sun."

"But Goose is in the yard."

"No, Goose is nowhere in sight. Everything is warm and safe and sunny." The Voice paused. "What are you doing?"

"Floating on my back in the water," Johnny said in a small voice. His mind's eye was looking straight up in the sky, which was milky with humid warmth. Whenever he did this, he looked for the hole through which his mother had tumbled out of heaven. She was back up there now, scattered into the sun, stars and moon. All good things dwelt in the sky.

Then a shadow fell over him.

White Nana was standing at the edge of the play pool, her long, heavy-jowled face quivering with contempt. Johnny quit floating on his back and bent forward into a defensive crouch.

"How red you are," she observed. "As red as your drunken father. What're you doing swimming?"

"You said I could, Nana."

"You lazy little redskin!" she bawled. "The hell I did. I said I might let you go swimming after you finish weeding my nasturtiums. My nasturtiums are lousy with weeds, and here you are swimming!"

It hadn't been that way. She'd said he could go swimming first. White Nana lied. She promised something, only to pretend to forget just so she could say that he had disobeyed her. And he hated the peppery smell of her nasturtiums, the stink they left on his hands. He hated her lies.

There was a splash as she grabbed his arm. She yanked him out of the water, dangled him in the air a moment like a fish, before dragging him squealing over the hot, sticky grass to the hammock. She tossed him into it, slapped him until he stopped squirming and kicking, then stripped off his jockey shorts he used for swimming trunks.

"No, Nana, please!"

"Shut up!" She took the long nylon strap she kept all the time in the pocket of her apron. "You are as useless and lazy as your father," she said, strapping Johnny into the hammock, lashing the canvas like a cocoon around him but leaving openings for his face and genitals. "The only thing he ever managed to do was kill my daughter with his big red dick!"

Then she stormed away, but Johnny could take no comfort from her absence.

It would be brief.

He had learned long ago that struggling against the cocoon was useless. He had to get away before she came back. Not his body, that was impossible. But his mind. In the midst of his powerlessness, his mind could go away, sometimes. His mind could float up into the sky, as free as a balloon.

Honk . . . honk . . . honk!

White Nana was back with Goose flapping in her arms, and Johnny's mind was still trapped inside his head. Goose turned a wicked eye on him as if gauging his helplessness. Tiny feathers of down swirled around Nana's head like snowflakes. Grinning, she held the huge white bird closer, and the orange beak jabbed at Johnny's penis, seizing it, stretching it taut like a rubber band before letting it go.

"No more pecks, Nana! Please!"

Nana cackled with glee, that horrible glee of hers that only came out in moments like these, and Johnny was trying to go up into the sky with his mind when the Voice returned over his cellular phone.

"Can you hear me?" it asked.

Snuffling back tears, Johnny said, "Yes. I hear you."

"Find Tawiskalu. We need Tawiskalu."

23

*S*NOW FALLS BEHIND VAUGHN *Devereaux's office window as he scrolls through the Oneida Nation Police Department's computerized communications logs. Emmett watches him, tapping his chin with an impatient finger. Anna rejoices: He is unhurt. But in the midst of this joy, she knows what she must do. Slowly, she rises and steps behind Devereaux, who remains absorbed with his computer screen. She slips her pistol from her belt holster and, without the slightest hesitation, jabs the muzzle against the back of the detective's head and squeezes the trigger. Blood and brains spray his framed diplomas, certificates and commendations on the wall—*

"Turnipseed?"

She turned and stared at the male speaker, still wondering why none of her otherwise prescient dreams had told her exactly how Emmett would be attacked. But had she been forewarned about Devereaux, could she have killed him?

Perhaps.

But *you can't raise the sky,* as the Modoc of old said, meaning that once the heavens have fallen on you, they have fallen forever. *A broken stick can't be made whole again,* and prophetic dreams might simply be a curse.

"Turnipseed, you okay?" the speaker intruded once more. It was Ithaca. That wasn't the agent's name. It was the FBI office he worked out of. So many agents were assisting her examination of the tribal P.D.'s files, she'd given up trying to recall their names and instead substituted their cities of origin.

"I'm fine," she said. "Just thinking."

Drifting had been more like it, drifting in useless regret.

Ithaca, a trained accountant, sat on the floor again and continued poring through the files Devereaux had kept under lock and key. She'd sent out Rochester, who had lacked accounting experience, to get whatever fast food was still available at two in the morning. Utica was in the office across the corridor, interviewing the P.D.'s watch commander about the detective. Earlier, she'd witnessed Devereaux's autopsy. Her most real experience in days, for she could have dipped her sleeves in the blood from the three bullet wounds Emmett had left in his body.

Ithaca's interruption had reminded her that she'd been woolgathering again. *Have to sleep sometime.* But, more than anything, she didn't want to be awakened and told that Emmett was gone. If that news came, she wanted all her defenses up and running. *You can't guard against horrors, just against being horrified.*

The investigation had come to a fork in the road. Option one, pin everything on Devereaux and call it a day. Option two, widen the case in search of a conspiracy that God only knew went how high. An investigation was like the universe itself, the same laws of physics applied: It was either expanding or contracting, with nothing in-between. The biggest argument for expansion involved the message that had been left for her on Turning Stone voicemail at 9:56 A.M. while she'd been at the Syracuse office. Returning to the hotel at noon and retrieving her messages, she'd immediately had security make a copy. Next, she rushed the cassette to the lab techs, who confirmed in short order that he was the same caller who'd left a similar message for her last week. But there was something new in this one. A clear reference to the Oneida creation story—this was all tied to Sky Woman, somehow, and here the caller was professing to be one of her mythic sons. The good one.

Everyone on the task force agreed that Hazen Two Kettles was probably dead, so what did the suggestion that he was still alive mean? *He's got the Two Kettles boy?* He, inferring the dark side of the Oneida cosmos, the Evil Twin? Was this only a ploy to lure Anna to a meeting that could leave her crushed and lifeless, like Brenda Two Kettles, in a frozen cornfield?

Armed with an edited version of the tape, FBI agents swarmed out over the rez, playing the tape to anybody who would listen in the hope someone would recognize the voice. No luck. Nobody was talking, particularly to whites. Seemingly, the Oneida were now convinced that unmentionable powers were locked in a deadly struggle, and they didn't want to offend either side, even unintentionally.

"Got something that might help, Turnipseed," Utica said, leaning against the doorjamb. A first-office, or rookie, agent, he was painfully reminiscent of Leo Manoukian in his eagerness to accommodate. "Devereaux had *two* encrypted cell phones."

"Two," Anna echoed. She'd known that the tribal detective had had a department-issued cellular secure enough for use in narcotics investigations. "Was the second phone issued by the P.D. too?"

"The captain here," Utica replied, giving a slight flick of his head toward the watch commander in the office behind him, "doesn't think so. But I'll check."

"*Eureka*, Turnipseed." Ithaca held a paper over his head. She grabbed it and read. A hotel statement in Devereaux's name for the Iguana Inn in Mazatlan. She'd asked Ithaca to bring anything related to Mexico to her immediate attention. Before she could decide what this meant, Utica clucked his tongue for her attention and cast his eyes down the corridor.

Stepping out, her heart went cold.

It was only a man in a matching black fedora and overcoat, but his grave look made her feel she was being visited by the Angel of Death, here to tell her the inevitable about Emmett. He removed his hat from wavy, silver hair that shone under the fluorescent lights. His pale face faded and she saw Emmett as she'd first seen him at McCarran International in Las Vegas just over a year ago, bigger than any Comanche she'd ever seen, thick-chested with a deceptively languid stride that overtook the other passengers off the flight from Phoenix. "*Investigator Parker . . . ?*" she had asked, speaking to him for the first time. And he had smiled, an appealing smile that was swiftly gone.

"Turnipseed," the man said, standing before her, "we've got to talk." Her silence made him ask, "Do you remember me?"

Finally, she did. William Jordan, the chief deputy marshal who'd pressed a deputization order and a business card on Emmett their first morning here, then promptly vanished, so completely he hadn't even bothered to return Parker's call. "Yes, what is it?"

Jordan gave Utica a glance that made the agent step back into Devereaux's office and shut the door. "Anna," the marshal said with unexpected familiarity, "I've just been ordered by the A.G. himself to get you onboard a DOJ Lear jet. It'll be landing at Syracuse International any minute now. We've got to hustle." With that, he turned and motioned for her to follow him out of the facility.

She caught up with him, relieved that this had nothing to do with Emmett's condition. "Will I need my things from the hotel?"

"One of my men already swung by your room and gathered them up," Jordan said, voice jiggling from his quick stride. "He'll meet us at the airport."

She kept her silence, but as they were speeding west on the Dewey Thruway, she snapped, "What've you been doing here?"

"Playing the guardian angel," he answered, surprising her with his reference to angels. Coincidentally, it was how she'd seen him minutes before. "Under impossible conditions," he added bitterly. "And now we have another significant missing person."

Hazen Two Kettles had spit out the last two reds as soon as he saw that Johnny Skyholder wasn't looking. Gradually, the boy's mind began to clear, although he was careful to keep his eyes spacey and his speech dopey whenever the big man examined him. And, when toward the middle of the day, Johnny got up from his rocker and went out the door, his departure confirmed minutes later by the sound of his van's engine being fired up, Hazen began squirming against his restraints.

He worked against the green nylon straps through the day and well into the night. The effort made him break out in a clammy sweat, and his skin was chafed raw at the contact points with the webbing, but he kept at it.

Something hit him. It sliced through his lingering barbiturate haze and made his heart race. Aunt Brenda had been in this very room. The presence of her purse and overnight bag said so. She'd wound up dead in a cornfield, but the thing that had dropped her from the sky had its beginnings in this room. He could not imagine what, but he sensed its awful presence all around him.

He had to get away. No matter what, he had to flee.

But sometime in the darkness, he became too exhausted to struggle any further. Even though his bindings had begun to loosen. He mashed the side of his face into the smelly pillow and wept. He wept until he dozed off.

Only to awaken at the sound of a vehicle approaching through the woods. It was either Johnny or Tawiskalu.

Over the long day, Hazen had even begun to hope that the deputies might show again. Juvenile hall was to be preferred over this shabby dwelling place of two brothers, one evil and the other too weak and stupid to be good. He would be safe in juvie, at least temporarily, until the courts made him pay for what he'd done to Daniel Garrity.

Hazen thrashed as hard as he could.

The straps loosened with a sudden jerk, and his hands were free to explore for the knots that bound him.

The vehicle could be heard pulling up front.

Hazen yanked furiously at the strap around his chest—until the engine died. If it was Johnny, the boy would lie still again and hope that Skyholder would be too dumb to notice that Hazen was within inches of freeing himself.

But it was the front door to the adjoining duplex that opened and closed again.

Tawiskalu was back. Hazen could hear the Evil Twin moving around his apartment, the floor groaning under him. Water came on, running through the pipes with a hiss.

Whimpering, Hazen slithered out of his bindings and off the bed. But his exertions left him with a fiery, blinding headache. And he realized that he was entirely naked.

The water was shut off.

Silence.

Gnashing his teeth, Hazen forced himself to start for the door. He knew he could not get far beyond in his condition, but a plan began to take shape in his brain. He would make for the vehicle that had just pulled up. If Tawiskalu had left his keys in the ignition, as most people did who lived off the main roads around here, Hazen would speed away. It kept him moving, the imagined thrill of speed as he accelerated away, with Tawiskalu fuming in the rearview mirror.

But what if the keys weren't in the ignition?

In that case, Hazen would hide himself in the cargo area, if it was a van, or the backseat, if it was a car. Tawiskalu might not think to search his own vehicle when he found Hazen missing, and if he drove away the boy would hunker down on the floor until he could creep out and away into the night.

He groped in the darkness for the door knob.

It was locked.

Tawiskalu was talking. With occasional pauses. He was on the phone with somebody.

The boy undid the push button to the lock, then spun the knob and pulled the door back toward him.

A stunning cold flowed over his bare skin. The wind was rocking the pines, making a soughing sound that almost blotted out Tawiskalu's growling voice. He was angry about something with the person on the other end. He was arguing, loudly now.

Quietly, Hazen slid back the door, only enough to pass through, then scuttled around on his sore ribs and shut it again.

He had to rest a few seconds to regain his breath.

A porch light fanned out over the yard. Its brightness stretched all the way to the parked van. Not Johnny's, which was mustard-yellow. This one was black.

Crawling on his elbows and knees to keep his weight off his ribs, Hazen crossed the frozen ground at a snail's pace. He had to reach the warmth of the van's interior before he got frostbite. But he could barely move, and the hot juices of his stomach were high in his throat.

A pause had gone on so long he realized that Tawiskalu was no longer on the phone. No noise broke from the duplex.

Hazen came to the passenger side of the black van, but the door seemed an impossible distance above him. Somehow, he would have to stand, if he were to get inside. Digging his fingertips into the door seam, he tried to lift himself, but his hands slipped away.

Quietly crying now, Hazen crept around to the front and with both hands seized one of the chrome bars that formed the grille. This gave him more leverage. It felt like doing a chin-up in P.E. class. He never did well with chin-ups and hated how his struggling with them made the other boys laugh.

That memory now helped him rise.

He was standing, the frigid wind whipping around him. His feet felt chunky and numb, and he shuffled around the front of the van to the driver's door. Thankfully, Tawiskalu had left it ajar, so Hazen didn't have to fool with the latch. He tumbled half-inside and sprawled with his upper body on the bucket seat. He was intoxicated by the escaping warmth, made soft and weak by it. Still weeping, he swung his legs around, tangling his feet among the pedals before he collapsed into the space between the seats. Without rising, he reached behind for the ignition on the steering column. Found the chrome slot. No keys.

A sob broke between his clenched teeth.

But after a few seconds, he clambered through the seats and into the cargo area. The porch light was shining through the windshield and illuminating the whole interior of the van. Tanks of some kind were racked against the side-walls, connected together with hoses and gauges, but the metal cylinders were too skinny to hide behind. Some were marked: PROPERTY OF THE BOATHOUSE MARINA.

A blue tarp was spread over much of the deck. He lifted a corner and slid under, shivering. It was unexpectedly warm under the covering. And the air was perfumed. His fingers brushed long hair. Startling, he whipped the tarp back.

And cried out, muffled, but still he cried out.

A woman lay beside him, her hair a red storm around her shoulders. The exposed skin of her face, neck and hands was so milky pale he was sure she was dead. Her eyes were fixed on his, but without moving. She was bound by straps, just as he had been, and a piece of duct tape covered her mouth.

He cried out again when she blinked at him. The dead stirring to a grim mockery of life. Her glassy, violet-colored eyes then held his, insistently.

And he finally understood.

She wanted him to remove the tape.

Through his shock and fear, Hazen pinched a corner of the duct tape between his thumb and forefinger. He pulled, drawing her lips away from her teeth. It looked like a corpse's mouth, all discolored and misshapen. But then the lips moved, first as if trying to restore sensation and then in slurred speech. "Who are you . . . ?"

"Hazen Two Kettles."

Incredibly, the woman giggled. Like she was drunk, though Hazen could smell no booze on her breath. She had *breath*, he realized, convinced for the first time that she was genuinely alive.

"Who?" she repeated as if she didn't believe him.

He told her again, and she giggled again. "That fucking does it," she said. "Are you with him?"

Tawiskalu, he was sure she meant. "No, I'm trying to get away." He believed that he had seen the redheaded woman before. Yes, he had, he was sure of it—in the gold Beemer the night she picked up Aunt Brenda for the last time. "Who're you?" he whispered, fearful now that Tawiskalu might have heard him from inside the duplex.

The woman said, "Portia Nelson." The name meant something, but he wasn't sure what. "How'd you get here . . . ?" she asked. He started blathering on about his motorcycle and the lake, Johnny Skyholder and Tawiskalu, and being tied up all these days, but she interrupted, "Later—untie me, quickly, before that big son of a bitch comes back!"

He began working at a knot in the strap around her belly. But it was drawn tight, and he had little feeling in his fingertips.

"Do you have a gun, Hazen?"

"No, nothing like that."

"What about a knife?" Her voice was weird, both drunk-sounding and very keen, like one part of her refused to be drunk.

"Maybe the kitchen, I don't know."

"Is he inside there right now?"

"There's two apartments. He's in one of them."

"Can you get inside the other and look for a weapon, anything we can use to kill him?"

Hazen was making no progress on the knot. He shifted to another one on the webbing that bound her legs together. "I barely made it out here." He gave up. "I can't undo these knots."

"Run, then. I can't. He gave me a shot of something. Run, Hazen. Get help. Hurry."

"I can't run neither. Can't even *walk*. Tawiskalu beat me bad. I think he broke ribs—" Then Hazen felt a gust of icy air on the back of his neck. Even before he turned his head, he knew that the rear doors to the van had been parted.

The boy twisted around to look.

A huge white-clad figure stood there, arms holding the doors wide. The face was deathlike. A mummy's. Hazen was gasping and cringing when he finally made sense of it—Tawiskalu was wearing a cornhusk mask. His dark eyes sparkled through the holes at him. "What're you doing out here!" he roared.

Hazen hurled himself under one of the man's arms, giving no thought to what he'd do once he landed on the frozen ground. But he never reached it. Tawiskalu swung down that arm, catching the boy by the neck in mid-air. Hazen dangled limp for a second, then struggled to relieve the pressure of the choke-hold around his throat by touching his feet to the ground. He extended his toes as far as he could, but nothing solid met them, and soon his vision went to a frenzy of tiny dots, like a TV screen when the station was off for the night. A waterfall sound filled his ears, but through it he could hear Portia Nelson screaming at Tawiskalu. Telling him to go to hell.

Then silence.

When Hazen could see and hear again, he sensed that time had passed. He was lying flat on his back, gazing up into the stars. Big stars tonight; the wind had swept the sky clean. But he was horribly cold. Dead cold. He could hear a hiss. At first, he thought it might be the water running again in the duplex. But this was louder, like the sound the air hose makes in a gas station.

Portia Nelson was no longer screaming at Tawiskalu. She was moaning and begging. "Don't do that, don't do that," she was saying.

Hazen's lower face was stiff with frozen spittle. He wanted to wipe it away, but discovered that his arms were pinned to his sides.

Tawiskalu stepped over him, holding a knife in one hand and in the other a rope that, incredibly, stood straight up into the darkness. "You've outlived your usefulness," he said, that frightening pity back in his voice.

Hazen could think of nothing to say.

Tawiskalu's mask-hidden face drew close. He jerked his knife hand. At first, Hazen thought he'd been cut. But then as he felt for his belly he realized that the strap around his arms had been severed. He was steeling himself to go for Tawiskalu's eyes when the giant said, "Say hello to Sky Father for me, little redskin." A click followed. Like metal being fastened to metal.

Then Hazen was lifted up as if the wind had fists and had grabbed him. He was flying up into the stars, spinning back and forth as the ground fell away between his feet. Tawiskalu leered up at him. Got small. The boy had a soaring view of the isolated duplex. He saw two vans, the black one in front of the place and the yellow one pulled around back. Tawiskalu waved, then was gone. Hazen looked all around. Great pools of light stood off in the distance. Cities. Eventually they too got small, and the stars stopped twinkling. They flared steadily from the dark, inhuman void.

Through his terror, he cried out at the wonder of it all.

24

ANNA LEFT THE U.S. Marshal in the warmth of his car and strolled out onto the prow of the ferry. Not William Jordan; he'd remained behind in Syracuse. This younger, leaner marshal had picked her up at Gabreski Airport near Westhampton, although he, like Jordan before, remained close-mouthed about the purpose of her summons. The waters of Peconic Bay were iron-colored with winter, but dawn erupted all around in a vibrant pink mist. Through it a flat shoreline began to appear: Shelter Island, a summer resort between the lobster-like pincers of eastern Long Island.

The flight in the Lear jet from Syracuse had been lonely and beautiful. She sat in the otherwise empty cabin, watching New York state whisper past below. The moon was new, but there were entire galaxies of lights tucked here and there among the dark rolling hills, clinging to the black traceries of rivers and bays. Towns and cities where millions lived. She felt far above the living. This was where the dead dwelt, and alone in the pre-dawn darkness she'd sensed that this was how they saw the world, insulated by death itself, impervious to the eternal cold and captivated by the scintillant beauty below.

But she stopped thinking in this vein when she remembered how close Emmett was to joining them.

"Special Agent Turnipseed!"

She glanced back at the marshal, who'd powered down his window to shout.

"We're getting ready to dock!"

She returned to the car. The only one on the small ferry, another indication that no expense had been spared in getting her here. After the fresh marine air, the interior of the sedan reeked even more of the marshal's aftershave. He smiled at her as she sat inside again. He kept smiling as if to reassure her that there was nothing punitive about this trip.

She wasn't convinced.

But neither did she care, much. Her body was tired, but her mind—sharp and agitated—almost seemed to be shedding it like an old snakeskin. After a brutal year in the field, she now recognized these transcendent moments to be the prelude to emotional exhaustion.

The fact that Portia Nelson was now missing only added another weight to her sense of fatigue. Jordan had offered her a few scraps of detail. He'd been following the attorney as she searched the airport parking garage for an empty space, intending to tail her inside the terminal. He rounded the ramp onto the next level, only to find her gold-colored BMW sedan abandoned in a slot, the trunk lid yawning open and her luggage still in the back. Roadblocks clamped down the airport exits, but obviously too late, yielded nothing.

The ferry gently bumped into the dock, the guard cable retracted, and the marshal drove onto the island. A marina slipped past Anna's window, the cocooned pleasure-boats dusted with frost. Saltbox vacation homes, shuttered until summer, gave way to fields dotted with shingled windmills and vacant roadside stands advertising new potatoes and farm-fresh tomatoes.

The marshal slowed for a bayside resort. A CLOSED FOR SEASON board had been nailed diagonally across a sign that read COCKLESHELL LODGE. Anna thought that he was going to turn left into the parking lot. But he stopped above the narrow strip of beach and pointed at a figure sitting on the rear of a diving board at the end of a wooden pier. "I'll wait for you," he said. Smiling once again.

She got out and crunched toward the man. A brittle crunch with each step. The beach was made of scallop shells and pebbles. The man stood as she came down the pier toward him. He wore a navy blue overcoat like one her mother had picked out at the Salvation Army store in Alturas, the town nearest their rancheria. An elfin man, just a few inches over five feet. He had enormous ears and a shallow chin. His face would have been comical had it not also been so compellingly gentle. "May I call you Anna?" he asked, reaching out with a gloved hand for hers.

She nodded, waiting for him to introduce himself.

"I'm to tell you that a while ago Investigator Parker was off the ventilator. Briefly. He asked for you, then they had to reinsert the tube."

Her eyes clouded with tears. She would have turned away, except the little man continued to grasp her hand. Only when she muttered a soft thanks did he let go.

"I'm Judge Solomon," he said with a droll inflection that let her know it wasn't his name. "And I've made a pretty poor Solomon, if I must say. But we'll get into that in a moment. Have you been to the island before?"

"No, sir."

"Let's walk. Too cold to stand still." He led her back up the pier. "My late wife and I used to come here each summer. *For a swim and a burn,* as she used to say. Dear Lord, how I'd burn. Her skin could take the sun, but not mine." It was there in his grin: the pain of his loss. "Of course, I came here long before I was married. With my parents. The waiters used to be recruited from black colleges. Fine young men. We were especially fond of one named Charles. We asked for Charles's table each time we came. But then, one August, the waiters went on strike. Hours and working conditions. The management worked them like dogs. Even I, a boy, could tell that. The end result was that all the waiters were fired and sent packing. I never saw my friend Charles again . . ."

Anna was finding it hard to follow. She wanted to talk to Emmett. Right away, even if the ventilator and sedation prevented him from responding.

"Anyway, Anna," the judge went on, "that's when I decided what I wanted to do with my life. I wanted to bring justice to the world." He chuckled. "But it isn't easy being Solomon." They avoided the shell-strewn beach by taking a cement walkway. "Three years ago, the U.S. District Court in Syracuse designated a neutral settlement master to form a committee from the warring parties in the Oneida land claim."

"You, sir?"

"No, dear, I was still enjoying my retirement from the federal bench. That first settlement committee resulted in an impasse. Worse than an impasse. It wound up a fiasco, all because the members tattled on each other to the press as soon as they could dash out of the federal building in Syracuse. Nothing but posturing, bickering and maneuvering. There were anonymous threats of violence against both Oneida and white participants. Members quit right and left. Injunctions were filed even before an initial status report could be drafted. The settlement master was a fine man, a really fine man, but what a fiasco." They'd started up a flight of steps, and the judge paused to rest after mounting only three of them. "Six months ago, the court decided to try again, and I was offered the can of worms. I agreed, conditionally. The new committee was to be absolutely secret. Divulging the names of the members would be good for jail time. The mediation sessions would be held out of the land claim area at a secluded venue. You want a peace accord? Give me the peace and quiet and security of a Camp David . . ." He gestured at the lodge and its wooded grounds sprawling above them. "Transportation to and from the site would be arranged in such a manner so as not to leave a paper trail or otherwise draw attention to the members. Back in Madison and Oneida Counties, they were to keep contact with one another to a minimum until a settlement was reached. An unprecedented level of secrecy, you see, one the Marshal's Service complained—perhaps justifiably—that made their job of protecting the committee members impossible."

It all fell into place with a mental click. Curiously, Anna felt no satisfaction in knowing. "Brenda Two Kettles was a member. So's Portia Nelson."

Tight-lipped, the judge began ascending the steps again, making Anna catch up. "When poor Brenda was found dead," he said, wheezing slightly, "I was informed it might have nothing to do with the land claim. Internal Oneida politics, the marshals suspected. I bought that reason. In part. But I also wanted a fresh perspective from outside."

"So Emmett Parker and I were called in," Anna said. "And you had Emmett deputized by the Marshal's Service so he'd have clear sailing to get the information you needed for that perspective."

"Precisely. Now Portia's missing, and I'm just sick about what that means. We can't blame the disappearances on Oneida politics. And I'm sick at heart, generally. See, this particular committee had the potential to settle this thing once and for all. It still does—if I can get the process back on track, quickly. After eighteen years with this case pending, we have the power to resolve it."

The judge halted on the deserted road, waved at the marshal in his car as if he knew the man well.

Anna asked, "How many serve on the committee?"

"Fourteen total. Six Oneida and six whites. One alternate for each side."

"Why have Brenda and Ms. Nelson been singled out, if that's what happened?"

The judge nodded as if he'd debated the question himself. "Strange thing about the mediation process, the two people who start off screaming at each other the worst usually wind up friends. I think that's what happened with Brenda and Portia. It's a miraculous thing to witness, enemies slowly warming to each other. It gives hope for the world, Anna. But I'd wanted them to avoid each other at home until we had a settlement. I have a bad feeling they didn't. Come . . ." He took her hand to cross the road to the lodge grounds.

But she pulled away. "Why weren't my partner and I told any of this?"

He continued on toward the main lodge, again forcing her to tag along. "*Need to know*—that's the operative phrase, my dear. The Marshal's Service assured me you and Mr. Parker were looking in all the right dark corners, and if Brenda's death was foul play, Oneida politics was written all over it. The actions of that tribal detective only reinforced this assumption. Until—"

"Until Portia Nelson disappeared."

The lodge entrance was unlocked, and he swung back the door for her. "Yes." The lobby was dark with early morning gloom, cloths draped ghostly over the furniture. He led her down a corridor toward the dining hall, which was lit. "Look at our quandary—anything we did to try to protect the members might backfire by drawing attention to them." Then he sighed, "Poor Portia. I pray she's all right."

"She was supposed to show up here last night?"

"Yes. I dismissed the rest of the committee and sent them home in the wee hours this morning." All the tables had been pushed against the walls, except one, which stood in the middle of the dining room. It had been cleared, although its cloth showed stains and cigarette ashes. Six chairs stood on one side, six on the other, with a slightly larger chair at the head. "This is where Solomon holds court, Anna. But instead of two women claiming the same baby, he is confronted by two children claiming the same mother. That mother is much of upstate New York. One side says she's mine because she has always been my mother. Mother Earth, our sacred Place of the Standing Rock, taken from us by state treaties in direct violation of the U.S. Constitution. Good point. The other side says this is where our pioneer heritage was forged, where we have lived for over two hundred years, built communities and paid taxes under the reasonable assumption that we exercised dominion over our mother. Good point. Coffee?"

A waiter, wearing a U.S. Marshal's jacket, had appeared with a silver service. "Please," she said.

The judge paused until the marshal had withdrawn, then continued with a wry smile, "Many a time in this room, Anna, I've been tempted to say, *Bring me my sword, and I'll split your mother right down the middle!* But I was afraid both sides might say, *Divide her, it shall be neither yours nor mine!* Until lately. When it seemed both sides seemed to see the price of no compromise. A new light was beginning to shine at this table."

She asked, "What honestly happens if a settlement isn't reached?"

The judged slipped into his chair, which seemed too big for him. "The 1985 Supreme Court decision will simply be imposed at some point, the Oneida Nation will have title to monumental wealth, and there could be civil war in upstate New York." She took the chair to his immediate right so they could look at each other, eye-to-eye. "I'm asking you to help close out this case, Anna, swiftly and decisively, so I can get the committee rolling again. I want to regain the momentum we had. I want to witness more miracles of enemies becoming friends."

She considered. "There can't be any interference from FBI headquarters."

"Pardon?"

"There's a move underfoot to direct the investigation from D.C., and that means my contributions will be minimized. Sidetracked even, with a lot of busy work. Unless the brass is told what you want."

His shaggy gray and white eyebrows went up. "Who am I to tell your agency what to do?"

"King Solomon," she replied.

Johnny Skyholder studied the woman strapped to his bed. Morning sunlight fell across her battered face, showing the extent of the damages Tawiskalu had inflicted on her. Her lower lip was split, her left eyelid puffed up and eggplant-purple. Arriving home in the pre-dawn darkness, Johnny had been amazed to find Hazen Two Kettles gone and this redheaded woman in the boy's place. He'd demanded to know what had happened to the boy. Tawiskalu said he'd let Hazen go. It was now obvious that the boy knew nothing more, so he'd driven him to the south end of the county and pushed him out of the van. Johnny noted the risk in having done this. Hazen might lead the deputies back to the duplex. When Tawiskalu gave no answer, Johnny realized that he was lying. He'd killed Hazen, like his aunt before him. His brother and he then argued, even grappled briefly, leaving broken glass in the kitchenette. But in the end, a sneering Tawiskalu just ordered Johnny to attend to the woman until he awoke. He gave instructions. Everybody was always giving Johnny instructions.

The woman now opened her right eye on him.

He was reminded of Goose's obscenely reddish eye, even though the iris was violet-colored.

"Would you like some water?" he asked.

No answer. Her single, probing eye held fast on his face, confused but also hateful.

"Water will make you feel better. Maybe some Tylenol too."

Still no response.

"Tawiskalu killed Hazen, didn't he?"

The eye hardened in affirmation.

Sitting back in his rocker, Johnny cleared his throat. It was tightening on him. And tears were scalding his eyes. "I was afraid that would happen." He'd liked young Hazen. Liked him a lot. And felt protective toward him, particularly after fishing him like a wet kitten out of Oneida Creek. Whatever he saved, Tawiskalu destroyed. It had always been that way, and Johnny was fed up. Suddenly, he saw Tawiskalu's sneer floating in front of him. It was just like white Nana's. He lashed out with his fists at the phantom sneer, his hands flying through the air as he tried to cross time and thrash the sneer off his grandmother's face.

But it was no good.

Even in death, she was stronger than he was. Tawiskalu too. Everybody.

Johnny dropped his hands into his lap and wept. "I'm sorry, lady," he blubbered, "but sometimes there's no holding him back. If you know something he wants to know, just tell him, okay?"

The despising eye remained locked on his face until his wristwatch alarm beeped.

"Time for my medicine," he said, shutting it off. Wiping away his tears, he rose and went to the kitchen for a jelly glass of water, his boots grating over the shattered glass from last night's confrontation with Tawiskalu. He was downing his pills when his alarm went off for a second time. Thumbing it off, he remembered. His brother had told him to do something.

"Pardon me," he muttered, mostly because white Nana always made him politely excuse himself whenever he tried to squirm out of her presence. These same nice manners made Oneida Nana say that that white bitch was turning him into a prissy little white boy. Johnny groaned as their competing voices fired up inside his head for another day of quibbling.

Sky Father, give me peace!

Outside, all was cold and still. The sky above the woods was a velvety lavender. The two vans, his and Tawiskalu's, stood side-by-side, bejeweled with frozen dew. They looked stunning. Magical. Vans encrusted with diamonds. He smiled.

But the smile died as he crept inside Tawiskalu's half of the duplex.

He could hear his brother snoring. Gulping down air like he gulped down everything—savagely.

The only illumination was that coming through the open door behind him. Tawiskalu liked to sleep in utter darkness, while Johnny always had to have some light going, if only the firelight escaping from the seams in his woodstove. Tawiskalu had bought a big bed with four posts and a canopy, then shrouded it over with a black velour curtain he got from a theater in Utica that went bankrupt. He had no fear of white Nana and Goose skulking around in the night. Tawiskalu had no fears at all, and for that Johnny envied him. He would like to be Tawiskalu, except for his brother's meanness.

As always, the little leather case was waiting on top of the bureau. Johnny grabbed it and hurried out, quietly shutting the door behind him.

He could tell by the heat in the woman's face that she'd flailed against her restraints while he'd been out. "Don't do that," he cautioned her. "I know you been trying to get away, but don't do anything to make Tawiskalu mad, okay? Hazen tried, and you know what happened to him." He took a syringe and vial from the little case. "If you're real, real good, I might phone the FBI lady staying at Turning Stone and ask her to help us . . ." Even though his brother absolutely forbade it. Johnny filled the syringe, then flicked it with a knuckle as he squeezed the plunger to make sure no bubbles got inside the lady's bloodstream. "Just be nice, do everything you're told, and I'll get help. I'll need help. I can't fight Tawiskalu on my own . . ." He flipped back the covers. His brother had undressed her, and she was nude. Her skin was like milk. White Nana would have liked it very much. "Now, this is different medicine from what my brother gave you before. It'll make you sleep."

Her bloodshot eye flared as Johnny stabbed the needle into her upper arm. Almost instantly, her right eye slid down over the eyeball and her breaths started coming deep and regular. Like a baby's.

"There we go," he whispered, taking a blood pressure cuff from under the bed. "Better."

He'd no sooner put away the syringe kit and taken her pressure to make sure she was all right—than his cell phone rang from his coverall pocket. He answered, and the Voice said, "Did you take your medicine, Thaluhyawaku?"

Johnny sank into his rocker. "Yes, just a few minutes ago."

"Did you give the woman her medicine too?"

"Just now."

"Are you sitting?"

"Yes."

"Are you comfortable . . . ?"

25

"Copy, responding to Guard facility." Anna backed out of the space in the Community General Hospital parking lot. She'd just pulled in and hadn't even had time to turn off the engine before the local FBI office radioed her that Chief Master Sergeant Riley requested—*if at all possible*—she swing by the Air National Guard center before quitting time. Enough urgency was implied by the *at all possible* for her to postpone checking with Emmett's physician.

She rationalized that Parker would want her to follow up on any lead first. *Either you want to solve this goddamned thing or you don't.*

Speeding toward the airport, she wondered if his voice would be locked inside her head for the rest of her working life. He'd been with her on Shelter Island, lurking inside her request to the judge to run interference with FBI headquarters. A lover's voice faded with time, but perhaps a mentor's didn't. Emmett's words would remain sharp and insightful, even when his face was dimmed by the years.

Riley met her at the facility gate. "Sorry to bug you, ma'am, but something came over the wire I thought you should see right away."

"No problem," she said.

But she floated along on a wave of light-headedness as they made their way through the personnel door and into the hangar. The only sleep she'd had in the last day and a half had been on the return flight from Long Island.

"Air Force Office of Special Investigations is already on to it," the chief said, leading her into the office, "but they and my commanding officer said I should share it with my FBI contact. Leo was my contact, I guess. Now, it's you, if you don't mind."

"I don't mind."

Riley took a page off his desk and handed it to her. The communication was cluttered with so many abbreviations and acronyms she could scarcely make heads or tails of it. "In plain English," the chief explained, "a civilian brought a piece of unidentified gear into the public affairs office at Loring Air Force Base in Maine. A timber worker. He was out marking trees when he found this thing in the snow. The olive drab nylon webbing looked military to him and that's why he took it in to Loring."

"Isn't webbing pretty generic?"

"Just webbing, yes." As if he'd anticipated this question, the chief reached for another page on his desk. A copy of a photograph of an airman holding up something configured like a vest, except that it had been loosely assembled from webbing straps instead of cloth. The ruler for scale showed that the article was the approximate size of a human torso.

She asked, "What am I looking at?"

"Well, we're not sure. This is what the timber marker found. The best name we can come up with for it is *an improvised parachute harness*. It was hand-stitched. We use sewing machines."

Immediately, her eyes fastened on the parachute shop, which had been burglarized three times in the last few months.

"That's right," the chief confirmed.

Anna pointed at a metallic cylinder in the middle of the assembly. It was circled in red. "Why's this indicated?"

"It's one of those harness cutters I told you and the other investigator about the other night . . ." The night all hell broke loose, his tone inferred. "Uses a low-powered explosive, like I said."

"What kind?"

"Black powder."

Anna's pulse kicked up a beat. The pathologist had found traces of something on the blister between Brenda Two Kettles's breasts and on her sweater; the lab had later identified it as black powder. "Go on, how's it work?"

"Well, the powder's sealed inside a cylinder—that's the tube you see here. It ignites and burns at four thousand degrees but doesn't rupture the containment cylinder, which stays intact. The pressure from the combustion applies force to the cutter, which is an actual blade that severs the harness."

"Why's this one attached to a nylon strap?"

He referred to a line in the letter. "That's what the guys at Loring wondered. An airman tried the harness on, just to see where the strap that'd been cut fit over a person's body—right across the chest."

"I don't understand," she said.

"Well, imagine somebody dangling you in the air by your shirt collar. Cutting that strap would be like unbuttoning your shirt front. One second you'd be suspended in the harness, the next you'd drop right out of it."

Again, Anna saw farmer Van Hastart's mouth twitch as he described the sound that angled down over his house that night two weeks ago: *It was a howling. Like the wind screaming, except it was the most god-awful thing I ever heard in my life.*

"You telling me this is your cutter?" she asked.

"That's right. Most anything potentially used in life support systems is serialized. The guys at Loring ran the numbers of the internalized Cartridge Actuated Device and barometric switch through the computerized tracking system, and they popped up stolen out of our inventory."

"Barometric switch?"

"Yes," the chief said, slightly embarrassed, "I didn't notice some of them were missing last time I talked to Leo."

"What are they?"

"If you want something to happen at a certain altitude and you can't be there," he explained, "you slap on a barometric switch."

"You're losing me."

"A preset altitude's reached, and the baro switch triggers the CAD, which cuts the chest strip . . ."

Dropping Brenda Two Kettles to her death. Leaving no evidence attached to the Oneida woman's corpse that might explain how she had gotten up into the sky and then been let go by it.

"Shit," Anna whispered involuntarily.

The chief went on, "Of course, the balloons had a burst altitude manu-
factured into them—"

"Balloons?" Anna interrupted.

"Yeah." The chief's forefinger tapped the grainy photograph on some
dark gray or black scraps that had been tied together with a line. "These are
what remains of meteorological balloons, the reinforced necks."

"Yours?"

"We haven't had any in inventory for years." Then Riley added defen-
sively, "I'm sure. Checked. Twice."

She asked, "Did Jason Eberhardt have a key to this center?"

"Yes, ma'am," he said, frowning. "He'd do maintenance work for us at
odd hours."

So the Adirondack Airlines mechanic and Air Force reservist had burglarized his own center with no need of forced entry, something Manoukian
had noted was absent in all three burglaries. "Who around here does have
balloons of that type?" she asked.

"The weather station, maybe. But it isn't much of a facility anymore.
Cutbacks."

"Chief, I appreciate all this. I'll keep you informed."

She was almost to the door when Riley turned her around: "Ma'am . . . ?"
He observed with an odd smile, "Had me a slew of B-52 missions over Nam,
but I'd never seen anybody die 'til the other night." Leo Manoukian, he
meant. "How about you?"

She didn't want to explain that she'd lost count. Emmett had even tried
to warn her that much of Indian Country was the Third World, prone to
wholesale Third World violence. And there was a grisly lethality to law enforcement itself that the public scarcely realized, regardless of jurisdiction.
But she said to the chief, "Me too."

It seemed to reassure him.

The single remaining U.S. Weather Service employee at the Syracuse station had already left for the day, but Anna felt no hesitation in having the
FBI office roust him.

Waiting for his return to the airport, she used the time to run through the equation she was putting together: Eberhardt had supplied the logistics, possibly for Brenda's execution and almost certainly for some use of the Adirondack–*Aero Mazatlan* merger that still eluded the investigation. Regardless, Vaughn Devereaux had so feared Eberhardt talking he'd had no hesitation in murdering both the mechanic and Leo, who'd had custody of him at the time. Christopher White Pine had taken responsibility for hiring Devereaux, yet Anna had left the Oneida longhouse wondering why he'd risked his own job by concealing from the Nation Rep the DEA's investigation of the detective.

A balding man in a parka and baggy trousers appeared and unlocked the station door. "You must be the FBI agent," he said with a shy grin.

"Yes, Special Agent Turnipseed." He didn't notice her extended right hand, so she lowered it after a second.

Switching on the fluorescents to a small office crammed with charts and computers, he said, "I'm Walters." As if he didn't rate a first name.

"Do you keep meteorological balloons here?"

"No." He smirked as if the notion were absurd, but then said, "In our storage space downstairs. I haven't launched one in ages."

"When's the last time you checked if they're still there?"

"Years," Walters confessed.

"You mind if we check?"

"Not at all."

"But first," she said, "I have a question about wind patterns."

"Shoot," Walters said.

"Two weeks ago for the greater Syracuse area. The pattern on the evening of Monday, January sixth."

"All right." Walters eased onto a stool and booted up a computer.

Anna looked over his shoulder at a screen dense with squiggles. Among them she recognized the outlines of Madison and Oneida Counties.

The weatherman asked, "What time that evening?"

"Sevenish." Brenda Two Kettles's flight had departed for LaGuardia at 6:45 P.M.

Walters typed in the time, then shifted on his stool to let Anna see.

"Meaning?" she asked.

"That's the wind pattern at nineteen hundred hours on the sixth. Generally, strong winds out of the northwest."

"Okay," she said, slowing down, "would radar here at airport pick up a rising weather balloon?"

"Almost certainly—and they'd come bitching to me. It'd be a hazard to aircraft. That's why we leave the balloon stuff to research stations out in the boonies."

"Still, if you'd released a balloon here at that time on that date, what would its flight path have been?"

Walters seemed to welcome the challenge. He typed, pondered, then typed some more. The result was a wavering line of red dots that tended southeast across Onondaga County and into Madison County. It dipped too far south of Bridgewater Flats, where Brenda's shoe had been found by the Oneida S.O. deputy, and Van Hastart's cornfield, which was nearby.

All in all, the pattern at that hour did not account for the path through the sky Brenda had traveled.

Hour.

Time.

Van Hastart had heard the howling sound at about three. "Do me a favor," Anna said, "show me the wind pattern for three that morning."

"Zero three hundred hours on the seventh?"

"Please."

Seconds later, Walters had it. "The wind direction had shifted by then. From out of the northwest to more out of the west. That flip-flop accounts for our big temperature fluctuations around here. Warm a couple days ago, now back to near arctic conditions. You want another flight path designated from a release point here at the airport?"

No, Anna suddenly realized. That was getting it backwards. "How about this . . . ?" She tapped the screen where she reckoned the red shoe had been retrieved on the railroad track and where the corpse had been found in the fallow field. "Please show me a flight path that'd pass over these two points just prior to three that morning."

"Originating where?" Walters asked.

"That's what I don't know."

"Pardon?"

"Give me the *probable* flight path leading up to those two points."

"I see." Walters set out to work again.

After a few minutes, she bent over his shoulder to have a look. The wavering series of dots passed over the heart of Madison County, coming close to the Oneida Nation. "Make me a copy?"

"Sure."

She was still studying the read-out as they started for the elevator. The assumption had always been that Brenda had gone airborne from somewhere along the Adirondack 727's flight path, or perhaps even the airport itself. Anna now had a swathe full of possible departure points that would have to be checked out.

Walters smiled at her as he pressed the ground-level button in the elevator car. Evidently, they had bonded over wind patterns. "You Oneida?" he asked.

Something made her say yes. Curiosity, perhaps, over what the white weatherman would say.

"You people got a raw deal," he declared, yawning.

"Thank you," she said, surprised, following him out into a large combination kitchen and warehouse. Catering trucks with Chez Sky Food logos on their sides were being loaded. White-clad caterers milled around. Most were Hispanic, but Anna noticed an especially large one who appeared to be Indian—he'd stopped unloading a trash cart and was staring unabashedly at her. Then she recalled him: Adrian Flint, who'd loaded Flight 557 both the night Brenda had been booked to fly and the following Wednesday, when Emmett, Dutch and she had gone aboard, the surly caterer who'd asked Emmett at the interview later if the term *Indian* was politically correct. "Your storage is in here, Walters?"

"Yeah," the weatherman answered, "space is hard to come by. We rent some from Chez Sky. This way . . ."

Flint continued to stare at her until Walters unlocked a metal door and they stepped inside a locker. He yanked the chain to an overhead bulb, revealing stacks of boxes, most crumpled at the edges from exposure to humidity. "Meteorological balloons are usually made of natural rubber, which doesn't stand up to time real well. But fortunately, they're dusted in preservative and sealed in moisture-proof polyethylene bags . . ." He opened a large box. It was filled to the brim with Styrofoam packing pellets, and he plunged his right arm down into the popcorn-like depths, only to bite the inside of his cheek. He tried again. And failed again. "There were two large-payload balloons in here," he said on a rising tone of worry.

"Let me," Anna offered, and Walters obediently stepped back. Over-turning the box, she dumped the contents onto the floor. She kicked through the loose drift of Styrofoam to make sure, but there was nothing more than pellets.

Three other boxes were empty. In all, eighteen balloons were missing.

Walter shook his head, then mumbled, "Can you take the theft report?"

"And what relation are you to the patient?" the attending physician asked, jotting notes on his clipboard.

Anna hadn't intended to venture farther than the waiting room in the direction of the Intensive Care Unit, but Emmett's mother had cheerfully insisted that she accompany her on the last check of the evening. It was al-most ten o'clock. "I'm his partner," she finally answered.

The doctor's dubious look said that he'd been around law enforcement long enough to have learned that injured cops had countless partners, all blithely set on trooping their street germs into the cloistered sterility of ICU.

Celia Parker stepped in and said with a twinkle in her eye, "She's my son's significant other." Obviously pleased with herself for using such a modern phrase.

Anna was struck by the fact that Mother Parker had a precise fix on her relationship with Emmett. His *lover* did not quite fit, for a myriad of reasons. Neither did his *intended,* for both of them had kept their intentions for each other to themselves. But *significant* implied the importance both had given to the relationship. *Other* suggested other half, each of them a half of the whole, even if that whole was largely indefinable. Anna had al-ways sensed that Emmett routinely confided in his mother. In dingy motels throughout Indian Country, through the wafer-thin walls, she had heard him on the phone with her. At first, she'd been irked, even alarmed a little that he was seeking solace from one of his ex-wives. But his explanation that it'd been his mother and then Anna's own recognition of his son-to-mother tone half-convinced her that he was telling the truth.

Now she knew for sure.

On Shelter Island this morning, the federal settlement master, the elfin Judge Solomon, had assured her that Emmett had spoken. But Mother Parker had just told her that her son was now heavily sedated again so the ventilator tube could pass down into his trachea.

The doctor peered at her over the bifocal portions of his glasses, his eyes a clear and dispassionate blue. "Go ahead, but make your visit brief."

Arm in arm, Mother Parker and Anna continued down the corridor.

Anna had steeled herself for the first glimpse of Emmett inside the ICU glass cubicle since seeing him in the back of the airport ambulance. But she was spared any further shock by the illusion that it wasn't Emmett lying in the bed. The figure there was too broken to be Emmett Parker. Her mind stubbornly refused to believe. The unnatural anodized twilight and the monotonous wheeze of the respirator bag helped maintain this sense of unreality. Emmett seemed unreal. Tubing obscured his expressive mouth, and his chest was so wasted by the massive wound, Anna felt as if she was beholding someone else other than her partner and significant other of the past thirteen months.

"Cold," Mother Parker declared, rubbing Emmett's left foot where it protruded palely from under the bed sheet. There was something plaintive, almost heart-breaking about the sight of her small, arthritis-gnarled hands kneading his foot.

Anna sank into the chair at bedside. She didn't feel like touching him. She knew he wouldn't want to be touched in such a helpless state. From her abysmal childhood, she knew precisely what that felt like.

"The nurse says we should talk to him," Mother Parker said, then turned to Emmett and raised her voice as if addressing someone hard of hearing. "Anna's here, Emmett."

Anna searched his eyelids for the tiniest tic. Of course, there was none. He was far away. Safe from pain for the moment. "What happened this morning?" she asked.

"Well," the old woman replied, "the doctor had just taken the tube out of his throat to change it when he gave a great big shake and his eyes popped open like he'd been startled . . ." He had been startled, Anna realized. His last memory would have been the bite of the cockpit fire axe into his left pectoral muscle and ribs. "He saw me and his eyes smiled just like when he was little," Mother Parker went on. "Then he asked if you were okay. I said sure, and his mouth smiled too. Next, he asked to see you. I said you were out doing your job, but he wanted to see you as soon as you could make it . . ." Now, instead of feeling professional and efficient about checking with Chief Riley before coming up to ICU, Anna felt guilty. The feeling was admittedly absurd. Emmett had been sedated again at the time, and her presence would have been lost on him.

At last, Mother Parker stopped rubbing his foot and looked thoughtfully at Anna. "He told me he wanted to say good-bye to you . . ." She gave a quick shake of her head. "No, I'm not getting it right. He said he wanted to find a way to say good-bye." She glanced up at Anna. "That's different, isn't it?"

Anna had no answer. Only the formal Modoc farewell came to mind. The words themselves were tinged with seriousness, for life is so tenuous reunion is always in doubt: *Now you go back.* And the response was: *Yes, now I go back.*

"I'll leave you two alone to talk," Mother Parker said.

She withdrew, and Anna was left to stare at the shattered phantom pretending to be Emmett Parker.

After a long silence, she took the small jewelry case from her jacket pocket and removed the hummingbird, the mummified talisman her granduncle had given her for protection. Was all human spirituality born of desperation? Was her own desperation now sharp enough for her to have no qualms about what she did next in a white hospital, in a city that was largely white, in the midst of a job that gave no time or consideration to her traditions:

Anna Turnipseed, daughter of the Kokiwas branch of the Modoc, slowly ran the hummingbird up and down the length of Emmett's body, infusing him with the speed to flit beyond death's reach.

This was how she would say good-bye until she could think of something better.

26

AS THE LATEST ROUNDTABLE meeting broke up in the conference room of the Syracuse FBI office, Anna delayed Marvin Roth, the burly agent who'd helped Leo Manoukian and her serve the search warrant on Daniel Garrity's residence and then had gotten caught up in the pursuit. Roth seemed to be in a hurry to get back to his desk in the bull pen, but when he pivoted and saw that it was Anna who'd tugged on his sleeve he took a moment to study her face for omens. Everybody seemed to know that she was well connected on this gig. She was at the center of things, so she had to know more than they did. "What's up?" he asked.

"I'm sure you've got a lot to do today, Marvin—but I could use your help."

Roth ran a reluctant hand over his crew-cut, but then said, "Let me get my coat."

She trailed him out into the bull pen. From behind the glass partition to his office, Cochran tracked her every movement with casual but distrustful glances.

The emphasis of this morning's roundtable had been Portia Nelson— her probable abduction and continued disappearance—and not seeking anybody beyond and above Vaughn Devereaux who might have had a hand in Leo's homicide. Over the hour-long meeting, it had occurred to Anna that either no one other than she knew of Portia's involvement in the secret settlement committee or those who did were keeping mum about it. She was still unsure how much she should divulge of what Judge Solomon had told her.

Nor did she volunteer anything about the improvised parachute harness the timber worker had given over to the Air Force. Emmett had taught her to personally follow up on her own leads before feeding them into the gears of a task force, only to see them masticated into useless pulp.

"Ready," Roth said, bruin-like in a brown overcoat.

His collar was sticking up in the back and she smoothed it for him. "You sure you have time, Marvin?"

"Yeah."

While he signed out, she ducked her head through the SAC's door and said, "If you don't mind, sir, I'm borrowing Roth for a few hours."

"No problem," Cochran said. "What're you working?"

"Some follow-up on that caller who left the two messages for me on voicemail at Turning Stone. No real leads, but I have a couple ideas." Vaguely the truth.

And the SAC gave her a vague smile in return. But his smile faded as he unlocked the file drawer in his desk. "This came over secure communications around eleven o'clock, while you were in the meeting." He handed her a sealed envelope.

She opened and read an encrypted email from the Justice Department in D.C., addressed to her:

Dear Anna:
Members of my flock are resigning right and left. Do what you can, as quickly as you can.
Solomon

"I talked to Jordan last night," Cochran volunteered, revealing that he knew about the committee, and presumably Brenda's and Portia's involvement. "Anything you need?"

"Just Roth," Anna said, turning to go.

Outside, the snow was light but the flakes were large. They spun down onto the glistening black asphalt, crashing like kites, and slowly melted. She asked Roth if they could take her loaner car. Most of her materials were in the vehicle, including the copy of *The Oneida Creation Story* translated by White Pine.

Roth agreed, and she let him drive.

Her motive in asking him along had been to prevent spending most of the day lost in the hinterlands of Madison County. She hoped that motive wasn't too transparent, for she liked Roth and, despite appearances, he was probably as emotionally beat up as she after the last few days.

"Know where Niagara Mohawk's main office is?" she asked as he pulled out into traffic.

"Sure."

Earlier this morning, she'd made a telephone request of the power company's data processing department, service maps of a section of central Madison County that roughly correlated to the chart given her by the weatherman.

Her stomach rumbled, but she declined Roth's offer to stop for a bite.

She studied him a moment.

There were three tiers of investigative detail. Lowest and least useful was that which the bureau saw fit to release to the public. Slightly more useful were those details submitted to an in-house roundtable, like this morning's. But the germaneness of that detail was equal only to the willingness of the provider to go out on a limb. Most useful were those things whispered by agents to each other around drinking fountains and in the privacy of bucars. "What do you think happened to Portia Nelson?" she now asked.

Roth shrugged. "I hear she had a falling out with C.U.E., maybe even double-crossed them in some way."

"Based on what?"

"Well, she stopped publicly representing them a couple months ago. *Something* was behind that."

Yes, her participation in the settlement process that was convening regularly on Shelter Island. No doubt Portia had turned Committee for Upstate Equality business over to her partner to avoid a potential conflict of interest allegation.

Anna realized that she knew much more than Roth. "Where'd this rumor come from?"

"Oneida Nation, I guess. One of the guys out of our office was interviewing a tribal informant about Devereaux, and off the record he started speculating about Nelson being on the outs with C.U.E." Roth had double-parked in front of an office building. "Niagara Mohawk Power."

"Back in a sec."

Dashing up the wet steps, Anna wondered why anyone in the tribe would have spread this rumor. Did it conveniently muddy the waters, suggesting that whites were behind Two Kettles's death and Nelson's disappearance?

First Brenda and then Portia.

The two women represented both ends of the settlement spectrum. In eliminating them, if that's what had happened, had someone wanted to make absolutely sure that there'd be no settlement? Some Oneida might desire that, wanting to drive as hard a bargain as possible with white property owners in the claim area. But why would a white owner want to stonewall a settlement?

She showed her credentials to the guard at the security desk in the lobby. Like the other agents in the region, she'd fastened a strip of black tape to her badge. "Special Agent Turnipseed, FBI. Data processing was going to leave something for me?"

The guard slapped a thick sheaf of printouts onto the counter top. "Condolences on the kid you lost at the airport the other night."

"Thanks."

Out front, she slowed on her way down to the street. The monochromatic light filtering through the clouds showed where the steps had frozen in spots. It was snowing, harder and smaller, spongy little pellets that bounced off her head and shoulders.

Roth had found a parking space farther down the block.

Getting in the car, she saw his eyes were damp. Left alone, he'd probably been thinking of Manoukian. "How's Parker?"

"No real change," she said.

Then he switched the subject by asking about the printouts.

Anna had known this would be the price of his help. With Leo gone, she trusted Roth more than any other agent in the Syracuse office. "If I ask you to sit on some info for the next day or two, would you do it?"

"If it helped the case." Roth put on his left blinker to merge back into traffic. "Where we headed?"

She referred to the weatherman's chart. "Morrisville."

A minute later, Roth asked, "What's the information?"

There hadn't been time for Anna to thread this all together. Now, as Roth sped toward central Madison County, she had an opportunity to muse out loud. "Bear with me a moment, Marvin. I'm still trying to think this through."

"No problem." He turned on the headlights. The snowfall was now thick. It churned and billowed in the lights.

She finally said, "All the things that have been happening around here have an Oneida feel to them."

"Meaning a member of the tribe's behind them?"

"Could be. Somebody is either thinking like an Oneida, or trying to think like one. This is where you have to bear with me. I just don't know yet. But, whatever, one thing is obvious—Brenda Two Kettles came down to earth like Sky Woman."

"Sky *Who?*"

"Sky Woman. Daughter of Sky Father. He sent her down here from the heavens. Differing opinions even among the Oneida why he did this. But, as she fell, swans kept her from crash-landing into a dark sea that covered the whole planet. It's all kind of like Adam and Eve, plus Noah, but the end result was the world and the human race as we know it today."

"Okay, I guess I got it." The highway had begun to whiten over. Roth's attentive eyes shifted from it to the documentation in Anna's lap. "What's creation got to do with Niagara Mohawk Power? *Let there be light?*"

She smiled. But it was quickly gone. "I'm going to submit a form two-eighty to Cochran later today on what I'm about to tell you," she said, disliking her own evasiveness. "Bottom line, you're getting a first look, Marvin."

"Appreciate it." Roth slowed. The highway was getting worse. "Leo and I really hit it off. I've worked with other guys and gals. It was okay. But Leo and I complemented each other. He was all brains, all insight, and I was the jock. The two of us made up something better than each of us alone. Does that make sense?"

"Yes," she said. Emmett and she had been something like that.

His voice had grown hoarse. He cleared it. "We got mud-and-snow tires on these cars. They do okay most the time. God, I hope the highway department doesn't put up chain control. I hate putting on chains." Then he asked, "What've you been holding back from the brass?"

"I think I know how Brenda Two Kettles was killed . . ."

Roth got back in the car, having just put on the chains. He smelled of wet wool.

For a while, she'd stood outside with him, but he'd told her that there was no sense in both of them getting soaked. So, she had sat inside the warm interior again, occasionally rubbing out a circle in her steamed-over window for a view of the snow-drenched woods.

Accelerating now, Roth said, "Basically, you're saying *I'll know it when I see it*. That's no help to me."

"You're right." Her brief pause was filled with the clatter of the chain ends whipping the wheel arches. She took her copy of *The Oneida Creation Story* from the space between the bucket seats and began leafing through the pages, which were soft from the dampness. *Down and down she falls, and as she is enveloped by darkness, she keeps falling down.* "I don't know if I can put it in exact terms, Marvin."

Roth said in frustration, "If Two Kettles was launched into the sky somewhere around here, what would tell us that?"

"I'm not sure," she murmured, reading: *Swan said, 'That woman's coming down from above, let's go and meet her.' So the swans went up, flying up in circles, trumpeting as they flew, going so high they could no longer be heard or seen.*

"And if a place looks promising, we match it to a name on a Niagara Mohawk service map?"

"Hopefully," Anna said.

"If swans helped Sky Woman, should we be looking for a place with swans. A poultry ranch, or something?"

"Something, a place."

"What kind of place?"

"A significant place."

"Significant how?"

Anna thought a moment. "If you knew nothing about the Torah, the

Old Testament, you'd look at a mountain in Turkey and just see a big mountain. But if you were aware of the stories, you'd see where Noah's ark supposedly came to rest. You'd see the place where the world began again."

"Go on," Roth said.

"Back home, there's a hill near Tule Lake. Just a small hill shaped like a belly-button, an outtie belly-button, except if you know the tradition of my people, you'd see it as the navel of the world. The center of existence."

Roth kicked up the tempo on the wiper blades, which were icing over. "Okay then, how do the Oneida say the world started?"

"Sky Woman floated—"

"No," he interrupted, "the earth itself. How'd the earth come into being?"

Good question, she realized, flipping through the pages of the book. "Let's see, the swans gently lowered her out of the sky onto Turtle's back. *There she stood, the back of Turtle just big enough for her to stand on it with her feet together.* A day passed. The first day of light. By the next morning, the earth was of a *size she could lie upon it.* Another dawn, the earth was large enough for her to walk around on it. And so on . . ."

By three that afternoon, they were nearing the Oneida Nation, having worked up the heart of Madison County from southwest to northeast and revisiting many of the small hamlets they'd barreled through the night of the pursuit. Nothing in the landscape suggested anything special to either of them, and Anna was down to running names past Roth to see if they sounded Oneida to him. "Power customer up this lane . . ." She thrust her chin at a shadowy tunnel through the pines. ". . . named Hancock. Didn't a lot of local Oneida take that name?"

"Suppose," Roth replied, "there's a Hancock on the Men's Council. But there's also a lot of white Hancocks, going all the way back to the Civil War general." He started up the lane in a higher gear, to avoid spinning out on the icy surface now cushioned beneath four inches of fresh, wet snow. "This must be new to you," he said.

"What?"

"Snow."

"Why?"

"You're from California, aren't you?"

"Not any California you'd recognize from the travel postes."

"What do you mean?"

His idle observation made her realize something. Her conctration had lapsed, and she was back to viewing the country with Modoc eyes. A landscape too cluttered with vegetation to be familiar, and the muntains here would be called hills back home. She rekindled her effort to e the land as the Haudenosaunee might.

Her call sign came from the radio speaker. She hesitated ore reaching for the mike. It was the Syracuse office. She had asked the hital to phone dispatch if there was any change in Emmett's condition. ' ahead," she transmitted, her empty stomach knotting up.

"Welfare check and location?" the dispatcher inquire sking if she and Roth were all right.

"Code four . . ." She looked to Roth for where they w

"Stockbridge area," he said.

She advised dispatch, then hung up the mike.

Roth fought off a yawn. "What's your California like

"No palm trees or surf. High desert and rocky mour. Blizzards in winter." She checked the dash clock. Pushing four o'clod nothing to show for it. She'd compensate Roth for wasting his da aking him to dinner. He was easy to be with and no doubt as sick as s putting up a brave front. Law enforcement and the military, both we ds that conditioned you to bury your grief in the routine.

The long day was beginning to feel routine.

The Hancock residence didn't mark the end of the l ich wound on ahead and gradually vanished into the snowy murk. o-story farmhouse showed a light from a front window, so Anna d o add a pointless interview to an already pointless afternoon of dri

As she opened her door to get out, Roth ask nt me to go with you?"

"No, keep the defroster running."

"You sure?"

"Yeah."

Her lack of suspicion was justified when an elde woman with a ruddy face answered her knock. "Hello, Ms. Hanco

"Yes . . ?"

"Is Mr. Hancock in?"

"Oh no my husband passed away." No special emotion was attached to the remark so it must have been some time ago. And no invitation came to step past h half-cocked storm door into the cozy living room.

"Was Oneida, by chance?"

"I beg ur pardon?"

Anna g out her credentials. "Special Agent Turnipseed, FBI, Ms. Hancock. Which was the right fib to use? "We're out searching for an Oneida teeger, Hazen Two Kettles—"

"Oh y of course," the woman said, relieved that this awkward situation sudde had an explanation, "the deputies were by about a week ago, asking abo im. I've kept my eyes open. But no sign of him."

"Have seen any unusual activity in the neighborhood lately?"

"Such

Anna a breath. "Somebody launching weather balloons?"

The w sucked in her cheeks for a moment, then chuckled. "How strange. N thing like that."

Anna ed that she'd just been given a preview of how her superiors would rea y Oneida live nearby?"

"How "

"With ile or so."

"A few

"And ames?" Anna pressed.

"Oh, rley on Jones Road. I believe she's part Oneida. Or maybe it's Onon orget which. Truth is, I'm not sure she really knows any-more—sh st a hundred and rambles on and on about nothing. Then there are hers who live up our road here."

"Are t eida?" Anna asked.

"They"

"Do y their names?"

"No, ver spoken."

"How e they lived here?"

"Abo ears. One waves when he drives by, the other isn't so friendly. Nly at all."

"How now they're brothers?"

"They just look it."

Anna glanced over the rolling woods and farmland. A breeze had risen, creating open spaces in the snowfall. "Any of these parcels tribally owned?"

"Not yet," the woman said, acidly, letting slip where she stood on the land claim.

Anna thanked her and trooped back to the car, the snow filling her shoes.

Roth was hunched over the steering wheel, wide-eyed as he stared through the windshield, seemingly transfixed by the vista before him.

Sitting, she left her door ajar to dump the slush out of her shoes.

"*Look,*" Roth said emphatically.

Glancing up, she asked, "What?"

"Don't you see?"

At first, she didn't. Just a low, rounded hill behind the Hancock house. Then her imagination found a design in the ridge line. It was humped, like the shell of the turtle. One end even terminated in a knob of granite that resembled a turtle's head.

The snowfall descended again and obliterated the sight.

"Go on up the lane," she said, shutting the car door and reaching for the power company service maps. "The woman told me two brothers live farther along it. Probably Oneida."

Roth eagerly turned around in the driveway and veered left onto the lane. No tire tracks broke the smooth ribbon of snow ahead of them.

Anna had lost her place in the sheaf and began riffling through the maps, searching for the Hancock place to orient herself again.

"What're we getting excited about?" Roth suddenly asked, chuckling. "A freaking turtle we see in a hill?"

Anna had to laugh at the absurdity too, but her sense of the absurd was overshadowed by the conviction that they were on to some sort of design. A design was unfolding before them. Still, she couldn't find the map that had the Hancock place on it. "Shit."

"What's wrong?" Roth asked.

"Nothing, keep going."

The lane rose through scrub woods, and Roth went to a lower gear for the climb over the apogee of the turtle's back. The boughs of the trees, especially the pines, were heavily laden with snow, blocking a clear view through the forest, but gradually an opening began to materialize below. A meadow, maybe, cluttered with junk cars. She had fleeting glimpses of something large, something rectangular—a dwelling, she believed.

Other roads, old logging tracks, branched off into the trees, but Roth kept to their lane, which was the broadest.

Anna powered down her window to listen. She heard nothing but their engine and the wind in the restless, snowy boughs. But she did catch a whiff of smoke.

She referred back to the maps. *Hancock*. There it was. Roth side-slipped on a curve, and she pressed a fingertip over the dot that marked the farmhouse to keep track of it as she glanced up. They broke from the woods and the dwelling lay straight ahead. Smoke was leaking flush to the roof from a stovepipe at one end of the long, rectangular building. There were numerous junk cars on the far side of the dooryard. The only apparently drivable vehicle was an older model Dodge van, a putrid yellow in color.

She looked down at the map and projected the direction they'd just come from Ms. Hancock's house. *Flint*. That set off bells inside her head.

"Flint," she said out loud.

Slowing for the dwelling, Roth began looking all around for danger. "You mean like the stone?"

"Yes."

He was now driving at idle speed. "Watch it—one of the doors is open."

She saw it. One of two doors on the front of the building. An unpainted structure thrown together from a mishmash of materials—clapboard, plying sheeting and even tin siding. This and presence of junk cars gave a rez feel to the place. "You think we're on Nation lands?"

"Doubt it. Reservation is still a couple miles north of us."

"You know of any Oneida named Flint?"

Roth gave a disinterested shake of his head as he scanned the tree line for movement. Anna realized that the fluttering, wind-driven snow made it hard to pick out movement. She rechecked the open doorway. Nothing but darkness beyond.

For the first time, she noticed tire impressions other than their own. They started directly in front of the dwelling but struck out along a narrow byway that wound north into the trees, avoiding the lane Roth and she had just descended.

Between this starting point and the open doorway was an indentation showing where something had been dragged across the snow. Straddled by large boot prints.

Anna was about to tell Roth when he said, "See it. Be careful." Bailing out, he drew his weapon.

She unholstered her pistol, but lingered inside the car long enough to advise Syracuse of their location and to expect a status report within minutes—or roll back-up.

Then she stepped out.

Roth clicked his eyes toward the open door, meaning that he wanted her to cover him. She nodded and raised her semi-automatic to eye-level, shifting her sight picture back and forth across the face of the building. Roth jogged stiffly, almost waddled, in his overcoat to one side of the doorway.

Snowflakes tangled in Anna's eyelashes and melted on the warm gunmetal of her semi-automatic.

Roth paused momentarily with his muzzle held skyward, then ducked inside.

Anna was right behind him. Going through the doorway, she recalled that the Oneida word for flint was *Tawiskalu*.

27

ANNA AND ROTH RAKED the shadowy corners of the squalid apartment with their handguns. They spun around the rooms in wary circles, and only when they were convinced that nobody was inside the place did she glance at the bed a second time. Nylon straps—military-style olive drab webbing—hung in limp strands off both the mattress and the frame. Most had been severed, apparently by the butcher's knife that still lay on the floor beside the bed.

Anna felt the exposed bottom sheet: warm to the touch.

This apartment accounted for only half of the total space of the structure, and no interior door gave access to the other side. It was a duplex. Roth grasped this as quickly as she, and together they swept outside and approached the door to the adjoining apartment. This time, Roth covered her as she tested the knob with a twist. Unlocked. She flung the door open and crouched as she crossed the threshold into a chilling darkness. To her back, there was a clink of metal rings as Roth parted the window drapes, letting in the twilight.

She swiveled her handgun from side to side, scanning the apartment for movement or worse—a stock-still human silhouette waiting for them.

No one.

Both kitchenette and bathroom were empty too. But there was a possible hiding place: a canopied bed shut off from the rest of the room by heavy curtains. On Anna's signal, Roth went to it and tore down an entire panel of drapes while she trained her weapon on the mattress within.

No one again, although the dark coverlet and pillow showed disturbance where someone had rested on them. Cold to the touch.

This apartment was unheated, unlike the first which had a woodstove going, and adding to the atmosphere of tomblike chill was the catafalque of a bed. Who would take pleasure from sleeping in such a thing?

Roth rushed back outside, and Anna followed.

They listened for the vehicle that might have departed in just the past few minutes. But the only sound was the creaking of the tree branches in the wind. Roth was getting in behind the wheel of the FBI car when Anna decided to do something before they gave chase. She dashed across the drifted yard to the front of the yellow van that had been left behind. A swipe of her hand revealed the license plate number. She committed it to memory and returned to the FBI car.

Roth had leaned across the front seats to unlatch the door for her.

Click-uh . . . Click-uh . . . Click-uh . . .

That is what Johnny Skyholder heard, telling him that a vehicle was approaching the duplex along the lane from the far side of the hill. He recognized it at once as being the annoying sound tire chains make when the spare links aren't fastened down. But to make matters more confusing, in the same instant his wristwatch went *beep . . . beep . . . beep*. It was time for medicine. Not for him. But for the redheaded lady, who was now wide-eyed as she lay strapped to his bed.

He had already started for his door, intending to go into Tawiskalu's apartment for the syringe kit, when his cell phone rang from his coverall pocket.

It was the Voice. "Time for her medicine."

Johnny stood at the open door, snowflakes whistling around him. The clicks of the tire chain ends sounded much closer than before, and he expected the vehicle to crest the hill momentarily. "Somebody's coming."

"Deputies?" the Voice asked.

"No, they got four-wheel drive. I hear chains on these tires."

"Take no chances. Get out right now."

"What about the lady's medicine?"

"No time. Get out. Can you leave by the north road?"

"I think so." Johnny checked the redheaded lady. She was writhing against her restraints, eyes glowering and nostrils flared above the strip of silver duct tape covering her mouth.

"Take Tawiskalu's van."

"But I don't like to drive—"

"Just do exactly what I say. Warm up Tawiskalu's van first. Then load the woman in the van. Keep an open line to me. Don't hang up. Do you understand?"

"Yes, yes." Johnny trudged dejectedly across the yard to the black van. He threw open the driver's door and flipped up the corner of the floor mat where Tawiskalu hid the key. Jumping into the seat, he turned over the balky engine. It coughed to life, but sputtered out. *Come on, come on, come on now.* On the second try, Johnny nursed the choke to keep the motor running.

Barely audible, the Voice squawked from the cell phone: "Everything okay?"

"Car's cold," Johnny said on his clumsy trot back to his apartment, slightly heady from the noxiously sweet exhaust fumes that now filled the air around him.

"Drive away . . ." The Voice unraveled into static from the storm.

"What?"

"Put some distance between you and the duplex. Then stop again. As soon as you safely can."

"Why?"

"Just do it," the Voice insisted.

Johnny clipped the phone to his breast pocket and began to try to untie the main knot. His long fingers shook with frustration. The woman looked spitefully up at him, adding to his hand tremors. "Dammit!" He gave up on the knot and headed for the kitchenette, where he ripped out a drawer and dumped the contents into the sink. He picked a butcher's knife out of the jumble of utensils and went back to the bed. Tawiskalu always carried a knife, but Johnny never did. He hated things that gave pain.

The woman's eyes bulged with fright, even as Johnny promised, hushed, "I won't hurt you. I'm the good one. I never hurt nobody."

He severed the straps, except those that bound her wrists and ankles, and scooped her up off the bed. He shifted her weight onto his shoulder and turned for the doorway, accidentally bashing her head against the jamb on his way outside. She showed that she was still conscious by kicking him. One of her toes dug into a kidney and he growled angrily, sounding more like Tawiskalu than himself, even to his own ears. Tawiskalu was always so close. So close.

He dropped her to the ground and dragged her across the snow.

He swung open the rear cargo doors with his free hand, lifted and laid her on the deck. There were things inside his brother's van he didn't like to look at, and he averted his eyes from them. Evil things used to carry out evil chores. It'd always been this way, even in Michigan, where Tawiskalu had kept a rusty Boy Scout knife to stick in stray dogs, a jar of gasoline in which he dropped live frogs.

By now, the approaching car was halfway down the near side of the hill, advancing slowly through the trees. Glimpses of it appeared and vanished through the woods.

"What's happening?" the Voice squawked.

Johnny unclipped the phone from his pocket. "I'm leaving right now."

"What about the car that's coming?"

"I think it's FBI. Looks like an FBI car to me."

The Voice had nothing to say about that.

Johnny's eyeglasses had misted up, but he just lowered them on the bridge of his nose as he accelerated along the north road. The four-wheel-drive van did fine in the snow and held the hairpin curves among the trees.

Bang . . . bang . . . bang!

The woman was bashing her bare feet against the rear doors. "Stop it!" Johnny shouted. "Or my brother will beat the stuffing out of you!"

She quit, but he was left feeling jittery and scared. He didn't like driving Tawiskalu's van. People might mistake him for his brother, and he detested that more than anything. He was nothing like his mean-spirited brother. He was gentle, even to people who didn't care for him.

"What's happening now?"

Johnny raised the cell phone to his ear again. "I'm in the woods."

"Is the car following you?"

"Can't tell yet." Johnny hiked one of his ponderous buttocks off the seat so he could remove his handkerchief from his rear pocket. He wiped his glasses, then jockeyed his body this way and that to check his mirrors. There was no sign of the car behind him. But he almost wanted to see it. He wanted to know if the Indian agent, Turnipseed, was inside. He'd always felt that he could talk to her. That she would understand the predicament he was in. He'd liked the sound of her voice that night in the museum, the way she'd stood eye-to-eye with White Pine. But Tawiskalu, who claimed to have been watching her for days, said she was a typical conniving red bitch who deserved to die, soon.

"Still clear behind?" the Voice asked.

"Yes."

"Stop the van."

Johnny did what he was told, so unthinkingly he felt disappointed with himself. He despised the power in the Voice, and his own powerlessness to resist it.

"Take your own medicine," it now ordered.

"I got no water out here."

"*Take it.*"

Johnny fumbled for the little bottle in his pocket, gulped down two reds dry.

"Drive on," the Voice continued smoothly, as smooth as the untracked snow ahead of the van. "Keep driving, but I want you to start to get comfortable."

"Can't. I'm scared."

"No reason to be scared. You're safe, relaxed and warm. Is the heater in the van starting to work?"

Johnny held his knuckles up to a vent. "Yes."

"Does it feel good?"

"Yes."

"Watch the road. But just with your eyes. Let your mind relax. Everything's okay. The FBI is miles and miles behind you. It's probably not the FBI, just some hunters looking for tracks. They're looking for little bunny rabbits, not you."

Johnny sighed wearily.

"Now," the Voice urged, "I want you to go back to Michigan. I want you—"

A jolt from behind rocked Johnny, snapping his head against the side window. He braked, turned around in the seat and seized the woman's ankle strap. She had squirmed down the length of the van's interior to a place just behind him. He gave her a fierce shake, more of a shake than he'd really intended, and she gave a muffled gurgle before lying still.

"What's going on?" the Voice asked from the floorboards. The woman's kick had made Johnny drop the phone.

He picked it up. "She's being bad."

The Voice said something, but it was lost in static again.

"What?" Johnny asked, slowing for the dip of a shallow creek, his tires crunching through the surface ice.

"I was saying," the Voice went on, "she's a bad woman. She's never been happy. She even murdered her own husband. Shot him dead in their bedroom . . ." Johnny glanced back at her body, motionless but for the swaying of the van. He hadn't known these things, otherwise he would have been far more cautious around her. She was like his brother, someone to be watched. Feared. "Do you know what Tawiskalu would do to her?"

"Yes," Johnny meekly replied, "he'd punish her."

"Exactly. Can you do that?"

"No. It's not up to me to punish her. That's up to Sky Father. I don't do bad things."

"Neither do I, Thaluhyawaku. In the end, everyone will see that. Everyone will benefit." Then the Voice said after a moment, "All right then, I want you to help her."

"How?"

"Free her from her unhappy life. She's not Oneida, but I know she would be happy in our heaven. She could be up there and be happy. It's always springtime up there, and she could draw water for the sweaty young lacrosse players and laugh with them."

Johnny saw these things in his mind, and they made him feel better. He believed that Hazen Two Kettles was up there now, laughing and playing lacrosse. This was the only way he could bear to think about the boy.

"Can you do this, Thaluhyawaku?"

Johnny was growing tired of resisting the Voice. "Maybe, maybe."

"I'm sure you can. Anyone behind you?"

Johnny looked. "No, not yet."

*   *   *

Anna thought a moment with her thumb off the microphone key. She had no description of the vehicle that had gone north from the duplex, other than the wide-tire tracks it had left on the road Roth and she were following through the increasingly dark forest. She did have compelling evidence of a person being held against his or her will—the severed nylon straps around the bed. She had little doubt that that person was Portia Nelson. But how to frame all this in a coherent way so a law enforcement cordon could be thrown up around the turtle-shaped hill that had no name on the Niagara Mohawk Power service map? "Control," she finally raised the Syracuse FBI office, identifying herself.

"Still code four?" the distant dispatcher asked.

"Negative, requesting assistance in the Stockbridge area. We have indications a kidnap victim has just been moved from a remote residence . . ." Pausing, she turned to Roth. "Where the hell are we?"

Shrugging, he looked at a loss too. "A hill north of Williams Road is the only way I can describe it. The Madison deputies should know where the Hancock residence is."

Anna repeated the less than specific location over the air, only to have the dispatcher ask for a vehicle description.

"Unknown," Anna transmitted, "but I need registration and wants on a New York plate. Not the vehicle we're pursuing."

"Go ahead with your plate."

Anna gave the dispatcher the license number to the yellow van that had been left at the duplex.

The dispatcher repeated the number, then advised Anna to switch to the mutual aid frequency. She did so in time to hear the Madison sheriff's dispatcher repeat the information she'd just provided. In its second telling, it sounded fragmentary. Sketchy, almost useless. Rural New York was proving to be as sparsely posted with signs as a reservation out West.

She strained through the windshield for a glimpse of the vehicle ahead of them. The driver probably knew better than to tap his brakes, but she hoped for a blink of red. The road, defined only by its winding course through the trees and the tire tracks, abruptly plunged down toward a half-frozen creek. Shards of freshly-broken ice were being heaped against a log by the flowing water.

The bucar side-slipped on the steep down-grade. Roth let go of the steering wheel and kept his foot off the brake pedal. The slide slowed to a crawl, but still Anna's side of the car crunched into the trunk of a pine. "Goddamn!" Roth cried, then dropped the automatic shift lever into low gear and continued down toward the streamlet, leaving a strip of chrome trim mashed into the bark. "We keep asking for four-bys for our motor pool, but Washington says we got no business being out in the boonies anyways. Damn!"

Before Anna could commiserate, the FBI dispatcher raised her. "No wants on your 1989 Dodge van. Registration is current—"

A squeal marked an overriding transmission from a state trooper, who advised that he was just leaving the barracks in Oneida, the whine of speed in the background.

Frowning, Anna asked the dispatcher to repeat the registration information.

"Registered owner is a Johnny T. Skyholder, Rural Route 14, Peterboro, New York."

Anna stared down between her shoes at the slushy floor mat.

"I know where that is," a new voice on the radio declared. "Williams Road feeds right into it."

"Unit identify," the FBI dispatcher requested.

"Madison S.O. patrol unit Robert-Four-Paul, responding from Morrisville," the patrol deputy explained. "FBI unit, you have any idea where you are . . . ?"

Anna glanced up, still dazed, abstracted. The defroster-melted snow was beginning to stick as ice on the glass wherever the wipers didn't reach. The onset of darkness was almost complete, but the snowfall seemed to create its own diffuse light out in the trees. A shattered white sky falling in pieces to blanket the earth.

"You read me, FBI?" the deputy asked.

Anna scarcely felt Roth slipping the mike from her grasp, and she was only peripherally aware of the confusion on his face as he glanced away from her. "We're above Williams Road on an unpaved road that's sloping away to the north," the agent said. "Following wide-track tire impressions, possibly to a light truck or van. We can use some help out in front of us."

"Okay, I think I know where you are," the state trooper responded. "There's a hill like that northeast of Peterboro, isn't there, Rich?"

"Sounds like it," the deputy answered. He and the trooper went on speculating about the location while Anna re-opened *The Oneida Creation Story*. Her penlite beam skipped over the pages of the introduction—until she found what she was seeking, a passage she'd highlighted after the peculiar juvenile-sounding voice had left the second message on her voicemail.

Roth tried to get her attention. "What's wrong?"

But she ignored him as words from White Pine's introduction leapt out at her: *Sky Woman's good son was named Thaluhyawaku, translated as "Upholder of Heaven" or "Sky-holder." Her evil-minded son was called Tawiskalu, the Oneida word for flint.* The magical stone that, with steel, creates fire. A combustible name, evocative of power.

"What is it, Turnipseed?"

Her only answer was to take the shotgun down from its roof rack and prop it between her legs, awaiting the moment when Roth and she would confront Tawiskalu along a road bend in this dismal forest. She now believed that she had already met his brother, Johnny, the night janitor at the cultural center. Johnny believed himself to be Thaluhyawaku, the Good Twin. Maybe he was, despite his ominous appearance. But the coming confrontation would be gut-wrenching if only because she had seen with her own eyes that Tawiskalu—or Adrian Flint—was his brother's match in sheer size.

"I need headlights," Roth said.

He was right. It was now fully dark.

"Go ahead," Anna said. "Turn them on."

"I want you to stop the van as soon as you can, Thaluhyawaku. Can you seen anything behind?"

Minuscule headlights showed in Johnny's left-side mirror, twinkling through the trees far up on the hill. "They've put on their lights," he said, scrunching the cell phone between his cheek and shoulder.

"Have you turned on yours?"

"Not yet," Johnny replied. "Don't need 'em yet. I know the way. And it's never that dark in the snow."

"Are they close behind?"

"Not close, no."

"Then stop the van. I want you to take a minute to relax."

Johnny laughed bitterly at the absurdity of relaxing. He'd never felt less relaxed in his entire life, except maybe when Goose's beak had been jabbing at his genitals. Once again, he was taking the blame for Tawiskalu's mischief. Once again, he was running when he'd done nothing wrong.

"Have you stopped?" the Voice asked.

"No." On the contrary, Johnny had left the logging road and was driving west on Stockbridge Hill Road. The snowplow had not made it here, but the six inches of snow were like a cushion under the van. At last, he hit his headlights and with a mild start noted the large flakes, previously invisible, that now seemed to be sucked into his windshield. There were no other vehicle lights on the highway as far as he could see.

"I want you to find Tawiskalu for me."

Johnny gritted his teeth in silence.

"Do you know where Tawiskalu is?"

Johnny checked on the woman. She was curled up in the back of the cargo area, legs doubled against her chest, as still as a department store dummy. Sooner or later, everybody quit fighting.

"I think you know where your brother is."

"Fuck Tawiskalu," Johnny seethed.

"What do you mean?" For the first time in memory, the Voice sounded worried. But Johnny didn't listen to it. He tossed the phone onto the passenger seat beside him and slowed the van, gradually, so he wouldn't spin out.

The Voice went on, words inaudible but with the same undertone of concern and indignation.

Johnny felt exhilarated by his own rebelliousness. He stopped completely and got out of the van, smiling with open arms up into the snow, which seemed to be planting cold little caresses on his face. The sky was blessing what he meant to do. He was going to let the redheaded woman go. He was going to ignore the Voice and do something good. Thaluhyawaku was finally going to triumph over Tawiskalu.

Johnny opened the rear doors, ready to tell the woman that he was going to untie her, free her to walk to the nearest house, which was less than a mile back down the way they'd come. But before he could speak a puff of air hit his eyes, instantly followed by something hard and bony. A crunch resonated inside his skull, the crunch of the bridge of his nose snapping. Pain blinded him, and he sank to his knees, burying his face in his hands. His palms filled with a warm wetness. The luminous sensation of pain became the milky summer sun over his play pool in white Nana's backyard. A shadow fell across him. Nana was standing over him, her heavy-jowled face full of pleasure as she nestled Goose in her arms. Goose was there too in the sunburst of pain, jabbing, clenching Johnny's youthful penis in his beak and flexing it.

How red you are. As red as your drunken father!

Johnny roared against the pain. Against the indignity being visited on his genitals. Howled against the mix of hatred and love he had for this grandmother. Both grandmothers. All women, especially those with contempt for him. Like the bitch Turnipseed. Damned conniving bitches.

Then the play pool, white Nana and Goose were gone again, and he saw that the redheaded woman had somehow managed to lower herself out of the back of the van and was slinking across the road toward the trees.

Mopping his bloody face with his sleeve, he plodded after her.

She rose on her knees and lunged for freedom, but he seized her by the wrist strap and jerked her to her feet. His rage made her feel as light as a feather. She turned her face up into his, eyes rapt with a disgust that infuriated him. Infuriated him as much as the black drops of blood that were spilling out of his broken nose and flecking the snow around his boots.

She was white. Like white Nana.

Then he did the unthinkable.

He reared back his hand and slapped her. He backhanded white Nana's heavy-jowled face. Her head snapped to the side. He could never have imagined how good it felt to strike her. He did it again. Again and again until her head hung limp on her neck and she was left moaning. Then he dragged her back to the rear doors and hurled her inside the van. She landed on the cargo deck with a bone-rattling thump.

Something made him look over his shoulder. Faint lights. The headlights of the pursuing car were almost to the highway. But then he realized that they weren't moving.

He strode confidently to the driver's door, threw it open. He switched off his own headlights before reaching across the seats for his cell phone. "Hello," he said in a low, surly growl.

Pause. Then the Voice said pleasantly, "Hello, my dear Tawiskalu. Glad to have you back. Everything under control?"

"Quite." He took his handkerchief from his pocket and finished wiping his face. His nose was already swelling up, but the pain now gratified him. It made him feel sharp and strong. "I know what to do from here."

"Get it done, then ditch the van. You know where. I'll pick you up there and we'll have a little breather at the lake. Good-bye for now."

He put down the phone and turned on the dome light—just as the woman made a gurgling noise and vomit flew out of her nose. Swiftly, for he didn't want her to aspirate on her own puke, he ripped the duct tape away from her mouth. She threw up repeatedly. He let her as he put down the back of his bucket seat and slid into the cargo area. He no longer saw white Nana in her, just a pathetic woman who was making a stink in the back of his van. "Not so smart, not so smart," he repeated, taking three large weather balloons from a box in the back and tethering them together.

She gazed up at him, her face very still.

"We should pick our friends with care . . ." He fitted the neck of the first balloon over the connection to the manifold assembly that tapped several helium tanks at once. Then he turned on the valves. The loud hisses made the woman flinch. "You chose poorly," he went on, removing from the same box one of the web harnesses he'd fashioned. "There's no worse friend in this world than an Indian witch. Both those terms are probably politically incorrect—*Indian* and *witch*. But when I'm right I'm right, and when all's said and done a red witch will bring you nothing but bad luck . . ." The swelling rubber globe began to fill the interior of the cargo area, so he nudged it through the rear doors as he began inflating the next balloon. "And now you're flat out of luck, Portia."

"Shit," Roth whispered as the bucar skidded off a curve. Anna cringed, waiting for a plunge down the hillside. But the chained tires grabbed, and the car shuddered to a halt, headlights flaring out into the billowing white.

Roth jammed the lever into reverse. But he didn't have enough traction to back onto the road again.

"Shut off the engine," Anna said.

"What?"

"Kill the engine and lights a minute." Wrenching open the damaged door, she bailed out and stood with a hand held against the snowy wind. There was an opening below, a valley perhaps, but with no signs of activity other than a stationary white-red glow, so dim and fuzzy she couldn't mark the instant when it seemed to disappear entirely.

"What is it?" Roth asked over the roof of the car.

"Suspect vehicle, I think."

They both sat back inside, and Roth grabbed the mike to confirm with the back-ups from the sheriff's office and state police if they were indeed in position to block the fleeing vehicle. Five different officers advised that they were, but the agent sounded unconvinced as he transmitted, "This is the hill north of a Mrs. Hancock's residence. Anybody know where that is?"

A lull went on so long, Roth asked, "Copy me?"

"Roger," a deputy said sheepishly, "I didn't hear anything about old lady Hancock's place. We're set up around the hill just to the north of Peterboro. Sounds like you're coming down off the backside of Stockbridge Hill." He could be heard firing up his engine.

As Roth swore, Anna stepped out into the night again. The white-red light was gone, so completely gone she wondered if she'd only imagined it. But then she heard something too distinctive to be imagined—a scream and then a choking sob directly overhead.

She looked up, but there was nothing to be seen except swirling snow.

Another scream followed, but this one grew faint into the night.

28

FROM THE MEADOW NEAR the duplex, Anna watched the night sky. Stars shone from a deep cobalt blue. The storm had moved on, leaving a foot of fresh snow that was muffling all sounds—except one. A steady thumping had been approaching out of the west for some minutes. She lit a highway flare and held it at an arm's length. The thumping cleared the turtle-shaped hill and became thunderous. A spotlight bored down out of the heavens, skittered through the trees and fixed on her.

The Air National Guard helicopter swooped down, raising a blizzard, and eased its skids to the pillowed ground. The cabin door swung open, and a helmeted crewman motioned for Anna to approach the craft.

She pitched the flare into the snow and jogged over in a crouch. The rotor blade twirled with a whooshing noise like a guillotine that seemed only inches above her head. The waiting crewman was Chief Master Sergeant Riley from the Syracuse Search and Rescue unit. "Take this," he shouted, handing her an Air Force parka that was too large for her.

There was already another passenger in the cabin: William Jordan. The deputy chief marshal patted the place on the bench beside him. She sat and was starting to strap herself in—when he stopped her with a light touch. "Wait, Turnipseed. If you want, you can call it a day." Then he added with a face that had gone very still, "Parker's mother has sent for other relatives to come from Oklahoma."

Anna understood at once. Without saying it, Jordan was telling her that Emmett's condition had taken a turn for the worse. He was giving her the chance to go immediately to the hospital. But how do you say good-bye to somebody heavily sedated so a ventilation tube can be shoved down his throat? However unintentionally, all their good-byes had been said days ago beside Sunset Lake.

The parka sleeves were too long. She folded them back and belted herself in. She would join the search for the woman who had screamed from the sky. It was what Emmett's voice told her to do. "How do you know about Parker's condition?" she asked.

"I've been checking every few hours," Jordan said. "I deputized him, so I consider him to be one of my own."

"But not enough your own to tell him you were secretly guarding committee members all these weeks?"

"When you're not allowed to explain something, Turnipseed, you don't even try."

She knew her question had been unfair. Jordan had been acting under Judge Solomon's orders. But neither did she feel like apologizing. All of a sudden, she was riotously angry because of Emmett. At the whole world.

Her heart rose into her throat as the chopper lifted off and banked sharply over the tree tops. She had a plunging view of the duplex, its lighted windows and the FBI vehicles of the Evidence Response Team parked out front. The pilot's searchlight told her that he was following the combined tracks of the suspect vehicle and her loaner car to the bend where Roth had become mired in the snow—and she had heard the scream fade to the northeast. Earlier tonight, as her car was winched from the snow bank by a tow truck, a state trooper had determined the exact coordinates with his Global Positioning Satellite device. That spot would mark the beginning of the search for the woman, presumed to have been borne by the strong southwesterly at that hour into Oneida County and beyond.

Portia Nelson, Anna felt sure.

Rising slightly from the bench, she could see Stockbridge Hill Road at last, on which she believed she'd spotted the lights of the suspect vehicle. Plowed free of its snow, the road now showed like a black ribbon. There was no moon, as it was still in its new phase, but the starlight was dazzling on the snow.

An error, a wrong assumption of the kind that occurred all the time in law enforcement, had left either Johnny Skyholder or Adrian Flint—or both, conceivably—free to drive off into the stormy night. In all the frenetic radio traffic, the deputy assigned to the Stockbridge beat hadn't heard mention of Mrs. Hancock's residence, with which he was familiar. As a result, the cordon had been thrown up around another hill four miles to the west.

Spilt milk.

Jordan leaned into her to be heard. "How close is the ERT to wrapping up?"

"Not very. More and more evidence keeps cropping up." She paused as the pilot turned northeast, following Portia's probable track across the sky. "The duplex is owned by the tribe. One of many properties they rent out to Oneida Nation employees."

"And this Johnny Skyholder, who works as a maintenance man for the Shak—" Jordan's mouth puckered in frustration. "How d'you say it?"

"Shako:wi Cultural Center. Yes, he rented one of the apartments. Adrian Flint, the other."

"Flint's not a tribal employee. He works for that catering service at the airport."

"Right, but he might be related to Skyholder."

Jordan observed, "But their last names are different."

"Archetypal names."

"Sorry?"

"Skyholder and Flint are the names of two legendary brothers—" Thankfully, she was spared delving into the significance of the Twins in Oneida cosmology when an impatient Jordan asked her to recount the evidence collected thus far. She took a breath and told him what had been recovered by the time she'd stepped out of the duplex and into the meadow:

Brenda Two Kettles's purse and carry-on bag, including her boarding pass for Flight 557 to LaGuardia.

Hazen Two Kettles's black leather jacket.

Long red hairs off the filthy pillow on the bed where someone had lain for long hours, strapped in to prevent escape.

Enough barbs to zone out an elephant, and a syringe kit with an unidentified substance in the vials.

And, preliminarily, the fingerprint technician suspected that the majority of latents gathered from surfaces inside both apartments came from a single individual. Too many repeated digits. But none matching either Brenda's or Portia's exemplar cards, telling him that the women had not had the run of the place. Yet, Madison S.O. had sent a facsimile of Hazen Two Kettles's fingerprint card to the portable fax in the FBI evidence van, confirming that the boy had made at least one foray around Skyholder's apartment. Before escaping? Hazen hadn't drowned in Sunset Lake. That much was clear.

Anna's eyes ached with fatigue. Another long night.

Jordan visibly reflected out the side window.

She'd already learned from him that both Skyholder and Flint had been no-shows at their jobs. Roth, a SWAT ninja in addition to a regular agent, had helped hit the cultural center. Other ninjas and field agents had swarmed over Chez Sky Foods' operations at the airport. Both teams had come up empty-handed. DMV checks showed no driver's license or vehicle registrations in the name of Adrian Flint. But Skyholder held title to two 1989 Dodge vans, something that struck her as peculiar. One of them, the yellow one, was still parked outside the duplex among the junkers left by previous occupants. His other van was now believed to be the vehicle that had eluded Roth and her on the logging road off what she now knew to be Stockbridge Hill, and its plate number was being rebroadcast on the mutual aid frequency every thirty minutes—with a caution that the driver was to be considered *armed and dangerous.*

Jordan was examining her. "How well you know Christopher White Pine?" he asked.

"Not very. Ran in to him a couple of times over the past two weeks here." Most notably at the longhouse when he'd been confronted by his boss, the Nation Rep. But she wasn't ready to admit that unauthorized meeting to anybody. "Why?"

"White Pine has left two urgent messages for Cochran at the Syracuse office." The special agent in charge, obviously, was the source of the marshal's current case information.

"Fred respond yet?"

"No." Jordan glanced out his window again. "He wants to talk to you first."

Anna estimated that they were flying about five hundred feet over the frosted hills. There would have been no stars for Portia, just the cold and stifling darkness of the snow clouds. *Enveloped by darkness,* as the creation story said, silence but for snowflakes pattering against the weather balloons.

"Why do you think White Pine is so eager to get hold of the SAC?" Jordan continued.

"Damage control. It's his specialty."

Chief Riley appeared from the cockpit. "Pilot would like to show you two what he's doing."

Unfastening her belt, Anna was glad for distraction. It was hitting her now, the fact that Emmett's mother had sent for the rest of the family.

On wobbly legs, she followed the chief and Jordan forward.

The pilot and co-pilot introduced themselves, but she was too distracted to recall their names a second later, distracted by the alien environment of the noisy, dimly-lit cockpit. The pilot tapped the reddish screen to a monitor. "Infrared radar," he explained, "the hot spot you see right here . . ." He pointed. ". . . is to the motor of a vehicle that was probably parked hours ago. Still warm enough for us to pick it up." The car was beside a house in a residential development, so of no special interest.

She found the screen itself to be like a predatory eye on the snowy, timbered hills. It probed the frigid night for the heat of blood. Jordan was thinking along similar lines, for he asked the pilot, "Would your radar pick up a corpse three hours after time of death?"

"Yes, sir. It gets down to contrast. The ground is extremely cold tonight. A dead body would still be giving off visible heat hours from now."

Anna took no satisfaction from the revelation that the marshal also assumed Portia Nelson was long dead. It still gave her chills to recall that scream gliding over her head and off into the night.

Suddenly one entire side of the screen flashed an explosive red. At the same time, Anna noticed an eruption of flame rise out of the southeast. Catching it as well, Jordan said knowingly, "There's our suspect vehicle." He slipped a Handie-Talkie from his jacket pocket and raised the Oneida Sheriff's dispatcher, reminding Anna that they had crossed out of Madison County by now. "I've got a visual on large fire . . . stand by for location."

The pilot was giving him the approximate coordinates when dispatch advised the marshal that phone reports had already come in on the 911 system and the Vernon Volunteer Fire Department was responding to a barn fire off State Route 26.

"Copy." Jordan asked the pilot to head that way.

As the chopper veered southeast, Anna saw the orange flame grow in size. It was crowned by a canopy of murk, smoke that blotted out the stars there. Within minutes, they were circling over the scene. A feathery plume of retardant was gushing from the nozzle on a ladder truck's boom.

The chopper was buffeted by the surprisingly strong updraft from the fire. The pilot widened the circle and switched on his spotlight to assist with the effort.

More and more volunteer firemen arrived in their private vehicles. The barn was barely reminiscent of a structure. As Anna watched, the last remaining wall collapsed, sending up a torrent of sparks that drove the hose teams back on their heels. The barnyard was girdled by a band of dark mud where the snow had been scorched off.

More emergency vehicles were coming down Route 26, which she saw connected with the Dewey Thruway a few miles to the north. By which Skyholder could escape, if he hadn't already.

"Set us down," Jordan told the pilot.

"Okay, but strap yourselves in first. Chief, prepare to land."

"Roger, sir."

Anna and Jordan returned to their bench seat. "What makes you so sure it's the suspect vehicle?" she asked him.

"Skyholder or Flint is smart enough to know he won't last long tooling around in his own van. Also, he didn't have time to sanitize the duplex, but he won't make that mistake with his ride. Matter of fact, I was *counting* on him using fire to destroy any remaining evidence. Hopefully, he's not familiar with the wonders modern forensics can work with arson cases . . ." Once again, a blizzard of rotor-stirred snow engulfed the chopper. "In any event, he's telling us where to pick up the hunt."

Stepping down with the chief's help, Anna recoiled from the awesome heat. It made her want to turn away, despite an equally strong urge to behold the raging fire. She flipped up the hood to the Air Force parka and half-shut the opening to protect her nose and mouth.

Holding his fedora to his head with a hand, Jordan strode past her to collar a fire captain. He pointed out tire tracks in the snow he wanted preserved. The captain was scarcely listening. Obviously, the fire was the largest in recent local history, and he was mesmerized by it. By now, several streams of retardant arched into the conflagration, but had little effect on it.

Anna inspected the tire impressions. She believed they were the same Roth and she had followed on the logging road earlier in the evening. Jordan was pointing into the heart of the fire, bawling over the crackling roar for the captain to have his men aim their nozzles there.

Giving the heat a wide berth, Anna ambled to the far side of the barn. There, she found boot tracks that emerged from the mud and struck across the snowfield—directly for the highway. They were at least men's fifteens, worthy of the behemoth janitor she'd seen in the cultural center that night she first met White Pine. Johnny T. Skyholder had passed this way. It had to have been him.

Returning to Jordan's side, she finally saw what had captivated him— the shell of a van half-buried by a shoal of embers. He grinned at her: "See?"

She nodded appreciatively, although she couldn't imagine what evidence of value could survive a fire that intense.

Then she noticed something sparkling nearby in the mud.

Shielding the side of her face with the hood, she darted for the object. The heat almost forced her back, but she grabbed for a pair of horn-rimmed glasses and took them to Jordan.

"What've you got?"

"Eyeglasses."

"Skyholder's?"

"Maybe. Ditched here, though boot tracks head for the road from the other side of the barn."

The marshal brushed away a cinder that was smoldering on the shoulder of her parka, then took the glasses from her. "I'm going to call in my people and get a ground search going. Starting right here. You mind continuing the aerial search alone?"

She shook her head.

He gave her arm a squeeze. "We'll put this one to bed, Turnipseed. Believe me."

Back in the chopper, she asked the pilot to resume the search from the point where they'd turned away for the fire. Soon, they were back on Portia

Nelson's presumed flight path, heading northeast again, the raptor-like infrared eye scanning the terrain for blood heat.

Anna retired to the cabin and strapped herself in.

The questions, of course, were where and at what altitude had the stolen barometric switch kicked in, igniting the Cartridge Actuated Device that severed Portia's tether to the balloons? Anna watched the sky slip past. Fatigue made everything seem forlorn, depressingly unreal. A cluster of lights blazed to the north. Either Rome or Utica, she wasn't certain which. Between this luminous city and her lay the sky. Beautiful and deadly, the membrane between heaven and earth. A realm apart. With no place in it for a human to rest. *Down and down she falls, and as she is enveloped by darkness, she keeps falling down and down. Then at last, a light suddenly appears in the direction towards which she is falling.*

Anna wondered if, somehow, the clouds had parted and Portia had seen the lights of that city just before she plummeted to her death.

Birds dwelt aloft, and they went flying up, the one leading them saying to the flock, "It is a woman coming down, it's a woman coming down!"

Anna startled as a hand rested on her shoulder. It was Riley. "Pilot wants to see you, ma'am," the chief said, not blinking.

The chopper, she realized, was now hovering.

She trailed Riley forward as if in a dream, with the prescient sense of her recent dreams that she knew which horror would unfold next. The pilot was saying something to her, but his words were lost as she fixated on the infrared screen. On it, against a background of pink snow, was etched a human figure in bright red, arms clearly outstretched and one leg skewed over the other. Gradually, the pilot's words penetrated her shock: "I can put us down about a quarter mile away. That close enough for you?"

29

JOHNNY SKYHOLDER LAY ON a leather sofa, a blanket stretched tight over his toes and up to his chin. The leather was stiff from the cold and crackled under him each time he heaved a sob. He had been crying off and on for hours and could not stop, no matter how hard he tried.

"Come on," the Voice said impatiently, "pull yourself together."

Johnny dried his eyes on a corner of the scratchy woolen blanket and looked into the big wall mirror opposite him. He saw the Voice's reflection—cold, quiet and composed. Dr. White Pine was seated behind him in a leather chair that matched the sofa. The therapist was much higher than Johnny, partly because he was sitting up and partly because the unheated main cabin was on a slant. He was still bundled up in his overcoat with a scarf around his throat. His words came out in white spurts of mist.

Johnny wasn't sure how he'd come to join Dr. White Pine in this beached houseboat. A piece of time in his life was missing again. He did know that the boat belonged to the tribe, as did the marina outside. In a corner of the mirror, he could see a sliding glass door, and through it, Oneida Lake beyond. It stretched away under a late afternoon sun. The recent cold snap had refrozen the surface. Across a half-moon bay was the boathouse after which the marina was named.

As always, Dr. White Pine was scratching out notes on a pad, but today he kept his gloves on as he wrote. "Tell me about last night, Johnny."

"I don't . . . ," he started, but then stopped, his own voice sounding queerly nasal to him from his broken nose. "I don't remember."

"Then why do you feel so bad?"

"That's the thing," he wailed. "I don't know. I never know!"

Johnny realized that he'd shouted only when Dr. White Pine frowned. "Certainly, dear boy, you must remember *something*. Please try."

Obediently, Johnny shut his eyes, trying, snuffling, his swollen nose aching with each snuffle. And it hurt to think. He never wanted to think again. Just when his brain felt like it was going to burst from the effort, an image popped into it. "I see a lady."

"Describe her."

"Red hair. Eyes the same color as the dogtooth flowers my white Nana grew in her garden."

"And what's the redheaded lady doing?"

"She's all tied . . ." Johnny tossed his head from side to side.

"What's wrong?"

"Can't see her no more."

"Why not?"

"Tawiskalu gets in the way." Johnny checked the image in the mirror.

Dr. White Pine was tapping his pen against his chin. "Relax. Close your eyes again and relax. Don't strain. Everything will come back to you."

Johnny shut his eyes and pulled in a shuddery breath through his mouth. It was so hard to relax. But he tried, and after a few minutes he saw flames flickering against the insides of his eyelids. He smelled kerosene and saw pretty orange flames. "Fire," he whispered.

"What?"

"I see fire."

"So," White Pine said, "*you do* recall last night."

"A little."

"Relax, you're nice and comfortable. Nothing can hurt you. I won't let anybody hurt you. I never do. Tell me about this fire."

"Can't."

"Of course you can. *Try, dammit.*"

Dr. White Pine was different this morning, and it disturbed Johnny. In all their years together, he seldom showed impatience. Or disapproval. Yet, his voice dripped with both this morning. At last, Johnny complained, "I can't see the fire because Tawiskalu gets in the way."

"*Tawiskalu gets in the way.*" A sarcastic echo.

Again, Johnny checked the man's reflection in the mirror.

Dr. White Pine pocketed his pen and pad as if he never meant to write anything ever again. "Enough," the therapist sighed.

"What do you mean?" Johnny asked, suddenly worried.

"It's time Tawiskalu stops getting in the way."

"But how can we stop him?"

From the depths of the mirror, Dr. White Pine held Johnny's gaze. "You remember the day the juvenile authorities brought you to my office in Sault Sainte Marie . . . ?"

Johnny nodded. Cautiously. He didn't like this. It felt like veering a car off a highway at night. They were leaving the familiar for darkness.

"They brought you to me for a court-ordered evaluation. Remember what you'd done, Johnny?"

"No."

"Tell the truth. You'll never be punished here for telling the truth. It was in the city park."

"Park?"

"Yes, you doused a swan with lighter fluid and set it on fire."

"I . . ." Johnny's alibi collapsed in the delicious, glorious image of Goose in flames, flapping around the park, leaving behind trails of smoke and singed feathers.

"You don't like swans, do you? Swans helped Sky Woman, saved her from a fatal fall, didn't they?"

"I don't like Goose," Johnny clarified.

"All right, Goose, then. The probation officer let off John Flint, an over-sized boy who cringed when I reached out to shake his hand."

"My name's Johnny Skyholder."

"Not legally. You cringed like a dog that had been whipped. And whipped you had been. Verbally by both grandmothers, physically by one. *Dueling grandmas,* as I put in my report to the court, one Indian and one white. Your Oneida Nana was a relative of mine, a distant cousin and a nasty-tempered alcoholic bitch. Your white Nana was a teetotaler, so there was no excuse for her cruelties. You remember being shuttled back and forth between the two of them, Johnny, two reluctant caregivers who couldn't stand the sight of you . . . ?"

He flipped the blanket over his face. *Too fast.* Dr. White Pine had never rattled things off so fast before. Always nice and slow and patient before.

"One despised your white blood," he went on, "the other your Indian blood. It was impossible to ever please either of them, let alone both of them, so do you know what I did?"

"You helped me not to get in trouble so much."

"But do you know how I did that?"

"No."

"I came up with an alternative to psychosis for you, Johnny. I rescued you with Dissociative Identity Disorder, which is no disorder at all. It's a fad diagnosis. A by-product of psychotherapy itself. The result of leading comments, hypnosis and barbiturates, a drug which increases vulnerability to suggestion. The therapist can inadvertently trigger DID . . ." He chuckled. "Or *not* so accidentally trigger it."

"Why're you saying these things?" Johnny said, staying under the blanket.

"Because it's time to say them."

Johnny peeked out at Dr. White Pine, who'd sat back with his hands clasped behind his head.

"I gave you a way not to feel so conflicted. Some inner turmoil is unavoidable, and that's what you're feeling today. But, by and large, I split your internal conflict off into two personalities. One that was weak but good and one that was strong but completely lacking what in the traditional view passes for conscience. I designed a multiple-personality mechanism for you, one based on the Sky Woman myth, because after chucking white Nana down the cellar stairs you were so turned on by the notion of a female literally falling from grace. This mechanism allowed you to avenge yourself while maintaining the fiction that you were a good person. Nobody can be as good and loving as Thaluhyawaku, not without also having a Tawiskalu to look out for him in this world. Not you, Johnny. Not me. Not anyone. I too have a Tawiskalu inside me. The difference between you and me is that I accept him."

Johnny asked, "What d'you mean *avenge*?"

"You confessed to two homicides to me, but I exercised the therapist-patient privilege and kept both confessions from the courts."

"Confessions?"

"You killed your Nanas."

Close to tears again, Johnny whimpered, "Not true, not true. I loved 'em."

"That's the terrible irony of child abuse. The child loves his tormentor." White Pine smiled consolingly. "It's okay, Johnny. Homicide is a non-judgmental term, means nothing more than the taking of a human life. Your actions were in self-defense after the most extreme kind of provocation. That isn't murder."

"If what you're saying's true, how come you let me do these things— you, a doctor?"

"You have no idea how long I've waited for that question, Johnny. Good for you. How often I've contemplated the same issue myself." Dr. White Pine rose and—due to the slanting deck—limped to the sliding glass door. He looked out on the cloudless day. "A psychotherapist sees so much evil. Unimaginable cruelty of the kind that was inflicted on you as a child— and me. I too had the equivalent of your Nanas, a pedophile of a stepfather. But the therapist, even the abused therapist, is supposed to stay objective. He's supposed to see that evil as sickness. In the expectation that it can be cured. But you can't cure evil. So why not make use of it to achieve ultimate good in the world? Nothing good can be achieved without involving an element of evil. So, dear boy, I asked myself—*If evil is ubiquitous, inevitable and incurable, is it truly wrong for me to use a little of it to satisfy my own need to help my people . . . ?*" He gazed off at the old boathouse, his trim body was limned by sunshine. "Some therapists prey on their patients for sex. I always found that rather pathetic. Small change. There are greater needs than sex. Such as claiming your rightful place in the world and helping your people achieve greatness again." Dr. White Pine's face turned back toward Johnny in the mirror. "Do you have any idea what I'm talking about?"

"No," he said.

"A shame. That's why it's always more enjoyable to talk to Tawiskalu. He understands."

"I hate him."

"Oh, but he's so useful." White Pine approached the sofa and stood over

Johnny, who craned his neck to look up at him. "We've reached a critical juncture in your therapy. The crucial step in which we must attempt to integrate the alternate personalities back into a single psyche." He stepped around the end of the sofa and knelt so that his eyes were on the same level as Johnny's. Sympathetic brown eyes, which made the things he was saying all the more confusing. "As I just said, I have my own Tawiskalu within me."

"Your own Evil Twin?" Johnny asked incredulously.

"Yes. We all have one. Unlike you, dear boy, I'm grateful for the things he does in my behalf." Dr. White Pine paused. "You remember what the other Oneida kids in Michigan called you?"

"*Shakes the Earth,*" Johnny said bitterly. "On account I was so big for my age."

"And what'd you do when they called you that?"

"Cried," he admitted, tears spilling from his eyes, now as then. He hated how the therapist could make things come back to him in a flash.

"Yes," Dr. White Pine said mockingly, "John Flint cried. But it was his alter, his fearless brother, Adrian, who caught those same kids on a reservation road at night and beat them so bloody nobody ever called you *Shakes the Earth* again."

"I don't remember."

"How convenient. Do you also forget the winter night your Oneida Nana passed out after screaming and ranting at you once again, berating you so vilely you carried her into the woods behind the shack and left her there to freeze to death?"

"Tawiskalu may've said something about it," Johnny said evasively.

"That naughty, naughty Tawiskalu," Dr. White Pine mocked, making Johnny's lower lip tremble. "Well, in any event, the coroner ruled accident. You were just a boy of thirteen, larger than most grown men, worthy of being branded *Shakes the Earth,* but still a boy. Who was doing no more than defending himself and aspiring to his rightful place on God's good earth. Don't you get it, Johnny?"

He didn't. He wanted to run, but couldn't. He'd shucked off his boots and the thought of fumbling into them, but Dr. White Pine's critical stare kept him from getting up. For the moment, the therapist's gaze was pinning him to the sofa.

"Remember this? About a year later, white Nana fell down her basement stairs. Again, an accident, though the authorities nearly got you on
that one. It took all my powers to confuse the issue and save you from the
consequences of that massive shove to the back of her head. Tell me that you
remember, Johnny. Don't lie. Don't blame Tawiskalu. Please, dear boy," Dr.
White Pine implored with a steady beat to his voice, "tell me about that afternoon. You never have. Tell me about that final day with white Nana. I
don't want Adrian to tell me. I want *you* to."

Johnny wanted to swing his long legs to the slanting deck, race for the
sliding glass door, fling it open on the bright day and make for freedom. But,
instead, he was shuffling behind white Nana down that gloomy corridor that
led to the cellar door. He was trapped in the past again. "Nana," he began
tentatively, "she says I'm too big for the hammock now. She's 'fraid I'll bust
right through it, so these days she takes me down to the cellar instead."

"Have you already gone down to the basement and are you climbing
back up the stairs when you shove her?"

"No," Johnny whined. "We're still upstairs. But I know what's coming.
Know all 'bout the handcuffs she nailed to a wooden post. Her papa was
a policeman in Mackinaw City, so that's how she got the cuffs. We're still
upstairs."

"What happened then?"

"I hear Goose Two honking down in the cellar even before we get to
the door."

"Goose Two?" White Pine quietly asked.

"First Goose died, and this is one of his babies. Except he's all growed up
and big like Goose. Scared, so scared. I'm crying to Nana not to do this to
me, but she laughs. She opens the door and turns to me. Down there in the
dark the honking goes on loud. All of a sudden, I know I won't go down. Not
never. And next thing I know, I'm not me no more."

"Not you?"

"I'm Tawiskalu, and just like with those bad kids on the rez it's easy for
Tawiskalu to hit back. I don't like to hit, but he does."

"There, Johnny, you said it—*I'm Tawiskalu.*"

Eyes closed, Johnny rocked his head again. "No, no, it's not that simple."

"Yes, it is. You'll be astonished how simple it is to accept everything you are. The amazing totality of *you*. Go on. You're at the open door to the cellar below. Nana is looking right at you."

"She tells me to quit blubbering, then starts down the stairs first. And—before I can stop him—Tawiskalu shoves her."

"You shoved her, Johnny. You shoved her through a hole in the heavens, and she tumbled down into the darkness of the unborn world. No swans flew up to slow her descent. She died because no animals took pity on her. You slew her, justifiably."

"No. I loved white Nana."

"Of course you did. But it was time for her to step aside so you could take your rightful place in the world. It was God's will that she step aside, just as it was time for Hudson to get out of the way." Dr. White Pine paused. "Do you remember Reverend Hudson?"

"Yes," Johnny said grudgingly, "he was chairman."

"That's right, chairman of our tribal band. What happened to him?"

"Tawiskalu caught him out swimming."

"Who?"

"You sent Adrian out to the beach on Whitefish Bay. Reverend Hudson liked to swim there on Saturdays in summer."

"I sent *you*, Johnny. You went as a favor to me."

Suddenly, Johnny was no longer trapped in the gloom of white Nana's house.

He moves through a blaze of sunshine on a birch-screened cove of Lake Superior. He can feel slimy, round rocks underfoot as he wades out into the shallows. Reverend Hudson's withered old body is visible from the waist-up. He dips his right hand into the curling swells and pours the water onto his chamois-like face and shoulders, as if baptizing himself. He seems to contemplate plunging all the way in. Just before he dives, something makes him turn—and behold the fully-clothed youth coming toward him.

Then follows a gap in time.

At its far side. Hudson is leering up at Johnny from just beneath the surface, eyes so huge they appear ready to rupture.

Dr. White Pine interrupted: "Tell me what happened to Brenda Two Kettles. Without resorting to Tawiskalu. You were there, Johnny, so tell me in your own words what happened."

"I scared her," he murmured.

"How?"

"She didn't expect anybody to step out in front of her on the loading bridge."

"Were there other passengers on their way to the plane?"

"Yes, but they didn't pay us any mind. We were both obviously Indian, and it was none of their concern."

"Are you still with me, Johnny? You're starting to talk like Adrian."

Johnny groaned in confusion. Tawiskalu was rooting around inside his brain, trying to wrest its control from him. "I'm still here, I guess."

"What'd you say to Ms. Two Kettles?"

"I said her overnight bag was too big for the overhead and she was to follow me."

"Did she, Johnny, despite your caterer's uniform?"

"Yeah, no problem. Through the security door and down the stairs to air-side, where I'd left the catering truck."

"Any problems in the truck?"

"No," Johnny said listlessly. "I gave her the shot, just like you said. There were no problems."

"Who gave her the shot?"

"I did."

"And who are you?"

"John Flint."

"Good," Dr. White Pine coached. "Before you sent her off into the sky, did she have any last words?"

Brenda Two Kettles, her face sweaty and her eyes puffy with exhaustion, gazes up at him from the bed. "Why do you hate your own people so?"

"And what did you say, Johnny?"

"Nothing. There was nothing to say about that."

"All right," Dr. White Pine said after a few seconds. "Tell me about your final hours with Hazen Two Kettles."

Hazen, his pink Mohawk flat against his stubbly scalp, looks up at him from the bed, taking the warm place just occupied by his aunt. "I liked Hazen. He was a nice boy."

"But you disobeyed my orders about him, didn't you?"

"Yes," Johnny confessed. "I wasn't supposed to save him, just follow him around and see what he did. I saw him kill Dan Garrity with a shopping cart."

"No loss there. And your saving Hazen wasn't a complete loss either. We needed to get Portia Nelson too, to avoid a settlement. The boy led us to her."

"The redheaded lady," Johnny said. But his mind wasn't on her. He was remembering Hazen, who'd spent a lot of time in juvie too, who knew what it was like to have everybody think you were bad, even when you weren't. *"I steal little stuff sometimes, Johnny, but what's it matter? Everybody already thinks I'm a thief just because I'm Oneida and because they think we're stealing their land."* Yet, for all the affection Johnny had had for the boy, he now felt the grim satisfaction of catching Hazen as he tried to escape from the back of the van, snatching him by the neck and holding him mid-air with his bare feet kicking off the ground. From that moment on, Johnny had wanted nothing more than to put the boy out of his misery, a misery he himself knew so well. As he fitted the harness to the boy's skinny torso, the webbing he himself had sewn together, he'd reminded himself that he was killing the misery, not the boy. *Say hello to Sky Father for me, little redskin.* The words had come out all mean, but Johnny wasn't sure that he'd felt mean at the time. How could he have meant harm to Hazen?

It was all a hopeless jumble.

"Back to last night," Dr. White Pine said. "Tell me about Portia Nelson."

But Johnny only half-heard. He was recalling the bitter resentment he'd felt when White Pine had ordered him to launch the boy up into the night sky. He'd been humiliated by his own obedience. Yet, even Tawiskalu, in all his power and fury, was answerable to the Voice.

"Did you hear me, Johnny?"

Something was happening inside him. He sensed that there had always been a wall between Adrian and him. Just like the wall between the duplexes. But now that distinction, as solid as a rock, was crumbling. He wasn't thinking like Johnny and he wasn't thinking like Adrian. A new combination was taking shape, part Thaluhyawaku's sad love for the weak and helpless, and part Tawiskalu's contempt for others, especially those who tried to defy him.

He opened his eyes on Dr. White Pine, who, still kneeling beside the sofa, looked deeply concerned. "What are you thinking, Johnny?"

"Nothing," he said.

"You must be thinking something."

"No," Johnny said adamantly. He'd never reveal himself to the therapist again. All those hours of revelation had left him at the man's mercy. Now, finally, with stunning clarity, he saw that this was a man without mercy. He had helped himself more than he'd ever helped Johnny.

"Tell me about Ms. Nelson's final minutes."

"Why do you care?"

"Was she frightened?"

"No, angry. She broke my nose, then tried to crawl across the road and out into the woods. I slapped her around some."

"You had every right," Dr. White Pine said. "What happened next?"

Johnny calculated. White Pine wanted something, and that made an opening, an opportunity for rebellion. "She started throwing up, so I took the tape off her mouth so she wouldn't choke."

"So she could talk to you at the end?"

"Yeah."

"What did she say, Johnny?"

He paused. This was monumental. The biggest and most dangerous thing he would ever do. Tawiskalu whispered to him, suggesting what to say. But not Tawiskalu outside Johnny, a voice from without, but rather a voice from within. "As I got ready to let go of the balloons, she said, *'You can tell White Pine I know he's behind it all. I know he's trying to take over the tribe. He wants to be Nation Rep more than anything in the whole wide world.'*"

The therapist didn't move a muscle for what seemed forever, then rose, unsteadily, and sank back into the leather chair. He sat, barely breathing. Watching him in the mirror, Johnny said nothing, for he was used to these silences in which Dr. White Pine gazed off into space. But this silence went on so interminably Johnny began to worry, wondering what life would be like without his protection.

At last, the therapist asked in a soft croak, "Do you know how the FBI agent, Turnipseed, found your duplex?"

Johnny recalled the messages he'd left on her voicemail. His heart beat fast as he remembered these first clumsy stabs at freeing himself from White Pine. "I don't know."

"You have absolutely no idea?" Dr. White Pine demanded.

"No. Maybe she followed me back from the cultural center the night before."

The longest silence yet followed.

At its end, the therapist slid his overcoat sleeve back from his wrist and checked the time. "Put your boots back on, Johnny."

"Why?"

"We have things to do. We have to go away now. There's no other choice. Save ourselves to fight another day."

"Where we going?"

"Out of the country."

Johnny's big fingers fumbled with the knotted laces to his left boot. "When?"

"Tonight." Dr. White Pine's voice sounded thin and faraway, as if he were thinking. "One of the converted Mexican airliners is returning to Mazatlan. Without passengers, except for us."

"What will we do in Mexico?" Johnny asked, rising.

"Live well. I've provided for us in this eventuality. But first . . ." Dr. White Pine took his cell phone from a pocket and tossed it to Johnny. ". . . you're going to phone Turning Stone. Number five on my speed-dialer. Leave a voicemail for Anna Turnipseed. If she answers in person, hang up."

"What do I say?"

"Say you're Mr. Thaluhyawaku. Ask her to meet you at Sunset Lake in an hour. Alone. You'll be watching, and she absolutely must come alone or you won't tell her where Hazen Two Kettles is buried."

"But Hazen isn't buried—"

"Just phone and do as you're told."

Again, for the thousandth time, he obeyed, although his voice shook with resentment all the time he talked into the voicemail. He decided this was the last thing he'd ever do for White Pine. Disconnecting, he glanced back at the therapist—who had leveled a pistol on him.

"Good-bye, *boys*," he said.

Instinctively, Johnny grabbed his right boot and whipped it against the handgun just as the muzzle flashed. Something tugged at his ear. He clasped the side of his head, feeling blood. Ears ringing, he staggered up from the sofa and lunged at White Pine, who was scrambling to retrieve the dropped pistol. It had slid down the sloping deck and come to rest against the glass door.

"Stay where you are!" White Pine commanded.

But, reaching out for the man, Johnny tried to plant his stocking feet on the deck, only to fall. His massive bulk drove White Pine crashing through the glass door, showering both of them with sparkling shards. Johnny came to rest half inside and half outside.

White Pine's face was crisscrossed with cuts. "Stop this right now!" he shouted.

Johnny heard his own voice mumble, "Okay, okay." But his huge hands—strong, tendons taut with rage—flew to the man's throat and closed around it.

White Pine gurgled, his face turning purple, "You're Johnny, not Tawiskalu!"

My God, Johnny thought, *he's got it only part right. My hands are Tawiskalu's!* His brain sent the impulse to his fingers to stop digging into White Pine's windpipe, but the impulse was ignored, and the man's face grew darker and darker. His fists began flailing against Johnny's head, which only made Tawiskalu's hands twist into each other. There came a muted click from White Pine's neck, and his eyes fluttered back, exposing the whites as he went limp in Johnny's grasp.

"Oh, oh."

Gently, he laid the man down in the snow on the outer deck. And studied him, stanching the flow from his ear with his handkerchief while he ran his curious gaze over the corpse.

Then he turned back for the mirror in the cabin.

The sight of his tattered ear made him cry out in anger. It was dangling by the merest strand of tissue. He gingerly plucked it off, held it in his palm, not knowing what to do next.

Finally, he roared and hurled it into the chair where Dr. White Pine had sat.

Grinning, overflowing with a feral rage, he made for the first aid kit in the galley. No matter about the ear. He no longer needed Johnny's body.

30

UNDER THE NEW MOON, Anna waited along the shore of Sunset Lake. She looked out across the starlit, frozen surface where three days ago, during an unseasonable warm spell, a sheriff's Search and Rescue boat had dragged the bottom with grappling hooks for Hazen Two Kettles's body. Where Emmett had confided his satisfaction in how she'd come along as an investigator. She took no pride in that right now. Sweat was collecting against the ballistic vest she wore beneath an overcoat two sizes too large for her. Not a pliant Kevlar vest. Instead, it was rigid body armor with steel trauma plates to keep the impact of a high-velocity slug from killing her.

> *Come to the fearful, Moon of the Sky,*
> *Make ready your powers, Moon of the Sky,*
> *Make ready to fight with death, to lose or win.*

Fear, now so familiar. Manageable. Different from that of an abused child on a backwater reservation. Now she had power to defend herself.

Or at least try.

For what seemed the hundredth time, she turned and scanned the parking area near the bridge over Oneida Creek. Only her bucar showed, chrome glinting in the starshine.

No other vehicles had pulled up. As expected.

Johnny T. Skyholder or Adrian Flint, or maybe even both brothers together, would never drive up to her. They'd be too wary of capture to do that. Nor, probably, would they trust her to come alone. The caller's promise to show her where Hazen was buried was no more than a come-on. The boy, she felt sure, had been launched into the sky like Brenda and Portia.

She had come solely on the slim chance the twins could be enticed out into the open.

If they came at all tonight, they would approach her from cover, the trees most likely, which crept down in clumps to the shore.

She clenched the grips of her semi-automatic, but kept the pistol concealed inside a coat pocket. Her palm, like the small of her back, was sweaty. *Fear.* She'd always believed it to be instinctive, yet Emmett, as usual, had differed with her: *It's the love of life boiled down to a drop of acid in your gut.*

Emmett.

His relatives from Oklahoma had gathered around his ICU bed, but he refused to pass. He was revealing an unexpected love of live, and Anna was no longer sure if that was good. It'd be a relief for the wait to be over, a bitter solace, but still a relief to know that his pain was behind him. She waited for a pang of remorse for thinking this way, but it didn't come. She was still too numb for anything like remorse.

A sound spun her around, and she held her breath to listen.

There was a breeze tonight, and maybe the sound had been one tree limb chafing against another, or the lake ice shifting.

Or it had been Skyholder making his move.

Skyholder and Flint.

As much as she tried, she couldn't imagine both brothers approaching her tonight. Obviously, Johnny, not Adrian, had phoned her, and like each of his previously recorded messages this latest one had had a hint of collaboration in it, a faint tone of regret, guilt even, that begged for absolution.

Anna checked the tree line. Easy for fancy to run away with her. Skyholder's gargantuan silhouette was in every tree trunk or fallen log, his quiet trod in every natural sound on a breezy night.

Nothing, she told herself. *Hold your imagination in check and wait for reality to present itself.*

She found herself recalling the duplex.

One apartment had been warm from recent habitation, the other cold. More than a few hours' cold. Almost as if it was never used.

She started pacing. But kept to a tight circle. The staked goat couldn't go far on its tether.

Skyholder held title to both 1989 Dodge vans. The yellow one had stayed parked near the duplex yesterday as Roth and she drove down off the turtle-shaped crest, while Johnny, or his brother, or the two of them, had made off with Portia Nelson in the other van, which was torched later that evening in the barn near Vernon.

Maybe not two of them—only one set of boot tracks had led away from the fire.

On that, she stopped walking.

What had the I.D. technician told her? Most of the latent fingerprints collected from inside both apartments most likely belonged to a single individual.

And the horn-rimmed glasses abandoned outside the barn, it turned out, had plano lenses. Non-prescriptive. Cosmetic.

Radio traffic cut through her thoughts, unfamiliar call signs crackling in the earpiece she wore. She realized that Oneida County S.O. was telling one of its detectives to switch channels. This investigator was part of the hopefully invisible cordon that had been thrown up by deputies, state police and FBI sniper teams around Sunset Lake while she waited for the caller to show. Dozens of pairs of eyes, most enhanced with night-vision optics, were fixed protectively on her. There was also aerial security in the form of the Air National Guard chopper, hovering just out of audible range, electronically scoping the forest for a large body on the move.

She had won an argument earlier, kiboshing the plan that the smallest male agent from the Syracuse office take her place as the lure, donning a dark wig and the overcoat she was now perspiring under.

Anna twirled her channel selector to see why Oneida S.O. needed to contact its click so urgently. "Can you break away?" the dispatcher asked.

The detective hesitated. "What've you got?"

"Report of a homicide at the Nation's marina on Oneida Lake."

"Who's the RP?"

"One of our units found the DB while on routine patrol."

Turning her face into the microphone clipped to her blouse collar, Anna interrupted, "Is that the *Oneida* Nation's marina?"

"Affirmative," the detective replied. "The Boathouse Marina."

"I.D. on victim?" she asked the dispatcher.

"Still ten-thirty-six." Confidential.

She lit up the dial on her wristwatch. It was now an hour and forty-five minutes past the time the caller had promised to meet her. "Go ahead and respond," she told the investigator. "I'll be right behind you."

Cochran came on the air. "You curtailing this, Turnipseed?"

"Affirmative, if that's okay with you. I'm not sure the caller ever meant to show. It could all be a deke . . ." A decoy to cover whatever had happened at the marina ten miles to the northwest. "I'm heading back to my car."

"All units remain in place," the SAC ordered, "until she's safely out of the area."

Plodding up the beach, she had no doubt that the locus of the entire investigation had just shifted to Oneida Lake.

Johnny huddled in the snowy woods, miserable, sniffling through his broken nose and clasping the bandage taped to where his ear had been. With Dr. White Pine gone, he didn't know what to do next. His sense of triumph, so strong at first, had now faded into loneliness. Plus something new. *Awareness.* He could recount everything about the therapist's death, down to how Tawiskalu's fingers had cramped while digging into the man's throat. Johnny now understood the gaps in time that had mystified him most of his life. They were filled with ghastly things like Tawiskalu's hands choking the life out of White Pine. Oneida Nana lying in the snow. White Nana tumbling down the stairs. No longer could he wrap himself in a warm blanket of amnesia.

Who am I?

Gazing up, he spread his fingers against the stars. There was something odd about his hands. They looked different, somehow. White Pine had done something ghastly to him inside the houseboat—his cunning words had fused parts of both Johnny and Adrian into a single being. A crazy mishmash of a body. *My God, my hands are no longer my own!* They were

Tawiskalu's, clawed for gouging. And his eyes were now his brother's, for they burned like hot coals as he ground his palms into them.

Dear Sky Father! What about my heart?

His hand flew to his chest. Tawiskalu's heart. No question about it. He could feel the slow, steady, unquenchable anger of his brother's heartbeats, his brother's blood poisoning his entire body.

Suddenly, a stream of light shot down out of the heavens and touched the ground a half mile away. *Sky Father—you've unearthed another white pine . . . you're letting out the light of paradise . . . you're sending my mother down to earth again!* But then the light rippled through the barren growth, and the *thump-thump-thump* of a rotor drifted to Johnny. No divine light, no return of his mother to help him through this. It was a cop helicopter hunting for him.

Something was wrong with his mouth.

He felt where his lips had curled back from his teeth—he was grinning. It was Tawiskalu's frenzied grin, indelibly frozen to Johnny's face. He tried to peel if off, ripping at his lips with his fingers, but soon gave up with a moan, staggered to his feet and started through the scrub for the far-off gleam of the frozen lake.

He had to find Special Agent Turnipseed and tell her how sorry he was about everything. He had to get her on his side before his twin brother took over his body.

Entirely.

Complicity.

The name Anna gave to the crime scene before her was *complicity*. It was written in how Christopher White Pine had come to rest in the trampled snow on the side deck of the houseboat. His head was skewed awkwardly on his broken neck, his frosted pupils a milky brown as they stared off to the point in space where, perhaps, his co-conspirator—and murderer—had loomed over him. A powerful assailant, capable of snapping a grown man's neck like a stalk of celery. White Pine had known his killer, had even brought him here. That much was suggested by the presence of the man's jade-green Lexus, which was parked just outside the gate arm to the marina.

The joint sheriff's and FBI evidence team— it wasn't quite certain if this property owned by Oneida Nation Enterprises was truly tribal land and under federal jurisdiction—had already photographed the two sets of boot tracks, one size fifteen and one normal-sized for an adult male, that dotted the shin-deep snow in a beeline from the car to this houseboat. Then a file of just the big impressions that returned to the Lexus, paused there outside the driver's door as if for a check of the unlocked interior for the keys, only to finally disappear on the stone-hard glaze left on the highway by the snowplows.

Anna wondered if the large man had headed for the swampy scrublands east of the lake. Johnny Skyholder, she knew, had left those impressions and perhaps was hunkered down, avoiding the ANG chopper which was spotlighting the area for tracks.

She glanced away from the corpse.

Not good to stare at one too long. A corpse could mesmerize you. And despite all its abominations, a crime scene could lull you into a reverie, part shock from the sheer audacity of the act itself but part comfort that, despite all the carnage and wreckage left behind, the danger was now gone. Like a tornado that had meandered off into the twilight to wreak its destruction elsewhere.

It didn't surprise her that White Pine was involved in all this. She hadn't been able to follow up on the information yet, but she'd learned from Mid-Atlantic Investigations that the special assistant to the Nation Representative had asked for only a cursory background check on Vaughn Devereaux, not *the whole nine yards* of inquiry into the detective's past he had reported to his boss and Anna that evening in the longhouse. This had been a departure from the Nation's otherwise thorough hiring practices for its cops.

It did surprise her that White Pine had fallen victim. He'd seemed cannier than that. Yet, as the old Modoc song implied: While you can make ready to fight death, losing or winning is most often beyond your power.

Human beings have so little power.

Under the harsh glare of the portable light stands, the medical examiner lifted White Pine's coat and shirt and slid a temperature probe into his liver to determine the approximate time of death. The spiked end of the probe penetrated the skin with sickening ease.

Quickly, Anna shifted her view to a row of houseboats, all beached and mothballed under tarpaulins for the winter. Except for this boat. The tarp over the sliding glass door had been raised, letting in the sunlight earlier today, for she'd already determined that there was no electricity. At the far end of the beach on a point of land stood a shingled boathouse, decrepit and silver with age.

She stepped through the shattered sliding glass door and into the main cabin, so far only casually searched.

A leather sofa and chair dominated it. Both had been draped with white cloths, which now lay rumpled on the sloping floor. The sofa cushions still showed an indentation left by a figure that had lain there. And on the chair cushion—something not recognizable until she drew closer and shone her penlite on it.

She winced—a mutilated ear.

Shoes crunched over the broken glass behind her, and someone cleared his throat over the puttering of the generator. It was the medical examiner, wearing green latex gloves and holding out a small notepad to her on the tip of his pen, which he'd thrust through the wire spiral. "This fell out of the victim's inner coat pocket while I was working on him. I think somebody should take a look before it's bagged."

Agreed. The last communication from a murdered man could identify his killer.

"You want to fume the pages for prints?" Anna asked, borrowing his pen to rest the pad atop one of the sofa arms.

"Yeah, so please be careful."

She brought the examiner's attention to the ear.

"Lovely," he said, then quietly returned to his chores out on the deck.

She flipped the pages with her own pen, illuminating them with her small flashlight. All was written in a highly personalized shorthand, most of it unintelligible, except for a few entries on the page that had been open when the examiner handed the pad to her: *St. intg. alters.* And the final entry: *He awkns.*

He awakens.

More crunching came over the glass pebbled on the deck. Marvin Roth, who'd beat her to the scene and locked it down for the evidence techs. "Nation Rep just pulled up," the Syracuse agent said. "He's raising Cain to be let inside the perimeter."

That perimeter, she realized, enclosed White Pine's Lexus as well, which she and Roth had already examined. "All right," she told him. "Advise the guys to escort him to White Pine's car and wait for me there. Take over here, okay, Marvin? This notebook came off the victim. And the examiner already knows about the ear on the chair."

"Ear?"

She pointed it out to him.

"Gross," Roth said nonchalantly, holding out his hand. "I need your H.T.—loaned mine to the SAC." Cochran was last seen haunting the marina with Chief Deputy Marshal Jordan at his side. Every office was chronically short of working pack sets. Anna took hers from her belt and gave it to Roth. Previously, she'd shed her ballistic vest in the car, which had left her sweat-soaked and shivering for the snowy trudge through the marina grounds to the houseboat.

She now set off for the highway, Roth transmitting her request behind her. She side-stepped White Pine's body and climbed down to the beach through a gap in the railing.

She wanted to see the look on the Nation Rep's face when the trunk was opened for the second time tonight. That look would never be admissible, however damning, but it would be one more tile in the mosaic called *totality of circumstance*. The overview that always seemed to come at such a price. Quickly, she blocked a mental image of Emmett, entangled in the tentacles of life-support tubing in ICU. Her anger of last night was replaced by an acceptance she was too weary to fight.

Don't hold on to anything. Everything eventually slips away.

The chief executive of the tribe was waiting for her beside the Lexus, flanked by two deputies. One had walked him through the perimeter. The other had been guarding the car. This was the same patrolman who, while on patrol, had noticed the suspicious vehicle parked outside the marina, which was closed for the season.

Nobody seemed to be in the mood for chitchat.

The Nation Rep's face was grave and drawn. No quiet smile tonight. "Anna," he said curtly.

She returned his greeting with a nod, then asked one of the deputies, "Mind popping the trunk?"

"No problem."

Presumably the car keys were still in White Pine's trouser pocket, but Roth had found the Lexus unlocked.

The lid levitated and the trunk light came on. Inside was a metal container. Stenciled on one side was AERO MAZATLAN.

"What's that?" the Nation Rep asked impatiently.

"Trash bin from an airliner lavatory," she answered, swinging it around so that the mouth of the container faced him. Roth had found a false bottom. She now opened it and slid out a canvas bank bag, just enough to reveal: TURNING STONE CASINO.

"Show me what's inside," he grimly said.

She gave him a peek at the bundles of hundred-dollar notes within, then shut the bag again. It had already been tagged as evidence by Roth, and a full accounting of the contents would be done only in the security of the Syracuse FBI office. Money bound for laundering in a Mexican bank. This, almost undoubtedly, was what the mechanic Eberhardt had alluded to in the minutes before Devereaux murdered him.

The Nation Rep's face hardened. The reaction was spontaneously natural, and it lasted for several seconds. "Very well," he finally said, his voice raw from having been betrayed. "May I see the body?"

"Not now," Anna said. Nothing would be served by that, and a civilian's presence at the heart of a fresh crime scene would only help some future defense team. If needed, he could ID White Pine at the morgue, even though there was no question in her mind about the body's identity.

The deputy led the Nation Rep back toward a string of law enforcement vehicles out on the highway, and left him with his driver and Cadillac.

As Anna crossed an open expanse of white, heading back for the glare of the crime scene, something flashed in the corner of her eye. She faced that way and waited. It wasn't long before another flash broke from a window in the second story of the boathouse. On for perhaps two seconds, then off. She delayed an agent who was hurrying past with a videocam. "Who secured the area?"

"Deputies, I think."

"Did they hit that boathouse down there?"

"No idea." He rushed on.

It struck her that, with muddled jurisdiction, no one might have taken firm control of the scene. That would have left chinks in the security.

Swirling activity was not the same as security. She wanted to get Roth and check out the boathouse, but she'd already tied him up babysitting evidence. That left William Jordan, the chief deputy marshal, who was breaking trail across the snow toward her in his black coat and fedora.

She was standing in strong light, something she realized when he was able to observe: "Something wrong, Anna?"

"You recall anybody making a complete search of the area?"

"Assumed your people did."

A bit of academy doggerel flitted through her mind: *Assume* makes an *ass* of *u* and *me*.

Roth had been first to arrive after the deputy's discovery. She'd been next, confident that the rapid gathering of deputies and agents had freed her to focus on the Lexus and DB. Emmett had warned her time and again about making assumptions, and now his censuring voice rattled around inside her head, annoyingly. "Mind helping me make a sweep along the bay here?" she asked.

Jordan took a rubberized flashlight from his coat pocket. "Not at all. You see something?"

"A light," she said, setting off with him toward the point, "from a window in the boathouse down there."

"What kind?"

"Maybe a flashlight. Could be a deputy wrapping up a search of the marina or . . ." She didn't finish.

"Or it could be the brothers."

"There are no brothers," she said, thumbing on her penlite.

"What do you mean?"

"I'll explain as soon as we clear the boathouse." And explain her belief now that Flint had been tied to White Pine, Devereaux and even the mechanic, Eberhardt, in an effort to shift the blame for Brenda's death on Daniel Garrity.

Together, Jordan and she worked their beams over the snow. Hers was fainter than his, but she could still see that the drifts were unmarked with either Skyholder's huge boot impressions or those of a deputy. Any cop, most likely, would have approached the boathouse from this side, checking the beached boats along the way.

"You think it was a deputy signaling you?" Jordan asked, hushed.

"Not really," she said.

That made him draw his pistol. She did the same. They were nearing the boathouse. Its outer deck was heaped with unbroken snow. There were three dormers on the facing side of the old building, all the windows darkened now, which only ratcheted up Anna's sense that Jordan and she were being watched from one of them.

A creak stopped them dead in their tracks.

She glanced up.

The creak came from a rusted weathervane that was swinging around on a shift of the breeze. It was now blowing out of the southeast, sifting fine snow across the lake ice. The crime scene spotlights were shining over the entire marina, making everything appear stark and skeletal, especially a high-voltage power line a few hundred yards to the north.

Jordan asked, "What do you say—let's go together through that side door?"

Now that she was on the verge of checking the boathouse out, her throat was tight. "You have a radio with local channels?"

"Yes."

"I didn't get a chance to advise anybody."

"Fine, I'll tell Cochran what we're up to." Jordan retreated a short ways back from the boathouse, and she could hear him murmuring his transmission. Several seconds later, he rejoined her. "SAC wants a welfare check from us in ten minutes." Then something—maybe he was feeling the same vague dread as she—made the marshal add, "Sorry I couldn't level with Parker and you in the beginning."

"I know," she said, scanning the windows above again. "I was just mad last night. Mad Emmett and I ever got suckered into coming here."

"Don't blame you."

They extinguished their flashlights, and he led the way toward the side entrance. The snow covering the deck muffled their footfalls. She trained her weapon on the dormers, while he focused on the door. It was ajar. Jordan's breath puffed around his shoulders. The temperature was in the teens. And still dropping. He paused beside the door, she a few steps behind him. There was no view between it and the jamb, just a stripe of impenetrable black beyond.

By hand signals, Anna indicated that she wanted to check out the lake-end of the boathouse. What if the doors were open to let a snowmobile escape? Jordan nodded his approval. She crept to the edge of the dock, clung to a piling and leaned out for a look. A second-story door opened onto a small balcony beneath the gable of the roof. Below, the twin boat doors were chained shut.

She backtracked to Jordan.

He signaled that, on entering, he would cover high and she would cover low. A division of labor to split up the interior space to increase the chance one of them would get off a shot before an assailant did.

He gave the door an exploratory nudge.

It was gripped by ice.

Jordan stood back and kicked. The crash was still echoing around the cavernous boathouse as she followed him inside, trampling over the collapsed door. He switched on his flashlight again and ran it up a flight of rickety wooden stairs. Anna saw this only peripherally, for she was sweeping her own light around the horseshoe-shaped dock framing the boat stall. No boat in that stall, just ice. No human figure either. The deck was tufted with frost crystals—disturbed by human tracks. More tracks both ascended and descended the staircase. Jordan advanced toward it, his beam passing over the clutter in the loft above.

Following, she stole an upward look.

Tanks of some sort were stored up there. *No, they're called cylinders,* she corrected herself, *like for oxygen or acetylene. Or helium, used to fill meteorological balloons.*

A motorboat was suspended against the ceiling on a sling lift.

She refocused on the dark space between the layer of ice inside the stall and the underside of the deck, scanning for anything that appeared remotely human. For anything resembling a weapon.

Jordan stopped at the foot of the stairs, listening.

She did the same.

A groan sounded from above. Weight passing over boards, she thought. Another sound broke the suspicious quiet, a thrumming, like a taut rope being severed. Anna saw no one, but down swung the boat like a pendulum. "Jordan, look out!" she shouted, dropping her penlite to push him out of the way. But the stern slammed into the marshal first, pinning him against the newel post to the staircase. He bellowed, or maybe it was just the air being squeezed out of him. Then the hull whirled away from him, and his pistol and flashlight clattered to the deck. The light rolled dizzily off onto the ice below, the beam doing curlicues on the wall across from Anna. She made another grab for Jordan. But the hull whooshed in-between them again.

He fell, crashing through the ice.

An eruption of white water carried him to the surface. His motionless body was cast in frothy green by his waterproof light, which bobbed around him.

Anna sat on the deck's edge and eased her right shoe onto the ice. As soon as she applied scarcely any weight at all, it cracked. Jordan's face jerked up out of the water. He began thrashing and spluttering for breath.

The boat was now dangling directly over him by its bow sling.

Anna rested her pistol beside her on the deck and stripped off her belt. A quick glance all around revealed no one. She flung the buckled end of her belt out toward the marshal. He went on treading water, tossing his right arm up onto the ice shelf, only to have it slip off again.

"Jordan, here!" she hollered.

He reared up in the water and seemed to look directly at her through the faint glows of their lights. With a shocked, stricken face. She whipped her belt toward him, but the reach of it and her arm was too short. By at least two feet.

From the corner of her eye, she caught movement at the top of the stairs. Picking up her handgun, she swung the muzzle toward the landing— only to see no one up there. No target. You only fired when you had a target.

Jordan waved a desperate arm over his head. He wasn't going to last much longer.

She set her pistol atop a piling, clung to it with her left arm and held out the belt. He seized it, yanking so frantically her end nearly whipped out of her hand. Straining, she tried to haul him up onto the ice, but his waterlogged weight was too much. Her eyes roved around for anything longer than her belt, something that would let her stand on the deck and use her entire body as leverage to pull Jordan out.

She was still looking when the boat fell past her eyes, swiftly, like a plunging knife. *Kawoosh!* It drove Jordan down and out of sight. The hull flopped over on its keel, raising a foaming swell that broke against the big outer doors, rattling the chain.

When the wave had ebbed, she could see Jordan spread-eagled a few feet off the bottom, his flashlight and fedora still on the surface.

Cold water immersion.

The spark of life could be sustained by icy water for a time. She'd run for help, which might already be on the way. Certainly by now Jordan and she had missed the check-in Cochran had wanted in ten minutes.

Using the piling to swing herself back onto the deck, she was reaching for her pistol—when a big hand pinioned her by the wrist. Jordan's splashing had created a mist in the dim light, and the face above her was shadowy, but she knew at once who she was confronting in silhouette. A luminously white bandage was taped to the left side of his head. "Looking for this . . . ?" He twirled her weapon around an index finger. "Now I've got two. Yours and White Pine's. But I don't want to just shoot you. Oh no, bitch, that 'd be a terrible waste of sky!"

She dug her teeth into the back of his hand. The salty taste of blood filled her mouth, but she held fast until he gasped in pain. His hand whipped out of her mouth, loosening teeth as it went. Yet, before she could run for the gaping door frame, something metallic struck the left side of her head.

The impact lit a sparkly white fire behind her eyes.

She'd been struck with her own pistol, she realized, as the light left her head like fireworks dimming in the night sky.

She totters blindly on the balls of her feet, leaning out over the lip of a precipice at the edge of a bottomless void. Then undeniably, she is falling. She can see nothing, but she has the tingling sensation of falling. Her arms flail and her hands grab at the blackness, but she plummets with ever increasing speed. The night air is like fire on her face. Her body howls through the void, and a scream is pulled from her lungs. Then she has no air left to scream. She begins to tumble end over end, making a whiffling noise as she somersaults faster and faster.

She spreads her arms like wings, trying to stop spinning.

Spinning.

Although she was rolling in nausea, Anna understood that she was on her feet. Sort of. Maybe not standing on her own, for when she gave in to the urge to sink back down into oblivion, some irresistible force seemed to be propping her up.

What?

There was a sound, indefinable. Maybe like soft, hollow objects rubbing against each other.

A face was very close to hers. A body that stank of wood smoke and sweat.

She startled, triggering an intense ache that left her wondering if her skull had been fractured. She decided it wasn't—she could still think. "Johnny . . . ?" she asked.

"There is no more Johnny," the whispery baritone, confident and contemptuous-sounding, said. She'd last heard it in the police interviewing room at Syracuse International, where his final challenge had been spat at Emmett and her—*What do you find offensive?* The juvenile voice quality in the caller who'd left the messages on her voicemail was completely absent now.

"Adrian?" she guessed.

A pause, red glittering deep in the backs of his eyes, then: "If you mean Tawiskalu Flint . . . yes."

Her spirits sank as she realized that the murderous half of this personality had taken over the meeker Johnny Skyholder. Where was that oversized child now?

Regardless, she needed time to figure out how much use of her body she still had. She gulped in cold air, which cleared her head a little and helped her nausea. "What happened to White Pine?"

"He went on ahead."

"What do you mean?"

"He went on ahead of *you.*" This was more than a threat. It was a promise. As was his next utterance: "Make a peep and I'll break your neck, just like I did his."

She listened for help on the way.

Nothing but the creak of the weathervane.

Furtively, she flexed her hands. They still had sensation. They still functioned as possible weapons. But the slightest movement brought the white fire back to her brain.

Adrian Flint was fussing, his fingers shaking with impatience as he adjusted something around her torso. She expanded her lungs and felt straps pressing against her. *An improvised parachute harness!* No doubt, equipped with a harness cutter, ready to drop her out of the sky at a preset altitude. She was no longer nauseated, but now she was cold. Chilled down to her marrow. And that would only get worse as she climbed into the night. She didn't want to die cold.

Everything within her cried out to flee, but she knew she couldn't try that too soon. A premature move would end only in him beating her senseless again.

And sending her aloft like all the others.

Take your bearings . . . take your bearings.

The light around her was faint, mere starlight perhaps, but she had the sense that something was projecting over her head. *Yes*—three large weather balloons, squeaking as they rubbed against each other in the wind. Above them stars? No. A roof line, with only a portion of night sky visible straight ahead. Over the icebound surface of Oneida Lake.

Time.

How many minutes had elapsed since he'd clubbed her in the head with her pistol? How many minutes now since the welfare check Jordan had promised to Cochran, the deadline that had come and gone with nothing but radio silence to show for it?

Rely only on yourself! Emmett's voice scolded her.

She looked for an opening as Flint's fingers busily went on cinching straps. Again, she tested her restraints, this time by splaying her arms, just enough so he wouldn't notice.

Disappointment.

At least two sets of straps were clamping her arms to her sides.

Think . . . think!

But then it appeared that there was no time left in which to think. He'd tethered the balloons to a balcony post and now untied them, straining against the lifting power of the helium within them. There was a click as he attached the end of the balloons' rope to a metal ring on the harness. She felt the eagerness of the balloons to carry her off into the sky, but Flint kept a heavy hand on her arm. "You figured it out," he said, voice quavering with anger. "You figured me out. Where I lived. And then you drove me from my home. What'd I ever do to you?"

"I was only trying to help you."

"Don't lie, bitch!"

She cringed, waiting for a blow. But it didn't come. Instead, Flint hefted her up onto the balcony railing and continued to keep a hand on her, postponing what now seemed inevitable. She fought a deadening sensation, a paralytic sense of utter futility in ever trying anything again. Is this what her great-great-grandfather, Kintpuash, had felt as the Army made its preparations to hang him?

Resist . . . resist!

From this angle, she clearly saw that Flint was wearing coveralls. Not the white jumpsuit of his catering company. Coveralls with suspender-like straps hanging loosely over his shoulders.

A shout came out of the distance. Her name. It was Cochran calling for her, although she knew that he would never reach her on the boathouse balcony in time.

Dimly, she realized that her legs were free. But Flint seemed to read her thoughts, for one of his long arms shifted to hold her by the legs as he let go of her shoulder and took something from a pocket. A knife. Its blade shone in the frigid starlight.

Emmett's voice was in her head again, sounding as resigned as she herself now felt: *We should've made love . . . if only once.*

"Say hello to Sky Father for me," Flint hissed.

She thought of the dried bird inside the clamshell case in her jacket pocket. Her racing heart spoke to it: *Enable me to hover in mid-air, Hummingbird, give me invisible-quick wings, don't let the sky take me away!*

Flint used the knife to sever the two sets of straps holding her arms. Immediately, he braced for her to lash out at him. Instead, she kept her arms down at her sides while she slid the toe of her right shoe under one of his suspender straps—and twisted the material around her ankle.

"Good-bye, bitch!" he cried, releasing the balloons.

But his farewell turned into a surprised wail as he was carried over the railing with Anna.

They were flying.

But she thought of nothing but the knife. *Stay in close.* You survived a knife attack by staying in close to your attacker. And her hands were now free. With deceptive tenderness, she touched him, bent back his wrist. It was not a matter of strength. In fact, the beefier the arm, the more sensitive the tendons. Flint yowled, and his fist opened on a spasm of pain. A second too late, he realized that the blade had been slipped from his grasp. "Bitch, bitch!"

He tried to wrench her right ankle out of his suspender strap. She was positive he would break it like White Pine's neck—until it occurred to him that only she was preventing him from falling at least thirty feet to the lake ice. She gnashed her teeth together in growing agony. His weight threatened to dislocate her right leg at the hip, so she had no choice but to offer him her left one as well.

He glommed onto her knees, gasping.

She wanted to plunge the knife into him, but feared that he'd deflect the blade back into her.

Something fluttered around her right elbow. It was the remnant of one of the straps he'd used to bind her arms. She gathered it in her left hand and looped it around his neck. "Stop it!" he protested, but that was all he could do. He was powerless to let go of her legs, although she saw by the crime scene lights in the distance that their combined weight was too much for the balloons—Flint and she were gradually losing altitude as they sailed along. If they landed, she had the knife. That was when she would use the knife.

He gaped up at her, eyes wild. "You filthy Indian bitch!"

She threaded the end of the strap through the metal ring on the harness and tied it off.

"When we get down, I'm going to break your fucking neck!" he ranted on, trying to shake off the strap now looped around his throat.

His weight was going to tear her in two. But it alone was keeping her from soaring off into the blackness of space. A gust carried them higher. But only by a few feet, for as it slackened they sank again—until his boots skimmed the ice as they were blown along.

At that moment, she cut herself out of the harness with the knife. Instantly, she inverted and everything spun in a topsy-turvy blur. Flint let go of her legs, his outraged voice rising away from her.

She fell. Falling precisely as she had dreamed, filled with a tingling sensation, making a whiffling noise through the air. She just had time to curl into a fetal ball before striking the ice with a bone-shuddering jolt. She somersaulted again and again, and finally came to rest. With her head throbbing and blood trickling from her nose.

She was facing the boathouse.

She flopped over to track Flint.

He was ascending, slowly ascending, building speed and altitude toward the shoreline, now that only his weight was being borne by the balloons.

"Say hello to Sky Father," Anna whispered.

Shrieking in rage, he jostled the balloon tethers, trying to change his course. Still, he glided gracefully up into the power lines. There was a loud pop and an arcing blue flash. He fell out of this dimming flash like a rock, his clothes on fire.

No swans flew up to cushion his fall.

31

"*SUKWAITTU*," CELIA PARKER SAID, blowing Emmett a kiss from the doorway as she left for the night. Love.

"*Sukwaittu*, Mama," he responded, "tomorrow." And back she would come to the Indian hospital in Lawton first thing in the morning.

The stillness created by her departure always gave him too much time to think.

The lamp over his bed was dim enough for him to have a moonlit view out his window of Mount Scott, once the heart of the reservation, a reservation that no longer existed. Congressional efforts to turn the nomadic Comanche into farmers had stripped them of their tribal lands in 1887. Those who had stayed in southwest Oklahoma did so on small farms or in the towns bordering the Fort Sill artillery post, such as here in Lawton, where they could gaze up at Mount Scott and imagine its lower slopes dotted with smoke-stained teepees.

Not that the Comanche were overly given to dwelling in the past.

They were taught from childhood to enjoy the moment, and the moment now shouted with spring. Strange, but being shut away in hospitals these past three months had keenly attuned him to the seasons outside. Now, in April, he could feel spring wriggling out of the ground in countless green spikes, the prairies swelling with succulent growth and chirring with newly-hatched insects. West of the Wichita Mountains, the flowering time was coming to the Staked Plains, so called because only a Comanche warrior could navigate their trackless expanses without driving stakes into the iron-hard ground.

The door swung open.

It was Kitty Toppah, the night nurse, bearing a tray. A Kiowa, she had attended the same Catholic Indian mission as he, although several grades behind. Skinny then and fond of girlish conspiracies. Ripe-figured now but still cute—a naughty smile set in dimpled brown cheeks. Constantly hinting that she found the hospital rules a hindrance, without specifying why. Remembering Emmett from the mission, she'd struck up a flirtation with him the evening he'd been flown here from Syracuse, and in the five weeks since they'd played variation after variation on the mutual attraction, although he kept cautioning himself. One of his ex-wives was Kiowa. *Great lovers, difficult wives,* he felt, although it was an admitted tribal prejudice.

"How are you tonight, Em?" Kitty asked. In keeping with a bombardment of questions about his condition over the last few days.

"Better."

"Honestly?" she prodded with a teasing look that gave him pause.

He had begun to suspect that boosting his libido was part of his recovery regimen. If so, it was working. The last few mornings he'd awakened with urinary erections. And tonight, as the crickets outside drummed out their desire, Kitty looked especially attractive. "Any calls?" he inquired.

"Who you expecting to call?"

"Nobody, really." He had wanted no work-related calls, particularly from the Syracuse office of the FBI, which was putting the finishing touches on the investigation. To make sure of this, he'd had the telephone removed from his room. But he had also been waiting for a message from Anna, who presumably was back in Las Vegas. The only thing he recalled from his foggiest periods of sedation was Anna's voice telling him to live. Yet, by the time he was off the ventilator and fully aware of his surroundings, she was gone. Without having said good-bye. *At least a goddamned good-bye had been in order.*

"Cheers." Kitty held out a tiny paper cup to him and a glass of water.

It contained his painkillers for tonight. Half the usual dosage, which raised his eyebrows. "Doc cutting me back?"

"No, but I thought you could use all your faculties."

A new level of flirtation?

At first, fearing addiction, he'd vowed not to take any narcotics at all. That was before he tried to breathe without them. It was nothing like the transcendent pain he'd experienced years ago in South Dakota during the finale of the Sun Dance, when he'd hung suspended on tethers fastened to his pectoral muscles with bone skewers. That agony had swept him up into another level of existence. This variety simply beat him down.

Kitty shut off his light. "Good-night, Emmett Parker." Then she left a kiss on his forehead before turning the window blinds and going out. Something she'd never done before. He basked in the afterglow of the kiss, although not prepared to speculate where it might lead. Kiowa women were a handful. Not that Modoc women weren't too.

Why the fuck hasn't she phoned?

Lying close to death in Syracuse, he had taken pleasure from the pleading in Anna's faint, far-off voice for him to live. Yet, that wasn't why he'd pulled through. She'd helped, but it was not truly why. Malcolm had come to him time and again, as if Emmett, in dwelling between life and death, was close to his late brother. Repeatedly, Malcolm said that he regretted having taken his own life. However, what was done was done, and only Emmett had the *puha* to spare their mother further grief. *She must not outlive both of us. That'll be more than even she can take.* "All right," Emmett had finally promised Malcolm. "All right."

After that, his recovery had been rapid.

At last, tonight's painkillers kicked in, and Emmett found himself out on the Staked Plains, riding a horse so smooth he could not feel its gait and so quiet he couldn't hear the pounding of its hooves.

Sometime later, a brief wash of light from the corridor fell over him before the door snicked shut again. Used to these nocturnal medical checks now, he didn't rouse. Not until he heard the silken rustle of clothing being shed to the floor. He opened his eyes on a female shadow set against the translucent window blinds.

Foolishly, he asked, "What—?" Cool fingertips pressed against his lips.

Foolish because he knew perfectly well what was coming.

Not a word was spoken. Everything was translated to him by her hands. That, in deference to his almost-healed chest wound, he remain on his back.

That he raise his hospital gown so she might gracefully straddle him. That he was free to explore her body. What followed was simple, earnest love-making. Like most plains tribes, the Kiowa were not a diminutive people, so he was surprised by how light she felt on top of him. At one point she threw her arms over her head as if she were falling. Plummeting down into her pleasure. Yet, in most moments, she seemed surprisingly tentative, surprising given her flirtatious nature. But her kisses were tender and heartfelt. His passion grew, but at no point did he feel the need to roll over and dominate. It was all very, very nice.

When it was done, she kissed him once more, then quickly dressed and ducked out the door by opening it as narrowly as possible.

Alone, he murmured sleepily, "Now *that's* health care," then dozed off again.

His mother's voice awakened him. She had already opened the blinds on a gray morning with mist cloaking Mount Scott. "*Sukwaittu,* my son," she said, coming to the side of his bed.

"*Sukwaittu,* Mama," he repeated.

"What's this?"

"What's what?"

She picked up something from beside his pillow and showed it to him. A dried hummingbird.